Praise for *The Year of Soup*

"*The Year of Soup*, as with his first novel *A Family Institution*, clearly establishes Howard Reiss' credentials as an especially gifted storyteller with a knack for creating fully developed characters and original storylines that engage the readers complete attention from first page to last. *The Year of Soup* is highly recommended and thoroughly entertaining, making it an appropriate addition for community library contemporary fiction collections."

--*The Midwest Book Review*

"*The Year of Soup*, mixes a fine stew of intelligence and wisdom, while also at times stirring in a sharp wit and a pinch of genuine, heartfelt charm and humanity."

--*IndieReader*

The Year of Soup received the Silver Medal for Best Fiction in the North-East Region at the Independent Publisher Book Awards in 2013.

Praise for *A Family Institution*

"By understanding our family history we can understand our future. A frank novel of family and what binds us all through our troubles, *A Family Institution* is a choice pick for general fiction collections."

--*The Midwest Book Review*

"The dialogue and the physical descriptions of characters ring with truth."
"If you liked *Where We Belong* [by Emily Giffin], you'll love.... *A Family Institution* by Howard Reiss."

--*IndieReader*

A Family Institution was a finalist in the 2012 IndieReader Discovery Awards.

The Year of Soup

Howard Reiss

Published by Krance Publishing

Cover art by Michael Witte
with contributions from Martha Gradisher

ISBN: 0615725457
ISBN-13: 978-0615725451

DEDICATION

To El: Everything I write is always for you.

The Preamble--Two Soup Lovers

I decided to open a restaurant on my 30th birthday after three different lovers and the same number of careers. I started after college as a beat reporter for a local newspaper on the New York side of Lake Champlain in Plattsburgh. That lasted for three years. I then became an art teacher at a private school in rural Vermont for another three years, followed by a stint as an assistant to a fashion photographer in San Francisco. It shouldn't be too difficult to figure out how long I lasted in that job—three years. Everything in my life seemed based on threes, including my cycle, which is closer to three weeks than four.

I decided to open a restaurant to break that numerical jinx because I read that it takes at least three years for a restaurant to start making money and with a ten year bank loan I had no choice but to stick with it. Besides, cooking and eating have always been the easiest way for me to forget and move on. I'm not referring to rich, chocolaty desserts or fried foods like homemade potato chips, although both, especially when combined with an old late-night movie, can be a wonderful amnesiac in the aftermath of a break-up, especially when it seems as if you're running out of time. For me, it's always been about soups. I suppose because my great-grandmother was famous for them, as was my grandmother and mother. When my mother died way too young, the victim of a smoking habit she couldn't shake, she left me the family notebook filled with hundreds of handwritten soup recipes that went back across the Atlantic to my great-grandmother's mother and her grandmother.

On those days when I feel singled out and alone, ready to weep if I see one more dark cloud, which has become more and more frequent as my success with relationships has failed to come close to matching my expectations, it's always soup I turn to. It's soup that helps me pull the emotional plug so those feelings can run out my mental drain, and it's more than just the soup—it's the preparation as well that helps make the bitter a bit sweeter.

Take potato leek soup, for example, a basic and simple soup with what seems sometimes like a heavenly reward. First, there's the steady, rhythmic chopping of the potatoes, the leeks, the celery and the onions. The sound of the knife against the cutting board, that old, familiar cutting board given to me by mother as a housewarming gift when I moved into my first apartment, cut and bruised by more emotional mishaps than it deserved, provides a soothing counterpoint to the sharp beating of my sad heart. The focus and concentration that it takes to slice the garlic thin enough to crackle and disappear when sautéed in butter, and it has to be 100 percent butter—margarine can be no substitute at a time like this—always manages to turn those moments of preparation into the only reality.

Browning the ingredients brings an amazing auditory and olfactory comfort. The smell of sautéing onions and leeks, a staple in my mother's kitchen, is like reconnecting with an old acquaintance who remembers me at my best or hearing from a favorite aunt who still holds me up high on a pedestal, regardless of how low I may feel my life has sunk. The onions brown, seemingly alive as they yellow and shrivel with time, always drawing my undivided attention, almost whispering as they simmer, as if to remind me that there is a life force that lives on even when my expectations are lower than they've ever been before. It's a scent that reaches back to my childhood and further connects with my ancestors like some kind of culinary DNA. It's a scent that always helps me empty myself of some of the heartache, at least for a little while, like a narcotic whose high is instantaneous and which takes it time dissolving so the trip back down to earth is slow - the same way the smell of sautéing onion and leeks lingers throughout the house long after the soup has been eaten and put away.

When everything is evenly browned, it's time to add the chicken stock. Now, if I can see the ugliness coming, and often I do, even if it's only subconsciously, I will put up some homemade stock in anticipation. However, when I'm blindsided, as I was in my last relationship, abandoned in complete surprise, and forced to move again this time from San Francisco, then it's canned or out of a box, passable but not nearly as good. The canned soup is always missing something, whether it is patience or passion, it just doesn't offer the same resistance. Good home-cooked stock can make the difference between a long season filled with regret or moving quickly on to forgiveness.

Unfortunately, cooks have to make do with what they have available, as do each of us in life when we are plagued with poor choices. When it came to poor choices I had Nick, Jake and Jolene, and I wasn't planning to make any more.

Now, I've always thought that there is a certain satisfaction that comes with bitterness, which is why we hold on to it as long as we do, even why you sometimes like the taste of it, which probably explains why I like the simmering part most of all. It tames the bitterness so that even the worse memories become more palatable. It goes on for hours making promise after promise which, in the case of soup as opposed to people, it usually delivers on.

When the simmering is done, about two-thirds of the soup gets liquefied in the blender and returned to the pot with a drop of cream—heavy for major disappointments, light for the others. The soup then has to cool a bit so it can be served warm, not hot, because you can't distinguish all the flavors when it's too hot, and without all the flavors it will never be able to take hold of my despondency and anxiety as I sip it down.

In my experience, good soup is defiant of every mood and always manages to release somewhat that tight grip time and recent memories may have around my heart. It turns wherever I am - the kitchen or the small dining area in my new restaurant - into a place where those veils of troubling thoughts and confusion about who I am and what I want are not quite as suffocating as they often tend to be.

Of course, it helps to be accompanied by a good red wine and the appropriate bread which, in this case, would be sourdough that I always keep frozen at home and have delivered fresh every day at the restaurant. I named it Circa for the last nine years of my life that I'd just as soon forget – especially the two men and one woman who inspired me to disavow any future that might involve romance and to keep the rest of humanity at a safe distance.

Instead of just cooking for my own memories, I decided to open a restaurant to see if I could help others forget and let go, if only during the course of a meal. What better way to do it than with a restaurant where soups are the only course, hearty bowls and warm, crusty bread. I figured that I couldn't be the only one out there susceptible to soup's medicinal qualities and I was right, although I'm getting a bit off track since this story isn't about soup, it's about me and one of my first customers, my favorite customer actually, an old man named Roger Peckinpaw Beanstock, known as Professor Beany, Professor Emeritus of English at Smith College. He walked in the first week I opened—Thursday night—as he would every Thursday night for a year, until my soup could no longer drown out the voices in his head.

CHAPTER ONE

The first time I met Professor Beany is as clear in my mind as my first kiss, which I suppose says more about me than the Professor. It was the week I opened for business.

I had three special soups available - my mother's Tibetan lentil soup with lentils, carrots, and potatoes seasoned with onions, cumin, coriander and a green chili paste I could only find in New York City; an old college friend's spicy carrot peanut soup, which I modified somewhat by using organic peanut butter to offset the sour and salty flavors; and my grandmother's eggplant soup, which includes potatoes, green beans, colorful bell peppers, chopped tomatoes and olives.

I also had a wild rice and vegetable chicken soup on the board. I always try to have at least one Campbell's type soup available for those couples—and it's mostly singles and couples who come to the restaurant, rarely families—with one member who will tolerate Circa's Bohemian atmosphere with its dark walls and low light, and the black-and-white photos of unknown people, but refuse to let go of their epicurean sense of bourgeois respectability and demand a soup that sounds as if it can be found in a can on a shelf in the supermarket.

The first couple of days were very slow, which was no surprise since Circa is on a side street and I was new to Northampton and knew almost no one. But word travels fast in a college town, particularly during the winter when people crave the new things that lie ahead in the spring and hungry minds never stray too far from the memories of good soup. Each night brought more people looking for something warm and filling for their restlessness and longing. Not just the under-graduate types, but locals looking for a change, recent grads still searching for their burning passion, college instructors struggling to complete their PhDs after years of trying, frustrated artists, musicians and actors who always seem to be one break away from something and work in offices and shops, older individuals tired of the grind or just tired of being alone, and couples sharing thoughts that have lost their charm.

It was late, near the 10 p.m. closing time, that first Thursday when Professor Beany walked in carrying his own bottle of red wine having heard, I supposed, that I had not yet received my license to sell alcohol. I was in the kitchen cleaning up, but when Georgina, a junior business major, and the only waitress—in fact, the only one who worked in the restaurant other than me—came in to tell me that one of Smith's preeminent professors, a published poet and scholar of 19th and 20th-century English literature, had just walked in and asked if there was still time for dinner. I couldn't resist peeking into the dining room to take measure of the Professor before I answered.

Beany was a big man, not fat but regal in size, and it was clear to anyone—any woman, anyway—that he was probably carved out of stone as a young man. He had a full head of gray hair that was long, even for a college town, and Greek features, a classic, straight nose, deep-set eyes and a serious mouth that had clearly suffered from an overabundance of alcohol, fermenting as it were over many years and filling with wrinkles. His head was large, probably because it hadn't shrunk over the years like his body and seemed to hover above his shoulders, which were draped with a scarf over his sport jacket. It gave his head a disembodied, spiritual quality to it.

"Sure," I told Georgina.

In truth, I was tired from the opening and the weeks leading up to it and if Beany hadn't looked so interesting standing there without a winter coat and been a professor at Smith, I might have turned him away and suggested that he order some soup to take home.

It turned out to be a rather late night, since Professor Beany was not one to be rushed. He lingered over his bottle of wine, ripping his bread into small pieces, the way it should be done, so that there is more surface area to soak up the broth—I refused to allow any butter or olive oil on the table—and finishing two big bowls of my Tibetan lentil soup.

"He wants to meet the chef," Georgina said, coming into the kitchen and sitting up on the counter.

Since he was the only patron left, and had been for quite some time, I obliged.

"Tess Alexander," I said, wiping my hands on my apron as I stepped up to his table in the corner, "owner, head chef and just about everything else…other than waitress."

Professor Beany smiled. He had a great smile that spread immediately to his eyes. He poured out what remained of his red wine and took a sip while he looked me up and down, not the way some men look at me, like they're hoping I might also be on the menu, but like an artist searching for the right perspective, as if he were trying to understand something about me that might be visible only to him.

"Named after Hardy's main character in *Tess of the D'Urbervilles*?"

"No, my grandmother Gussie, they always called her Tess."

"You know what Hardy did to your namesake?"

"Got her pregnant and killed her off," I said. I was a woman's lit major, so it was impossible to avoid *Tess of the D'Urbervilles.*

The professor smiled.

"She was from a great family fallen on hard times, used and abandoned by a narrow-minded, young minister."

"Which is why I suppose I've never been a big fan of organized religion," I said.

I had no idea why I was suddenly so talkative, perhaps because it was late and I was tired, or perhaps because I had yet to really meet anyone in Northampton other than my landlord, the banker and my suppliers. Of course, it didn't hurt that there was obviously no reason to be concerned about another romantic entanglement in Beany's case.

"What is your religion?" he asked.

"Isn't that a question you're not supposed to ask?"

"I don't have to worry about being politically correct at my age. Everything gets blamed on my dotage."

"I suppose college professors are not confined to the same rules of decorum that the rest of us are."

"They're much worse actually," he said. "Professors have to live up to the expectations of thousands of students, not to mention hordes of administrators and other faculty."

"OK, let me think about it."

"If you have to think about it then it's not a religion."

"My true religion is kindness," I said, having read it once somewhere and liked it very much.

"You and the Dalai Lama," Professor Beany said.

He took another sip of wine.

"Tess Alexander," he said looking up at his glass, "it's a name more fitting for an actress or writer, or even a swindler, than a chef in a small college town."

"There's no better place to hide from my fate."

"Well, I hope you stay hidden for a while longer, because a soup like this," he said smacking his lips, "is a narcotic. It is possessed of unspeakable joy and too easily ruined by the powers of commercialism."

Georgina, who had been listening over my shoulder, laughed and walked away.

"A business major, no doubt."

I nodded.

"They tend to hibernate during the English prerequisites."

"Well, I'm glad you are enjoying the soup. I intend to change them on a weekly basis."

"And I intend to be here on a weekly basis."

With that, he raised his glass to me and went back to eating. I went back to the kitchen, figuring Professor Beany to be a lonely, old man with nothing but time to think about all those important moments in life which, except for one, had passed him by. I imagined him a widower missing his wife and unhappy with his relationship with his adult children; a semi-retired professor frustrated with his reduced caseload, the modern hi-tech student and his own diminished productivity, who ducked into Circa to hide from time, which was hot on his heels.

I really didn't expect to see him for a while. Then late the following Thursday, Georgina came in to pick up two orders of the mushroom barley soup, my mother's specialty, one of the soups in my repertoire that I didn't run partly through the Cuisinart.

"He's back," she said, filling a basket with bread.

"Who?"

"Your professor friend."

So I peeked out of the kitchen and there was Beany at the same table with his bottle of wine and a book, looking over the chalkboard menu.

"Back again," I said, coming out after the other diners had left.

"Would you join me for a glass of wine," he said, "in celebration?"

"Of what?"

"Of the blessings bestowed upon you by the soup gods."

The way he said things always made me laugh. So I joined him for a glass and we spent so long talking that I sent Georgina home and locked up on my own.

"Tell me what brought you here."

"To Northampton?" I said.

"No, to the point where your life is in the soup so to speak and you're hiding in our small corner of the world."

"What makes you think I'm hiding?"

He looked around the restaurant.

"Other than the fact that you said so last week, there's the dim lighting, the side street location and the small window in the kitchen door that's almost impossible to see through, at least from this side."

"You're very good," I said with a laugh.

"Not really. We're all hiding something, although, believe it or not, people always think that they have more to hide at your age than at mine."

"That isn't true?"

"You accumulate secrets as you get older; you just find more places to put them so they stay out of sight and are less obvious."

I nodded.

"So tell me what brought you here."

So we talked about me…in general terms, nothing too specific. I told him how I grew up as an only child without a father. He was an only child as well and grew up with a father who worked long hours when he was young and died before Beany reached his teens.

"There are all kinds of ways for parents to be absent," he said.

When I eventually learned that Beany didn't have any children of his own, I wondered if was because he put too much of himself into his teaching and writing, and didn't want to be one of those fathers present in body, but absent in spirit.

"Why only soups?" he asked.

"That's my small talent."

"A small talent can be a curse," Beany said, "take it from me. What you have is a very big talent."

Beany then picked up his wineglass, which was nearly full and drained it completely. It was the first time that I noticed he wasn't just a gulper, he was a super-gulper. I suppose at his age there wasn't any time to waste . . . and it took more to deaden the pain, whatever it was.

I never saw or spoke with Professor Beany any time other than during his Thursday nights at Circa. On the one-year anniversary of our year of soup, I made him his favorite - winter minestrone, which, in addition to vegetables of every persuasion from parsnips to kidney beans, also included a generous helping of a good, dry Napa Valley Cabernet. However, when he didn't show at his normal time I got somewhat concerned. I grew even more concerned when I asked Georgina to call him and there was no answer.

The police found him dead in his living room chair, a book of poetry on his lap, a glass of wine by his side and a stomach full of pills in place of my soup.

CHAPTER TWO

I saw most of my regular customers over the next few days and Beany was the main topic of conversation. Captain Tom Dale, the chief of police, was the first to come in after the funeral because the next day I had New England clam chowder on the menu, for which I always abandoned my vegan leanings by adding chopped bacon, and he never misses it when I do. He says it makes him feel like a little boy again visiting his grandmother on Cape Cod.

He was also the only one of the regulars comfortable enough to pop into the kitchen before he left. I suppose policeman don't consider doors much of an obstacle.

"Great as always Tess," he said, "even bought a container to take home for the missus."

"Go easy on it Tom," I said, because I didn't believe him, "it's got about a gallon of butter and cream."

"It's a great way to go."

"Suicide by soup isn't going to be good for business."

It was a stupid thing to say. I realized it right away so I stuck my head in the pot in front of me and stirred. Tom gave me a moment to settle down. He was unlike any cop I'd ever met before. He knew exactly when to give you space. He was more grandfatherly and pastoral than authoritative. He made you want to do the right thing. He didn't have to tell you to do it.

"Too bad about the Professor," he said. "We all liked him . . . although half the time I didn't understand him."

"These onions," I said, picking up a dish towel to wipe my eyes.

He put the soup down on the table and took a step closer.

"Wasn't a Thursday night I can remember," he said in a low, soft voice, "that I didn't see the Professor walking by the station on his way here. You could see by the lift in his step just how much he was looking forward to it."

It was all I could do to nod and swallow, so I turned to the stove and stirred one of the soups.

"What did Georgina tell me you called it again . . . the Thursday nights?"

"The year of soup."

"Right," Tom said, his expression so serious it looked as if he was about to arrest me. "Sometimes the pain gets too hard to take, especially at his age . . . particularly when you're alone. There's nothing anyone could have done about it . . . not you . . . not anyone."

He put his hand on my shoulder and I turned away to keep from adding any tears to the soup.

"Soup's never gonna be enough," he said with a little fatherly pat on my back. "It can't do it all."

I nodded without looking over at him.

"Alone is always much harder," he said, walking over to the door. "And that goes for you too."

Georgina came in after Tom left and it was a good thing that there were still some freshly chopped onions on the cutting board so I didn't have to explain my teary eyes. Otherwise, she'd have had a thousand questions and no one would have gotten served.

"Lisa Montero wants to say hello."

"She wants to talk about Beany," I said.

"That too."

"Tell her I'll be out in a minute."

I knew I wouldn't be able to duck her for long so I figured I might as well get it over with.

Lisa owned a unisex beauty parlor on the next street and would run over between appointments whenever the weather turned cold and nasty to gulp down the chicken soup of the week. She also considered herself the local matchmaker and me her lost cause.

"I know how you must be feeling," she said as soon as I walked out of the kitchen. I was drying my hands on my apron, but she still grabbed them with her own.

"I wish he'd have let me cut his hair," she said, "I'd have made him look 10 years younger."

"I don't think that was it," I said.

"You'd be surprised at how important hair is to your self-image."

I managed a weak smile.

Beany was vain about most everything, but not his hair. He let his hair go, as if that was his way of rebelling against the college and his status as professor emeritus. It drove Lisa crazy and she offered him a free haircut about once a month.

"I could make you look cuter," she said to me, "than you already are if you'd let me change that college ponytail thing of yours."

"It keeps it out of the way of the soup. Besides, I don't want to look cute."

"You can't help it," Lisa said. "But you need short now, something more suitable for a 30-year old, something more sophisticated."

"How sophisticated do I have to be? I make soup."

"You're a culinary artist."

"Artists need long hair. It gives them strength."

Lisa dropped her smile.

"I want to get serious for a moment."

"OK."

"I can come by later tonight for some soup if you'd like. I'll bring a bottle of wine. I'll sit at the same table. Life goes on. He'd want that."

It hadn't dawned on me yet that it was Thursday. I'd sort of lost track of the days. This would be the first one without Beany, not counting the night of his suicide.

"I think I'm talked out for a while," I said. "I'm just going to close on time for a change and go home. I'm researching some new soups."

"I'm a phone call away if you change your mind. Lord knows you need a friend at a time like this . . . and you can have more than one if you say the word."

"I appreciate that."

"I've got a whole black book full of eligible young men, so when you're finally ready all you have to do is let me know. There are a couple of hunks I know, even if it's just for a quick tumble . . . girls too."

"Do you think Beany was holding me back?"

"You know what I mean. I'm working late tonight and I'll be sitting home alone after that."

"What happened to Phil?"

"Dumped him, the guy was a walking pigsty and he shed worse than a black lab. I'm working on someone new . . . makes furniture, tough as nails. I'll keep you posted."

Lisa went through a lot of guys, three in the time since I'd been open. I suppose that being a matchmaker means there's always something new and different in the inventory.

The last two regulars to come by to check me out that first Thursday were Orit Nelson, the 78-year old town librarian, and Joe Johnson, who owned a three bay gas station he inherited from his father. He was born on the same day as me, which he brought up about once a week as a good reason, astrologically speaking, that we should hitch our stars together.

Orit had arranged a display at the library of Beany's scholarly commentaries after he died and was very partial to any soup with beans and lentils, which thankfully, she once told me, didn't matter since she lived alone. She lived in the house across the street from me and sometimes she'd call and I'd drop off some soup on my way home.

No matter how late I went to bed, her light was always on when I looked out my window. She said it was because she never stopped reading. She said she intended to read every book in the library before she died. She occasionally invited me in for tea when I dropped off some soup, and I was always curious to look around and see just how well the local town spinster got along, especially since I was planning to follow in her footsteps.

"I thought you might like to read the Professor's obituary in this morning's New York Times, if you haven't already."

"I haven't seen it yet."

I hadn't wanted to but I took it from Orit and she stood beside me as I read it.

"Top left," she said, "that's quite an honor."

"He looks 50 in that photo."

"55, it was on the jacket for his book on 20th century English poets."

She waited until I finished before speaking again.

"The two of us were a couple of birds of a feather," she said, "old birds to be precise."

I nodded. I knew what was coming, because I'd heard it from her before.

"Both of us loved books, neither of us could find anyone to measure up to them. Not a question of too high expectations, just the way it is with book people like us."

She touched my arm when she said that to make sure I realized she was including me in us. As a woman's lit major I suppose I qualified.

I'd heard that Orit spent most of her life taking care of her father who lived to 85. He died in the same house where she lived, which was also right around the corner from the library. I suppose books were the only way she had of escaping her narrow world. It was different for Beany . . . me too.

"I'm not quite as bookish," I said, "but I have my soup."

"I'm sure that's enough dear, but if you need to talk when you get home I'll be up late or if you want a good book just knock, nothing can take you out of your misery like a good book."

"Thanks, I will."

Joe Johnson, the best mechanic in the State of Massachusetts, at least according to him walked in just as Georgina was getting ready to close up. He was wearing his greasy overalls, not his clean courting ones, which I suppose might mean he was getting a bit discouraged. He always ordered that spiciest soup on the menu. Georgina was writing down his order when I came out of the kitchen to see if she needed any help.

"You here to ask me out again," I asked with a little smile, "or for the soup?"

"The soup, unless you tell me the answer is gonna change."

"Now that my Thursdays are free," I said.

Joe, Georgina and I all stared over at Beany's table.

"I didn't mean it like that," I said and Joe and Georgina just nodded.

For a while Joe asked me out pretty much every time he saw me and he never seemed to mind that I always said no. I said no to everyone, man and woman and I had a lot of offers. Good cooking works on both sexes. The rumor I heard a few times was that I had had some kind of operation on my ovaries that left me estrogen-depleted and asexual, which might explain why Joe sometimes used to stand as close as he could to me examining my face like he was looking for the signs of a moustache or beard.

"I'll never ask on a Thursday," Joe said, "in honor of the Bean."

"That's very kind of you."

"But if you need a ride home . . . ."

"You know I always walk."

"Or someone to walk you home tonight, I got nothing better to do."

"It's a nice offer Joe, but I just want to be alone."

Georgina brought out Joe's soup.

"It's on the house," I said.

"You don't have to do that," he said.

"It's the least I can do for my last remaining suitor."

"Whose fault is that?" Georgina said and Joe laughed.

"There are a couple of big dirty pots in the sink with your name on it."

Georgina curtsied and left. Joe picked up the bag.

"You're like that big, shiny fish in Occum's Pond that everyone swears they almost caught. Eventually someone's gonna snag it."

"Been snagged, Joe, more than once, I'm too smart now to bite."

"No one's that smart," he said, waving behind him as he walked out the door, "or that lucky."

CHAPTER THREE

At first when Beany and I talked on Thursday nights it was mostly about my life. I hadn't had a listener like that since my mother died and I must say his discriminating ear coupled with the aroma of the soups and the long time that had passed since my last relationship ended, at least by my reckoning, made it easier for me to talk.

I tried to give Beany his turn, insisting from time to time that I wouldn't continue if he didn't share as well, which is when I'd hear about his job during the war, his bad back, his insomnia and sometimes about the politics of teaching young women at a great college like Smith. He was always glad to speak about what he called his truest and most faithful love, great literature. He talked about poetry, which he analyzed and wrote about, as well as writing himself, and great novels and novelists, particularly D. H. Lawrence, E. M. Forster, and Virginia Woolf, who were the subjects of much of his scholarly output.

"D. H. Lawrence was obsessed with the dehumanizing effect of industrialization," Beany told me during one of his early wine-induced mini-lectures, "and was reviled by the critics because of the importance he put on sexuality."

"Isn't sex important?" I asked, although I couldn't have sounded like much of a believer having practiced celibacy since leaving San Francisco. I usually had quite a bit to drink as well on these Thursday nights, trying to match Beany glass for glass, although he could hold his liquor like no man I'd ever met before. No matter how much he had to drink his gaze never wavered or watered and his words never slurred or lost their focus.

"If it's accompanied by love," he said.

That made me laugh.

"Not for my generation," I said. "The love part doesn't matter in the least. It's like who can have the most sex wins."

"And how are you doing?"

"I quit while I was ahead."

"I've noticed," Beany said, rubbing his chin and examining me like he was looking for a loose thread.

"And how's that?"

"Your frustrated mechanic friend and the hair stylist with her little black book, this is a small town if you hadn't noticed."

"Joe and Lisa are just customers. I'm trying to keep my private life separate from work."

"Then you shouldn't be so obvious about it."

"You mean pretend that I have a fella overseas that I'm waiting for?"

"About modeling your life after our esteemed librarian."

"She seems happy enough," I said.

"You're not her."

I took a quick gulp of wine.

"Anyway," Beany continued, "I wasn't talking about over-hormoned teenagers and twenty-something year olds. I was talking about adults. Love and sex should go together."

"Well I'm done with latter," I said.

"And love?"

"That too."

Beany poured us both some more wine.

"That's too bad."

"That's all you have to say?"

"The art of criticism my dear requires time and study." With that he turned the conversation back to literature.

E. M. Forster was clearly Beany's favorite author. Unlike Lawrence, he was a favorite of the critics, although he wrote only five novels, the last of which, *A Passage To India*, was written at the age of 45.

"His stories were all about characters trying to connect with each other," Beany explained, "as well as with their place and time. The context was always important. Sometimes they made the connection, most of the time they didn't. Unfortunately, the differences were often irreconcilable."

I found Virginia Woolf the most interesting of the three, at least in terms of her life, and no doubt in part because she had committed suicide, although Beany never talked much about that. Instead, he focused on her as a lyrical novelist, who brought the stream of consciousness to English literature, explored the flux of time and life, and considered art as a way to transform life. Of course, it was her sexual ambivalence - having a husband, a fulfilling marriage, and a long time female lover – that interested me the most.

From Beany's description, I could be the culinary version of Virginia Woolf. Instead of using a stream of consciousness, I relied upon a stream of ingredients and the flux of time to reduce them to their common essence, believing just as strongly that my soup could also transform life. Circa was my *room of one's own.* I suppose the sexual ambivalence and mood swings, if not tempered by my soup, could conceivably lead to the same end, although I doubted it. Other than exploring it philosophically in college as part of one of my classes, suicide has never held any interest or attraction for me, certainly not the way solitude and celibacy now did.

"Enough with the lecture," I said, after Beany started talking about the Bloomsbury Group, "tell me something personal. It's only fair."

So he told me that his father died when he was young and his mother passed away shortly after he returned from World War II, where he had the unenviable job of going in after the battle to retrieve the bodies.

That sent a shiver down my spine.

"I thought about becoming a funeral director when I got back," he said, "because death no longer scared me, but I already had my college degree in English and with all the GIs going back to school there were a lot of openings for professors."

He never talked much about any other difficult memories he must have seen when he closed his eyes, either because he had played the professor for so long or because I was always so busy talking about mine and, in particular, my big three difficult memories names Nick, Jake and Jolene.

"My problem," I said one Thursday after I'd had enough wine to make it impossible to avoid those hard realities and maintain those self-delusions I was so good at doing while I was busy in the kitchen, "is that I always seem to make poor choices."

"Not when it comes to soup," Beany said, signaling to Georgina for another bowl of my Tuscan minestrone soup, which he had declared one of his top three favorites. I only made it when I could get fresh tomatoes and other organic vegetables from one of the neighboring farms.

"I mean take Nick."

"He was the first one out of college," Beany said and I nodded, as if it were the right answer to a pop quiz.

"A complete change of direction . . . the first man in my life who was all about money . . . 24/7 . . . he thought the dollar bill was a work of art and studied the stock quotes like they were great literature . . . he was like a flasher."

"Really?"

"Not that kind of flasher, a financial flasher . . . he'd flex his bank statements like he was showing off his biceps."

Beany laughed.

"And Jake," I said, "that was another one of my really good choices . . . come on, a drug dealer . . . really . . . the one good thing I can say about him is that he drew the line at 18. He wouldn't sell to minors."

"Number 2 on the 3-year wheel of fortune," Beany said and I nodded again. "And then there's Jolene, the third and most recent, the one who broke the clock."

"What?"

"Stopped time from moving forward."

"Don't be ridiculous," I said.

"How was she a bad choice, because it ended?" Beany said. "Everything ends."

"Because it was all about the sex . . . she was always ready for action . . . there was no . . . no . . . ."

"Music," Beany said.

"Soup sentimentality."

Beany's eyebrows jumped at that one and when Georgina brought over his soup he had her bring me over some coffee.

"That's what we do in our twenties," he said, after she walked away.

"What?"

"Make bad choices. They help you make the hard decisions later on."

I reached for my wine, but the glass was empty. Beany made no effort to fill it. Instead he pointed at the coffee Georgina had already put down in front of me.

"OK," I said, "while I sober up tell me some of your bad choices."

Of course he didn't. He talked some more about the war. He had volunteered to retrieve bodies because he thought it would be easier than shooting people. Then he told me about the trouble he was having falling asleep.

"I've simply fallen out of love with it."

Sleep no longer soothed and caressed the way it did when he was a young man, he said. Instead it threatened to sneak in like some nocturnal beast, stealing everything and leaving him silent forever.

"What's the bad decision in that?" I said.

He just shrugged and ate some more soup.

"At least tell me how did you wound up at an all girl's school like Smith?" I asked. "Trying to make up for lost time?"

Beany smiled and lifted his glass in a silent toast. There were certain things he wouldn't talk about and if a professor emeritus wants to remain silent or change the subject there's nothing anyone can do about it.

I knew that Beany had never married but I attributed it to the fact that when he arrived here after the war it was like being the first one on line at the midnight buffet. There were so many choices and so much to experience, settling for one would have seemed emotionally and intellectually shortsighted.

And Beany was a real hunk back then, because he brought in some photos taken right after the war when I threatened to refuse to serve him any more soup unless he did. They were black-and-white, but I could see the brilliant, sandy color of his baby-fine hair as it fell casually across his eyes. He had muscles everywhere in his arms and neck. I could even see them pressing up against his collared shirt and long pants.

"You looked like Mr. Universe," I said, touching the photo lightly with my finger.

"I'd spent almost four years lifting weights every day," he said. "Unfortunately, the weights were the shells of fallen soldiers."

I let a few moments of silence pass and while those words reverberated in Circa's small dining room I studied the photo more closely. Beany looked about 25, but he looked unlike any 25-year old I had known. He was looking straight through the camera, like he couldn't see it. He certainly wasn't posing for it. His mouth may have been wiped clean of expression, but he wasn't quite that guarded with the rest of his face. There was something very solemn and resigned in his eyes, as if he was lost or had lost something in himself that he could never find again, like his inner child. That was something very melancholy and arresting for a 25-year old.

"The coeds must have swarmed around you," I said to break the spell, "like gnats on a warm summer day."

"I kept my work and personal life separate. Isn't that your rule?"

"Only after you've had your 3 strikes."

Beany shook his head from side to side.

"It's not baseball Tess," he said. He only used my name when he didn't care for my answer. "There's no limit to love, the heart is inexhaustible, particularly at your age."

"According to whom," I said, "our local confirmed bachelor?"

"Every poet throughout recorded history."

"Then what made you so special? How come you escaped it and never settled down?"

I hated those two words as soon as I said them – settled down. I made them sound more like giving up.

"Stubborn I guess and I had my work, my poetry and my writing. I was obsessed with it back then. There wasn't time for much else besides writing and teaching, and I had to make a name for myself. It was publish or perish."

Beany took his time sipping his wine.

"One day you look up and it's all behind you. The days may drag on but the years fly by."

I could understand not needing another person to be complete. I had my soup and I was obsessed with creating new ones and improving the old ones. I wasn't interested in any new distractions, not even the comfort and contentment it might offer. Creativity, be it literary or culinary, requires a certain amount of uncertainty and solitude. Hadn't poets throughout recorded history agreed with that?

Of course, Beany could have been asexual or even gay—I had no way of knowing and I wasn't going to ask. It was not the kind of conversation that would have brought him back to Circa every Thursday night. I could see it in his eyes sometimes, the way they seemed to lose consciousness of his own life as he sipped his wine, breathed in the soup and focused on my life and my words. He needed time off from being old and alone, not an analysis of what might have gone wrong.

At some point during our Thursday night conversations we'd get around to talking about my present "bent" as Beany put it "towards celibacy and spinsterhood." When he finished joking about Joe Johnson, who promised me a lifetime of free car care, and when he learned I didn't own a car, a discount on the cleanest, smoothest-running used car on his lot, and Lisa Montero, who would trim his hair on occasion and complain about how I refused to let her set me up with anyone, man or woman, he'd prod me for more about Nick, Jake and Jolene.

"I understand that you came to Northampton to hide with your soup," he said, "but I'm still not convinced that you have all that much to hide from."

This had to be sometime around the beginning of our second month of Thursdays.

"I need more details," he said, "if I'm going to understand it."

"You mean criticize it," I said. "Aren't you Smith's most noted critic?"

"Literary critic," Beany said. "Believe me when it comes to your personal life, it's purely a prurient interest."

"I'm glad to hear that part of you is still alive."

"I teach in a college filled with coeds, some of its bound to rub off."

"You sure you want to hear this?" I said. "It's just going to sound like more of the coed stuff."

"Try me," Beany said. "It's the same heart whatever the age and whatever the time."

So I told him the Nick details. What you saw was what you got with Nick. There were no layers below the surface.

"He got me with those untroubled eyes," I said. "They were never the least bit self-conscious."

"A good superficial relationship is healthy at that age . . . any age really. Happy, contented people with no shadows or secrets are as necessary sometimes, if you ask me, as a good Chianti."

"So where are all yours?"

"I make do with the good Chianti," Beany said.

I was living in Plattsburgh at the time, I explained, working for the local newspaper covering area business news when I met Nick. We were covering the opening of a new apartment building overlooking Lake Champlain, the tallest building within 50 miles, where he was renting the penthouse, an octagonal apartment with windows all around. The views were stunning. The sex was just as unbelievable, hot from the start, which was great in a place that cold during the winter. It wasn't a relationship built on much else.

"When we weren't having sex," I said, "we were lying wordlessly on the couch watching his big screen TV."

"So far I'm jealous," Beany said, waving Georgina over for some more soup.

He had just finished a bowl of the mushroom barley, which I made with 8 varieties of mushrooms and imported Italian barley. I remember the soups I was serving like most women remember the clothes they were wearing.

"Go on," he said after Georgina put another bowl in front of him.

"Nick had no immense secrets or troubling thoughts," I said, "at least none that I could sense and I'm pretty good at that. His main ambition in life was conspicuous consumption."

"A noble American aspiration," Beany said.

"All he ever talked about was getting rich, not just rich, but very, very rich, and he was well on his way to getting there. And he certainly intended to spend every last cent of it before it was too late. He was good at that."

"You can't take it with you," Beany said with a smile.

"You could give some of it away. He wouldn't even buy Girl Scout cookies."

"He might have softened after his first million."

"He was one of those people," I said, "valedictorian of his high school class, 4.0 straight through college, who could always understand things faster than anyone else."

"I don't know, he sounds perfect," Beany said, although it wasn't hard to detect the note of sarcasm that mingled with the dill and parsley notes steaming up from the bowl of soup in front of him.

"One night out of the blue he told me that he loved me."

"Chilling I'm sure, but I suspect you'd heard that line before," Beany said, knowing how trite those three words have become and how susceptible girls in their 20s were to it.

"But we weren't in a passionate embrace. We were sitting fully clothed, drinking wine, listening to his $3,000 stereo and staring out his picture window at the snow-covered Green Mountains. He was sipping his red wine slowly and deliberately, like the great un-anguished often do."

Beany smiled at that one.

"He was sitting there with a big smile on his face," I continued, "like he'd just had the funniest thought, happy as a clam."

"The original phrase," Beany said, "was happy as a clam at high tide, which was when the clam diggers couldn't find them."

"He was always happy on Friday night, not so much because of the weekend ahead, but because that was the day he went through his finances and took the measure of his cash flow and net worth. It was always heading in one direction, so he liked to light the fire and open up an expensive bottle of wine. He'd drink about 3/4's it."

"At least you got to taste it."

"He didn't let me gulp like you do."

"I was never a sipper," Beany said. "I guess the high tide was never high enough. So what happened after he professed his love? I'm guessing it was all a Ponzi scheme and there was a rap at the door followed by the police breaking in."

"I wish. He turned to me on the couch and repeated it. I mean it Tess, he said, I really love you. Then he patted me on the back for emphasis."

"A true romantic."

"I mean the sex is great, he said, and your body is just . . . wow."

"And a poetic soul," Beany said, closing his eyes for a second as he sipped down the soup. Potato leak had a way sometimes of taking you out of the moment to someplace better, at least for an instant.

"He said wow," I said, "I swear."

"A lot of words rhyme with wow. Don't tell me he next called you a cow or sow?"

"Stop," I said, pouring myself some more wine.

"Sorry, go on."

"So he adds 'but I'll never be able to figure out why. I always thought that the woman I loved would be someone really smart . . . at least as smart as me'."

Beany mumbled something. I could swear it was asshole, although he was not one to use foul language. He followed that up by remarking that the dumbest people he's ever met were the ones who measured smarts by grades and test scores.

"Anyway," I continued, "I turned away to keep him from seeing my eyes fill up with tears . . . now that I knew what my lover really thought about me."

"And walked out I hope," Beany said.

"I wish I had. I knew at that point what was coming, what would eventually come, but I just gulped my wine and stuck around three more weeks until he said it was over. Sex can only carry you so far."

"He said that?"

I nodded.

"The girl waiting in the wings was a little heavy and not any smarter, but she had a big, fat trust fund."

Beany didn't say a word. He always knew when words wouldn't make a difference. Later when he was leaving and I was walking him to the door, he did say that maybe I had been hunting the wrong species up until now.

"You mean I should start looking for extraterrestrials?"

"Maybe you need someone who desperately needs your soup, someone with a dark shadow across his soul . . . or hers . . . and an immense secret that needs someplace safe to hide."

"I'm done with all that," I said. "And what about that Dylan Thomas poem you like so much . . . *Do not go gentle into that good night.*"

"What about it?"

"I'm not going to do love anymore," I said, "not without kicking and screaming . . . and raging against love's dying light, which begins to die the moment it's born."

Beany shook his head from side to side.

"He was talking about the end of creativity and life," Beany said, "not fighting love and living alone.

CHAPTER FOUR

I didn't just pick Northampton by throwing a dart at a map or because it was a small college town in the middle of soup-sensitive New England. I picked it because it was surrounded by colleges and well know for being arty and very lesbian-friendly, which might or might not matter, since I wasn't sure what I was. It struck me as the type of place where people could appreciate the medicinal qualities of soup and accept it as a complete meal. Beside, it was also a continent away from my last 3-year romance.

I used to describe San Francisco as "the nicest place I'd ever been dumped."

Beany hated that word – dumped - at least the way I used it, and I frequently used it when talking about Nick, Jake and Jolene.

"I know it's not very poetic," I remember saying one Thursday night about a third of the way into our "year of soup" when the end of my relationship with Nick came up again.

I was telling him the last thing Nick said to me as I carried my stuff out of that beautiful penthouse apartment.

"If there's anything I can do for you, he said, anything, anytime, just ask. I really mean it."

"He probably did," Beany said. "Once you've finished loving someone you'll do most anything in the world for them, except love them again."

"That's not what you read in the papers."

"Usually, not always, there are exceptions to every rule."

"It's about as common a dumping line," I said, "as I've ever heard. In fact, I got to hear it 2 more times."

He groaned, as he did every time I used that word.

"What word would you use instead of dumped?"

Beany took his time answering. He couldn't be rushed when he had a bowl of hot soup, fresh bread and a glass of dry red wine in front of him.

"Youth's a stuff will not endure," he said, quoting Shakespeare.

"It's no less painful because you're young," I said.

"But it's not final . . . it's to be expected. The 20s are a time to find love and to lose love. Lost is a much better word than dumped . . . so is death. I like a love that's died or been lost much more than I do a love that's been dumped."

"But I hadn't lost it," I said, "I still felt it."

"Love needs its own reflection," he said, "if you hadn't realized you were losing it, you would soon enough."

"So there's no such thing as unrequited love?"

"Not for ordinary people thankfully, only for poets."

"Like you," I said. "So who was your unrequited love?"

"Literature."

"That's not fair."

"Not every life can be about love, it's too fragile for some and quick to disappear; some lives have to be about self-fulfillment, creation and art. I'm not talking about you," he added in case I was getting any idea that I was in the same category as Smith's esteemed professor emeritus of poetry and English literature.

"Would you go back to Nick if you had the chance?"

He knew the answer to that one.

"Lost as well," Beany said with a nod. "And how long did it take you to find love number 2?"

I started dating Jake two weeks later, he knew that.

"And the third?"

"Why does the time matter?"

"Because the numbness doesn't last very long when you're that young," Beany said. "Dreams are too aggressive at your age and every longing is a hug and kiss. It's like the Dylan Thomas poem . . . dying makes it possible for a new leaf to grow."

"That would apply at any age."

"Growing old is a resignation . . . some things stop growing back."

I didn't respond. Beany looked so unhappy when he said it that I didn't want to prolong the moment.

"You didn't have any problems until you moved here, closed your eyes and put your fingers in your ear."

"Because the last one was different."

"Because it was a woman?"

"Yes."

I'd never had a relationship like that with a woman before. Girls were important in high school and college as friends and confidants, because in truth no man can replace a true and close girlfriend on the telephone when all you want to do is sleep and die and come back in an entirely different body in the morning.

"What do you expect milk and cookies?" Beany said. "Love, forbidden or not, is a delicious torment."

"Who said that?"

"Emerson."

Jake was next. He taught math in the same private school where I was teaching art. He was a few years older and supplemented his income selling marijuana, amphetamines and coke, although never to any of the students. And he only used pot, keeping the best for himself, and switching to single-malt scotch when he needed a more conventional escape.

"I didn't like the drug thing," I said, "but he promised to stop when he had enough money."

"What was he running from?" Beany asked.

"Nothing that I could tell."

Jake didn't have any thwarted ambitions, I told him, or tragic losses. He was just a happy guy who liked having the extra money and good stuff around to get high, like he was trying to hold on to college as long as he could. I didn't mind getting high and I hardly made any soup during my Jake years.

"Three years and kicked out," I said, "same as always."

Beany then repeated what he'd tell me many more times during our year of soup that what I needed was someone—man or woman, he didn't seem to have any prejudice in that regard—who had a closet full of his or her own ghosts to exorcise, so we could do things together with warm baths, good books and credit cards, trading the pains of what was for the pleasures of what is. Someone, he liked to say, who really needed my soup.

"Mr. or Ms. Happy," he said, "who never look back and aren't burdened with hard choices, who don't understand themselves and didn't want to try will never have a shelf life of more than three years . . . when it comes to you."

"What about you?" I said.

"What about me?" he responded.

"What have you been doing over the past 20 years about the pleasures of right now?"

"Observe," he said holding up his glass of wine, pointing down at my soup and nodding at the book he had brought with him to keep busy until I found the time to pop out of the kitchen.

"So how did Jake end it," Beany asked, "a note from prison?"

We must have begun our third month of Thursdays by now.

"Pretty much the same way as Nick, he had this thing with a former student. She was over 21 at the time and he kept seeing her behind my back. She was a senior in college. She was into drugs, dropped out and moved back . . . so he dumped me . . . I'm sorry, I meant to say he discarded the love . . . or should I say itch."

"If you ask me," Beany said, "it was time to move on and find someone a little better, or at least with a better hobby."

"All right, so he turned out to be an idiot and I was better off without him, but it was another 3 years and another big mistake."

"Mistakes are portals of discovery," Beany said. "James Joyce."

Sometimes Beany made me feel like an attorney summing up to a jury of one, trying to convince him beyond a reasonable doubt that finishing the journey alone, accompanied by my soups, was the right way, the only way for me to go; a similar path to the one Beany had followed. But clearly he remained unconvinced.

CHAPTER FIVE

I had to make a lot of soups to get through the first two weeks after the funeral and Circa's menu board had double the normal variety, which for some reason seemed to upset people more than excite them.

"Too many choices," Captain Tom said when he came in to pick up something to bring home for dinner, although his real complaint was that New England clam chowder wasn't on the menu. He and his wife were big clam chowder fans. It's a good soup for helping you focus on the good memories, instead of the bad ones and I know Tom and his wife had their share of those, which included the loss of a child in a car accident.

"I think New England should be one of the regular staples."

"I'm picky about my clams Tom. I'm not getting them out of a can."

Tom sighed as he continued to stare at the board trying to make a decision. I think police by nature crave routine and need something that they're familiar with. Tom was always at a loss if New England or some similar creamy chowder wasn't on the menu.

"What's this Hungarian Pepperstock?"

"Too spicy, good for loneliness, I wouldn't recommend it."

Tom laughed.

"What's the closest thing you've got to New England?"

I studied the board.

"In terms of effect?"

"In terms of taste."

"I didn't use an ounce of cream tonight in anything . . . too soothing."

"You're not ready yet to let go of the pain," he said.

"Exactly."

"The longer you hold on to it," Tom said, "the harder it will be to let go when you're ready. Take it from me I've seen more than my share of suicides and accidents and what it does to the people left. You need to find someone to fill up the empty space."

"On Thursday night?"

"Every night," Tom said. "It's time you started looking out instead of in all the time. What you need is a good creamy soup."

"Yes Dad, maybe tomorrow."

"Just trying to be helpful, that's what they pay me the big bucks for."

"Well Captain Dale," I said, "you can help by keeping Joe and Lisa off my back. I don't react well to pressure. Is there such a thing as attempted date harassment? The only one on my side these days is Orit."

"That figures. You want to be the next librarian?"

"I'm happy cataloguing my soups."

"Was Beany on your side?" he asked.

"No comment."

Dale nodded slowly, like my answer was the same as a confession.

"So what do you recommend?" he asked looking back up at the board.

"I'd recommend the navy bean soup, tomatoes, oregano, beans, basil and quinoa. It's good for filling in some of those empty spaces. We all have things we miss."

Tom nodded slowly and I sent Georgina into the kitchen to get it for him.

Everyone gave me some space the first couple of weeks, but by the beginning of the third week the gloves were off. Lisa brought her little black book with her every time she came in for soup and insisted on telling me about her latest additions, both male and female. She even offered me a free makeover.

"You won't recognize yourself when I'm through with you."

That was about as tempting an offer as anyone had made to me since I'd moved to Northampton.

"Too much change," I said, "and I might lose my soup power."

"God forbid, half the town would kill me."

Joe was back to his dress overalls and was on reason number 200 as to how my life would never be the same if I went out with him.

"There's a lot more to me than you can see," Joe said.

"I know that Joe," I said, "but it's not you it's me. You feel more like a brother than a lover."

Joe stuck out his lower lip and nodded, like it was the best compliment he'd had in quite some time.

Only Orit was prepared to welcome me with open arms to the lonely hearts club by bringing me book recommendation after book recommendation to fill up my time. She even invited me to dinner to try her beef stew, her father's favorite.

It was the third Thursday night after Beany's death, at about the same time that Beany used to walk in with his bottle of red wine—never in a paper bag like everyone else but out for everyone to see—that Beany's attorney walked into the restaurant.

"I'm sorry to bother you at work," he said, "but Professor Beanstock's will provides I deliver this to you on a Thursday night at this exact time."

"Because he came every week at this time for dinner," I said with a chuckle.

He just stood there looking around like he couldn't wait to run out of here. I made a mental note to look into a good soup for tight-asses.

"What is it?" I said, as he handed me the accordion file he was carrying that was neatly bound and taped.

"It's not money," he said. "People are always disappointed when they hear that."

I wasn't and I hope my eyes told him that.

"Because he left his money to a trust to establish a prize for new poets."

"So what is it?" I asked. I was tired. Thursdays seemed so much longer without Beany around, even though I was going home earlier. All I wanted to do at this point was rummage around the internet for new soups and go to sleep.

"It's a collection he picked out from his correspondence that goes back to the war."

Then he cleared his throat into his closed hand and added, "I did not read them, but that's what my secretary told me after she catalogued the contents."

"Why did he want me to have them?"

"I have no idea. They tell the lawyers what they want done, they rarely tell us why."

"Didn't he have an old friend or a colleague who would really appreciate these? Perhaps collect them for a book?"

"All dead I suspect, besides, he wasn't that famous."

"What about some distant relative?"

"None."

"Did he say what he wanted me to do with them?"

"He didn't, read them I suppose."

He was serious every second he stood there, which might explain why I had very few lawyers as regular customers, actually none that I knew of. They apparently had little need for the restorative powers of soup, perhaps because they generally seemed to like themselves the way they were.

"I'll do that," I said.

He nodded, smacked his lips together and turned to leave.

"Would you like some soup? You could have a seat at Beany's table," I said, pointing to the table I'd kept empty in his honor.

"No, thank you, I've already eaten."

He put his hand on the door knob, but stopped before opening it.

"There is one thing," he said.

"What's that?"

He raised his hand to his chin and stood still for a moment, like he was carefully weighing his words.

"I don't remember his exact words, my secretary might. She was in the office taking notes when we met about a month ago to redo his will. He gave her your name and address. She had heard about your restaurant from the woman who cuts her hair."

"Lisa Montero," I said.

"I don't the name," he said, his hand still on his chin. "Anyway, she asked him after writing it all down why the correspondence, why not a lamp or some books from his library. Professor Beanstock had an enormous library which he left to the college. Of course, I frowned at Mildred when she asked that question, because it wasn't at all appropriate. Clients don't want their attorney curious when it comes to things like that. If the beneficiary is really a distant cousin or a mistress is none of our business. Of course I told her that after he left."

"What did Beany say?"

"Beany?"

"Professor Beanstock."

"I'm trying to remember."

He rubbed his chin like he was hoping that a genie inside might pop out with the answer.

"It will help her, yes, I think that's it. He said it would help you."

"Help me do what?" I said, more confused than ever.

He just shrugged.

"People that close to death speak in riddles, I know that for a fact. I've executed quite a few deathbed wills over the years."

With that he shrugged again, pulled his collar tight around his neck and left. I took the folder full of letters into the kitchen and put it up on a high shelf so it would be out of the way, where it stayed untouched for a month while I threw myself into my soups, working day and night preparing the next days soups and experimenting with new recipes.

CHAPTER SIX

I did stop over at Orit's one night for her beef stew. I felt badly after the third time she asked. It was quite good but too much beef always leaves me uneasy and I felt as if I'd put on 50 pounds as we sat there afterward in her living room sipping tea and letting the time run away, like a day without a purpose. Still, I wanted to get her point of view. I wanted to hear all the positives of the life I proposed living, as opposed to the negatives Beany used to suggest in his own Socratic way.

"Orit, do you ever wonder whether you did the right thing?"

She was sitting in her rocker looking as content as the cat curled on her lap.

"You mean becoming the town's old maid?"

I nodded.

"Honey, anyone who tells you when they get to be my age that they got here without any regrets is either a liar or has a heart of stone."

I sipped my tea and sat back in the chair. I knew I didn't have to say another word. Orit might be an old spinster, but she wasn't afraid to speak up and she was quick to point out the nonsense of others, as well as her own.

"I know what you're thinking," she said. "I see you at the restaurant. There isn't a single eligible guy who doesn't look at you like a buried treasure . . . a lot of the girls too."

She laughed as she stroked the cat.

"I'm telling you those soups are as much a love potion as anything else . . . for the cook that is."

"That's strictly unintentional."

"Maybe if I had your opportunities," she said, "It'd have turned out differently."

"Was it taking care of your father?" I asked.

The cat jumped off her lap and she brushed off her dress.

"In part, a small part really, if I'd have wanted to find the time to go looking I could have."

Orit turned and looked out the window, although I could see she was staring through time more than through space.

"Don't listen to everything that they say in town. My father used to say that you should only believe 25 percent of what you hear and 50 percent of what you see."

That made me chuckle.

"My father was a quiet man, didn't need for much and could have done without me around all the time if I'd had the mind. No, I'd say it was my mostly my decision because it was my way . . . something I felt even as a little girl. I was happy to play by myself all the time. I liked to read and learn things on my own. I never wanted a playmate, not even an imaginary one. That wasn't the kind of love I had a thirst for."

I nodded.

"Did you ever try?"

"You mean did I ever have a fella? No, not even someone I was sweet on in school. I had chores. I had other things on my mind. I spent as much time in the library as I could, that's where I was the most comfortable . . . that's where I found love."

I nodded because soup was like that for me; it was about healing, it was about serving others and it was something I loved. If it worked for Orit and Beany, maybe researching and inventing new soups would be enough for me.

"Some people are born for one," Orit said, as she rocked slowly back and forth, "that's what my father used to say, one job, one house, one kid. It's been a rich life and I'm not overwhelmed with regrets and that's good. I'd have liked to have traveled some, but books have taken me just about everywhere . . . not just foreign places, but into a thousand different hearts . . . most of them broken."

Of course, Orit set on her path from the very beginning, which is not the same thing as wanting something more, failing at it and giving up. Of course I didn't say that, instead I asked her if she was ever confused about who she was.

"You mean whether I liked men or women?"

I nodded again.

"I'd say I like them both, although if I had to make a decision one way or another I'd say I had a preference for men."

"Did you find that confusing?"

"Honey all of life is confusing. You can't think about things too much or it'll just confuse you to the point of stillness. Don't worry about it. It is what it is. Think about the things you can change because nature isn't one of them. Focus on something else - and the world is full of something else."

"That's why I make soup," I said.

"And your soups take us around the world," Orit said, as she stood up and moved toward the door. "And into our own hearts . . . just like books."

Orit stood at the door and I stopped at the bottom step to turn around and thank her. When I looked back it was as if the light behind her was holding her in place and pulling her slowly toward it. I'm no psychic, but I thought then that she didn't have that much time left alone.

"One thing books have taught me," she said before she closed the door "is that hearts trip and fall over things much less final than abandonment and death – that can't be helped - but it's a lot easier getting back up when no one's watching."

I got back from Orit's and lay in bed unable to sleep. I was like Orit in that I'd say I preferred men as well, but the similarities seemed to end there. I hadn't grown up preferring my own company and was a social butterfly in college. Our conversation did make me think some more about Jolene and the conversations I had about her with Beany.

I'd have thought Beaney would be more interested in hearing about the end of love number 3, almost 3 years to the day it began, because she was the first woman and because Jolene was the last before I decided that I'd had enough and wanted to devote my life to soup, but he wasn't.

"Jolene's no different than the others," he said. "Why should the gender matter when love is lost?"

"The breakup was more abrupt and painful," I said.

"Because it's more recent."

"Because I didn't see it coming."

"Because women tend to trust other women," he said, "but all endings are abrupt and painful when it comes to the heart."

"Hence poetry."

He smiled as he sipped down some soup. It was probably the fifth month. I don't remember the exact date, but I do remember the soups: Thai tomato, island pumpkin, curried chestnut, clear kelp and broccoli chowder. Of the 5, Beany preferred the Thai tomato and curried chestnut. He liked his spices out front.

"I saw it coming with Nick and Jake," I said, "or should have. The conversation stopped flowing and the silence no longer felt like a shared moment."

Beany put down his spoon and looked up from his soup.

"Love that's waning begins to feel like a new secret that neither one of you care to reveal," he said.

"Who said that?"

"I did."

He smiled and picked up his wine.

"Instead of staring endlessly into my eyes, they started turning away," I said, "as if they needed to catch their breath."

"You're beginning to sound like a soap opera."

"For some reason," I said, "I'm never the one to do the breaking up, not even in high school or college."

"Why do you think that is?"

"I suppose because I'm such a creature of habit, a worshipper of those little consistencies in life."

I was stubbornly unwilling to stop loving what I once loved, as if to contemplate a change of heart like that would be treasonous. Some people inherit a weak heart. I inherited one that gladly settled for mediocrity or even solitude, because it couldn't bare uncertainty.

"Uncertainty," Beany asked, "or change?"

"Who likes change?" I said.

"Certainly not us soup lovers," Beany said, picking back up his spoon.

"I didn't see any of the signs with Jolene."

"Love and routine can make people stupid."

"There were no real emotional changes, no fights. The physical part was still good, at least I thought so. I mean it wasn't like it was those first few crazy months, but that's normal, otherwise you'd burn out."

I waited for Beany to say something, but when he didn't I continued.

"Who doesn't feel as if they're going through the motions sometimes? Maybe her evening voice sounded a bit dull at times, now that I look back on it, and maybe there were a few more apologies, but that's inevitable as relationships mature. There was really nothing that I noticed, not like with Nick and Jake."

"Men are never subtle when it comes to love."

"One day she came back to the apartment and said she wanted me to move out, just like that. At first I thought she said she wanted to eat out. I had to ask her to repeat it."

Beany nodded slowly while he sipped his soup.

"I still had feelings for her," I said. "I still do."

"And always will," Beany said. "Feelings aren't extinguished like a candle; they're stored away like any other memory."

"It was only 6 months ago."

"So it's still clear," he said. "It will fade when there are new memories . . . you have to move on."

"And that's what I've done."

"To a life of soup?"

"It can keep you warm at night," I said with a smile.

"But not for the whole night."

"It was so easy for her . . . she found someone else and transferred her feelings like an old license plate to a new car."

"It's easier for untroubled souls . . . they don't have the requisite experience or enough anguish to empathize with the pain."

"Well those are the type of people – men and women – I seem attracted to."

"Tastes change . . . that's how we learn."

"A man of few words tonight," I said.

"It's the soup."

My Creole soup with cayenne and horseradish does tend to leave people speechless. It soothes the nerves and offers the consciousness the quiet it sometimes need to listen to its own thoughts.

The choice I had to make was not just whether I wanted to try and fail again, but who I was and what gender I really wanted. It would have been easier to be strictly heterosexual or gay, but I was neither or both, and if I couldn't settle on one, I told Beany that night, the best thing to do would be to settle on soup.

"Soup is so constant . . . and loyal."

"But is it enough?" Beany asked.

"A heart like mine," I said, "can be content with that kind of certainty.

"Humbug."

"Maybe it's more nature than cowardice," I said. "Maybe that was my mother's problem as well."

I thought my mother loved the solitude and quiet, cooking and reading, watching the birds visit the feeder, but maybe it was because she was trying to hide her own ambivalence. Indecision like that can be frightening, particularly when everyone else around you seems to know exactly what they want. Maybe she thought there was something seriously wrong with her, because she wanted both at a time when a woman loving a woman was not acceptable, except perhaps in the rarified world of high art, certainly not when you were abandoned by your husband, left with a young child and worked as an elementary school teacher.

I got up and made myself some chamomile tea, Orit's beef stew was resisting my stomach's efforts to break it down.

I don't want give the wrong impression. I don't think there's something wrong with me, although I don't think everything is right with me either. I just think that when in doubt about what you are and who you want sometimes the best thing to do is choose neither. When you're uncertain about which path to take, there is something to be said for standing still and letting it come to you. Life blows past you quickly enough, even when you're standing still. A life filled with good soup and dry red wine can be more than enough. Indeed, it is probably more than most.

"A life of teaching and poetry seems to have been enough for you," I said, when Beany didn't respond to the remark about my mother since he already knew her story. "And don't give me that old refrain that it's better to have loved and lost than never to have loved at all, because I have and there's nothing that says you can't stop at three and have to continue banging your head against the wall."

"There are no wrong ways," he said, "just as there are no wrong interpretations. I tell that to my students all the time. A poem is exactly what it says to you. You may see in it something that no one has ever seen before, because no one has ever looked at it through your eyes. It may be something even the author didn't intend. That doesn't mean it's not there; we say and do a lot of things subconsciously, without ever intending to, although you do need a sound basis for whatever your position is. A few bad relationships and a love and talent for soup doesn't translate to a contented life alone."

"Not like a poet and teacher?"

"Not like me," Beany said.

"Is it about the propagation of the species?" I said. "Is it the idea that no womb should ever go to waste?"

Beany laughed.

"I haven't thought of it quite that way. Certainly sperm is never the problem. It's the egg the world covets."

We both laughed.

"I don't think the world will miss one egg."

"No, I suppose not."

"But it's not about what the world will miss," Beany said, "it's about what you will miss."

"Did you ever want children?" I asked.

Beany finished off the wine in his glass. He always thought before he answered the more difficult questions. Sometimes his answer was simply to change the subject.

"No."

"Why not?"

He emptied the wine bottle into his glass.

"Because . . . how did you put it . . . some people are built for one."

"Come on Professor, answer the question."

"I suppose because words are what I'll leave behind. Words are my children."

Then he changed the subject to the other children in his life, the college coeds, and the senior seminar he was teaching on the 20th century English novel.

"Did you know," he told me, "that E. M. Forster wrote only 5 books."

"Yes," I said, not trying to hide my disappointment with the new subject. There was no turning Beany back once he'd decided to move on.

"He stopped writing at 45."

"So you told me."

"And lived to 91."

Of course, he wanted me to ask the obvious question.

"What did he do those last 46 years?"

"Besides basking in his glory, nothing much, wrote some short stories, worked for the BBC, and, of course, taught a little."

"That's something."

"Not for the man who wrote *A Passage to India.*"

"And this means what in terms of what we've just been talking about?"

"That quitting because of great success is no different than quitting because of great failure. It's still quitting. All it does is make the years fly by and you know what they say about an uneventful life."

"That can be a good thing," I said.

"If that's what you truly believe," he said standing up to leave, "then why wait?"

CHAPTER SEVEN

It was a cold and grey Thursday night, the sixth one after Beany's death. It had been unusually warm and rainy for a couple of days earlier in the week, a late January thaw, according to Lisa, who loved it because it was great for business.

"It brings all the bad hair out of hibernation."

But it turned ugly Thursday morning and the white Northampton world of *Silent Snow Secret Snow* was now a black, slushy gruel that extended from the ground up to your ankles.

The only color in Circa that night came from the green and red bell peppers, the diced carrots and tomatoes, and the okra in my catfish gumbo, which was never a big hit, but which I made anyway for my customers with Southern roots who looked up from each spoonful with tears in their eyes. Joe Johnson was born in Georgia and he said it was better than his grandmother made, which I took as a big compliment considering how legendary childhood culinary memories can seem.

Not surprisingly on a cold, grey night, the restaurant was busy. Two other special soups on the board that day were my mother's roasted winter vegetable soup with truffle oil, which is filled with butternut squash, rutabaga, parsnips and new potatoes, and my Brazilian Black Bean soup, which I make without the traditional sausage and ham, relying instead on red and black beans and tons of fresh cilantro to which I add hot green chili peppers and mango. A touch of sweetness is always appreciated after the sun goes down. It has a way of helping to bring some unity to the discord among the myriad of ingredients or the mix of feelings after a long, hard day.

Joe Johnson came in after the dinner rush since Georgina called to tell him that the catfish gumbo was on the board. He never missed it when it was. He said he had a head cold and felt like "a car with a clogged carburetor."

"That's what I get from spending so much time on my back on a cold, cement floor."

I insisted he take some of the roasted winter vegetable home on the house because it would help him get a good night's sleep, which is what you need when you're fighting a cold.

"How about if I return the favor," he said, perking up. "I just got in this 2004 Ford Taurus that's a peach . . . like you. I'll give it to you for what I paid and throw in a brake job."

"And what's the punch line," I said, as Georgina stopped to listen over my shoulder.

"You can come bring some soup over after you close the next couple of nights and help nurse me back to health."

We both laughed.

"You never give up."

"Never saw a car I couldn't fix."

We both laughed again.

"It's not personal Joe . . . you're just not my type."

"Too dirty?"

"No," I said, "too happy."

He scratched his head in response to that one.

"I'm still waiting for her to find someone who is her type," Georgina said, before she walked into the kitchen to get Joe's soup.

"You may be sorry one day," he said. "You don't know what you're missing."

"I know that."

"I'm not talking about the car."

"I wasn't either."

Then Joe proceeded to tell me about a customer he was dating, a divorced young lady with long black hair, a 4-year old boy and an old car with serious problems.

"She's a good cook," he said, "but not like you."

"I'm only good with soups. I burn just about everything else."

I told Joe I was happy for him and added some extra bread while reminding him how important it was to feed a cold.

"Thursday's a bad night to ask, Joe," I overhead Georgina say as she walked him to the door. "Not even George Clooney would have a chance."

Orit was the last regular to pop in that night. She picked up a container of the Brazilian black bean and left me the library's copy of Walt Whitman's *Leaves of Grass.*

"He paid to print the first edition himself," she said. "He was alone his whole life. Some say he was confused in the way we talked about the other night."

I nodded.

"Look at what he accomplished."

After she left, I suddenly felt the strong pull of a downhill slope ahead and poured myself a bowl of yesterday's winter cabbage and potato soup, which was good for keeping things down. It was hard keeping all my feelings inside again now that Beany was gone and it was hard to focus my thoughts, which looked like an overexposed photo when I closed my eyes. I was alone in the restaurant by this time, having kicked Georgina out. She didn't like to leave me alone on Thursday night, but she had classes in the morning and needed some sleep.

I'd been hanging out at Circa lately until I was so tired that I could barely hold my head up. I've always hated the insomnia that visited me after unexpected endings like the ones with Nick, Jake and Jolene, and now Beany, and even roaming the world on my computer looking for new soups didn't seem to help, not with the unmade and embarrassed bed sitting there right beside me. So I'd putter around the restaurant until well after midnight and come home so tired sometimes that I'd fall asleep without even undressing. On those nights, I'd wake up suddenly just before dawn and look around unsure for a few moments where I was, a very disquieting feeling.

Tonight I decided to open up a bottle of good red wine and sit around hoping for some snow. When I reached up to the top shelf where I kept my private stash, I saw the accordion folder with Beany's letters. It's not that I'd forgotten it was there, but I'd pushed it way to the back of my mind. I'm a big believer in signs, at least the ones that instigated from our own subconscious, so I took it down and brought it to Beany's table along with the wine and another bowl of soup.

Beany was a very organized and considerate man, and I wasn't surprised to find all the letters, about a dozen in total, opened, pressed flat and put into chronological order. The first was to his mother, Elmira. It was dated December 22, 1944. Beany was 22 years old.

My Dearest Mother,

Another Christmas is upon us, and while the thoughts of birth and resurrection are a welcome change, another year has passed filled with neither. I know I am very fortunate to be one of the chosen few who sweep up after the battle; however, we may be the only ones who truly get to appreciate the full panorama of fatalities, because our war is the whole battlefield and not a group of foxholes or a single plot of cratered earth. As I do my work, I feel as if my lungs absorb the dust from these sad, broken, young men, so that I carry a piece of each one away with me. We also get to see the way broken hearts rise to the surface of those handsome, young faces caught by surprise when their souls are forced to flee so suddenly, long before their time is due.

You would think that the world's leaders could come up with a less barbaric method of determining a way of life. Perhaps an odd-even choice, like we did when we were little boys, or a race, although having seen firsthand what that little Nazi-boy can do to anyone who does not measure up to his Aryan fantasy, we could never allow him to win no matter what the cost. And he will not, Mother, I promise you that. You need not worry, the tide has clearly turned, and it is only a matter of time before he is as limp and withered as the fallen petals that litter the fields where I toil.

I stopped reading and poured myself another glass of wine. Beany was already a poet at 22. I don't know how he got through it. Before I read his letters, I was suitably impressed by the fact that he managed to live to a ripe, old age, still functioning and still seeing the point of just about everything. But now that I realized the extent of the endings he lived through as a young man and saw that he had that same sensibility back then, my admiration grew by leaps and bounds. I only wished that I could see the world like that and not simply myself in it.

I do have to tell you, Mother, about a good friend of mine, Eric, because there really is no one else I can talk to like I can talk to you, which you will be happy to hear I intend to continue doing long after you are gone. I met Eric about three months ago at the mess tent. He was sitting alone reading Dylan Thomas, so I had no choice but to join him. He had a very unenviable job, and I suppose by using the past tense I have given away the ending. Eric searched for and disarmed land mines, a job that sent many a shiver down my spine. I had suggested that he put in for a transfer, but he would have none of that, since he said he was quite good at it, always being one to tread lightly, and besides, he said, it wouldn't be "fair to the boys." We planned to spend Christmas together; he was to read me his two favorite poems and I was to read him mine. I planned to surprise him with some Robert Burns, not my favorite as you know but appropriate, I thought, for Christmas.

As I have no doubt you have already surmised, it was not to be. He missed a mine, which is to say that he did not miss it, he found it, but not in the manner that he had planned, which I learned when the battle was over, and it was my misfortune to come upon Eric for collection, which is the word our CO insists we use, as if the coldness of the word could somehow protect our senses from overheating. My one solace is that the mine took only his legs, leaving him with this virtuous little smile, as if he, unlike most of the others, was pleasantly surprised by the sudden stillness and the long view of eternity ahead.

Mother, I have learned here what I am sure you know well—hearts break in so many different ways. I suppose poets know that best of all.

With all my love and best wishes for this Christmas and the New Year, the next I hope to spend with you without the need to sit here in the cold, damp night, searching the darkness for the right words.

Your loving son,
Roger

I held the letter up to the light and examined it closely. For Beany, there was art in everything from his choice of words to the way those words were placed and formed. The paper stock Beany used was much thicker than normal and more porous, so it absorbed the ink much deeper and bled ever so slightly, leaving less even edges around the letters. It gave the words a certain depth and feeling, a significance and understanding that today's copier paper and ball-point pens could never do.

I read the letter again but I couldn't bring myself to read the next one and it took the rest of the bottle of wine and another bowl of soup before I could convince myself that I was tired enough to go home. I decided that Beany's bequest had to be savored like my soup to be appreciated, so I wouldn't read more than one letter at a time and only on Thursday evenings after everyone was gone. I would sit at Beany's table, drink a toast to his spiritual health and sip a soup that I know he would have liked.

Besides, it took me nearly a week to digest that first letter. The initial thing that struck me, obviously, was the terrible nature of what he did during the war. He had told me what he did, but it hit me so much harder hearing it from the 22-year old Beany, as it was happening, as opposed to 60 years later. I think I would have preferred to take my chances fighting and deal with the prospect of facing death each day instead of the certainty of doing so. The next was that I never realized just how close Beany was to his mother. He hardly ever mentioned her during our year of soup, except to say that he was raised by her, not because his father ran away but because he was almost never home, and that she died young like mine shortly after the war.

"My father was a prep school jock," he told me, "uninterested in anything academic. He got the good grades awarded to those who earn it in competitive sports."

Apparently, his father got a cushy job at a bank after graduating college, thanks to a sports-minded alumnus.

"I thought bankers had great hours," I said.

"Not this banker."

His job didn't involve reviewing loan applications as much as entertaining clients at a lot of lunches, dinners and golf outings. He also had to travel quite a bit, there being at least one out-of-town convention per month back then. I gathered that since Beany's interests lay in the arts and academics, not sports, there wasn't much reason for him to stay home on weekends. When he did, Beany said, he played golf unless the greens were covered with snow and then he went to the driving range.

"What brought your parents together?" I asked.

"My mother's inheritance."

After thinking about it all week, I concluded that the first letter served as reason enough for any man, let alone someone with Beany's poetic soul, to refuse to settle down with any one person. He saw how unaccommodating marriage could be and he certainly knew well the risks of sudden endings. So why not spend the rest of his years surrounded by books and young, vivacious college girls, none of whom, statistically speaking, would ever die before he did.

CHAPTER EIGHT

By the third month in our year of soup, I didn't wait for Georgina to come into the kitchen to tell me that Beany was back. I kept an eye out the little window between the kitchen and the dining room at his normal time to watch for his arrival. It was never a long wait because he was very punctual. He was a creature of routine, just like me, probably from having lived so long by the same academic calendar and according to class schedules. Beany did admit in the face of my relentless questioning one night that it was part of the human condition - the need and desire for those little certainties in life to counteract the bigger things which were anything but.

"Although some people," he said, his eyes boring right into mine, "are too willing to embrace it like a lover."

"What happens to those people?" I asked with a big smile.

"They are robbed of comfort one day . . . and left to their own darkness and gravity."

"Aren't you the cheery one tonight," I said, reaching out to touch Beany's arm.

I knew that he had his own demons by now, but I also knew that nothing I said would chase them away. I just hoped that my soup would help keep them at bay.

Of course, Georgina who was watching from the cash register chuckled. She had no idea what we were talking about but she got a big kick, she said, watching this "May December thing." She was fond of telling the other regulars that I watched the dining room on Thursday nights like a puppy dog waiting for a treat. Of course, it frustrated her to no end that she couldn't eavesdrop on our conversations since we both stopped talking whenever she was nearby.

"I know you don't have a lot of experience with this," I told her one day, "but Beany gives me something no man has given me before."

"I'm afraid to ask what," Georgina said

"His undivided attention."

By the fourth month, I didn't even let Beany order because I made a special soup every Thursday night just for him. Beany wasn't allowed to travel anymore because of what he called his "thick blood," which required him to take blood thinners and, according to him, allowed him to drink inordinate amounts of red wine. So I took him on a gastronomical soup tour of the world. I started with some of my favorite Asian recipes, which weren't all that popular with the locals, perhaps because they were filled with bok choy, seasoned tofu, fresh ginger root, leeks, and Sichuan peppercorns.

For our stop in Japan, I made ozoni, a soup traditionally made to celebrate the New Year, which contains sesame oil, tamari, hijiki, a type of seaweed, radishes and barley miso. I like to add fresh soybeans when they're in season, frozen are never acceptable. When it was time to travel to Vietnam, it was lemongrass, shallots, star anise, sweet potatoes and shiitake with fresh sugar snap peas if I could find them. I always embellished the traditional recipe here by adding beets, spinach and a touch of mandarin orange. For India, it was roasted eggplant with coconut milk and bell peppers to which I added generous amounts of the five C's, cumin, coriander, cardamom, cinnamon and cayenne. In India, it's all about the spices.

I had to hand it to Beany, he tried everything and his palate, like his mind, was broad and open to new tastes and new soup experiences. For him cooking was art, like literature and music that required a certain intimacy and sensibility to truly appreciate it.

The only Asian soup Beany didn't like was the Korean Pine Nut Porridge. I remember that night well, it was well into the fifth month of our soup odyssey. Beany walked in at exactly nine-forty five, as he always did, fifteen minutes before closing time. I remember watching him through the kitchen window as he stomped the fresh snow off his feet. It was a really heavy snow and I could tell by the way he shook the flakes from his head, his shoulders straight and his head up, that he didn't find the snow a burden. I suppose it would be hard to live 50 years in Northampton if you did.

We talked about the storm after I brought him out the porridge and the ciabatta I had made to go with it, sort of Korea meets Italy.

"The weather I don't mind," he said to me while Georgina uncorked his wine, "but this looks like cream of wheat."

"It isn't."

Of course, it did look like it and texture and appearance for a soup matters to people every bit as much as it does with an entrée or a shirt.

A shiver ran down Beany's back and it wasn't from the cold.

"I never liked oatmeal or cream of wheat or any other warm cereal."

"Force-fed as a child?"

"No, my mother was always very solicitous when it came to my meals. My father used to insist that a bowl of oatmeal be waiting for him—piping hot—on those mornings when he graced us with his presence, usually before a late t-time. He said he needed it to get through the front nine, which is when, I suspect, it was considered proper etiquette to bring out the flask. He had a hard and fast rule, no alcohol before 11 a.m."

Beany took a taste of the soup.

"I guess I get that from him."

"It's Korean Pine Nut Porridge," I said.

"A euphuism for cereal."

"It's a soup."

He took another taste.

"It has grain in it?"

"Yes."

"It is breakfast," he said, pushing it toward the center of the table. "Don't feel bad, you're still batting over nine hundred."

He was right in a way; it wasn't breakfast, but it was probably too confusing in looks and texture to call it a soup and it most certainly did not go with red wine. So I went back to the kitchen and got him a bowl of my classic roasted corn chowder, which I knew he would like and which turned out to be one of Beany's favorites.

"I wasn't sure you'd come out in this weather," I said.

"You mean to avoid the risk of the headline—Professor Emeritus slips and fractures hip."

"Because it's cold and the snow is deep."

"I love the snow," he said, spreading his arms like it was right there in front of us. "How could you not love something that buries the world out of sight?"

It was the first time I could recall Beany using the word love like that. He was very careful when it came to words that invoked too hot a passion, although I would be the first to agree that the word was overused and had very little heroic about it any more. Even when he talked about poetry and great novelists, he stuck with the words favorite and like.

I wasn't a big fan of snow since we never had a man in the house and I always had to help my mother shovel the car out while the other children were playing. By the time we were finished, they were usually inside drinking hot chocolate from a packet and soup out of a can. While I always had my mother's homemade soup to warm me up, I was usually too exhausted by that point to go back outside to play.

Beany seemed more talkative. You never know what will get someone to lower their guard. Maybe a ton of snow did it for him. Anyway, I was hoping that he'd open up over the corn chowder and show me a memory or two, perhaps one about being trapped in a blizzard with his first girlfriend, a scented soul who he could call back with just a breath of snow, but who died in a horrible car crash. Instead, he told me about the first time he fell in love with snow. He was 11 years old and his mother had given him a new short story by one of her favorite authors, Conrad Aiken, called "Silent Snow, Secret Snow."

"I never heard of it."

"Of course not," he said "no one buys short stories anymore. Readers don't want to be forced to think too fast or too hard, they want it all spoon-fed, idea by idea, character by character, page after page. Buying books these days is like shopping at the supermarket; people are looking for more words for their money."

"I don't mind short stories."

"I'm not talking about magazines. Name one author you have read since college that writes short stories."

"Joyce Carol Oates."

"Good, I just wanted to make sure I wasn't wasting my Thursday nights on a dolt."

"At least not when it comes to soup and reading."

"We're all dolts," he said, "in some aspect of life."

"That's me with relationships," I said. "What about you?"

He didn't answer right away. He had some soup while he mulled it over. With all the women he must have had in 50 years at Smith College, I had to imagine that there were one or two he was sorry to have let go.

"I'm a dolt," he said, taking a sip of wine, "when it comes to taking good care of my liver."

Of course, I was disappointed with the answer, but before I had a chance to say anything else, Beany launched into his snow memory.

"I'm going to bring a copy of Aiken's story for you to read, because it is marvelously written, like a prose poem. It's about a young boy who likes his snow-filled world much better than his real world at home and at school. As the snow falls harder and faster he slowly descends into madness."

"And you like snow because?" I asked.

Beany smiled that Mona Lisa smile of his—which I thought very professorial. It was not like he knew something that I didn't, more like he was pleased to see that I was trying to keep up.

"Not because I want to be that young man finding solace in snowy solitude and madness, although I can't say that it doesn't have a certain attraction, don't you think so?"

I shrugged. I've often wanted to be left alone, really alone, Walden Pond-type of alone, and I even had a fleeting interest in college in what drives people to live like hermits. I wrote a paper about it for one of my psych classes, but I couldn't say that I ever seriously entertained the idea of becoming one.

"What fascinated me when I first read it was how Aiken used the snow as an escape, as a way of rejecting reality, so when it snows like this, bringing commerce to a halt and blanketing the world with something other than its usual dirt and darkness, I can almost believe that nothing else exists beside what's in here," Beany said, tapping his head.

"Certainly none of this," he added, sweeping his arm around the room to encompass not just Circa, but all of Northampton and the world beyond, at least the nonliterary world.

"Including my soup?"

"Unfortunately, given today's porridge, I would have to say yes."

We both laughed. I remember nothing else from the night, except watching Beany in his heavy winter scarf and hat as he left Circa to walk home. I stood outside in the cold to watch him, to make sure that he didn't slip and fracture one of those hips, but I was more astonished than worried as he walked down the middle of what was a deserted main street by the lilt and buoyancy in his step.

CHAPTER NINE

There was another snowstorm when I sat down to read the second letter and when I looked out on the street it wasn't hard to pretend that everything outside was gone, buried forever, and that my world was now reduced to my little restaurant, Beany's letter and my own imagination. I must say it was a nice feeling.

The second letter was three years later, December 12, 1947, and Beany was home from the war. In fact, from the address on top it was clear that he had already moved into the house where he would spend the next 60 years, the house where he would take his own life.

I had never really looked at the house, so I walked past it the next day. It was a large brick Victorian set back on a big piece of property abutting the campus. I could see two fireplaces and a big library looking out on the quad, as the students called it. I also saw the big for sale sign on the front lawn partially buried in the snow. I stood there for a while trying to imagine the parade of students, colleagues and lovers that had entered into it over more than a half century. I wondered if I would have been one of them if I had been a student at Smith when Beany was 40 or 50 years younger. I certainly hoped so.

The second letter was not to his mother, but to his Aunt Emma, a woman he had once mentioned, a spinster living in Arcadia, Maine who taught high school English in a small school and never found anyone, because she had impossibly high standards. I think the way he put it was that a white knight on a white horse wouldn't have had a chance.

Her name came up one Thursday night when we were talking about family. Since both my parents were only children, I didn't have anyone other than two great aunts on my mother's side, who I had met on a couple of occasions when I was much younger. Beany admitted to one aunt, his Aunt Emma, who left him a lovely house on the coast of Maine, along with a fine collection of 20th century American literature.

"What happened to the house?" I asked.

"I sold it," he said, before changing the subject.

Beany did that a lot, he changed the subject when he had nothing more to say or wasn't prepared to say anything more, and I always respected his wishes. He wasn't as respectful in that regard when it came to me, probing on many occasions, but he only did that I think when he sensed that my silence was a curtain I subconsciously wanted to part. He never pushed if I resisted too hard or for too long.

Of course, I wondered why the next letter Beany bequeathed to me was to his aunt and not his mother, but the answer became clear in the very first line.

Dear Aunt Emma,

It is hard to believe that this will be my second Christmas without Mother. I know that there are many ways to die from the sublime - expiring in your sleep – to the ridiculous - diving from too high into the shallows. The reason I picked that example is because of a student at Smith who died this past summer when she dove into a lake, hit the rocky bottom and broke her neck. But to die as my mother did is something I cannot easily get out of mind. As long as I can remember she smoked in bed and was always careful to put out her cigarettes in the big ashtray she kept on the end table on top of her pile of books. She generally put it out long before she got tired and stopped reading, which sometimes leads me to believe on those nights when the Gods of sleep have not heard my prayer that perhaps it wasn't entirely accidental. I know she was unhappy, who isn't these days with all the lost friends and lovers still so fresh in our minds. She wanted me to find someone and settle down, and she wanted grandchildren and quickly, as if her untimely demise had been foreshadowed in a dream. I sincerely hope that my intentions to the contrary were not a cause of her unhappiness. In any event, I can only hope that she died from the smoke, before the flames reached her. You know mother was not one to accept pain gracefully.

Another thing in common, both of our mothers killed by cigarettes, one due to smoking in bed and the other by lung cancer. I couldn't decide which one was more insidious. I wondered why Beany had decided way back then not to marry and have children. Perhaps because of all the dead sons he had carried in his arms in Europe. Although the Baby Boom generation would suggest that most returning soldiers felt differently, although very few of them saw nearly as much death as Beany did, certainly not on a daily basis.

I hope you are well, Aunt Emma, and I wish you the most joyous of Yuletides. I thought I would write to let you know what your only nephew is up to, since I know that you have long relied on Mother for the family news. As you know, I am in my second year at Smith College. I am teaching introductory courses in 19th and 20th century English literature and a freshman seminar on the Immortal Poets, as silly a name for a course as I've ever heard, but challenging nonetheless since most of the young women in my charge seem to have little room in their heads for anything other than men and the decorative arts.

In answer to the question that I know you must be asking, I am not serious with anyone, although the opportunities are here in abundance, and include colleagues, townspeople and students, who, by the way, are not that much younger than me.

It was hard for me to imagine Beany in his 20s, even though I had seen a photograph and knew just how handsome a specimen he was, tall and lean with a face equally as balanced and well proportioned. Even as an old man he was handsome, although his features and his body sagged with age. Marinating in alcohol certainly didn't help. I suppose it was hard to picture Beany that young, because I wasn't reading the words as much as hearing them spoken by Beany. And the voice I heard was the only voice I knew, the 82-year-old man who had given up hope long ago of meeting someone to share that big empty house.

I have a lot of you in me, I think, preferring my books and my solitude after a long day teaching, setting impossible goals in a society that expects everyone to settle for a mate, as easily as those new ready-made suits you can now buy right off the rack. If I live my life as you I will have no regrets, although I certainly wonder now what you think about the trail you have blazed, and what advice you may have to someone thinking to follow in your footsteps.

I think spinster teachers were probably more common back then. What kind of woman would travel up to rural Maine to teach in a small, remote schoolhouse? A preference for your own company and books would be a prerequisite to taking that job. I wished that Beany had left me a photo album as well, so I could see a picture of Aunt Emma.

I cheated a bit glancing at the next few letters to see if there was a response, but there was none. In fact, all the letters Beany had bequeathed to me were from him. The letters in the folder weren't carbon copies and they certainly didn't have photocopy machines back then, which meant that he either carefully handwrote a second copy to keep or retrieved the originals. I suspect that he may have gotten the originals back from his mother and aunt after their deaths, but the later ones must have been duplicates, which made me wonder how often Beany re-read them. You wouldn't copy them over by hand unless you intended to. There were no letters from anyone else, which might have been an issue of privacy for Beany.

I wish you well, dear Aunt Emma, and look forward to a trip up to see you during the summer recess. Since I am expected to publish something, I can think of no better and quieter place to work than Maine, nor a better muse to work with than you.

Your loving nephew,
Roger

Beany wrote the two letters I had read so far with a fountain pen in a rich, thick indigo ink that was closer to violet than blue. He wrote in a cursive style, his letters always even, straight and well-rounded, the ink flow constant, like a man who could accept no deviations. When you only read one letter a week and re-read it and study it closely, like a work of art, you notice things you might not ordinarily notice the first time through, like the way the tail of the last letter in the last word of almost every paragraph reached up and out with a little flourish, as if it were trying to grab hold of the reader's attention to make sure he or she continued reading.

I felt as if I were getting closer to Beany, although still not close enough, and I was tempted to read all the letters right then and there, in the teeth of the snowy madness outside, but I didn't. Rushing was never my style, nor was it Beany's. Patient preparation and long-simmering soup was my style of cooking and my philosophy of life.

So I sat around the restaurant watching the snow fall while I finished the bottle of wine, thinking instead about my decision to keep my own company like Beany and Aunt Emma, and to rely on soup and work to carry me forward. What did we all have in common, I wondered? Perhaps there was a girl who couldn't wait for Beany to come back from the war or a man in Aunt Emma's case who didn't make it back from World War I? Or maybe it was something much less dramatic. Maybe they were also frustrated with failed relationships or simply confused as to who they wanted and couldn't make a decision. It couldn't have been easy back then. It certainly wasn't as acceptable as it is now.

Of course, the reasons don't matter, whether it was the result of a traumatic experience, like the one Beany experienced in World War II, finding yourself an alien in a world where you didn't belong, as I surmised with Aunt Emma, or the feeling of exhaustion that can overwhelm you when you feel like you've had enough. Perhaps what Beany said was true that not every life can be about love, because it's too fragile for some or comes too late or too hard . . . some lives have to be about self-fulfillment, creation and art.

Making soup is an art, although it can never be as transcendent as poetry or a great novel. What ever the reason, what matters is that you find a way to seem content, like Orit, and that you feel comfortable with the idea that other people no longer have to be your compass. A person can find his or her orientation and place in other ways.

CHAPTER TEN

I got a late start the next Thursday. Lisa Montero lingered over her soup and wouldn't leave, Georgina said, until I came out of the kitchen and sat with her for a while.

"The stranger from behind the closed door," she said when I sat down.

"I'm tired," I said.

"Who isn't at the end of the day?"

"I don't think I'm up for hearing about the latest prospect you found for me."

"Boy, do you need a drink."

I nodded.

"And a trim."

"I'll come in."

"I didn't want to talk about you," she said. "I've given up on you. I want to talk about me."

I went back into the kitchen to pour myself a glass of wine before she started.

"You know that cabinet I had built at the back of the shop to display all the shampoos, sprays and conditioners?"

I didn't, but I nodded anyway.

"It's a work of art. I'm almost afraid to use it. It makes everything else in the shop look as if it came from a flea market. I may have to do the whole place over now."

"Is that good or bad?" I asked.

"Expensive, but that's not my point. The guy who did it – Jim - is drop dead gorgeous. There's something dark about him. He needs mothering."

"I'm not interested," I said.

"I'm not offering," she said "I'm trying to get him for me."

She went on and on about him, but I confess I wasn't really listening. I was trying to decide on the soups for the weekend, although I was even having trouble focusing on that. I just wanted Lisa to leave so I could close up and get to letter number 3.

"He was there the whole day setting it up and I can't tell you how many customers hung around after they were done to watch him . . . without saying a word. It was like a wake in there for a while."

Georgina tried to help me out by reminding me about all the things left to do in the kitchen before we could close.

"I've got to get back to work," I said.

"Just a second," Lisa said, putting her hand on my arm.

"I did everything but strip and throw myself in front of him," she said. "I'm no skank and I can always get a guy aroused, even if it's only to open his eyes, but this guy was shut tighter than a stuck pickle jar."

"That's too bad," I said, trying to inch away.

"He just looked at me with those black eyes and apologized."

"Black eyes?"

"I told you . . . dark and secretive . . . like yours."

"Bring him some soup," I said, "maybe that'll help loosen him up."

"That's exactly my point," Lisa said, "it's not going to work for me, but I think this guy may be perfect for you. You know . . . two lost souls. He's got a secret I bet that will rival yours."

'What's my secret?" I asked.

"You tell me, I'm still waiting. Is it a bad break-up or are you waiting for that old beau to come back."

"Neither," I said, standing up

"So what do you think," she said, "wanna meet him?"

"I thought this wasn't about me."

"I lied."

"I'll pass," I said.

Lisa sighed and threw up her hands.

"I give up," she said.

"Good."

It was almost midnight by the time we were finished cleaning up and Georgina left. I was exhausted and knew I would have no trouble sleeping if I went home, but I couldn't leave before reading the next letter. The third letter was written the following summer, August 22, 1947, to someone named Evan. There was no last name and it was not a name I recalled Beany ever mentioning. Actually, Beany brought up very few names during our year of soup other than poets, novelists, his aunt and some occasional colleagues.

My Dear Evan,

Chemistry and literature are not as disparate as one might think. They both deal with relationships and interactions, be they people or elements of the Periodic Table. They both strive to understand life and the world around us, examining what makes the heart beat and adding together the various parts – or in your case particles – hoping that they somehow equal or explain the whole. I would say that letters and molecules are one and the same when you think about it. The words of science may seem dispassionate, but they are not any more unfeeling than the scientist who speaks them. I know because I have seen the flush in your cheeks and not just when you were speaking about the heavy elements, their protons and electrons, something no less savage and chaotic you would agree than a man's heart.

I don't know what was wrong with me, I thought to myself. Could I have been so focused on my own narrative not to notice, or is it just not that obvious in an old man. How could I have missed it - Beany was gay. He had been living so long in the closet that he couldn't even bring himself to come out to me, no matter how much soup and wine he consumed, and no matter how confused I was about my own sexuality.

I find the parallels between us fascinating. I see them as foreshadowing where we belong, and where we are supposed to end up 50 years from now, not lonely old men, but a trailblazing couple for the modern era, one part humanist and one part scientist, and free to choose. Think of it, both of us raised without fathers, which may be a possible cause or at least an excuse. Our roles in the war were too similar to be mere coincidence; it rises above that to the level of kismet. Neither one of us was capable of killing; me, carrying the bodies of our young soldiers broken beyond repair and you taking those bodies and preparing them for burial or return home. I think your job was infinitely more difficult. I saw them the way they were, their life force having barely departed, and then only for an instant. You, on the other hand, saw them the way they would spend eternity and spent more time with them than I could safely have done and still hoped to maintain my sanity.

Both jobs sounded equally impossible to me, although I disagreed with Beany. I thought his job was far more difficult. When he got to them the blood still flowed, the muscles still twitched and the pain and surprise was still written on their faces. By the time Evan got to them they were lifeless, their souls long gone, their bodies rigid, silent and long emptied of consciousness. A scientist would see them for what they were – a mix of elements and chemicals that no longer reacted the way they once had, that had turned inert and were ready to decompose and start all over again.

I don't think Beany really believed that Evan's work was harder; I think those were words of love and probably as plain as he could put his feelings at the time. Beany may have loved poetry and literature, but as a critic and a teacher it must have been hard to find the words for himself.

The fact that we both find ourselves teaching young coeds without a single prurient thought, seeing them for what they are, each one a doe in heat eager – no driven - to bear her fair share of the world's offspring (nor do we even care), suggests that we are well suited, and that nature has put us here for a reason, to create a unique life of our own for scholarly procreation. We both know - as a scientist and literary scholar - just how much nature abhors a vacuum. A life together would fill that vacuum, don't you think? What element in your Periodic Table ever exists for very long on its own? Man is no different.

No man should be as alone as we are now. If we are unwilling to forgive God for what he has done to us, and are prepared to turn our hearts against him, then we are not required to obey his commands, whether they are indeed his commands or nothing more than the tortured extrapolations of his self-appointed terrestrial representatives. How can a world that refuses to listen to God's words when it comes to war, find them so persuasive when it comes to love? It should not, it cannot, and I for one will not accept that tortured interpretation.

I know your concerns. I share them. We will be discreet in the beginning and after a while it won't matter. Who cares what two old men in their dotage do or have done? The girls will still run at us, but they will grow tired when we cannot be caught. And do not forget, we exist in the cocoon of academia, which, ideally, tolerates all ideas and insulates the bohemian from the social conformists.

We are humans like everyone else, composed of the same elements, driven by the same chemical reactions, searching to be satisfied and fulfilled. Remembering the other night, as I do, how could we not be entitled to more? And not want more? Because one thing we both know for sure is that there is much more that lies beyond what we have seen and felt, just ask the poets and astronomers.

Roger

I could imagine Beany antagonizing over the salutation. Lovingly was probably too difficult for him, fondly too cold a word, your friend, your special friend, sincerely, he probably ran through them all. In the end he decided to say nothing, to simply put his name, which was more than enough in light of everything that came before it. There was no mistaking this for anything other than a love letter.

The next morning I went to the Smith College library and found a copy of the 1947 yearbook. There was Beany at the bottom rung of the English Department. It was only a head shot, but he looked like a cross between Gregory Peck and Humphrey Bogart. With a poet's soul and a love of literature, I don't know how any coed could have resisted him.

At the same bottom rung of the Chemistry Department was Evan Dillon. The photo was black and white, as they all were, but in my mind's eye I saw the sandy hair framing his ocean-blue eyes. Evan didn't have Beany's chiseled features; he was more boyish, meaning everything was smaller and closer together, almost the way a child might draw a face with a crayon.

Of course, I studied the face for upward of an hour. If you look at a photo long enough it almost appears to come to life, which makes you see things, imagined or real, that no one who just glances at it ever would. I saw an expression that was determined and serious, a budding scientist prepared to devote every waking hour to the laboratory - filtering, clarifying and diluting – so that any other urges were forced to surrender. I saw a life that wasn't about love but about discovery. I also saw a bit of concern at the corner of his mouth where it turned down ever so slightly, and a hint of self-consciousness around the eyes, perhaps even fear of what might happen if his confused heart ever got the upper hand.

There was a little bio underneath the photo. It said that Evan had grown up on a farm in Idaho and studied science at the University of Iowa. He received his doctorate in organic chemistry and was studying the role of lipids in the body's chemistry. I found a paper by him in the faculty card catalogue that was written in the spring of 1948 entitled "The Metabolism of Lipids and Lipoproteins in Relation to Atherosclerosis." Orit was able to translate that into English for me. It was the beginning of what she called "food chemistry." Evan was studying how lipids might contribute to heart disease. If he was too timid to use his own heart, at least he could study its chemistry.

CHAPTER ELEVEN

I never gave a moment's thought to bisexuality; I hardly knew that category existed, until I found myself in bed with Jolene, while at the same time still attracted to those tall, dark-haired, men in line at Starbucks who had been my flavor of choice since I'd dated the forward on our high school basketball team my junior year. As far as I was concerned, you were either heterosexual or homosexual, either of which was fine with me. However tolerant and open-minded I thought I was, it still seemed to me that someone willing to sleep with every brunette that walked by, male or female, had a real problem which left unchecked could lead to a life filled with confusion and sorrow.

I felt like one of those Goth kids you see hanging out on the fringes of society with nowhere to go, no way to fit in, uncomfortable, dissatisfied, undisciplined and the object of my own bi-phobia. I looked in the mirror and appeared unbelievably normal, knowing what a lie that was, as I stood there taking my sexual temperature on the Kinsey Scale like I was fighting a fever. Zero meant completely heterosexual, never having had a homosexual thought, feeling or experience. Of course, the needle in the mirror was no longer stuck anywhere near that number. Six meant completely homosexual, which I would have preferred over where I found myself now, centered right on three, sometimes a little to the left toward 0 and sometimes a little to the right toward 6.

In our society one's sexuality often defines one's life, which is why I decided that it would be easier to remain celibate, to keep both of me in the closet, so to speak, and define myself by my soup, and whatever casual friendships went along with running a popular local eatery. Don't get me wrong; I wasn't planning to reject friends, just the kind of friends who could become sexual partners. That was a much bigger danger in my experience than the other way around - sexual partners who become friends. Certainly, Nick, Jake and Jolene argued against it.

I asked Beany about that one Thursday, probably a month before he took his life. Like so many women who can tell you what they were wearing on any special night of their life, I can tell you the soups I made that day. One was what I call my back-to-our-roots soup, because it's based on turnips and parsnips, vegetables our ancestors cherished much more than we do. Root vegetables are misunderstood and unappreciated these days, which is why I have to disguise them with a funny name. When you add them to some sliced leeks, minced garlic, tarragon, fennel seeds, lemon juice and vegetable stock, you have a smooth, thick, mildly sweet puree that most everyone enjoys and which will stand up to any salad or bread, as well as your most assertive worries.

The other soup was a first for me – Kelp Soup. I made it to introduce my customers to the abundance of minerals in sea vegetables. It's based on Kelp, of course, which you might be surprised to learn can be found at your everyday specialty grocer, to which I added carrots, radishes and, yes, turnips, which always seems to send a little shiver down most people's spines, soy sauce, scallions, parsley, and watercress. It was not one of Beany's favorites.

"It's bad enough swimming with sea weed," he said. "Why would I want to eat it?"

Nor was Beany fond of my theory that while friendship can lead to sex it rarely runs the other way and when sex is added to a good friendship it inevitably means the end of the friendship.

"That's Catholic school talking," he said, "society really. Good friends should be able to serve as sex partners from time to time and there's no reason why sex partners cannot become good friends."

"It's much easier conceptually," I said, "than in practice."

"That's because society and religion teach us at an early age to distrust ourselves, especially our sexuality. Instead of our instincts and natural inclinations, we are supposed to rely on ancient writings and external authority, inexperienced men of the cloth, to tell us what's right and normal.

"All great literature," Beany continued, "whether it's Dickens or Alan Ginsberg make one thing very clear: we do not always get to choose the object of our attraction. Lust and romance are never entirely under one's control."

"I'm making a choice," I said, "it's as simple as that."

"Choices tend to be impermanent when it comes to love."

"Not this one."

"We'll see," Beany said with a sigh as he finished the wine in his glass.

He leaned across his soup, so I could hear him as he said in a low voice, "sexuality should be an expression of our common humanity and divine spirit . . . it shouldn't be all about boundaries."

He leaned back and poured himself some more wine.

"It's all about the ability to see the world through someone else's eyes."

I nodded.

"I'm not running away," I said. "I'm not hiding. I'm not looking for the easy way out. I'm not afraid."

"I've got the point."

"I just want to focus on my art."

Beany nodded slowly and went back to his soup.

His fourth letter was four years later in the spring of 1951. I'm sure there was correspondence in between. Beany was a man of letters and all of his efforts couldn't have been restricted to his scholarly analysis and writings. I suspect these letters were carefully selected by Beany as my inheritance. It was another letter to Evan.

My Dear Boy or should I say Wrangler Evan,

How is the West? Are you wearing boots with spurs or a cowboy hat? Riding down the same tired trails, smiling at the same tired songs? I know how very important it is for you to fit in. I've certainly heard it often enough, often enough that like a popular song played endlessly on the radio I cannot help humming it sometimes to myself. I find the image of you in denim pants and boots roping calves quite amusing since, as we both know, you are not an outdoor sort of man, certainly not in the company of someone like me.

Clearly, Evan broke it off and fled Smith, probably because he couldn't bear the thought of anyone finding out. I suppose in the late forties and early fifties that would have meant the end of his science career, although what safer place to allow a gay male to teach than a woman's school? It was certainly safer than some of the lecherous teachers I encountered in the course of four years of college, even one in high school.

Is it as cold and snowy as they say? I know that Sam Clemens once said that the coldest winter he ever spent was a summer in New England, but I suspect that was only because he never spent any time in Nebraska. Of course, you know that I miss you and that I am angry. Taking that job at the University of Nebraska may have been right for your career, or it may have been nothing more than an excuse to run from me and yourself, from us actually, the latter being far more likely than the former. But I understand cowardice in this regard; society is like a parent we all fear to anger, although it's strange to feel it so much more here at home in the imagined looks and whispers of strangers and colleagues, than we did from death on the battlefield. I know the feeling; I have carried it around every day since we met, but I was prepared for that burden, although not now. Now it grows far too heavy without you around to share it.

How could I have missed it? I wondered. Yes, when I first met Beany he looked like the kindly old professor, widowed and childless, the kind who haunted the halls of academia everywhere having traded family for students who never age and never stop admiring their professors. How could I have gone through all those Thursday nights believing he was exactly as I wanted to see him, carefully cutting out the widower part, but leaving the rest intact? Of course, he had 50 years of practice in the art of pretending, while I had only recently discovered that sexual orientation was far from immutable. Pretend hard and long enough, as Beany did, and the passion of that pretense will fool just about anybody, perhaps even yourself.

What must the rest of our lives be like now? Is the secret we would have kept here any harder to carry than the secret you must still keep there? Do you really believe as you said that it will not happen again, that you of all people can mutate into one of those inert elements of yours able to resist the chemical reaction nature has dictated? At least I have chosen a field of study where pain and suffering, denial and solitude, are celebrated as muses, making it easy to answer that timeless question - who is more likely to have the happier life, or at least the easier life. You need me, if only to turn you inside out on occasion and offer you the forgiveness you so crave, so that the anger and bitterness does not turn your heart inert, leaving your life little more than a series of chemical reactions beyond your control and understanding. I, on the other hand, need no one. I can draw from E. M. Foster and D. H. Lawrence to deal with the trauma of memory. I can silence my heart when it comes to the Evans of the world, and let it beat strong with literary procreation and love, so that I can live a life that at least approaches in some small measure the one we might have shared.

You have disappointed me, but not nearly as much I am sure as you have disappointed yourself fleeing from your own desires and happiness, your own destiny, to the confines of a laboratory, leaving two more lives dead on the field of battle.

Yours faithfully,
Roger

I could barely catch my breath after reading the last part. I never saw Beany angry or bitter, not once during our year of soup. It didn't sound like the Beany I knew and, of course, it wasn't. The Beany I knew had made his choice long ago, the same one that I was trying to make now, and it was too late for regrets or bitterness by the time I met him, perhaps even too late for reflection. The memories and feelings that had generated this letter had settled so deep and been covered with so much silt over the years that it was beyond my ability to stir them back up.

I wondered what went through his mind the night he lit that fire and took those pills. Did he see and hear his mother and Aunt Emma, or reach out to the Evan he met after the war, when everything still seemed possible?

The internet makes everything public, so it wasn't hard the next day to look up Evan Dillon and easier still to find his obituary. He died in the spring, about six months before Beany, in the middle of Beany's soup sojourn, as he sometimes called it. His entire life was reduced to two paragraphs in the University of Nebraska Alumni Magazine.

> It is with profound sadness that the Trustees of the University announce the passing of Professor Emeritus Evan Dillon, age 84, former Chairman of the Department of Chemistry and the founder of the Whitehall Food Sciences Laboratory, built in 1955, thanks to a generous donation from the widow of Archibald C. Whitehall, to study the effect of chemicals in foods on the chemistry of the body. Professor Dillon's research has been widely published and he was a world renowned expert in the field of lipids.
>
> Professor Dillon died unexpectedly from heart failure. He will long be remembered for the tireless hours he devoted to his research and his teaching duties. Professor Dillon, a lifelong bachelor, liked to say that he was married to the University. He was a veteran of World War II and leaves no survivors. Professor Dillon was a true son of the University and has left his entire estate

to fund a fellowship for the continued study of the effect of lipids in the body.

I dealt with Beany's recent letter and Evan's obituary by throwing myself into my soups, spending hours in the library and on the internet researching new recipes and taking my customers places they had never been before. For many, they were places they didn't wish to be. I made a cabbage and apple soup using Granny Smith apples, red cabbage, caraway seeds, red wine, honey, vinegar and sour cream that even I had difficulty finishing and I never met a soup I didn't like.

I tried a Dixie Stampede Soup that was filled with peas, corn, green beans, carrots, potatoes, zucchini, and cream, that was so thick and heavy every customer who tried it had to loosen their belts and stretch out the elastic in their underwear, and I found an African chicken peanut soup recipe with sweet potatoes, black beans, peanuts, and heavy cream to which I added some hot cayenne peppers. I could hear the sniffles and cries for water from the back of kitchen.

For some reason that I could not understand, Beany's letter put me in a cream soup state of mind, although it's an ingredient I generally try to avoid. Fortunately, my customers were loyal and if none of the board specials were to their liking they always had the basic soups to fall back on, which I continued to make for my own peace of mind.

CHAPTER TWELVE

It was around this time that I needed to hire someone to upgrade Circa's computer system, which was freezing all too often and unable to keep up with my growing business, not to mention the exponential growth in my new soup recipes, which I had not yet bothered to back up. Matt was recommended to me by Captain Dale.

"He upgraded our computers at the station," Tom said, "even the ones in the patrol cars."

He said Matt was a real computer geek, who enjoyed reading manuals as much as I enjoyed studying soup recipes.

"He's about your age," he added, "and a nice looking young man."

"It's not going to happen," I told him.

"Still not over the guy who broke your heart?"

Nodding was a lot easier than explaining.

"Anyway, he'll do a bang up job," he said, "and that's what counts."

Tom handed me the telephone number and picked up his lunch, a miso based clam and potato soup that I insisted he get because I knew he would love it.

"You know," he said, smelling the bag to see if I was right, "my grandmother used to say that you can't let what you think you know get in the way of what you don't yet know."

"Which means," I said, smiling as I handed him back his change.

"You always have to leave some space in your heart for new experiences."

"You'd have made a good yoga teacher," I told him, and he laughed as he hiked up his gun and headed out.

I spoke to Matt on the phone about what I needed and he was eager to comb the software world to find the right restaurant program. He sounded like the type of guy who wore a clip-on tie in high school and stood in the corner of the cafeteria during the Homecoming Dance discussing chess moves with his friends. The thick black glasses he was wearing when he walked in certainly fit the image, although it was belied by his strong dimpled chin and cavernous eyes; eyes I would later decide that were not troubled by day to day existence as much as the dark secrets of programming and scalability, robotic functions and platform compatibility.

For him, my soups were just meals, like breathing in air. Still, the first time Georgina saw him she called him Clark Kent and me Lois Lane.

"Why don't you be Lois Lane," I said, "and I'll be Perry White."

"He's not my type," she said.

Georgina liked the strong hands, working class type, like her father, which is why I suspect she flirts with the townies so often.

After spending a couple of days researching all the different programs available for small restaurants, Matt needed some of my undivided attention, so he came by one night just before closing time to lay out my options. He came on a Thursday night, because it was the only weekday night he had available, and because it was still crowded we wound up sitting at Beany's table discussing software and servers, while Georgina handled the kitchen and the customers. I offered him a glass of wine, but he declined because he didn't drink, so I gave him a bowl of my mulligatawny, which he ate so slowly that I offered to warm it up for him.

"It's OK," he said, "I like it cold."

The thought of cold mulligatawny gave me the shivers, but it didn't seem to bother Matt as he absent-mindedly spooned it into his mouth, his eyes riveted on the software specifications. I wondered if he even tasted it.

If you're thinking that this is where I abandon my resolve, because he pushed the needle closer toward 0, you'd be wrong. I didn't sleep with Matt, nor was I tempted to; the chemistry wasn't there, which is sometimes just the way it is, although he did a great job and became another regular customer. Even computer nerds have to eat. Eventually I found out that Matt was gay, which might help explain it since the only people it seems I'm not physically attracted to are gay men.

"Compatibility is the key issue here," he said, showing me the 3 choices he had narrowed it down to.

"Compatibility with what," I replied, "me?"

That made him laugh and he had a real laugh with an open mouth and a lot of teeth, not that little pretend chuckle I would have expected from a computer geek.

"Compatibility with the other software," he said. "There's the server, which is your computer, which comes with what we call hardware. That's made by one company like Dell, IBM or Apple. Then there is the operating program, which is like the conductor of an orchestra that's supposed to coordinate all the programs you run. That's usually Microsoft Windows, but it can be something else, like Linx. Finally, you have all kinds of different operating software, for accounting, for word processing, photography, gaming, ordering, recipes and inventory, whatever it is you need. Each one of those is usually made by a different, unrelated company. Are you with me?"

I nodded. Obviously, he'd given this tutorial before.

"That's where the problems come in. The trick is to try to get all the programs to play in harmony like an orchestra . . . to be compatible. Unfortunately, what often happens is that one software program conflicts with another and the computer freezes or certain functions stop working. Most people just install the programs and find out the hard way. That's what has been happening to you. We're going to avoid all that by finding the least conflicting restaurant program that does what you need and then custom installing it to avoid any incompatibilities."

"That sounds perfect," I said, "I'll leave it up to you."

He wrote some numbers down on the pad.

"I would recommend a terminal out here, as well as the kitchen."

We both looked over at the reception desk, which was small and too modern for my taste.

"You'll need something a little bigger," he said.

"I've been thinking about replacing it for months," I said. "I'd like something old fashion looking, maybe a small writing desk, something with character. You have a catalogue for that?"

"Better than that," Matt said, "I know this great furniture guy who can build you whatever you want. He's up by the Vermont border, but he's down here a lot."

"Let me guess, his name is Jim."

"You know him."

"No, but his name has come up before. He built something for one of my customers, Lisa Montero. She has the hair salon on Becker."

Matt shrugged. He didn't seem the type who spent a lot of time worrying about his hair.

While he wrote up the order, one of my occasional late night customers, a saleswoman who sold fabrics to hotels and inns, stopped at the table on her way out to compliment me on the Farinata, a robust Italian vegetable soup. She'd been away on an extended trip into Canada and had missed my soup.

"I can't tell you how many times I thought about it," she said, "while sipping the stuff these other places had the nerve to call soup."

I smiled and thanked her.

"What happened to that old man who's always here on Thursdays?"

"Professor Beanstock, he died about two months ago."

"Sorry to hear that," she said, touching me lightly on the shoulder, surely aware of the special attention I always paid to him.

She nodded slowly at me and then Matt and walked out.

"I knew Professor Beanstock," Matt said without looking up from his writing.

"How?"

"I worked on his computer a couple of years ago."

I may not be all that religious, certainly not when it comes to organized religion, but all these connections made me wonder if there was some larger spiritual force at work.

"That's what happened to Professor Beanstock," Matt said.

"What?"

"His computer kept freezing. He installed something he shouldn't have. And he didn't have any anti-virus protection. He should have known better."

He made it sound like unsafe sex.

That's when he explained to me about viruses and spy-ware and why I had to add a security program. We were just wrapping up when Matt added, "I saw Professor Beanstock again the summer before last in Provincetown."

"Was he alone?" I asked, looking away so Matt wouldn't see my surprise.

He must have noticed; computer geeks may be lacking in some social skills, but that doesn't mean they are totally insensitive to subliminal messages, because Matt suddenly looked a bit uncomfortable as he turned his neck to loosen his collar.

"I know he was gay," I said.

Matt let out a breath.

"Did you know?" I asked.

"No," he said, "I would never have guessed it until I saw him there."

"He wasn't alone?"

"He wasn't with some young stud, if that's what you're thinking."

"Who was it?"

Matt started packing up his things.

"No one I'd seen around here," he said. "Someone his own age, he had a limp and didn't look all that well. They weren't holding hands or anything like that but they were leaning against each other as they walked. I thought it was sweet."

After Matt left and Georgina and I finished closing up, I took a warm bowl of mulligatawny and some wine and pulled out the next letter. It was dated November 15, 1956, the year of the bus boycott in Alabama, the Suez crisis and the Hungarian uprising. It was also the year Elvis first dominated the music charts. Of course, none of that mattered to me now.

My Dear Rose,

I am both honored and grateful for your invitation to dinner on Thanksgiving; however, I must regrettably decline. The thought of spending time with you is, of course, the main attraction, notwithstanding your outstanding culinary reputation among the faculty. However, Thanksgiving is a holiday like Christmas and New Years that I have spent so often alone that I have become quite used to it, and, if you can believe it, I actually look forward to the quiet time. It is not that I have rejected the social graces, as you well know from the wonderful moments we have shared recently at the department tea, or seek to emulate Marcel Proust, of whom I know you are quite fond; it's just that I find these holidays a wonderful time for reflection on my world and those who have departed from it in whatever manner. It is also a time free of the rigors of grading papers and planning lectures that I can devote to the pleasurable reading that is stacked beside my armchair demanding my attention, as well as the research and writing that the college expects and which sustains me as well.

I wasn't surprised that Beany had to fend off advances from coeds and female colleagues, who must have felt led on at times. What I wondered was whether his needle ever deviated from 6, and whether he ever took them up on any of their offers, even if only for a one-night stand. Is it possible to go over 50 years like that without ever again inhaling that lazy Sunday morning scent of a lover pressed up against you or feeling the warmth of someone's palm in yours when an anxious moment sneaks up on you? I suppose, in a way, being bi-sexual opens up many more opportunities for that sort of thing, particularly if physical proximity is all you crave. Still, my feeling was that if Beany could do it, why not me? Although he did tell me once that resolve at my age is a lot like the weather, it only takes one or two warm, sunny spring days to bring things back to life.

You realize Rose that I am on my way to 40, a decade that took my mother, and an age at which bachelors like myself have to learn to be practical and to measure tomorrow by the sameness of today. I have, to use the vernacular, become very set in my ways. You were quite correct in your observation at tea the other day that I am comfortable keeping my own company. I did so during the war, because I had no choice since none of my charges could ever talk back, and I have done so for the past many years, because I made the choice. It is not something I regret. It is not a fear of commitment or the absence of opportunity, because I am surrounded by women as you might expect from morning until night. The companionship that they add to my working day sustains me and allows me the private moments I so cherish to follow my scholarly and creative ambitions. In any event, it has become a way of life for me now that will not change, and derives more than enough social comfort from the certainty of friends like you.

I wondered if this was Beany's form letter. Rose couldn't have been the first and she couldn't have been the last. It certainly didn't sound from the tone of it that Beany regretted or suffered much from his choice. He sounded quite content and resolved in the life he had chosen, and I suspect that back then the spurned women just shook their heads sadly and attributed it to a domineering mother or a war injury, psychological or physical. I doubt that they suspected anything else. Beany had a way of fitting himself into your expectations, but without ever really doing what it was you expected.

I am not as bad a cook as you might think, and while I know that I will be missing the gastronomical event of the year at Smith, rest assured that I do acquit myself adequately when it comes to the bird and the stuffing, although I would love to have the recipe you mentioned for the squash and pumpkin casserole, which sounded delicious.

Again, thank you very much for the invitation, and I look forward to hearing all about your Thanksgiving accomplishments at the December tea.
With Great Affection,
Roger

I looked up Rose. Her last name was Petry and she joined Smith as an associate professor two years earlier and taught two introductory courses, one on the modern American novel and the other on Elizabethan poetry. She left a year after the letter. I couldn't find her anywhere on the internet and suspect that she married and dropped out of teaching, a much more common path for women to follow back in the fifties. Or perhaps Beany just had the knack back then of chasing away the people who liked him, as well as the people he liked. That would make most anyone pine away for celibacy.

CHAPTER THIRTEEN

The following Thursday was the coldest night of the year, 8 below without the wind chill factor and 32 below with it. Noses got sealed shut every time you inhaled, as if the cold had turned all the little hairs inside into Velcro. You would think it would be a great night for soup – and it would be, provided you were home dressed in flannel pajamas and sitting by a roaring fire – but it was not a great night to go out for anything. Captain Dale was my only customer after 8pm.

"I'm offering you a 3 for 1 tonight Tom," I said, "because I made too much and it looks like you're going to be the only one left out on the road."

I had made three special cold weather soups: Russian Green Bean and Potato Soup to which I always added a rather unusual ingredient for soup, sauerkraut juice; Garlic Butternut Squash Bisque; and Turkey Soup with Parsley Dumplings, which was so popular before Thanksgiving that I brought it back in January.

"I'll take you up on the soup offer," he said, shaking his head slowly from side to side. "I wish you were right about the roads, but nothing stops some people from driving, not even common sense. I expect I'll spend most of the night counting car accidents."

I put six containers of soup in a bag.

"I'll give some to the boys."

"How will you keep it warm?"

"As long as it's not frozen, it'll seem warm tonight."

I put in a ton of bread as well.

"You should close early and be careful walking home. The black ice is a killer."

Tom started toward the door, but stopped and turned around before opening it.

"I'm serious," he said, waging his finger the way my mother sometimes did. "We've already had to close a part of Route 91 by the border. An old couple spun out and got stuck off the shoulder. They had no phone and would probably have frozen to death if it weren't for this good Samaritan driving by with a truck full of furniture who stopped to pick them up."

"What was his name?" I asked.

I was getting this feeling again that the universe was trying to tell me something.

"You really want to know?"

I nodded and Tom pulled out his radio.

"Who was the good Sam on 91?"

"Guy named Jim," I heard crackling over the radio, "the old lady called him the holy carpenter."

"Someone you know?" Tom asked.

"No."

After Captain Dale left, I closed the doors and sent Georgina home, which she was happy about because she had a date, although she wouldn't tell me with whom. I took Beany's correspondence file from behind the canisters of whole wheat flour, where I kept it safe and out of sight, and sat down with a big bowl of Pasta E Fagioli, one of my favorites.

The wind was howling and I do confess to thinking hard about taking the next letter home to read. However, people like Beany and me who are determined to go through life fueled by self-love, without the complications that arise when you add a second heart to the mix, have to depend on the other little consistencies of life and this had now become one of them.

Breaking with tradition is not something that comes easy to me. Certainly it would take much more than a cold and windy night, even though the walk to my apartment was largely uphill. If it got too bad outside, I could always push a few chairs together and spend the night in the restaurant. I'd done that once before when I couldn't bear the thought of being too far from my soup.

The next letter was dated six years later, November 22, 1963. It was a date I didn't recognize at first, because I hadn't even been born yet and recent history always gets short shrift in public school, but it was one my mother and her contemporaries would not have been likely to forget. It was to Evan again, which I found both hopeful and disappointing at the same time; hopeful for Beany, disappointing for me, at least for my resolve.

My Dear Boy,

Of course boy is an inappropriate word to use with respect to you and me at this stage of life, since we haven't seen or spoken a word to each other in almost 15 years, but that is how you are still in my mind and, I suppose, always will be. I wonder if you can close your eyes and see me as well, or have you managed to delete me entirely from your personal Periodic Table, like some sort of bad element that once created a reaction that could not be controlled . . . except, of course, from a great distance.

I did appreciate, almost as much as I was surprised, by the hello you sent through Angus McGill, our organic chemist, who bumped into you in Portland where he, as well as you, were presenting papers. Of course, that is the kind of minimal social obligation even you would have to acknowledge. He did say without any prodding on my part that your work with lipids was quite interesting.

So you believe what I eat can damage my heart? I am sure you are right, but it's not nearly as much as the damage one can do by ignoring it. Literature has proven that time and time again. When you think about it, for the past 15 years we have actually been working together toward the same goal, understanding the human heart. Of course, I come at it through the mind, while you approach it through the stomach. Perhaps our two disciplines will come together someday in the future to create a heart that can never be broken or stopped, although I'm not so sure that would be such a good thing.

I assume that you are moved as well by the assassination, even though President Kennedy was clearly not of your political persuasion. I am sure that his victory over Vice-President Nixon two years ago was the cause of some angst for you. Still, you have to wonder where the world is heading now. On one hand I think we are moving toward more tolerance and free expression; on the other, I suspect there will be more violence, both random and coldly calculated to try to keep the world from changing.

I suppose tonight would be easier to accept if you could look at death and decay as just a different permutation of elements and reactions, different from birth and life, but no less natural and essential to life. I suppose to have that attitude you need to have been trained since college, and probably much earlier than that, to break everything down to its smallest component, as if the whole is always less than the sum of its parts (from my literary point of view it is always something more).

I suppose what Beany was trying to tell me by including this letter was that not even patience and time could eliminate all the sadness and disappointment, certainly not enough of it, all least in the absence of another relationship to block the view. How different would Beany's letter be if he was one or two relationships removed from Evan? Of course, what if Evan was that one true and perfect passion that could never be repeated? A poetic soul could believe that, although probably not a scientist, who would have to believe that any chemical reaction can be duplicated if the conditions are right. Beany the poet, at least back then, couldn't allow himself to feel that way. He preferred to live under the shadow of his intimate past and perhaps in this way keep his muse.

Of course, my situation was different, as I no longer ached for Nick, Jake or Jolene. My decision, like Evan's, was more concerned with simplifying my future and making a success of my present work. I've always been one to follow the path of least resistance. It would appear to be a lot easier sticking with soup and keeping my relationships skin deep.

Of course, I do know with absolute certainty that Kennedy will be replaced by another politician and one after that until he fades in the distance like a speeding train. Yet I feel as lost this night as I did when my mother passed away. I don't think I felt nearly as empty or alone when the news came about Aunt Emma. You remember her? She left me that little house by the ocean in Ogunquit, Maine, where we spent that marvelous weekend. I doubt even you could forget that, even if you did, as you once said you would when you had a bit too much to drink, take a wife and force yourself to procreate.

You were something to see back then on the beach, and it wasn't just me who noticed. The war had left you as trim and solid as the granite of New Hampshire, but that was a small part of your attraction. There was something much stronger, some kind of innocence that children have, which somehow made it through to adulthood despite all that horror. You were the first man that I ever knew who attracted desire much more than he radiated it.

I wonder sometimes if it wasn't the way you looked out at the world, like a child, your scientific eyes filled with curiosity, never conquest. It was almost as if you were born to some greater purpose and blessed with the smallest of personal egos. What's more, I don't think you ever realized or sensed your irresistibility. I doubt you were even aware of how generous the world had been with your physical gifts, which made you all the more . . . what's the right word . . . innocent, refreshing . . . naïve, greedy . . . exciting . . . I don't know, take your pick.

I had to open another bottle of wine after reading that. Beany had just turned 40. How long did it take for feelings like that to dim? They certainly didn't shine on the outside during the year of Thursdays we shared, but what did they look like inside of him when he wasn't sipping my soup? How did that contribute to his final decision? If the past – the long past – can't find a quiet, uncomplicated place in your heart by time you pass 80, what hope was there for my journey? Would trying to keep my heart empty make any difference?

In case you are interested, I have not been with anyone since you. I came close a couple of times, but decided against it. I'm not interested in a passing dalliance, and none of them were you. Besides, why would I want to risk jeopardizing the fine reputation that I already have as a stand-offish academic, a scholarly eunuch who channels what little hormonal passion still circulates in his being on his research, writing and lectures? I wonder if you can say the same. Actually, I suspect that you can, because what motivated you back then could not have changed very much, certainly not the way Angus described you. It sounds as if research and funding rules your world, forestalling any and all other natural inclinations.

The hardest thing for me has been the coeds; not resisting them, but explaining myself. They offer themselves up like a banquet and wonder why I'm not famished like all the other male members of the faculty, who seem quite thrilled to talk about their conquests. It keeps them young, I suppose, because the faces they see at climax never age. There can be no thrill in the chase, however, since they would line up and take a number if you asked them to.

There was one coed, Rebecca, long since graduated, and I'm sure married by now with children. The words shimmered for her like the late autumn sunset and came from a great distance, not down from the top of her head, but up from the cellar of her heart. She never saw quite what everyone else did - she saw the magic, the gods and the demons. I did not have one-tenth of her natural poetic talent. The time I spent working one on one with her on her honor's thesis was every bit as exciting as discovering Chaucer or Keats. To watch the forces of creation respond like that must be similar to the way you must feel when one of your chemical reactions challenges the laws of nature.

I did love her, the pilgrim soul in her, to quote a favorite poet of mine, but nothing more. I would devour her words without her being aware of it. But it was not the way, understandably, that she wanted to be loved. One day I came home and found her naked in my bed. I'm sure the look of horror on my face was not the one she was hoping for. She fled in tears as if being spurned by an older bachelor like that was a rejection of her talent, condemning her to a life in suburbia.

She never said anything to anyone, even though I suspect she realized at that point, but our teacher-student relationship was not the same, which is why I think it best to keep them all at a safe distance, for their sakes as much as mine. I do not invite them to my home for dinner like some of the other professors. I see them at the department teas and when I have office hours, and if they want to sleep with a professor, there are plenty of others to go around. In any event, soon time will take care of that little problem.

I have to apologize again for wandering far from the subject at hand, although I do feel quite remarkably as if I have loosened my grip a bit on the sadness. In any event, it is a terrible thing. I feel as if we have all been banished from Camelot. I fear that the world that lies ahead will be filled with change, too much, too quickly, with violence, as always, the necessary catalyst; World War II, Korea, and now another conflict simmering in Southeast Asia. How many young men must be picked up from battlefields for the world to get it right? Although I am not against change, I just prefer it at a measured and steady pace. Who knows, perhaps someday that change will come for us?

Wishing you a Nobel future, I remain
Yours faithfully,
Roger

I did sleep in the restaurant that night. The wind was howling by the time I finished the letter and the radio said that the wind chill was down to 40 below. I was tired despite the thoughts racing through my mind. Too much wine does that to me. I lay there waiting to be overcome with sleep wondering whether Evan wrote back and what kind of professor I would have made being available to sleep with students of both genders. At least this way no one would feel left out.

Not surprisingly, I dreamt that I was a cooking professor with a class in soups, alternating the young men and women I took home at night, like it was a game of musical chairs. However, I grew obese in my dream, bloated with all their youthful secretions until I couldn't bend or lie down, and was forced to carry on my lustful activities from a standing position.

CHAPTER FOURTEEN

Even in soup I am of two minds. Today it's all about being low-fat, the refrain being that we are what we eat and drink, which I don't disagree with, except like most everything else most people carry it too far to the extreme. They can even give you a number for the fat content of your body, a measure I have never asked for, but which is likely to make all but a few people very unhappy. Now I'm all for healthy food, soup being one of the best as far as I'm concerned, but I also believe that the body needs some fat from time to time, and that the flavor it adds can feed a spiritual hunger that shouldn't be ignored.

There are some soups, particularly the vegetable ones, to which I bend with the prevailing winds and work hard to reduce the fat. Little things make a big difference, like sautéing the vegetables in a teaspoon or two of olive oil instead of a pound of butter. You can do that by reducing the heat and cooking them slower and longer. Of course, vegetables have their own moisture that a drop of salt will help bring out.

The flavor of the fats can be replaced, although not duplicated, by aromatic herbs and fragrant vegetables like onions, leeks and mushrooms. Sometimes just a cup or two of miso will do the trick. And when I need to thicken a pureed soup, I can rely on rice, potatoes and even oats, all low-fat, and all dairy-free, which my customers demand, as they should, to be kept informed about. Accordingly, alongside each of my soups on the menu board are symbols indicating how guilty one need feel before eating them.

There are some soups, however, just as there are some moments in life that need fat and cry out for the rich and intense flavors of our childhood. For example, it is impossible to tinker with the Welsh Rarebit Soup my grandmother used to make, which is a full-flavored cheese soup that includes mounds of sharp cheddar, potatoes and tomatoes, along with butter, milk, beer, mustard and Worcestershire Sauce. With dense and dark bread, there is no other soup that transports me back faster to a moment in time when I had no thoughts about sexual orientation or fractured relationships, and my biggest fear was whether my grandmother would make me eat the liver and onions she was so fond of making with it.

Of course, you can replace milk and cream these days with buttermilk and evaporated skim milk. Some people will even use soy and rice milk to thicken those rich, creamy soups from our past, but it doesn't work for me. It's soup without its soul and misses the whole point. Rice milk is too sweet and evaporated milk just doesn't provide the thickness and flavor some soups require to raise the serotonins in the brain for that mood-altering moment we are all so desperately searching for. And forget about low-fat cheese if you want anyone to really remember it, let along savor every spoonful.

I cannot say which I like better. I love both kinds - the low-fat Tuscan Vegetable Bean and the creamy New England clam chowder. And although I have had some customers who refuse to accept my fence-sitting, demanding that I take sides in this great culinary debate, I cannot. Some people tend to be dismissive and have trouble believing that I can't make up my mind, but I assure them it's true. When it comes to soups, as with sexuality, I am a 3, the needle pointing dead center.

Matt didn't make me feel any better about it when he came by late the next Thursday night to see how the new system was operating. I told him it was working better than I had hoped. Georgina merely entered her orders in the dining room and they popped up in the kitchen with the elapsed time beside each order to remind me who had been waiting the longest.

"That's the easiest part," he said. "Wait until you see how well it works with inventory and back-up. You'll never lose a single recipe."

"Provided I find some time to input them all."

"I've got someone who could do that for you," Matt said. "He can enter data faster than anyone I've ever seen."

"He'll never be able to read my handwriting."

I made him sit down for some soup and in the course of our conversation about how tolerant Northampton was compared to where he came from, a steel town in Pennsylvania, I blurted it out. I suppose I felt safe that he of all people would understand what it felt like to deviate from the norm, but I wasn't pleased with his response.

"Claiming to be bi-sexual," he said, "is a way of dealing subconsciously with your own homophobia. It's a reaction to the fear of coming completely out of the closet and having to declare yourself a traitor to the sitcom nation."

Of course, I disagreed. There is no such thing as a closet in Northampton. Anything goes in this town. I could announce that I was a hermaphroditic visitor from outer space and it wouldn't affect my business. So who was I hiding it from?

"The only person who matters," he said, "yourself."

I spent six years with Nick and Jake, I explained, in large part because of the chemistry. We meshed like potatoes and leeks in a bowl of vichyssoise. The love-making with Jolene wasn't better, but it was just as good.

"So what better evidence is there that I'm an equal-opportunity employer?" I said to lighten up the conversation.

That didn't mean anything, according to Matt, since sex is always enjoyable, whenever and with whomever, which is why, he said, we practice so much auto-eroticism.

"How do you explain the Kinsey Report," I said, "which found that 90% of Americans had some attraction to both sexes?"

"I call it voyeurism," Matt said, "not attraction."

"You don't understand," I said, "because bisexuality occurs so much less often in men than women."

I had read that in a study recently on the internet.

"Because it's less sexual with a woman," he said, "all you really want is someone, anyone, who is willing to hold you for a while and stroke your arm."

That stereotype pissed me off, although there was some truth to it. Matt apologized and tried to put it in terms that he was more comfortable with.

"That kind of either-or paradigm does not exist in the real world any more than it does in the computer world. You have to pick an operating system with a computer. You have to make a choice about how the program should operate or everything is just going to freeze up."

Which was precisely my point, I thought to myself, regretting that I had confided in Matt and promising myself not to try that again with anyone else.

"Freezing up may be bad for computers," I said, "but maybe it's not so bad for people."

Matt looked like he didn't have any idea what I was talking about.

Since it was a Thursday night, I kicked Matt out so Georgina and I could close up and I could get to the next letter, which was dated June 30, 1969.

Dear Eliza,

Five years ago, when we first discovered that we shared a secret, which we had long concealed from our colleagues and the college that we were more than a couple of cantankerous aging asexual professors disinclined to invest in happy-ever-after, did you ever envision that any of that would change in our lifetimes? Certainly I did not. I expected to live as always without sentimentality, and still do, although recent events offer hope for those behind us.

I know you do not own a television in that cabin of yours in the New Hampshire woods, your summer hermitage as you put it, nor are you a fan of the newspapers and periodicals, preferring to focus on the knowable, as opposed to what you call society's insatiable need for action and uncertainty, so I will assume that you have heard nothing about what started two days ago in New York City in Greenwich Village on Sheridan Square in a small bar called Stonewall. Of course, I had never heard of Sheridan Square or Stonewall until now, but I suspect that it will one day become a landmark for people like you and me.

Have I your attention now, Eliza? Have you stopped your bird watching at the lake for a moment? I suspect that you have.

They are calling it the Stonewall Riot, but I think it should be more aptly called the Stonewall Revolution, because I believe that freedom and self-determination may follow as well. Mayor Lindsay, as pretty a politician as I can recall, which always created a little doubt in my mind, needed a political boost, so what better way to do it than raid a bar frequented by gay men. I think that's the first time I have ever written the word gay with that connotation. I certainly like it much more than the words used in our youth like queer and faggot.

This was a new Beany writing. It was the first time he'd written so openly about his homosexuality. It was also the first time that he didn't sound angry and alone. Of course, he was almost 50 and most of it must have washed over him by now. He certainly didn't need or expect anything else at this stage in his life. Besides, he must have felt ancient in terms of the years he'd spent concealing his true nature. If he had any regrets about the lifestyle he had chosen, perhaps this was the opportunity to make up for it.

Last Saturday morning at about 1 a.m., the police decided to raid the Stonewall, a favorite watering hole, to use the vernacular, of the homosexual community, and, according to the news reports, the trans-gendered as well. The papers called them drag queens, I suppose, because they dress like women, although I have no idea of the significance of the word drag. The raid, as you *might suspect, was not all that unusual, although it was normally done on advance notice to the bar owners and in the early evening hours so as not to disturb the peak hours of business. Apparently, even middle class morality must bend a bit in the big city when it comes to commerce. Normally, one or two of the more colorful ones are arrested, the "scantily clad go-go boys" is how they described them, and the remainder of the patrons would leave quietly. On the 28th, however, the mood was very different. The funeral for Judy Garland, one of your favorites, I know, was the afternoon before, and the papers said that at least half of the 22,000 mourners were gay men. So on this early morning, sad, inebriated, and fed-up, they did not go quietly into the night.*

Of course, I had heard about Stonewall, although I didn't realize its temporal proximity to Judy Garland's death. I know that a month or so later, the Gay Liberation Front was formed in New York City, and by the end of the year branches could be found in cities and universities across the country.

Fight they did with four police officers beaten and numerous protesters injured as well. They rioted for two days; men and women used to living their lives with caution, hiding behind their dark, hooded eyes, suddenly found their fear melted away. It simmers still as I write this letter. I read about a heterosexual folk singer, David van Ronk, who was pulled into the Stonewall Bar by the police who had taken shelter there from the stone and glass shower, and mistaking him for a homosexual, beat him into unconsciousness. Riot squads, trained to fight the Vietnam anti-war protesters, were brought in. And, much more importantly, the Stonewall Riots made the front pages everywhere across the country.

The secret that was never a secret is finally out – WE EXIST, and we are everywhere. We are neighbors and relatives and friends, we are athletes and actors, politicians and teachers, dentists and policemen, and we have been around since homo sapiens first stood erect. Perhaps in the future we will as well.

What an exciting moment that must have been, I thought, even though experienced from a great distance. Beany lived his life in the sheltered academic world, in his mind and among words and ideas – the consummate professor – and the Stonewall Riots were not going to change that. Still, it must have made the truth, his truth, seem less fragile and fraught with danger.

What has simmered for so long beneath the surface is now notorious and open for all to see. You know what they say about letting the cat out of the bag - it won't ever go back in. I think things will never be the same . . . at least I hope not. The utopians among us, and they are well represented throughout literature, will look forward to a world where we will not have to live in silence and secrecy, risking looks of unbearable disgust and gestures of unutterable loathing simply because of the way nature has made us. After all, we are found everywhere in the animal kingdom from sheep to man's best friend, which means that there must be a reason for it. Perhaps it's simply one of nature's efforts at birth control. Even the church teaches that it is beyond our limited intelligence to understand God's ways and purposes, so who are we to judge the way God has made some of us?

I would not mind visiting Stonewall one day, if it is ever rebuilt. Mark my words, Eliza, I think the long winter is finally turning into spring. I hope we will be around long enough to bask in the sunshine.

Fondly,
Roger

I wondered if Beany gave any thought about coming out at this juncture in history. He wouldn't have had to change his lifestyle, just his reputation. The two of them – Eliza and Roger – would have made formidable foot soldiers in the Massachusetts Gay Liberation Army. If it was twenty years earlier perhaps he would have, but the 50s are a hard age to begin a revolution, particularly when the alternative is the soothing melody of academic life and all the time in the world to study and write. Some men are born to action and others to pick up the bodies after it's all over. The world needs both.

CHAPTER FIFTEEN

Nick, Jake and Jolene all had the same complaint. After a couple of years together it didn't seem that I was all that big on spontaneous, sappy demonstrations of love, although I think what they really meant was sex, which they said was good, but not nearly frequent enough.

"Couples our age," Jake said, "do it on average once or twice a day, not once or twice a week."

That must have been a study limited to teenage fishermen because I couldn't imagine too many women owning up to a whopper like that; twice a week was plenty for me, although I didn't say that. I just promised to try harder, although when it came to those pressure-bursting hormones, I realized that I must have been somewhat short-changed. What I did also say was that love-making shouldn't become just another routine, like brushing teeth, although Nick, Jake and Jolene completely disagreed saying it sounded like another way of saying less often.

I know I shouldn't have felt guilty about it; it wasn't a conscious decision and it wasn't a reflection of how attractive I found them, but I always did. For a while afterward, I tried to act interested and excited whenever I saw that stinging need in their eyes or heard the impatience in their words. It even had its own scent – that hormonal desire - a damp, salty smell that for some reason reminded me of the ocean. Most of the time all I really wanted to do was read my book, cook some soup and get some sleep. Don't get me wrong; I enjoyed doing it, it's just that on some occasions I would have preferred hugging instead.

Perhaps that's nature's way of balancing off what it's bestowed upon me - bi-sexuality, a label I came to accept during the Year of Soup. If you are attracted to everyone – male and female – and have too active a sex drive, then you'll never get anything accomplished. I'm sure that my mother was the same way, a diminished libido in exchange for an enlarged field of play. Jake used to call it the leave-me-alone-and-let-me-sleep gene. Jolene called it the got-a-headache syndrome. I just figured that if we stayed together long enough, they would catch up to me in about 10 or 15 years.

Of course, after the Stonewall Riot letter I went back to the library to look up Eliza. She was the head of the Romance Language Department in the 1970s and taught conversational French, as well as an advanced course in French literature taught in the native language. She left in 1978 to teach at New York University, probably because unlike Beany she wanted to come out at least for a little while, even if she were past her sexual prime.

Her obituary in 2004 gave nothing away about her personal life, except to say that she left no survivors. It was in the Cape Cod Times, where she had retired and was living at the time. The obituary said that she was well known for her biography of Camus, written after a trove of unknown letters to one of his lovers was found in an attic. She had also published a number of scholarly studies comparing French and German 19th century poets. She was an avid gardener during her retirement and a supporter of the local theater, which was to be named after her thanks to a generous bequest.

I couldn't help wondering if she had died alone. Perhaps after a long, slow debilitating illness with no one to drive her to the doctor or help with the food shopping other than a rotating list of well-intentioned ladies from the church or the garden club, some of whom barely knew her. Clearly, that is one of the downsides of a celibate life – you have to face the end the same way you faced the middle, alone, but I suppose that can't come as a really big surprise. Perhaps spending his debilitating years depending on others was one of the things Beany wanted to avoid by leaving the way he did.

The next Thursday night it was Joe Johnson who hung around while I was waiting for everyone to leave so I could close up and get to the next letter.

"I'm not going home for a while," I told Joe, in case he had any ideas of waiting to walk me home.

"I'm not waiting around for you."

It took me a moment to get it.

"Georgina?"

Joe nodded.

"Don't be jealous, you had your opportunity."

"Just another regret to add to my long list."

"I was only kidding."

"So was I," I said, excusing myself to get something in the kitchen.

"You're going out with Joe?" I asked Georgina who was cleaning the chopping block and didn't bother to look up.

"He's not supposed to move on?" she said. "He's supposed to climb into his shell and live alone like you?"

"It's like he's moving down the food chain."

"Oh please."

We both took a deep breath.

"I'm sorry," I said.

"I kind of like him, I'm not planning to marry him."

"Just be careful, he's got about 8 years on you."

"Six," she said with a nod.

"She's almost ready," I told Joe when I came back out.

"You know," he said, "I've been thinking about you and the Professor. I think you should consider doing a soup cookbook combining some of the soups you made for him with some of his poems."

"Interesting idea," I said, "but his poems have nothing to do with soup."

"They have to do with life."

"True."

"And soup's part of life."

I nodded, as Georgina came out of the kitchen and put on her coat.

"There must be some good soup poems," Joe said.

"Beany once brought some in," Georgina said.

"Your soups are sort of like poetry."

"Thank you," I said.

Suddenly I understood what Georgina saw in Joe.

"You two kids be careful out there."

Joe grinned and Georgina gave me a little wave.

The conversation with Joe reminded of that Thursday, in the middle of our eighth month, when Beany decided to turn our evening into a literary discourse on soup. He did his research and was well-prepared, like any good professor, and started the evening with a poem by Carl Sandberg:

I saw a famous man eating soup
I say he was lifting a fat broth
Into his mouth with a spoon.

His name was in the newspapers that day
Spelled out in tall black headlines
And thousands of people were talking about him.

When I saw him

He sat bending his head over a plate
Putting soup in his mouth with a spoon.

"So eating soup is a great leveler," I said.

"More than that," Beany said, "it's a great unifier."

"All food is."

"Certain foods more than others - soups, pies – but there's something about the way soup is prepared . . . everything gets thrown into it, whatever odds and ends are lying around, then it simmers for the longest time. And the way we eat it, coming down to meet it halfway, that sets it apart."

I couldn't have agreed more.

I remember what I made that night, a Scotch Broth, a soup from Scotland bristling with bits of lamb, lots of root vegetables and pearl barley, a Winter Pumpkin Soup with turnips, parsnips and tomatoes, and a Saudi Lentil-Zucchini Soup with lentils, potatoes, celery, zucchini, onions, lemon and loads of cumin. The Saudi soup is a thick soup, but never rich or creamy. During the Hadj, many pilgrims to Mecca make a meal of it. Beany enjoyed the Scotch Broth and the pilgrim soup, as he called it, but didn't care all that much for the creamy sweetness of the pumpkin soup.

Beany brought out a second poem, this time by Anne Sexton called *The Fury of Rain Storms.*

The rain drums down like red ants,
each bouncing off my window.
These ants are in great pain
and they cry out as they hit,
as if their little legs were only
stitched on and their heads pasted.
And oh they bring to mind the grave,
so humble, so willing to be beat upon
with its awful lettering and
the body lying underneath
without an umbrella.
Depression is boring, I think,
and I would do better to make
some soup and light up the cave.

"It's nice to see that I'm not alone in this," I said.

"Great writers," he said, "are always searching for ways to ease the pain . . . at least for a while. Soup and wine are always high on their lists."

"How about love?" I asked.

"That too," he said, "but wine and soup are much more dependable."

"What else have you got?" I said.

"There's an old Estonian proverb that one cannot make soup out of beauty."

"Meaning no soup worth its while can spring from happiness and contentment?"

"You tell me," Beany said.

I thought about it for a while, finishing the pumpkin soup he refused to eat and pouring myself some of Beany's wine.

"I can think of one occasion, harvest time, when soup is motivated by beauty and abundance."

"Once a year isn't much."

I thought more about it, but couldn't come up with anything else. I couldn't think of a memorable birthday soup, or a celebration soup, and I had to agree that few soups were motivated by beauty.

There was an African proverb Beany found that said "soup is never measured by its quantity," and an Iranian one that said "of soup and love, the first is best."

"There's a Welsh proverb that says a spoon does not know the taste of soup, any more than a learned fool the taste of wisdom."

"So there's wisdom in my soup," I said.

"When it's appreciated."

"And what do you think?"

"I agree with what Virginia Wolfe wrote in *A Room of One's Own.* One cannot think well, love well, or sleep well, if one has not dined well."

Which is why, Beany added he always got his best night's sleep on Thursday nights.

"So come more often," I said.

"And dilute the magic, not on your life. Once a week is more than enough when it comes to soup and love," he said, borrowing part of a line I had used a week earlier when discussing my prior relationships.

"Who said that there is no love sincerer than the love of food?" Beany asked.

"My mother?"

"Obviously an intelligent woman, take a guess."

Beany waited patiently for my answer.

"I have no idea . . . Sartre?"

"No, but that's a good guess, George Bernard Shaw – *Man and Superman*, which means that you have a real talent for love, despite what you think."

"I have a talent for soup," I said, "motivated by a constant need to escape my own thoughts."

"Beethoven wrote in a letter to his true love - unrequited as we all well know - that whoever tells a lie cannot be pure of heart, and only the pure of heart can make good soup."

"He did not write that."

"He most certainly did."

"Well then, sexually pure is going to have to suffice," I said and Beany laughed.

Certainly my soups were better now than ever before. Maybe because I was more focused and didn't have all the distractions that a relationship can bring, or maybe because I had found a way to add my own thoughts and feelings, like tears, to the ingredients, adding a measure of truth and self-sufficiency to the spices and vegetables that simmering fashions into an elixir fit for almost any level of betrayal or loneliness.

Of course, Beany was probably reading my mind when he finished his tour of food in literature with the old Yiddish saying that troubles may be easier to take with soup than without it, but it won't drown them out forever.

The letter that Thursday was short, a year later, dated May 12, 1970, probably graduation week when Beany told me that he always took his senior thesis advisees out for a celebratory dinner.

"For some reason," he said, "it always seemed that getting drunk with a college professor was the highlight of their academic experience."

Dear Mr. Garret,

I certainly recognized your name and know who you are, and I am certainly flattered by your interest, but you are mistaken in your assumption. How you interpreted the look I supposedly gave you the other night after quite a few glasses of wine, of which I have no memory, is certainly not in my control, but it was not what you had thought. While I can certainly appreciate your discretion, it is not necessary in this instance. My decision is not, as you were concerned in your letter, based in any manner upon snobbery, intellectual or social, as I consider the culinary arts every bit as important to our souls as the literary and artistic ones, and it is certainly not the age difference, because it is obvious to me from your letter and our infrequent contacts at your establishment that you are much older in terms of experience and wisdom than the years would show. It is certainly not a question of appearance. I do not dislike long hair any more than I do beards. Besides, to a man on my side of the age divide, anyone without the crow's feet I look at every morning in the mirror is as refreshing as a field of lavender on a warm summer day. No, Mr. Garret, my decision is based entirely on the absence of need and desire.

The forgotten absence of need and desire would have been more appropriate, or better yet the natural atrophy of a muscle unflexed for almost 25 years. I didn't know whether to be proud of Beany for his resolve or to feel sorry for him for denying himself, even after Stonewall. I think I felt more the latter, which is why Beany must have included the letter. This way when my time came maybe I'd be a bit more honest about it, not denying the attraction, but only the will and desire to act on it. The question is whether that's cowardice or bravery. I suppose it depends on your point of view.

Again I appreciate your offer, and I will certainly keep it between us, but I must respectfully decline. I have, unfortunately, decided that discretion on my part dictates that I no longer frequent your establishment. It will, of course, be my loss.

Respectfully,
Professor Roger Beanstock

What was Beany in 1970, 48? Still young by today's standard. Did he already feel it was too late for him or was he just a creature of habit, unwilling or unable to change? Could he still be loyal to Evan, who at this point was not much more than a figment of his imagination? My vote was for routine, which is especially strong in a bucolic college setting like Smith where the seasonal rhythms march in step with the semesters and nothing ever changes with respect to the students or the dead poets and the authors Beany lived with.

It's safe to assume that there were a number of other occasions over the years that Beany walked away from opportunities that could have changed his life. Was he trying to show me that a person could stay firm in the face of temptation and that the mind could overrule the heart in all things? After all, Beany, who loved soup and good food, was not only walking away from a relationship, but a good restaurant, a significant decision in a small town where the choices were somewhat limited. Or was he simply trying to point out, coming right after the Stonewall letter, that if you wait too long and become too set in your ways it's impossible to change, even if society does? Did he know that I'd feel badly for him and wish he had decided otherwise?

I reread the letter over and over again as I finished my bottle of wine. Things sometimes change if you stare at them long enough. Paintings at the museum change shape as lines shift and shadows appear. Photographs seem to come to life, almost as if you can hear what the person was thinking. The more I read the letter, the clearer the picture I had of Beany's hand and heart, reluctantly taking directions from his stubborn resolve.

Of course, the letter did not contain any indication of how long or hard Beany had to wrestle with his response. I imagined that it took him a while, because even he had to be of two minds. A writer/teacher needs a variety of life experiences to draw from, both painful and pleasurable. Living the lives of others through poetry and novels can hardly suffice. Focusing more on scholarly criticism and analysis than your own poetry is one indication of that; taking one's own life, I suppose, is another.

CHAPTER SIXTEEN

It was the following Thursday night that Mr. X, as Georgina first called him, came into the restaurant. He came late and alone like Beany, although without the wine, and sat down coincidentally at Beany's table, even though he had a few others to choose from. I peeked out of the kitchen window after Georgina told me about him and felt that unmistakable tug from the left side of my heart, which is where I had decided that my heterosexual urges reside. He was tall, even sitting at the table, and rugged looking with sandy brown hair falling down almost to his shoulders that might have pegged him as a surfer if he wasn't wintering in Massachusetts.

Georgina thought he might be the new art professor in residence, the winter term having just started the week before and the rumors about him being rampant all over the school.

"I heard he was drop dead gorgeous," she said. "Somebody supposedly saw him doing laps in the pool and said he looked as good inside as out."

Georgina peaked out the kitchen door window.

"Or maybe he's one of the new young artists showing at the Michelson Gallery. Their winter exhibit opened the other day."

I took another look through the kitchen door window.

"Probably just a local farmer bored to death," I said with a smirk, walking back to the stove to ladle out his soup.

He had ordered a new creation of mine, a cauliflower, beet and thyme soup; the thyme for melancholy, the beets for pain and the cauliflower to help move a reluctant mind toward the light. Mark Twain called cauliflower "the cabbage with a college education." The fact that he picked that soup made it clear to me that he was no bored farmer.

"He's not wearing a wedding ring," Georgina said, coming back into the kitchen after dropping off his soup. "He's certainly not the talkative type."

"Because he didn't try to hit on you?"

"He's too old for me," she said.

"And Joe's not?"

"There's something old about him, something around the eyes . . . and unhappy."

You'd be surprised at how much you can tell about a person sitting in front of a bowl of soup. Of course, that piqued my interest even more and I gave Georgina some extra bread to bring out to him. I knew she couldn't come back without another one of her observations.

"His hands are all nicked up," she said as soon as she returned "like he builds things."

I know how much the universe likes a good coincidence and I know a persistent sign when I see one, so that was all I had to hear.

Georgina had already put down his bill since it was getting late and we both watched from the kitchen window as he took out a credit card. I was hoping he wouldn't pay with cash.

"I'll bet you anything," I told her, "that the name on the card is Jim or James."

"What are you a psychic now?"

"It's closing time," I said, "just go run the card and kick him out."

Georgina ran back in as soon as he left.

"How the hell did you know," she said. "His name is Jim Chapman."

"Lucky guess."

"Come on."

"Lisa Montero wanted to set me up with him," I said. "She probably sent him in to meet me."

"It didn't seem to me like he was interested in doing anything other than eating soup."

"How did he seem when he left?"

Georgina looked at me with those fish eyes that pop out sometimes when something hits her as comical or odd.

"The same as when he walked in . . . except full."

It looked to me – watching through the kitchen window – that he seemed a little lighter on his feet and stood a bit straighter, but I just shrugged and sent Georgina home. She said she would Google him and come in with a full biography the next day. It sounded like an invasion of privacy to me, but I didn't object.

The letter that night was very appropriate. It was dated September 8, 1974. Of course, that was still before I was born, so the date didn't register in my mind, as I am sure it might for some of the more politically astute baby boomers. It was another letter to Evan. My question as to whether the two of them had been corresponding over the years was answered in the first line.

Dear Evan,

It has been over ten years since I last wrote and longer since I heard from you, but since that was when our President, who you would not have supported, was shot by an assassin's bullet, I thought it appropriate to write again as I sit here late in the evening reading about another President, one I have no doubt you did support, who, in a figurative sense, shot himself.

But first the pleasantries, I hope you are well and happy. I am certainly the former, and the latter, of course, from time to time. I took a trip to Italy over the summer to sample the ruins and wine as part of a college summer program. I taught a little Dante and some poetry by Petrarch, which paid my way. I was happy then. English professors here are notoriously underpaid. I would make significantly more as a corporate librarian. Still, sporadic happiness should be enough for anyone, particularly for someone who has made a career out of poetry, which springs from pain and suffering more often than not. It is very unlike Chemistry, where a professor can expect to get aroused at least once a week, like any well-adjusted spouse, by the tantalizing results of his naked calculations and experimentation.

I have no idea why politics interests me, but it always has. I attribute it to two reasons; one, because it's a nice change from my academic pursuits. Neither intelligence nor scholarship seems to be very important, and instead of searching for the truth, it appears to be a sport more intent on obfuscating it. The second reason is that it tends to reveal the baser aspects of human nature, like a great novel. Richard Nixon is a prime example. You have to wonder why he would bother to lie since he was already on top, and elected to a second term, so there was no question of his hoping to hang on or ascend higher. Is it simply because he could get away with it or at least thought he could and enjoyed crushing the opposition? Perhaps it was simply a matter of control. That kind of arrogance when compared to the morality by which the rest of us are expected to live is clearly a character trait of the successful politician. I think the world would be a safer and better place if it was governed by poets and scientists. What a remarkable combination that would be - the pure heart and the pure mind.

What has me up late tonight is not Mr. Nixon's abrupt resignation or even his second Checkers speech the night before, but President Ford's pardon. If the most powerful men in our nation are not held accountable, why should any citizen respect the rule of law? Ending the political nightmare is hardly a reason to exonerate someone who has yet to admit his guilt.

I wondered if it was the sudden departure of another President that stirred up Beany's memories of Evan, much the way the spring smells of hyacinth, fresh cut grass and warm rain stir up memories of my college boyfriends, a time when life seemed as light as a feather.

So tell me, Evan, have you been recruited yet by the Gay Liberation Army? They are everywhere these days; by they, I mean us 30 years ago, men and women holding hands and strolling the campus like procreation is all a big mistake and this is what God really intended. Where did they all come from? Were they there all the time? Did one of their parents fight against their own nature? Were they able to forget and convince themselves that they were not what they felt? I know I never did, I never tried. I could not live that kind of lie. The lie I chose to live was hard enough.

How about your life? Still the mad scientist devoted to his research? Still married to your lipids? What reputation you must have on campus, the old man with elements and formulas circulating through his body. As for me, my reputation is secure. I am the asexual egghead of English literature. Of course, I would have to object to the asexual label, since an asexual in biology is a species that reproduces from a single organism, while I am an organism that does not reproduce at all.

Whatever the reputation and rumors, they have long since died down as I have become too old to be considered as a partner in any physical activity more strenuous than grading papers. With any luck, most of my students see me as the quintessential sexless intellectual like Sherlock Holmes. Now that is a model I can live with.

I suppose once you reach 80 and become "Professor Emeritus" the gossip stops and the rumors fade away. If they hadn't, I'd have heard something from Georgina when Beany first started coming in for soup, something more than what he did for a living. In a way, it seemed worse to me that no one cared enough to wonder anymore . . . including me.

So Nixon retires to California to live the rest of his life in ignominy, much the way you fled to Nebraska to live the rest of your life under a cloak of invisibility, at least in terms of your personal life.

So much for the regret and bitterness; it does not come out that often anymore. Fortunately, I do not write you very often, so rest assured it does not last. By the morning I will again be Professor Beany, as the students call me behind my back, the mad scientist of 20th century English literature and poetry, the hermit living high up on the literary mountain, but a damn good teacher, who respects their artistic souls and does not eye every coed like a potential meal.

Until the next time a President is assassinated or disgraced, I remain
Yours Truly,
Roger

CHAPTER SEVENTEEN

I remember one Thursday night when Beany came in carrying some student papers from a seminar he was teaching on D. H. Lawrence. The subject was sex and love in his novels, which every college student knows were once banned in this country for being too steamy. After reading a few of them on my own I could never really understand what the fuss was all about. Of course, I was many generations removed.

"What's funny is that Lawrence was not considered very sexual by the people who knew him," Beany said with a chuckle, "which my students always find hard to believe considering the intensely erotic nature of some of his writings."

"Still waters run deep," I said.

"Trite but true," Beany said with a professorial nod.

"The feminists these days object to his attitudes toward women," Beany said. "They don't see the larger picture and they certainly don't try to put him in context."

Lawrence was above all else, Beany explained, a realist. His novels were all about the gritty struggles of everyday life, mining communities like the one he grew up in that had a vein of melancholy running as broad and deep as the coal underground. He lightened them up with his powerful descriptions of nature, as well as sex.

"He treated nature just as graphically and realistically as he did the sex," Beany said, "describing sunsets with the same passion and detail."

Beany picked up one of the student papers.

"Not one of them bothered to mention that *The Rainbow* was banned because it depicted a lesbian relationship. All they focus on is the rough sex and the women who seem overcome, as if they had no choice . . . when in fact they just succumbed to temptation like everyone else."

Beany sighed.

"What do they expect? Lawrence was trying to loosen the grip the old Victorian guardians of morality had on England. Of course there was sex going on - all kinds - behind closed Victorian doors, so he completed his characters in real ways that no one had the nerve to do before."

"Try the soup," I said, concerned that Beany was getting a little too upset.

"It seems that intolerance can never be completely cured, even in my young, open-minded, liberal coeds."

Beany finally took a sip of soup. It was my black bean soup of love, as I called it on the menu board, spiced with bay leaves, coriander, cloves, cumin, cinnamon, and malt vinegar. It was a soup to lower your guard and open your heart.

"He was writing about a lower-class community," he said, another spoonful hovering close by his mouth. "At a time when women were not liberated, so the sex was different. Lady Chatterly had money, but she was the same in Lawrence's eyes when it came to sex as the other wives who struggled to put food on the table. She just smelled better. Isn't there a real truth to that?"

I nodded and poured us both some more wine.

"Why is it," Beany asked, "that people always have such difficulty seeing past the sex act? They never see the people behind it. It's always dirty if someone doesn't do it the same way or the generally accepted way. They never question who they are and why. It's just like driving a car. Anyone who goes slower than you do is an idiot and anyone who drives faster is a maniac. D.H. Lawrence isn't a skirt length or a color; he shouldn't change with the fashions."

Beany was moody the whole night and I sent him home early with a quart of soup and a warning to come in the following week with a better attitude.

Georgina came in the next day and told me what she was able to find out about Jim Chapman, which wasn't very much. He didn't teach at Smith and he wasn't a farmer. He didn't even live in Northampton, but about 25 miles north by the Vermont border in a small town called Colrain, which Georgina kept mispronouncing as Coltrane, like the musician, who, it turned out, she had never heard of. Mr. Chapman made furniture, armchairs, rockers, sideboards and tables, all hand carved from solid wood, no veneers, no tacks and nails, all tongue and grove construction. He also carved bowls and platters. Georgina brought in a pamphlet from The Signature Crafter, a large store in town that specialized in local artists and craftsmen, where Jim's custom orders were prominently featured.

Of course, once Mr. Chapman discovered Circa and my soups, I knew he'd be back. Even without Georgina's comments, I could see through the small kitchen window the troubled consequences that darkened his eyes, like they were less sure of the past than the future. There was something about him that looked lost and sad, and I'm pretty intuitive when I'm steeped in soup. Once he'd sampled my soup, I knew that he'd never be able to resist that subconscious thirst for something warm and forgetful.

Sure enough, the following Thursday evening he walked in looking exhausted. I was standing out front talking to Georgina and he barely nodded at us as she pointed out either of the 2 open tables. He looked like a weary cowboy after a long week herding cattle. His jeans were streaked and frayed, gripping tightly to his worn leather boots, and he had on a green Orvis rain jacket and a black hat with a wide brim and a soft crown. He sat down at Beany's table again by-passing the table in front of it, as if something was drawing him there. Routines can develop very quickly even at 30.

I don't remember all the soups I made that night, but I do remember the one he ordered, Tuscan white bean with broccoli. It's a great blend of textures, flavors and colors. I use onions, leeks, celery, cannelloni beans, dry only, which means six hours of soaking, coriander, thyme, parsley and balsamic vinegar. My mother used to add prosciutto for taste and color. I add diced and blanched tomatoes instead. With a glass of wine and some crusty bread, there is nothing more fortifying on a cold winter night and soothing to a damaged heart.

Jim did not have any wine that night or any other night he dined at Circa, but he did have two bowls of soup and two baskets of bread. Nothing makes me feel better than finding a new customer who needs my soup as much as I do.

"He wants to take home a quart," Georgina said, coming into the kitchen.

I filled a container and put it in a bag with some bread while she jabbered away.

"I tip my hat to the cook," she said.

"What?"

"That's what he said."

"So he does talk."

"That was about it," Georgina said. "But he seems very nice."

"Don't turn into another Lisa."

"You should go out there and say hello," she said.

"I'm busy."

"Yeah, right."

I walked over to the kitchen door and peered out the window into the dining room. He was sitting there in Beany's seat, his back straighter than when he walked in, but his eyes closed. He looked less worn and more relaxed. Good soup works fast, even if only for a little while.

"He's not wearing his hat," I said.

"He didn't actually tip it," Georgina said, miming the act, "he just pretended to."

She made it look exactly like the way gentlemen tipped their hats to ladies on the street in the old black and white movies.

"I'll take it out to him," I said.

"Now you're talking."

"I'm just curious."

"You're lonely," Georgina said.

I made a face at her and headed for the door.

It wasn't because I was thinking about getting back into the game, I said to myself, but because it was the right and proper thing to do, the same thing I would have done for any customer who asked one of the wait staff to bring me a nice compliment like that. It's good business.

His eyes were still closed as I approached the table. He had a younger face with them closed, serene and confident, almost like a sleeping child. Yet his lips, which were slightly parted, told a different story. They quivered just a bit as his breathing slowed and deepened, as if they were relieved to let go for a moment of that immense look of bravery he forced them to wear during the day.

I cleared my throat and Jim didn't jump. He just opened his eyes slowly and closed his mouth so once again his lips were strong and tight and gave nothing away.

"Sorry, I must have dozed off."

"Soup does the same thing to me," I said. "That's one of the reasons I love it."

"My mother used to give me warm milk when I had trouble sleeping."

I laughed and put the bag with the soup on the table.

"How far do you have to drive?"

"About 25 miles north."

"Then I won't let you leave without a cup of coffee . . . it's organic."

He nodded and I went back to the kitchen and brought it out myself. Somehow I knew he'd take it black.

"You must be the proprietor."

I liked that word – proprietor – it sounded so substantial.

"As well as cook, dishwasher and just about everything else."

"I came in last week for the first time. It was one of those days and I just needed something warm and filling. You know what I mean?"

I nodded.

"Someone steered me here, one of my customers, the owner of a hair salon that I built some shelves for."

"Lisa Montero," I said, "she's in all the time."

"That's what she said."

"I saw what you built. It was a lot more than shelves. It was a work of art."

"Thanks," he said, with no change in his expression to indicate that he got any satisfaction from the compliment.

"Actually it was a week ago that I was here. I was hoping to get that same soup again it was so good."

"The soup specials change every day."

"It was a cauliflower something."

"My CBT soup - Cauliflower, Beet and Thyme."

"That was it," he said. "What a great combination. I'd never have thought cauliflower and beet would go together."

"Nature is full of surprises."

He nodded slowly.

"My Ecuadorian Quinoa Vegetable Soup, Carrot Potato and Tomato Eggplant were also on the menu last Thursday," I said. "You'd have liked those as well."

"How can you remember from week to week?"

"I have a photo-soupic memory."

He laughed and his mouth softened again. It almost felt like a moment of trust.

"I don't see you as the Liberian Black-eyed Pea or Mexican Butter Bean Soup type. Those were the other specials last Thursday."

Jim laughed again.

"Well, you are a magician when it comes to soup."

"And the coffee?"

"Ordinary in comparison."

I liked his honesty. I didn't care about the coffee and I didn't push it.

"Good, the soup is much healthier for you . . . unless you're sleepy with 25 miles of road still ahead of you."

Jim nodded into his cup of coffee and I wondered if there was a soup that I could bring some caffeine into to serve instead of coffee, like a green tea consommé. It didn't sound nourishing or medicinal, but for the purpose of keeping you awake it sounded better than black coffee.

Georgina walked over, probably because she couldn't stand missing out on the conversation, and dropped off the check, at which point Jim thanked us both, paid his bill, put on his black cowboy hat and left. I could see from his eyes as he turned to wave good-bye that whatever relief my soup gave him wouldn't last all that long given the room for thought provided by the long, solitary, late night drive ahead.

"I bet he asks you out," Georgina said as we were cleaning up.

"And he'll get the same answer as Joe and all the others. I don't think it's a good idea to be dating customers."

"That's bullshit, you're just gun-shy. You're here 24-7, who else are you going to date?"

"Dating is not the only reason for living," I said with an exaggerated smile.

"It is when you're 21, perhaps you forgot."

"I was never like that."

Georgina raised her face and looked up at me.

"Every Valentine's Day, my mother announces to everyone that without my father she'd never have known who she was."

"Well, she's either stupid or lucky," I said, retiring to the kitchen.

"Probably a little of both," Georgina said, following close behind me.

Of course, her remark made me think of my own mother, who only found out who she really was after my father had left. I used to think that I wanted to be like Georgina's mother, now I doubted whether it was even possible for someone like me. In any event, I didn't need anyone else to help define myself. I had my soup for that. Some of those old dreams have got to be packed away as you get older.

I wondered what Jim Chapman had locked away that his lips were working so hard to conceal.

After Georgina left, I opened some wine, and pulled out Beany's next letter. It was to Evan again and it was dated February 1, 1977. It didn't appear that Evan had written back as of yet, but it didn't appear that Beany needed him to.

Dear Evan,

I thought I'd write, even in the absence of a Presidential catastrophe, and even though I have no way of knowing whether you have received or read any of my earlier letters. I send them to the University to be forwarded to you, instead of your home, just in case you actually went through with your threat and left the dark side, selling your soul for that house with the picket fence and all the accoutrements that come with it. It does not really matter, as long as I can pretend that you do read them. It's sort of like writing to Santa Claus or God; what I say matters much more than what gets heard.

Anyway, I am quite pleased with our 39th President. Who would have thought that in this age of television and big money a peanut farmer would ever make it to the top? I know you are not a fan of the Democrats, but as Jimmy Carter is one of your own, a scientist by training, I suspect that you hesitated a moment before buying another Ford. One thing that surprises me about Jimmy Carter is that we finally have a President who cares about the entire planet and does not appear to equate religious ideals with campaign slogans, which are only good until elected. Of course, I think the politics in Washington will eat him alive and his chances of a second term about as good as our chances of a repeat performance.

However, what surprises me even more is that he and I share the same birth year. When did we become old enough to become President? Presidents are supposed to be older and wiser, grandfatherly, close enough to St. Peter's gate to feel compelled to strive for purity. The next President will probably be younger than us, which confirms that we have crossed the boundary line between middle and old age. The good thing about that, if you are interested, is that we can do pretty much anything we want now and no one will care. We are at the age where we are no longer threats, but simply embarrassments, a danger only to ourselves.

Too bad, I thought, that Beany considered himself an old man in his mid-fifties. Priorities change when you begin thinking like that, I saw it in my mother, who stopped using her imagination and started worrying more about her balance, especially in the winter. The funny thing was that the Beany I knew, even at 82, seemed creative and active. Somewhere along the line something changed for him and then changed back. It wasn't the changing back that Beany couldn't stand, but something else, I suspected, that pushed him to his decision to leave early.

Of course there is an exception to every rule, which was not funny when it happened, although I can laugh about it now. I do not know what it is like out west, but here at Smith the administrators are very concerned, overly concerned if you ask me, with keeping the community happy. When the college anti-war rallies six years ago spilled over into the town, the college was quick to pay all the overtime and clean-up costs demanded by the mayor, without regard to all the taxes and profits the school generates for the town. And whenever a community group decides that they need a field house or a bigger auditorium, they get it without paying a dime. The latest good neighbor policy has been to allow high school seniors to take certain courses at Smith. They call it the college enrichment program, for which they are supposed to get actual credit somewhere down the road. So instead of expanding the college experience, we seem intent on shrinking it by helping them get it over quicker.

The administration asked me as chair of the English Department to help teach these urchins a course in poetry. How impressive, the Dean said, to offer up the Chairman of the Department instead of some graduate teaching assistant or associate professor. What could I say? You know I am not one to rock the boat. It was a pretty uneventful semester until the end, and I must say I was pleasantly surprised by the intensity and effort some of these young women put into their assignments. One such young woman, who I completely misjudged, came to my home unannounced to drop off a late paper. She tried to get me to give her the Cook's tour, but I refused and had her out without being too rude within five minutes. All an old man has to do is plead gas to cause any guest to flee.

The next thing I knew I was called down to the Dean's office. It seems that this young woman had accused me of attempted rape. She even had a torn blouse to prove it. I would have burst out laughing if it wasn't so disturbing. The police were called to investigate and they agreed to keep everything quiet for the time being, but they did warn me that I could be arrested at any time. To cut to the chase, the young woman, who had no bruises and seemed remarkably well gathered for the victim of so vile an attack, eventually confessed to lying in an effort to make her boyfriend jealous. Apparently, there was an issue lurking in the background about who he wanted to take to the senior prom. I suppose I should have considered it a compliment. It did get out on campus, at least the rumors did, and the silver lining appears to be that my reputation as a ladies man, albeit a young ladies man seems to have replaced the old standard about "Beany" the hermaphrodite.

I suppose the moral of the story is that we will be punished no matter what we do or don't do because we are different. That's what the universe does. Even running will not change that. I wonder if you have found the same thing.

I am sure that bothered Beany much more than he let on. That sort of thing brings a lot of other rumors and innuendos up to the surface, and I suspect that the real reason the Dean didn't immediately suspend him from his teaching duties and the police didn't arrest him was that neither thought it remotely possible. Beany may have thought that everything about him was well hidden, but certain proclivities and thoughts, no matter how deeply they are buried, begin to show as time wears us away, much the way skin grows thin and transparent as we age, making visible all kinds of veins and bony structures.

I leave you with a short poem by Ogden Nash, who is undoubtedly a poet you could find the patience to read. It is called The Turtle.

The Turtle lives 'twixt plated decks
Which practically conceals its sex.
I think it clever of the turtle
In such a fix to be so fertile.

Of course, how you define fertility is the key here. If we take your definition, relying on lipids and publications, then the two of us have spawned quite well. If you use mine, applying terms of love and considering one's success in overcoming what appears to be insurmountable differences, then we have not, which leads me to another poem by Coleridge, long a favorite of mine, entitled Epigram.

Sir, I admit your general rule,
That every poet is a fool,
But you yourself may serve to show it,
That every fool is not a poet.

Yours Truly,
Roger

Was Beany suggesting that he was a fool for having waited all these years for Evan? Or was he saying that Evan was the fool? Perhaps he was admitting that as a poet he foolishly failed to inspire his verses with life, because he never really lived it? I know that Beany was much more successful as a literary critic, measured in terms of his publications and citations, than he was as a poet, a fact he admitted one Thursday evening that really bothered him.

I wondered if Evan ever wrote back. I knew from his obituary that he never married, but did he have any other lovers? I doubted it, since it sounded like he was so frightened by the possibility that he fled to the Nebraska wilderness. Besides, he was a scientist first and foremost. Some people, whatever their sexual proclivity, can make a life of work. It's one thing that can take your mind off everything else, even mortality. Those are Beany's words, not mine. He just didn't believe that I was one of those people.

CHAPTER EIGHTEEN

Jim didn't appear nearly as tired the following Thursday, nor as dirty. His jeans had been washed and his boots wiped clean, although he looked like he was a couple of days into a new beard. Those were the first things Georgina told me when she came into the kitchen to announce his return.

"He's really cleaned himself up," she said, "and it's not because of me."

"It's because of the soup."

"Maybe . . . or maybe it's because of the coffee."

There were only three special soups that night. The first was my Latvian Potato and Wild Mushroom Soup, which contained dried porcini mushrooms, potatoes, onions, heavy cream and paprika. Potatoes and mushrooms are two of the best combinations in all of soupdom. The second soup was my mother's Red Onion Marmalade Soup, which does not contain marmalade, but heaps of red onions, red wine vinegar, red wine, celery and parsley stems. I add parmesan cheese as a garnish, because I refuse to layer it with heavy, crusted cheese like the French do, not because I don't love it that way, but for health reasons. The third soup was Tessie's Secrets Soup, named after my grandmother, which is a dark soup that combines almost all the colors of the spectrum, including yellow onions, black beans, red lentils, brown barley, purple and white cauliflower, green cabbage, brown mushrooms, red tomatoes, yellow corn, orange carrots, green peppers and blue potatoes, not to mention garlic, ginger and chili peppers.

I knew what Jim would order because I had him in mind when I selected the menu and I knew he liked cauliflower. My grandmother called it her Soup of Secrets, because she said it helped set them free either by weighing them down so they could sink out of sight or by opening a window in the heart wide enough to let them out; two very disparate ways to escape which my grandmother explained depended on the "weight" of the secret and "length of its captivity." However, once the secret gets out, she said, it was no longer a secret and so less lethal. Of course, it only worked if someone was hungry enough to want to let the secret go.

"Remember," she once told me when I was a little girl, "it's very hard to completely get rid of a secret."

"Why?" I asked.

"It's not like the truth," she said. "Secrets can call any place home."

Of course, I was young and thought it made perfect sense.

But for the soup to work its magic," she said, "you have to open yourself up as well in the preparation."

"How do you do that, grandma?" I asked and I still remember her answer . . . word for word.

"You have to put part of your self in the soup by adding one of your own secrets to it while it simmers."

"How do you do that?" I asked.

"With a tear," she said.

I didn't add a tear, but I did think about what was pressing up against my own heart as I watched the Secrets Soup simmer. I know it sounds a little silly, but how different is it really than believing in a good luck charm or wishing on a star.

"Even if it lets go for just a little bit," my grandmother said after I had some of her soup and told her that I felt a little better, "it can mean a real lot when the secret has been holding tight for so long around your heart."

After Jim had finished two bowls of the Secrets Soup and a cup of the Latvian Potato and Wild Mushroom Soup, which I sent out to him because I knew he'd like it just as much, I came out with a cup of coffee.

"For the ride home," I said.

"Do I look that tired again?"

"Not like last week."

"Last week was a tough week."

There goes one little secret, I thought. You can't rush secrets and you can't chase after them so I wasn't going to pry, although there's nothing wrong with a word or two of encouragement. After all, nothing leaks out, not even a small secret like that, if there isn't some pressure behind it.

"Why?" I asked.

Jim took a sip of coffee and looked up at me, his lips slightly parted as if they were getting ready to let another little one go.

"A lot of orders," he said, turning his dark and disturbed eyes away from mine and looking into the coffee.

"I think you need another bowl of my grandmother's Secrets Soup," I said, "because I don't believe that for one minute."

Jim tried a half-smile.

"I've always been a bad liar," he said.

"My grandmother used to say that a secret won't leave you alone until it's finished with you."

"And how do you know when that is?"

"She said when you can finally spit it out."

"Sounds like a wise woman," Jim said. "My mother used to say something similar about the truth."

"What was that?"

"That a truth told too soon can be dangerous."

"I like that."

"It's a Greek proverb. She also used to say that whoever you tell your secrets to gets your heart as well."

"Another Greek proverb?"

Jim nodded.

"Although my father used to turn it upside down."

"How?"

"By saying that whoever you tell your secrets to you surrender your liberty."

"I hope you take after your mother."

"So do I," he said very seriously, although he smiled back when I smiled at him.

He had a nice smile, not big enough to reach his eyes, like Beany, but warm and sincere. It almost seemed as if something was holding it back or blocking its way . . . like a guilty conscience.

I took a few slow, conscious, yoga breaths. Sometimes soup can overheat my imagination.

"What about you?" Jim said. "Did you have any of your grandmother's Secrets Soup today?"

"Of course, I try everything I make."

"Enough to set free any of your secrets?"

"What makes you think I have any secrets?"

"I don't know," he said with a little boy's impish grin. "It must be the soup; perhaps it makes you sensitive to secrets wherever they're hiding."

I nodded, because certain soups did just that; they gave you clarity and vision, helping you to see things that you might otherwise overlook.

"So am I wrong?"

"Everyone has some secrets."

"But not every secret has a strong grip," he said.

"And not every secret with a strong grip is that important or worth knowing."

Jim didn't respond right away, but looked up at the ceiling to give it some thought.

"I guess that depends on who is asking," he said.

Georgina, with her impeccable timing, walked over and put Jim's check down.

"Can I get you anything else?" she said.

Jim shook his head no.

"How about a quart for the weekend," I said after she left, "my treat?"

I think we were both glad to change the subject.

"That would be great. It'll help wash away the sawdust."

"Which one would you like?"

"You pick."

I went back into the kitchen and filled a container with the Red Onion Marmalade Soup, in part because he hadn't tried it. Despite its misleading name, it wasn't sweet at all. It was a great winter soup, forceful and invigorating, and very appropriate for Jim, especially since the ancient Egyptians believed that the strong scent of onions could help bring back the breath of life. I know Jim wasn't dead, but he did look like he needed to start breathing again. I don't know why I felt so sure of it, but I did.

Of course, I felt bad when I sat down to read Beany's next letter and remembered that the Red Onion Marmalade Soup contained red wine, since Jim had refused my offers of wine. What if he was a recovering alcoholic or reacted badly to wine? I thought about calling him, but I didn't have a number.

Beany's next letter was dated January 1, 1981.

Dear Evan:

Another President, another letter; I am sure you are quite pleased to have Ronald Reagan take over as our 40th. His career path is certainly unusual; from a democratic supporter of the New Deal to a virulent, anti-communist, anti-socialist, anti-government Goldwater Republican, quite a transformation in one lifetime. Of course, appearances in the Knute Rockne Story, Bedtime for Bonzo and Death Valley Days might account for it. In any event, he is off to a good start, having ended the Iranian hostage mess just by winning the election.

Time will tell how far his conservative economic and welfare agenda will extend to social issues. I wonder whether the less government he espouses when it comes to personal freedoms like owning a gun will be applied equally to choosing a partner or whether that personal freedom will be trumped by the many rules and regulations laid down by his God. Imagine a God that is okay with war, but angered by love. It is a conservative inconsistency that I will never understand.

The nicest part about President Reagan is that he is the oldest President ever elected. At 69, he makes me feel young again, young enough to still hope that the wick may yet be relit so that the candle burns again. So what say you? We could meet this summer in Provincetown, which is a place I am sure that is unlike anywhere in Nebraska; two old friends unexpectedly bumping into each other. When is the last time you saw the Atlantic Ocean? Could it have been our last weekend in Maine?

For two weeks we can be neither scientist nor scholar, simply two leafs on a branch clutching to each other in the teeth of an oncoming storm. If not now, when? Our when's are quickly running through the hour glass. We have both been through enough of life by now to know what is really important and what deserves attention and care. Write back if you are interested and prepared to give up two weeks of that Nobel Prize dream.

Fondly,
Roger

I was quite sure that Evan never did respond. If he had, I think I would have heard about it or sensed it. Beany would have said something and he certainly wouldn't have still been teaching full time at 82. If Evan had responded, perhaps Beany wouldn't have needed my soup as much as he did. Evan died during the middle of our year of soup and I wondered if Beany even knew.

CHAPTER NINETEEN

The following Saturday Nick popped into Circa right after the lunchtime rush. I don't know how he found out where I was or what I was doing, because we hadn't been in touch for over 6 years, but I suppose we are all hanging out there like wanted posters somewhere on the internet.

Joe Johnson had come in to pick up his lunch, which was as usual the chicken soup of the day. He and Georgina were dating, but he still gave Nick the fish eye when he walked in and gave me a big hug and kiss, which I did not return at least not in any meaningful way. I don't like surprises, whether they're surprise endings or surprise visits.

"Should I stick around?" Joe asked. Having given up trying to be my lover, he seemed prepared to play the part of big brother.

"I'm fine Joe, thanks," I said.

"New boyfriend?" Nick whispered after he left.

"Just one of the regulars," I said as the two of us sat down at a table.

He looked exactly the same down to the short haircut and tight cut of his clothes. He filled me in on his last six years in less time than it took for Georgina to bring him his soup. It's worth noting that he ordered the chicken with vermicelli and spinach like Joe, because none of the specials appealed to him.

"Wow," he said, "I'd forgotten how good you were with soups."

"That was my biggest talent," I said, "how could you forget?"

Nick was too busy eating to respond.

After he finished his soup, he went back to talking about himself. He had left the real estate business to go back to school to get an MBA and was now an investment banker. He was in Springfield for a conference that ended Sunday and my name came up when someone showed him an article about unusual restaurants in the Northampton area.

Of course, I didn't buy any of it. More likely, my name popped up in a Google search. I wondered if he signed up for the conference because it was nearby. Men cannot resist a sexual trip down memory lane, although Nick didn't act like a man interested in a quick tumble in the sack for old time's sake. He looked like a man who had weighed the evidence, taken the time he needed to decide and finally reached a verdict.

"So what have you been up to?" he said.

"My elbows in soup."

"Come on Tess, be serious. It's been 6 years. I heard you met someone in San Francisco."

"From who?"

"Some girl at your old job."

"Did you date everyone in the newsroom?"

Nick laughed. He was not the type of man to be insulted by anything that could conceivably be considered a compliment to his manhood.

"Are you involved now?" Nick asked.

"With my soup."

"You can't have a relationship with soup."

"Want to bet?"

Nick scratched his head and laughed.

"What about you?" I asked.

Nick told me about the girlfriends he had after me, including the one who walked through the door as I was leaving. Despite her money, he apparently couldn't get past her weight. He didn't quite say that, but I was able to read between the lines.

"We broke up after 6 months. You were teaching by then and had moved on to what's his name?"

"Jake."

"Yeah, right, I always kept you on the radar screen."

"That was very thoughtful."

"I was engaged once," Nick said, "but only for a short while."

"What happened?"

"I broke it off after a couple of months. I don't know what I was thinking. It wasn't love, it was more . . ."

"Habit?"

"Maybe, it was different with us."

It wasn't, but memory is the original rose-colored glass. Beany called it the great equalizer, because it always seemed to equal whatever it was you thought you lost getting here.

"I mean we had some really great times."

Nick smiled and looked like he was about to reach out to take my hand, which made me lean back in the chair as far as I could.

Nick reminded me of a character in a situation comedy. I expected him to tell me next that despite all his financial success, and he made sure that I noticed his Rolex, he lacked something or someone. I'm sure he did, and it's only natural to look up an old love if you have the opportunity to see if there was something that you overlooked. For all I knew, Nick was on a cross-country tour interviewing old girlfriends for this new and improved position. But what he needed I couldn't provide, nor did I want to. He needed an admirer, someone to feel eternally grateful to him and someone he could control. That wasn't me, not anymore.

"It's just an empty stretch, Nick. You'll find the right person."

Or at least another person, especially since he appeared to be at the stage in his life and career where he didn't need a love that would burn as much as a love that would last.

"Are you at least dating?" he asked, scraping his spoon along the bottom of the bowl.

"I'm too busy."

"This is really good. You know I could freeze this and get it into the supermarkets. We'd make a fortune."

I didn't answer, but I'm sure he saw the shiver run down my spine.

"Was your soup this good when we were going out, I don't remember."

I shrugged. He didn't remember because soup doesn't work on everyone. It won't work that well when it doesn't have that far to fall. Nick wasn't the type to give too much thought to his place in the universe, which might explain the initial attraction. What I needed when I met Nick, about the time my mother died, was someone shallow, an untroubled, ambitious soul, not just to hold me, but to hold me down. Who always picks the person best for them? Who always knows? It took me 9 years to figure out what I didn't want.

"You're not seeing anyone?" he asked again, like he couldn't believe it, or perhaps he was hoping that by repeating the question again he would make me realize just how much I needed him.

"Not really . . . maybe a little," I said, thinking for an instant of Jim.

Nick shrugged and looked into his empty bowl. I wasn't about to offer him another.

"You used to talk about the universe," Nick said, "like it had plans for each of us, remember that?"

I nodded. I felt sorry for him. He had this all scripted out, like a presentation to a potential investor and none of it was going the way he expected.

"Maybe this is part of the plan . . . us meeting again like this."

I let him down easy. I told him that I was happy here, committed to my soup, and not interested in a relationship right now, at least not anything meaningful. I was in a philosophical place, I told him, and I needed time to find my way out on my own. Nick was not the kind of guy who could wait.

"I wouldn't suffocate you," he said. "I give plenty of space these days. Lord knows I work long enough hours."

"It's not that," I said. "There's a solitary streak that runs in my family. You remember my mother?"

"You didn't want to be like your mother."

"You can't always be who you want. Sometimes you just have to be who you are."

Nick laughed.

"You were always saying strange things like that."

"It's the soup," I said. "It makes you realize sometimes just how little things ever really change."

"Well, if the next batch of soup helps change your mind," Nick said, "give me a call."

He looked a little relieved as he handed me a business card, perhaps because I seemed flakier than he remembered and he could cross me off his list, or maybe all the soup he had spooned into his mouth was having its desired effect, making it easier for him to accept what he couldn't change.

I didn't invite Nick back to my apartment that night for a second look and I gently declined his suggestion that I come by the hotel in the morning to let him buy me breakfast. I told him that I did my major produce shopping for the week on Sunday mornings, which wasn't entirely untrue since that's when some of the bigger farmer markets were open.

"It's hard to go back again," I said to Georgina after he left.

"I wouldn't know," she said. "I don't have anyone to go back to."

"You will."

"My problem," Georgina said, and like most people her age she was always eager to talk about herself, "is that I'm way too picky."

"You should be picky at your age," I said, "especially when it comes to love."

"And when you get older?"

"You mean like me?"

"No, like him," Georgina said, not realizing that Nick wasn't as old as he tried to look.

"It doesn't matter as much."

"Why?" Georgina asked.

"I don't know, I suppose because you get better at keeping secrets."

Georgina tilted her head at me like she needed a translation. I didn't have the energy to continue our discussion, not after Nick, so I just added, "and expectations get lower, much lower."

What concerned me after I went back into the kitchen was my total absence of any feelings toward a man I slept with and thought I loved for almost three years, the first man in my life after college. Unlike Beany with Evan, I felt no strong attachments to Nick, Jake or Jolene. I didn't stare at the ceiling at night fantasizing about a different outcome or even a new chapter with any one of them.

Instead, most nights I lay there feeling sorry for myself – in part because I was determined to be alone and knew from Beany just how hard that would be and in part because I hadn't come across anyone who could change my mind, although I would have to admit to a little fluttering in my stomach when I thought about Jim.

In a way, I wondered if the life I was contemplating would turn out sadder than Beany's. It is one thing to restrain your impulses and desires to conform with social norms and out of concern for your present position, allowing your feelings to roam free only in the past and confining them to letters and dreams. It's quite another to pretend that they don't exist, going through life self-medicated and anesthetized on soup, recognizing no feeling other than exhaustion, which would explain why I kept Circa open 7 days a week from 12 noon until 10 at night. It wasn't the bank loan or a string of old debts, as I led everyone to believe, but my need to keep busy making soup.

CHAPTER TWENTY

I wasn't sure Jim would come the next Thursday, since he looked a little uncomfortable when he left the week before. Letting go of a secret even a little bit of it for a little while is never easy. I wouldn't have minded, at least I didn't think so, because a part of me was a bit freaked out by the parallels with Beany's Thursday night visits - same time, same table, different secrets, but secrets nonetheless.

Jim did show up, although later than he had before, and Georgina said he wanted me to pick the soup I thought he'd like best, since all three of the specials sounded good. Beany didn't let me pick his starter soup until the beginning of the third month. Matching soups with people is not as hard as you might think. My mother used to say that all people could be divided into four basic categories coinciding with the seasons; winter people were reserved and looked best in whites and black, spring people were outgoing and partial to yellows and reds, summer people could never hide their emotions, they were quick to anger and favored blues and greens, while fall people were contemplative, more introspective and serious, and drawn to browns and oranges.

With soups, the color is just one of the criteria; ingredients have much more to do with it. Winter people are more apt to order creamy soups and are generally fond of potatoes, leeks and onions. Spring people like colors: split pea, zucchini, beets and red kidney beans, but they want their vegetables to be earthy and growing close to the ground, and they like their soup warm, but not too hot, and mild. Summer personalities demand spice and want thinner soups. They're the ones who pour in the salt without even tasting it, while fall people like chunky soups with muted colors and subtle spices. They like pumpkin and squash and are rather slow eaters, lingering over each spoonful.

I had no doubt that Jim was largely a fall person, with a hint of winter and a touch of spring, which is the way my mother used to describe me when I was growing up. When it comes to soups and seasons - likes do attract.

I had three special soups on the board, because I had too much on my mind to make five. I had a Potato, Broccoli, and Cheese soup; a Vegetarian Barley soup; and my own creation, a Roasted Yellow Pepper and Tomato soup with Cauliflower and Zucchini. I sent Jim out a large bowl of the last, since it was the soup I would have picked for myself, together with a few slices of a pumpernickel loaf with sunflower seeds that wasn't on the menu, but that I had been experimenting with.

"He loves it," Georgina said when she returned to the kitchen.

"How can you tell?"

"He closed his eyes after the first spoonful and sighed. It almost sounded like a moan."

"Maybe he's in pain," I said.

"Sounded more like foreplay to me," she said.

"Oh stop."

"He's a damn slow eater that much I can tell you, not like your old beau."

"I figured he was fall," I said.

"Or maybe he wants to make sure he's around at closing time," Georgina said, giving me one of her fish eyes.

Jim was sipping coffee by the time things slowed down enough for me to leave the kitchen.

"So did I guess right?" I said, sitting down with a glass of wine. I knew better by now than to offer Jim one.

"You did," he said, "but was it really a guess?"

"I'm not a witch or a mind reader if that's what you're implying."

"Good."

"It was an educated guess."

"Where does the educated part come in?"

I told him about my mother's seasonal people and what soups say about your personality.

"So I'm fall?" he said.

"In large part, no one is just one season."

"It's my favorite season now," he said, "but it wasn't growing up."

"We all liked the summer when we're kids," I said. "It's the school vacation thing."

Jim smiled.

"Actually, I liked winter the best."

It turned out that Jim grew up on a farm in Maine, where there was work from dawn to dusk during the summer. Winter was the slowest time of year and he was a big fan of cross country skiing and winter hikes.

"I made my own skis," he said. "I loved going out at night when the moon was full."

"Alone?"

Jim nodded.

"I liked the quiet and the solitude. I used to hike up to Spectator Pond by myself, through snow up to my waist just so I could ice fish."

"Indian name?"

"Named after all the birds that sit around in the summer staring back at you, but they were gone in the winter. It was so quiet you could hear the ice crack."

I closed my eyes and had this picture of being in a cabin by the lake surrounded by a blanket of fresh snow with a big pot of soup simmering on a wood burning stove to keep me company.

"Sleepy?" Jim asked with a smile.

"No, thinking of this story I read called *Silent Snow Secret Snow*, ever hear of it?"

"By Conrad Aiken," Jim said without a moment's hesitation.

"Yes."

"It's funny you should mention it; I just read it a couple of months ago."

"I read it for the first time about a year ago," I said, which led me into Beany and the year of soups. Jim almost sprayed the table with his coffee when he heard.

"I knew Professor Beanstock," he said.

"How?"

"When I first moved to Colrain about 4 years ago and started making furniture, he was one of my first customers. He ordered this walnut and maple desk, hand-carved drawers, mortise and tennon construction."

He ordered it through The Signature Crafter and Jim didn't get to meet Beany until he delivered the desk to his home.

"It was the first desk I ever made and I spent so much time on it that I probably wound up earning about 25 cents an hour. I remember throwing away two drawers because I didn't like the way the grain looked when they were open. I doubt I even made the cost of the materials, but I didn't mind. It was a good experience and I really needed to keep busy."

I fought the urge to ask him why. That was the winter part of Jim; if it was going to come out it wouldn't be in response to a question. It would have to be at the right time and in the right place when he was ready, and I wouldn't have to prod . . . at least not that much.

"He really appreciated the work that went into it and the quality of the wood," Jim said. "He couldn't have been nicer . . . and he probably had more books in that room than the entire Colrain library."

I told him about the letters. Not what they said, only that I was reading one each week.

"It's sort of like he's still coming by," I said.

"And I suppose in a way he's responsible for me coming in as well."

"I thought it was Lisa."

"She said it so many times when I was installing her cabinet that it sort of had the opposite effect."

"Sometimes she's so insistent I want to run in the opposite direction."

Jim nodded.

"But you came anyway, why?"

"The Professor left me the desk in his will."

"You're kidding, you have it?"

"I picked it up after he died. I thought that was very generous. Your first is always sort of special." He paused here, closed his eyes and swallowed hard.

"You OK, you want a little more soup."

Jim shook his head no.

"I still think it's one of the best pieces I've ever made."

That was saying a lot, since I saw some of Jim's pieces on display at The Signature Crafter. They were works of art.

"He really took good care of it, except for a few stains that looked like they were made by glasses. I could easily buff them out but I sort of like the lived in feeling they give it."

"Beany liked his red wine."

Connections like this in a small town shouldn't have surprised me, but they did.

"When I got it home, I found two things in the back of the center drawer where I'd made this little secret compartment at the Professor's request - the Conrad Aiken story and a menu for your restaurant."

I took out a tissue and wiped my eyes.

"It almost looks like we've been set up," I said.

Jim laughed.

"He didn't know very much about me."

"He knew you were good with your hands," I said, although Jim wasn't really listening.

"I don't know what he could have found out," he said, staring at his hands almost as if he were addressing them.

I had to bite my tongue so as not to ask what there was for Beany to have found out.

"Beany was pretty intuitive," I said. "He probably figured that you needed some good soup."

"Who doesn't?"

"A lot of it."

Jim nodded and I finished my wine.

"Maybe he didn't want too many of us following in his footsteps," I said.

"What do you mean?" Jim asked.

"Winding up alone."

"I don't know," Jim said, "he seemed to have done all right. He seemed pretty content with himself."

"He committed suicide."

"In his 80s, at his age there could have been any number of reasons. Maybe he was sick and dying, and didn't want to find himself helpless or in constant pain."

I looked at Jim and wondered whether he was thinking about himself when he said constant pain. The second sight I sometimes get from my soups seems to work best when it comes to sensing a point of almost paralyzing sadness in someone else. Sometimes, as with Jim now, and Beany on occasion, it was almost as if I could feel the anguish inside them.

"Did he leave a note?" Jim asked.

"No."

"Then I guess we'll never know the real reasons why," he said.

"Beany always said that no one can ever really know what's in someone else's heart," I said. "It's hard enough knowing what's in your own heart sometimes."

Jim nodded slowly and sighed. The only sound for what seemed a long time was the sound of Georgina setting up the tables for tomorrow.

"Well, I'm certainly glad he turned me on to your soup," Jim said standing up, his lips again shutting tight. He said he had to get going because he had a lot of deliveries to make the next morning in New Hampshire.

"Business must be good," I said walking him out.

"It is."

Jim's business must have been all word of mouth, because Georgina said she couldn't find a web site for it. It was called Reincarnations in Wood. I liked the name, since a tree had to die to be reborn as furniture, although I suspected that there was more to it.

"So what did you think of the short story?" I asked when we both paused at the door unsure, I think, about whether to shake hands, touch cheeks or just wave.

"I wished it were me," he said.

"Going insane?"

"Snowed in . . . I like the snow."

"Snowed in forever? I wouldn't say that's the best character in literature to identify with."

"I guess not," he said with a shrug, "how about you?"

"Everyone is a little attracted to the thought of going crazy, like that feeling you get at the edge of a cliff that makes you think about jumping."

"I suppose it's an instant cure for every worry and regret," he said.

"There are much better ways to forgive and forget . . . or at least to find a way to live with the things you can't. Cooking does it for me. I suppose I'd identify more if it were Silent Soup, Secret Soup."

Jim smiled.

"That's what I like about making furniture. I'm lost when I'm in the middle of building something."

"Sort of like being buried in imaginary snow."

"Exactly."

There was an awkward pause as we stood there with nothing more to say, which is when Jim came up with another way to part that I hadn't thought about, reaching up and giving my elbow a little squeeze. He looked away as soon as he let go, but not before I saw the light from the candles in the restaurant shimmer for a moment in his moist eyes, like the moonlight must have from time to time on Spectator Pond.

"Next Thursday," I said.

It was all he could do to say he'd try.

I finished off the bottle of wine before I could bring myself to take out Beany's next letter, dated October 2, 1985. Beany was 63 years old. Life passes quick enough when you live it – my mother used to say that the days drag on but the years fly by – but when you cover a decade in the span of a couple of letters it's as if time is receding at the speed of light.

My Dear Ms. Kalman,

What I once was is not what I am now. Indeed, I never really was what I once was. Denial has no respect, not even for nature. You get to an age when you cannot continue to hope, not that you stop living the moment, you just stop looking in the mirror with any expectation or promise. I am an older man now without a sexual thought in my head, at least not one that isn't literary, and while I appreciate the honor of being asked to speak before the Gay and Lesbian Alliance to talk about Smith in the 40s and 50s, I am afraid that I must respectfully decline. I could not offer much on that topic since I was not a part of that community, even though I may have met the basic criteria for membership.

So Beany was out-ed by then. How long, I wondered, and under what circumstances. I suspect that it turned out to be much ado about nothing. By 1985, Northampton was already Provincetown West and men strolling arm in arm were no longer a head-turner. Assumptions and presumptions change over time and many on the campus probably suspected long ago that Beany's adamant refusal to sample any of the coeds who regularly threw themselves at his professorial feet was more than just ethics and obsession with work.

Beany denied it before, because then it was all innuendo and the risk of admission was too uncertain, but what was the point of denying it now? No one cared, just as no one would be surprised. It wasn't going to affect his teaching or his scholarly reputation. In fact, I'm sure that a number of students would have looked upon him with more kindness and understanding. He was the injured war veteran, but it wasn't just World War II, it was the war against repression and intolerance. Beany's admission hardly seemed the momentous announcement that he once would have imagined, although I think his refusal to participate was because he didn't want anyone to feel sorry for him . . . and perhaps open the floodgates of regret.

Besides, it is imperative at my age to turn from the things and people that you cannot bear to think too much about, because of the silt that gets stirred up each time. I prefer not to let the recent changes confuse me and they do seem recent to me, or to harden me to the world I grew up in before those changes. Instead I prefer to focus on what has remained true and steadfast through all my years, great literature and poetry. To that end, I always have much to say. Does your group really need to hear an old man talk about keeping his eyes straight or
reminisce about people who may have once looked at him that way? I think not, nor do I want to be that old man.

Sincerely,
Roger P. Beanstock

The Beany in this letter was very different from my Thursday-night Beany, who was half inebriated by the time I left the kitchen and full of "piss and vinegar," to borrow one of my mother's phrases, aware that the hardest part of life was behind him and happily engrossed in helping me steer my own.

My soup was supposed to warm him up and help purge him of some of the bad memories and emotions, at least for a little while, although a barrier 60 years thick is hard to penetrate one night a week, even if it is largely water. Clearly, he was someone else when he was home alone, having sacrificed the world for his sinecure in the Department of English; sitting down to write a letter he was the poet of unrequited love trapped inside an old man.

I felt badly that I didn't give Beany enough of a chance to talk, assuming he would have. I monopolized those Thursday night conversations with my problems and my determination to follow in his footsteps. Although there was one night in particular I remember that I did not, although a lot of good that did. It was sometime in the middle of July, about three months before he took his life.

I had made a Sweet Pea and Green Garlic Soup, and a Celery Root, Mushroom and Potato Soup. The flavors of celery root and mushrooms are very complementary, although celery root will darken quickly when exposed to air, so you have to peel it at the last moment and put it quickly into the simmering soup. The third special soup that night was the one Beany really liked, Asparagus with Chervil. Asparagus needs to be cooked uncovered to preserve its color, and Chervil, a French favorite, is hard to find in central Massachusetts, but I was lucky that day. I won't make it without Chervil. However, if I'm a little short I will substitute some Italian Parsley in its place.

Anyway, it was obvious that Beany was a bit distracted when he walked in. He handed his bottle of wine to Georgina to open before sitting down without any of his normal pleasantries. Then he stared out the window without looking up at the soup board, draining his glass of wine, while he waited for Georgina to bring out whatever soup I had picked.

"Your professor must be constipated tonight," Georgina said while waiting for me to fill a bowl of the Asparagus Soup.

"Why, what did he say?"

"That's just it - he hasn't said a word, not even hello. He's just sitting there staring into space."

I looked at him through the kitchen door window. He looked smaller and more bent over than usual.

"He looks so old tonight," I said.

"Because he is," Georgina said, heading out to the dining room.

Instead of peppering me with questions when I finally came out of the kitchen, he just nodded and looked at his empty bottle of wine and asked me for one of mine, which I didn't have a permit to sell, but I could give away.

"Are you going to be able to make it back home?"

"Can anyone ever go back home again?"

"OK, that's a literary answer, except I'm asking it in its basic ambulatory sense."

"Yes, Tess, I will have no trouble walking the four blocks to my house. The rest of humanity may be 90 percent water, but I'm only 80 and have been for years. I've got an extra 10 percent in fermented grapes, so enough questions. Please bring out some of that private stash of yours."

I immediately went back into the kitchen and brought out another bottle.

I didn't have to say much more, because he started drinking and talking about how I should jump into the world now, instead of hiding in the kitchen, or I'd wind up smothered by desperation.

"Are you smothered by desperation?" I asked.

"No, I'm talking about someone like you . . . not me."

"I think you've already had too much to drink," I said, signaling to Georgina to bring out some Asparagus and Chervil Soup and bread.

"Because in the end," he said, clearly not listening to me, "it's all about loss."

"What is" I said, watching the kitchen door for Georgina to return with the soup, "the world?"

"Life . . . the world as well," Beany spoke like he was in front of a class giving a lecture, "it doesn't make a difference. In poetry the two are interchangeable - the world with its waterfalls and meandering rivers, its birds and fish, its blue sky and clouds, even the sun and the moon, all represent the same thing."

He stopped and sighed.

"What?"

"What?"

"They all represent what," I said, "the birds and fish, the blue sky and clouds, you said they all represent the same thing and I'm asking what."

"Life."

"And life is all about loss?" I asked.

"The world is all about loss."

"It sounds like the same thing."

"Tess, you are a fast learner," Beany said, "so learn this - whatever path you ultimately follow, the losses are still the same. It's only the end that's different."

"I thought the end was always the same."

"There are all kinds of endings, my dear girl. There are the endings that go unnoticed and the endings that are very public. Endings are different, it's what happens after the ending that's the same," Beany said, holding out his glass for some more wine. I filled it only halfway.

"You lose years . . . you lose people . . . you lose dreams . . . you lose direction . . . you lose energy."

"I think you need to go home and lie down . . . you look . . . tired."

"Very diplomatic of you, but I feel fine. You should never interrupt an English professor, certainly not in the middle of a thought."

"Sorry."

Georgina came over and put down another bowl of soup with some bread.

"Eat some more," I said, but Beany ignored me.

"Of course, you lose material things . . . a key . . . a favorite book . . . a photograph, and places like the house where you grew up . . . and that lovely spot on the beach where you first saw yourself in someone else's eyes. Those things are lost and can never be found, certainly not if you don't look. You want to look Tess. Are you following?"

"Yes," I said, pushing the soup closer.

Beany just ignored it and sighed into his wine.

"The losses weigh less or more depending on how you live and how you live determines how you end."

I was having difficulty following, because I was too worried about Beany. I don't think I could have followed in any event without knowing what had happened or what was really on his mind. He was clearly more inebriated than I'd ever seen him and the sadness was much closer to the surface. My soup hadn't had a chance tonight.

"You have to go home," I said. "I need to close early to do inventory."

"A bad liar Tess," he said, "but you are right."

Beany started nodding and didn't stop, sort of like a bobble-head doll on a moving car dashboard.

"I'm not very good company tonight."

"Why is that?"

"Not enough soup, I suppose," he said, looking down at the untouched bowl.

"I'll wrap it up for you to take home."

"No, I've lost my hunger for it."

"You make it sound permanent."

"At my age, anything can become permanent."

"Let me walk you home."

"I'm honored, but it's too late for that."

"What?"

"I'm fine. I'll make it."

Beany put on his coat and put down a tip. I had stopped letting him pay for the soup months ago. I told him that was because he wasn't charging me for the therapy.

As we walked to the door, Beany repeated what he had said earlier. "The world is all about loss, Tess, whether you choose to forget the world and love alone, soup or literature, or to lean on someone and be leaned upon . . . whatever the gender . . . the losses are the same for everyone. The only real difference is what remains of you at the end."

"A lot remains of you," I said, but again he wasn't listening.

"The big question is whether you will still have yourself at the end or have lost that as well . . . because one day you may wake up and find that you're not there. There's no sign of you. You're in the mirror looking back, but it's no one you recognize, because there's nothing of you that you remember left."

"You've had way too much to drink."

"Maybe."

"Did something happen today?" I said, unable to hold back the question any longer, as I stepped out into the evening to make sure Beany headed in the right direction. He was remarkably steady on his feet and didn't physically appear the least bit inebriated, which confirmed to me that Beany drank much more on the other nights of the week.

"Of course, something is lost every day . . . time, memories, moments . . . every day is about loss, didn't I just tell you that?"

"Yes, you did."

"So why should today be any different. Just ask the 5 billion of us who woke up this morning . . . you included. What did you lose today?"

I shrugged and gave Beany a worried little smile.

"Life goes on even when you have nothing left to lose, which is the ultimate oxymoron, which is why the endings are all so different."

"Go home," I said, realizing what I had lost today. I had lost the Thursday night conversation with Beany that I had been looking forward to all week.

CHAPTER TWENTY-ONE

The next morning, after spending a restless night thinking about the 1985 letter and the "lost" Thursday night with Beany, I went back to check Evan's obituary to confirm what I suspected. Evan died in early July on a Wednesday. Somehow Beany found out almost immediately, as if he were the next of kin. I wondered how.

For some reason that made me think about my relationship with Jolene, all three relationships actually, and how different it is when you're alone all the time. There's no hiding from your own thoughts; they whisper constantly in your ear. Without someone else in your life, someone who's actually there more than one night a week, there aren't too many moments when you can put down the guilt and confusion or let someone else carry them around for a while. How else can a heart get some rest? There isn't a soup in the world that can do that 24-7. It had to be incredibly hard for Beany to live that way for 60 years.

I wound up making Pablano Corn Chowder the next day for the first time at Circa. It's a recipe that I got from Jolene that came from her great-aunt who was half-Mexican. It is a spicy chowder with shrimp, corn, Pablano peppers and cream that I consider part earth and part water. It's a combination that gives strength and eases anxiety, particularly the kind that makes it seem so difficult sometimes to take a deep breath. White sugar is also one of the ingredients, which is the reason Jolene liked it so much. She had a sweet tooth that never seemed to give her any rest.

I didn't see the relationship coming with Jolene. I can't say that the thought of a lesbian experience had never crossed my mind, because it had along with thoughts about older men and strangers passing on the street, but I'd never acted on any of them. I thought of myself as completely heterosexual, although a little unlucky when it came to my two recent relationships. Finding men didn't seem to be the problem, finding the right one and holding on to him clearly was.

After Jake I decided to move out to San Francisco, because I had never lived in California and felt that everyone should at some point in their lives. I met Jolene my first week there at the Starbucks on Hyde Street in Nob Hill. It was a crowded Saturday and I was sitting alone with an empty chair on the other side of the table. She was looking for a seat, trying to balance her coffee, a muffin and US weekly, a magazine I never read except at the dentist's office, at least not until we started dating. She asked if she could share the table.

Two women cannot share a table without entering into a conversation, any more than they can stand next to each other at the checkout line in a clothing store and not share their philosophy about aging and clothes. It's amazing how quickly women can decide that they trust each other and tell the truth. In my mind, that fact and the compulsion most men have to think about sex every 30 seconds are the two main differences between us.

So Jolene and I started talking. She reminded me of the comfortable, less-complicated friends I had in college. She was from La Jolla in Southern California and had moved up about a month earlier to take a job as a graphic designer for an internet company. She was smart and funny, and could carry a conversation for an hour without interruption. An idea hit her and the words took off like a flock of migrating birds. And she had those clear, untroubled eyes, like Nick and Jake, except with make-up. That should have given me pause, but it didn't.

We became fast friends, meeting most Saturday mornings for coffee and having dinner together once or twice a week. Some nights we were on the telephone for hours like a couple of high school girls talking about boys, except we didn't talk all that much about boys.

I knew Jolene was a lesbian from that first day over coffee, which is why she decided to move to San Francisco, but things like that don't bother women, not like some men who can feel threatened just by their proximity to a guy who is gay, as if they might find out something about themselves they don't want to know.

By the second week, we were talking about everything, our failed relationships, our current prospective ones and our expectations.

"Since I've arrived in San Francisco," I told her, "my dates have all been a joke. The last man I went out with looked into my face, knit his eyebrows together like he was trying to get up the nerve to ask me to marry him and said me I had eyes like the moon."

Jolene laughed.

"It sounded like something he'd been practicing in the mirror."

"Women are never that self-conscious."

"One guy took my hand and licked my finger . . . maybe it was a kiss, but it was awfully wet. I swear I could feel his tongue. I suppose some dating guru once told him that would make me go weak in the knees."

Jolene laughed again. She had an easy laugh and she found me funny, funnier than Nick or Jake ever did.

I enjoyed hearing about Jolene's dates, because they were so different. Women rarely get tired of words. They can talk until their strained voices are reduced to whispers. They can hear things being said even when the words themselves don't actually say it. And they forgive and forget easily, because they're not afraid to let things go.

"But the breakups are just as hard," she said, "the reasons are never that different."

"How can you tell when a woman is interested in that sort of thing?" I asked. "I mean it's so easy with men when it comes to sex – whatever kind - they're about as subtle as a dog in heat."

"Gaydar," she said.

I had never heard that term before and I couldn't stop laughing.

"You just know, sometimes it's a quick look or a not so accidental touch. Sometimes it's an ambiguous remark, even a smell."

"Come on."

"Really, gay women go for more subtle fragrances. They're not always looking for miracle potions."

"Like me?"

Jolene leaned in close and tried to smell what I was wearing.

"Nothing," she said.

I suppose that made her gaydar go up.

Female relationships are not all about sex, they're not even largely about sex, at least not the way I saw it before Jolene. They're about support and sharing. Good women friends can remain good friends whatever their sexual preference, and perhaps that's the way it might have remained if not for the night the earth moved.

It was my first earthquake and other than a cracked picture frame my apartment suffered no damage. I was still shaking though when Jolene came over, a native Californian who hardly even noticed it. She brought a bottle of wine and spent the night and the thought that had barely crossed my mind on occasion over the years, of being with another woman, just happened. I thought it was mostly curiosity and the fact that I hadn't been with a man or had made a good bowl of soup in quite some time.

However, not only did I not regret it in the morning, I realized that I actually enjoyed it, and told her I wouldn't mind doing it again. That can't be a surprise; if you enjoy doing it to yourself, why wouldn't you like someone else you enjoy being with do it for you? Besides, a woman really knows the sweet spots . . . better than any man could, no matter how many notches he might have on his belt. There's nothing like having one of your own, Jolene liked to say, to really know how it really works.

We went out for almost three years, keeping our own apartments, which I suppose was a sort of admission on both of our parts, me not sure that this was what I really wanted, and Jolene not sure this was anything more than a sexual dalliance since she wasn't sure she wanted to commit to someone who also turned her head when certain men walked by.

Once again I was dumped, understandably I might add, because bisexuality in my case translated into confusion and uncertainty as much as opportunity. I think that by being attracted to both men and women I wound up less than fully committed to either and, as a result, did neither one very well. It was a different kind of break-up as compared to Jake and Nick. Women tend to be more honest about their feelings. They don't bury their hearts in the sports section and a bottle of beer, so if you don't bury your head in the sand like I tend to do you ought to be able to see it coming.

Jolene had taken a new job with Microsoft about three months earlier, which meant long hours working with another programmer, a younger woman right out of college. Intimacy often sprouts from little more than proximity. People have all kinds of hidden attractions; we are all as multi-faceted as diamonds, soup as well, and sometimes it just takes a bit of time and a lack of space to notice.

Jolene fell hard and was honest about it, too honest perhaps because she told me what I already knew that the sex hadn't been very good for quite a while.

"It's been much less frequent for one thing," she said.

Of course, she was working late and my hormone levels, not known for their jack-rabbit starts or spontaneous inspiration, were usually fast asleep by the hour she returned. Jake and Nick had the same complaint at the end, so apparently that was something about me that transcended the genders, some routinization that hit me harder and quicker than most.

Second, and perhaps more important, was the fact that while I was always very considerate about pleasing her, I wasn't nearly as accommodating when it came to letting her please me. That's also been a part of my personality for a long time. I cook and serve the soup. I am the nurturer, not the nurtured, a trait another woman might find frustrating, but which none of the men I'd known to date ever seemed to resent.

We stayed friendly for a while and I met her and Roslyn on occasion for coffee, but the whole thing confused me. I didn't long for Jolene and I wasn't paralyzed with jealousy. I couldn't decide who I was and what I wanted, whether I should be looking for another woman or another man. I tried both and when neither proved very satisfying I decided to do what I normally did in circumstances like these. I moved on. I left San Francisco and moved to Northampton. Turning to soups was how I coped.

CHAPTER TWENTY-TWO

Jim was late that next Thursday and for a newly converted celibate I spent a lot more time than I would have expected staring through the kitchen window into the dining room watching for his arrival.

"You look like a junkie waiting for a fix," Georgina said, when she almost swung the door into my nose for the fifth time that evening.

"How would you know what that looks like?"

"Television."

I had made a special soup for Jim that I hoped would help him with whatever it was in his past that was so dark and sticky, sort of like a memory spot remover. Soup can be a good mental paint thinner at times. It was a soup recipe my grandmother got from a Romanian neighbor. She said it was her great-grandmother's recipe and she called it her healing soup. I wasn't that dramatic, I called it "A Soup for What Ails You."

There were a lot of things I liked about it. It had a luscious fragrance that made people stick their noses right down into the bowl to breathe it in, and it was pungent enough to clear most normal sinuses. It had potatoes in it to soothe the digestive tract and the broth was filled with spinach, parsley, leeks and garlic for the emotional tract. I added some winter root vegetables for their sweetness, as well as some mustard, turmeric and a drop of cinnamon as healing anti-oxidants. It turned out to be very popular - who isn't in need of healing - and we would have run out long before Jim showed up if I hadn't held back a couple of bowls for him. He showed up about ten minutes before closing time.

"He's here," Georgina said, although I already knew that and had a big bowl of soup along with some fresh onion semolina bread ready for her to bring out to him.

"Did he say why he was so late?" I asked.

"No, but he was out of breath," Georgina said with a big grin.

We both peered out the door at Jim, who took off his coat and sat down as he always did at Beany's old table. He looked up at the menu board, but only for a second because he knew I'd send him the soup I thought he'd like best . . . or needed most. Then he looked down at his hands and sighed, turning them over and over as if he was still angry at them for something.

"Well, don't keep him waiting for the soup," I said.

"I don't think he's waiting for the soup," Georgina said. "I think he's ready to move on to the main course."

"I'm not on the menu," I said. "All we offer is soup,"

"At Circa maybe," Georgina said, "but out in the real world you're completely edible, just like the rest of us."

"His soup is getting cold."

"That's not the only thing getting cold," Georgina said, pushing the kitchen door open with her rear and disappearing into the dining room.

I wondered if it could rust shut if you didn't use it. Did it ever get cold enough that the engine down below refused to turn over? I wondered how Beany would have answered that question.

While I straightened up the kitchen and gave Jim some time to eat, I thought some more about the celibacy discussions I'd had with Beany. Obviously, Beany was not against it, he was just against it for the wrong reasons . . . which always seemed to be mine.

"The Church is all for it," I remember saying during one of my more desperate moments.

"Sure," he once said, "if you have a spouse, please a spouse, but without one all you can do is please the Lord. Now that's a philosophy that really takes human nature into account."

"There always confession and forgiveness," I said in response.

"Then what's the point?"

Beany's celibacy, as he explained it, was borne out of the Buddhist tradition, where the main goal of living is to decrease - if not eliminate - desire.

"Buddha considered it one of the primary causes of suffering in the mind, the heart and the world."

"It's what gets things done, isn't it?"

"Perseverance, Tess, perseverance. Beside, it's not that kind of desire he was referring to. He was talking about the desire for pleasure. Without that kind of desire clouding your brain, you can live freer and think and create at a higher level."

"And how do you do that?" I asked. "How do you eliminate desire?"

"Denial, denial and denial," Beany said, "because desire is like drinking salt water - the more you consume the greater the thirst."

"So isn't that my reason?" I said, figuring that there was plenty of room for me under Beany's Buddhist umbrella.

"Nice try, but you and I are not that alike. Your reasoning is more along the lines of the Hindu tradition."

"Which is?"

"Renouncing sensual pleasure because it can never lead to perfect happiness, a person who is looking for a higher form of happiness, a divine happiness based on a life centered on the spirit or in your case on soup."

I laughed. Beany always had a way of bringing a little humor into every conversation. Maybe it started as a defense mechanism when he was younger to deflect a conversation that was coming too close to home, but by the time I got to know him I really think it was because he saw the comedy in a lot of God's creations, or at least some of man's reaction to them, an important thing to see at his age or any age.

"So I'm a closet Hindu."

"Unfortunately, it's not a reason that holds up to close scrutiny," he said. "You can't avoid unhappiness by eliminating sexual desire any more than you can avoid breathing by living underwater. If your goal is finding a more perfect happiness, you're not going to do it by denying the body's needs and functions."

Beany held his wine glass up to the light to punctuate that thought.

"So you're saying that a life centered only on the spirit can never be complete? I bet the monks and priests might take exception."

"But not the ministers," he said with a smile. "I'm not saying a more spiritual existence isn't a richer existence, I'm just saying that a purely spiritual existence is not going to equal greater happiness in the end, and certainly not in your case."

"I'm not denying myself everything," I said. "I like wine and good food."

"That feeds the body and the mind, but you need love and passion to feed the heart. You just can't depend on it for everything, like half the world. It's just a part of the whole. It has a place, it's not the destination."

"What about you?" I asked.

"I have Shakespeare's love and Virginia Wolf's passion. That's the beauty of a life devoted to literature. I've lived many lives through words. I can feel love as surely as if I lived it along with the author. In the Buddhist tradition that's considered a pure learning experience and a worthy substitute for one's own desire."

"So it's desire without any of the side effects."

"In a manner of speaking."

"Don't you have to feel the withering heat and hear the heart beating in your ears at least once," I said, "to really appreciate love?"

Beany paused for a moment and looked out the window. Of course, I didn't know back then that he'd felt the heat and heard the heart beat many years earlier.

"The first time I read Robert Frost did that for me," he said. "Happiness is a concentrate distilled slowly from various experiences, which includes all kinds of relationships. For someone like you, happiness can only suffer if you dilute it by removing any one of life's basic ingredients, just like one of your soup recipes."

"Then how do you find happiness?" I asked.

"Eliminating desire in the Buddhist tradition is not an effort to obtain a more divine form of happiness, as much as it is to find a way of life that enables you see the world with greater clarity . . . free from the steam that can cloud your vision when your heart or mind are burning with desire or rage."

"Fine," I said, finishing off the wine in my glass, "I'll adopt that as my reason: celibacy for clarity, instead of a more perfect happiness."

"You're can't go back and change your answer," Beany said. "Not after the test has already been handed in."

I looked at my watch. It was getting near closing time and I started straightening out the kitchen. A few minutes later, Georgina came through the kitchen door.

"You look like you're asleep on your feet," she said.

"No, just thinking," I said, snapping back to the moment.

"Your boyfriend's ready for another bowl."

"He's not my boyfriend."

"And the last customer just left."

I sighed to myself and looked at Jim through the kitchen window. He was breathing slowly with his eyes closed, almost like he was meditating. I poured myself a glass of wine and walked out of the kitchen with his soup.

"They should stock this stuff in the pharmacy," Jim said, opening his eyes as I sat down. "I don't think my nose or my head have felt this clear since my cross-country skiing days back in

Maine, when my mother always had a bowl of hot soup waiting for me."

"What kind?"

"Almost like a vegetable stew."

"You can't beat that on a cold winter day."

Jim nodded. He was clearly looking at something behind his eyes, instead of in front of them.

"Are your parents still alive?" I asked, realizing that I knew almost nothing about Jim other than the fact that he was an only child like me.

"My father is."

"Are you guys close?"

"We haven't spoken since I left Maine."

"How long ago was that?"

"Five years ago," he said, diverting his eyes to watch Georgina straightening up by the front door.

"Any more soup?" he asked.

I pointed to the steaming bowl sitting there right in front of him.

"Wow," he said, "you are a magician."

"Sometimes . . . are you trying to change the subject?"

"Is it that obvious?"

"The two main ingredients in this soup are transparency and forgiveness."

Jim laughed.

"Can you see this?" he said, looking so deeply into my eyes that I could almost feel my blood begin to warm. There was a cold blue flame in Jim's eyes, which burned a bit for me I could see that, although it was still separated from the red heat of his heart. I wonder if he saw the same.

It seemed to me that Jim's abstinence wasn't quite in the Hindu tradition of renouncing happiness, because he couldn't find perfect happiness. It was more like he was renouncing happiness in his search for perfect unhappiness, as if he felt he deserved nothing less. I am sure Beany's opinion of that as a reason would have been the same as his opinion of mine. You can only beat yourself up so hard for so long.

I nodded, although I had to turn away and look down at my wine because for an instant I could almost feel his pain and there was no thought of comfort anywhere that I could see.

"It's like I do and I don't," Jim said.

I nodded because I knew exactly what he meant and I felt the same way.

"It's been a while," I said and Jim nodded.

"So what do you think?" Jim asked.

"Are you sure you're ready to do this?" I said.

"No, but I can't let not being sure keep stopping me."

I thought that sounded very wise.

"Unless you're saying no?" he added.

I could feel Beany looking over my shoulder.

"No," I said, "meaning I'm not saying no."

Jim let out a breath that I hadn't noticed he was holding.

"But we have to take it slow."

He nodded.

"And I have to bring Beany's next letter with me . . . to read alone."

Jim's eyes made it clear that he understood completely.

I asked Georgina to finish straightening up and lock up.

"What am I going to tell Lisa Montero?" she said.

"What do you mean?"

"She calls me every Friday to ask how it's going," Georgina said.

"With Jim?"

"Yes."

"How did she find out?"

"She's got spies everywhere."

"Meaning you."

Georgina didn't deny it.

"She thinks she's the greatest matchmaker in history these days. She even said she's the one who suggested to Joe that he ask me out."

"There's nothing to tell her, we're just going somewhere to talk."

"But you keep telling her that you won't go out with customers," Georgina said, unable to hold back her smile, "or potential customers, which covers pretty much everyone in a 100 mile radius."

"Very funny, tell her that only applies to the people my soup seems to help, not the ones it has trouble reaching."

"I think I'll leave that for you to explain."

CHAPTER TWENTY-THREE

With nothing but the clothes on my back and Beany's next letter, I got into Jim's truck and we headed north on Interstate 91 toward Colrain. Now Route 91 isn't a heavily traveled road, not once you get north of Northampton, especially once you get outside the commuting radius for Smith, Amherst, and UMass employees, but it was completely deserted at this late hour.

I expected Jim to turn on the radio, so the bass from his favorite rock group could drown out any reluctant thoughts on my part, like so many of the other guys I've dated who seem to think that loud music is some kind of aphrodisiac, but he left the radio off and he had no CDs stuffed into the armrest like the others. The truck was pretty clean for a furniture maker, except for a couple of empty coffee cups on the floor and the smell of varnish and sawdust. I wondered if he had cleaned it for me.

"Do you really believe all those things about your soup?" he said, taking a quick glance over at my black leather boots, which I didn't wear in the restaurant, preferring comfortable flats while I was working. They were expensive, left over from my San Francisco days.

"Yes."

I watched Jim's face to see if he was trying to measure my flake factor. His expression didn't change.

"I understand the medicinal aspects of herbs and vegetables and things like that," he said, taking one hand off the wheel and rubbing his chin, "but how can it react that quickly . . . or make you react that quickly."

"The body and the mind are interconnected," I said. "You can't touch one without affecting the other."

He nodded, looked over at me and smiled.

"I have been getting my best night's sleep lately on Thursdays."

I get my worst, I thought to myself, although it had nothing to do with my soup. It had to do with Beany and his letters. Jim had started to contribute to it as well. Confusion and indecision has always kept up.

We drove a while in silence. It was almost midnight, but there was a bright quarter moon reflected off the snow and ice like a child's flashlight.

"I think Professor Beanstock left me the desk with the menu inside for a reason," Jim said.

"It wouldn't surprise me. He approached most everything like he was living inside something he was writing."

Jim bit down lightly on his lower lip.

"So what do you think he had in mind for us as his plot twist?"

"What did he know about you?" I asked.

"Not very much."

"He knew you weren't out chasing skirts every night."

"Everyone knows that."

"He knew that there had to be a reason you were alone."

Jim put back on his driving face and stared straight ahead.

"And he knew what my soup could do."

"It can't turn back the clock, can it?"

"No."

"And it doesn't bring on amnesia?"

"No."

Jim took a deep breath.

It didn't take a witch to figure out something happened that Jim hadn't been able to put behind him; the death of his mother, perhaps, something ugly with his father. The more I thought about it, the more certain I was that there had to be a girl involved, because there almost always is. You can only bleed for so long over a parent, there's a certain natural order about things like that, but it is different when it comes to passion and love, especially with someone your own age and especially if it happened so fast that there was no time to duck and protect himself.

Perhaps it was the high school prom with a car full of teenagers and too much beer. Maybe Jim was driving, his arm around his high school sweetheart, whom he'd known since first grade, her seat belt unbuckled so she could sit closer. It had to be something he felt he could have avoided or prevented, no matter what everyone else said.

"Soup can only help you let go for a bit," I said. "Sometimes that's all you need to help you realize that you don't have to forget everything to live back in the moment."

"Another disconnected moment," Jim whispered staring straight ahead out into the highway.

I knew it was time to change the subject, although what I really wanted to say was that the disconnecting moments are the ones we pass through alone, those we share with others are the connecting moments. I certainly wasn't thinking along the lines I'd grown accustomed to over the past year.

"Did you know Beany was gay?" I said.

I didn't think Beany would mind at this point in his afterlife, nor did I think it would matter since Jim wasn't likely to spread it around.

"I just thought he was one of those scholarly hermit types."

"As opposed to one of those running-away-from-the-past hermit types?"

Jim nodded and watched a car filled with college students shoot past us, probably on their way up to Dartmouth for a long weekend.

"Are you gay?" I asked. Although I thought I knew the answer, I wanted to be sure. I was not longer so confident in light of Beany, as well as myself, in terms of my ability to tell.

"No," he said with a laugh. He must have seen me frown out of the corner of his eye, because he quickly added, "don't get me wrong, I only laughed because you're not the first woman to ask."

"Is that because you're such a snappy dresser?" I said with a smile, looking at his worn jeans and work shirt.

"I've been propositioned quite a few times when making deliveries and I've seen that look in their eyes when I decline. It seems to be the easiest way for them to rationalize it."

"Guys don't usually refuse unencumbered sex, particularly with a bored housewife."

"It's easier when you fall out of the habit," Jim said, glancing over at my newly clasped hands.

"Not too much farther," he said.

I nodded and turned to look out the window at the night speeding by with its shadows in the shape of trees and its vast fields of outer space. I wondered if I was doing the right thing, if I wasn't doing this for Beany, so I can say that I tried again or perhaps for Jim going beyond my soup in a way I never could for Beany.

I shut my eyes, took a deep breath and held on to it the way I do sometimes when my heart needs some more room and a chance to speak for itself. It was like stretching an almost forgotten muscle.

"I suppose I might have once been a little homophobic," Jim said, breaking the silence.

I turned back to him, trying not to frown. I certainly did appreciate his honesty.

"The town I grew up in in Maine was like that . . . and my old man, he was really bad. He hated just about everyone who wasn't like him. He used to call me queer when I was young because I didn't like to hunt. The way he killed deer was like target practice. I hated to see the animals stopped dead like that, alive one moment, lifeless the next. I liked fixing things around the house. There was always something my mother needed to get done that my father wouldn't do. He hated it that most of my good friends as I got older were girls."

"That's a sign," I said with a smile and now it was Jim's turn to frown.

"Of what?"

"Of a man in touch with his feminine side."

Jim smiled.

A bi-sexual sort of man, I thought to myself.

"I liked their conversations better. It wasn't always about guns, sports and bodily functions. I suppose that was my mother's doing. She talked to me all the time since I was very little. There wasn't much she could talk about with the old man. He was always mad at something or other."

"What did your mother talk to you about?"

"She talked about her childhood and her dreams. She always wanted to go to college and live for a while in a big city. And books, she talked about books. She loved to read."

"And your father?"

"The newspaper, that's about it. He wasn't much of a listener or a talker. He didn't ponder things the way she did and if she ever second-guessed anything he ever said or did we never heard the end of it."

"My father ran away after I was born," I said. "I never knew him."

"You can avoid a lot of anger and disappointment that way."

We both stared straight ahead for a little while, as the night hurdled past us.

"When did your mother die?" I asked.

"I was young . . . 14."

"How?"

"Slowly and painfully . . . it was breast cancer."

"I'm so sorry."

"How about your mother?"

"It was the year after I graduated college, lung cancer, she was a heavy smoker. She always said she'd go young."

"Soup intuition?"

"Family history."

It was time to change the subject again. I didn't want Jim thinking that I had a short shelf life. I didn't want to think that myself.

"What did your mother do?" I asked. "Did she work?"

"No, my father believed that a woman's place was in the home. So she cooked and cleaned and drowned herself . . . ."

"In alcohol?"

"Travel magazines."

"Did she ever get to travel?"

"To Kennebunkport, when she was lucky."

I could see Jim's eyes water and mine watered in response. My eyes frequently grew moist, but they rarely cried anymore. The last time was after my mother's death. Nick, Jake and Jolene couldn't make me cry, although they did rob me of the ability to sleep for a while.

It suddenly occurred to me what Beany might have had in mind. The men I had gone out with to this point - like Nick and Jake - would never have turned down unencumbered sex. Their eyes might have grown misty on occasion watching an old movie when the cavalry rode to the rescue, but I certainly never made them cry. Their minds dwelled on football, finances, sex, food, drugs, in Jake's case, and drinks – and themselves - when they weren't busy working. However liberated that they thought they were, they still had a role in mind for me similar to Jim's mother.

Jolene was the opposite, analytical, not unhappy or troubled, but super-sensitive to the moment, tears that paraded out often in response to all kinds of insults that lurked behind words and gestures that only she could see. Maybe Beany had his own recipe book when it came to troubled people and saw Jim and I as two ingredients that might normally clash if served separately, but which somehow compliment one another if simmered long enough together.

"What did Beany have on you?" Jim said.

Before last year I doubt I would have answered that question truthfully, at least not completely, but the year of soup and celibacy had washed away any pretense, at least when it came to relationships.

"We were talking about my plans to become a hermit as well."

"Which type?"

"The type who can't make up her mind whether she wants to be with a man or a woman, so decides to avoid both."

Jim nodded slowly as he signaled and exited Route 91.

"Surprised?" I said.

"Isn't that what Northampton is all about?"

I swallowed hard before asking the next question.

"Does it bother you?"

"That you've had relationships with both men and women?"

"Yes, that I'm bisexual."

Jim smiled.

"It means I have a chance, since I fit one of the categories . . . although it's going to be hard to compete with another woman when it comes to the sex part."

I laughed.

"The sex part is overrated for a lot of women. It's never been the issue for me."

"That's great, because I don't know if I'm any good at it anymore."

We both laughed.

"I believe in monogamy," Jim said, "whichever road you're on."

"I do too."

"You're lucky in a way," Jim said.

"How's that?"

"You have twice as many options. The rest of us are limited to half the population."

"Sometimes too many choices can drive you crazy."

"Like too much snow."

I nodded.

"Have you ever had an experience with a man?" I asked.

Jim shook his head from side to side.

"Afraid?"

"Not interested. You know there are people like us around - run of the mill, standard issue, completely average, black and white."

"You're anything but - you're about as grey as any guy I've ever met."

"And you can tell that from the soup?"

"Among other things," I said.

He reached out and rested his hand for a moment over mine, which I had moved onto the seat by my side.

"I suppose I can't help who I'm attracted to anymore than you can," he said.

"Were you always like this," I said, "or is it my soup?"

"Neither," Jim said, "it's you. I feel different around you. Things seem less out of focus. I feel calmer . . . and less destructive."

"Destructive doesn't sound like a good thing."

"So forget I said it."

"You're a craftsman, Jim. You create beauty every day. We've all destroyed things at one time or another."

Jim took in a slow breath and let it out just as slowly.

If Beany were here, I thought, he'd probably say that we had a lot more than our creativity in common. We've both been searching for anonymity, a way to be present, but to disappear at the same time. The funny thing was that we were both in a business that brought us in contact with a lot of people, which made that hard to do. It suggested that we were both of two minds, sort of bi-social.

Jim didn't say a word as we drove into Colrain, right down Main Street, which was at least as residential as it was full of business. With its snow-covered streets and old fashioned street lamps it looked like a movie set out of *It's a Wonderful Life.*

"It's a cute town," I said.

"Don't blink or you'll miss it."

"It's charming."

"Everything looks good under a blanket of snow."

"I bet there are church socials once a month and a Memorial Day parade."

"Population 520, neighborly, but not nosey, you have to nod in the morning, but you don't have to stop to talk. Who you were and what you once did doesn't matter. Of course, that might be different for the native Colrainians."

Who were you and what did you once do? I wondered.

Jim couldn't have been all that different - no one can change that much that quickly - so it must have been something he once did or that happened to him. It didn't feel like a crime or time in jail, which would rule out drugs, although the fact that Jim didn't drink could be a clue. If it was a DWI he could have served time in jail, particularly if someone was hurt or killed.

Jim's house wasn't far out of town. Since Colrain was only about 5 square miles, no one was very far from Main Street. He had a long driveway covered with packed snow that led to a small farmhouse with a light on in the kitchen and smoke pouring from the chimney.

"Wood-burning stove," he said, when he noticed me staring.

"Do you farm too?" I asked.

"No."

"It would be a great place to grow organic vegetables and fresh herbs."

"Most of the fields aren't mine. I was renting the house until last summer when I finally saved up enough to buy it along with a couple of acres."

"That's enough for a nice little organic farm."

Jim helped me out of the truck.

"Be careful stepping down, it gets pretty slippery."

I'd already taken a few falls in Northampton so I was careful not to embarrass myself now.

"Want to see the workshop before we go in?" he asked.

"Sure."

We trudged through the snow for about 25 yards to what was once a small working barn. The peeling red paint, the dry cracked wood and the creaking I heard as we approached the door were deceptive, because the inside had been completely rebuilt sealing out the wind gusts and filling it with light. The workshop was one large room that was neat and very organized with loads of tools, most of which I didn't recognize, hanging in their assigned places. There were a few machines, wiped down and shiny, as if they had yet to be used. Even the floors were swept clean, although you couldn't avoid the smell of sawdust in the air.

"You're a good housekeeper," I said. "It's as clean as my kitchen at Circa."

"It's only the workshop. The house is a different story."

"What about music?" I asked, looking around for some speakers and a CD player. I couldn't imagine spending hours crafting furniture without listening to something, anymore than I could preparing my soups all afternoon without the company of Nina Simone and Houston Person.

"There's a radio under the bench when I need to check the weather."

"Isn't it a little cold to work in here?" I asked, wrapping my arms around my chest.

"Not for a Maine boy. If it begins to numb my fingers, I bring out the space heater."

"I'm surprised you allow yourself a chair to sit down," I said, pointing to the Adirondack chair by the tool bench.

"It's for guests," he said with a little smile.

Jim showed me what he was currently working on, a large country French dining room table that was for a Bed and Breakfast in Acorn, Vermont, two big, curved-back rockers part of the same order, and a headboard for a professor at Amherst. I liked the way he stroked the wood and bent down to examine the grain while he described what remained to be done.

"I use hand tools whenever I can."

His designs seemed to flow right from the wood, almost as if he wasn't shaping it as much as liberating some true inner purpose that had been embodied in the tree at creation. He took the same pride in his work that I took in my soup, and clearly provided some of the same psychological benefits, albeit on a more long-term basis.

"Ready to see the house?" he said.

"Sure."

"It's not much to see. I haven't done anything to it yet."

"You must have done something over the last four years."

"Not really, other than changing a few light bulbs."

I didn't believe him, but he wasn't kidding. The farmhouse looked the way it probably did 50 years ago. We entered through the kitchen with its scuffed and cracked linoleum on the floor, the black and white pattern faded beyond recognition, and its smoky white walls spotted with pox marks, like the remnants of some childhood disease. There was an empty white metal table against the wall with one small, square-backed chair above which was a single bulb in a small porcelain fixture. The stove and sink had to be original issue and there were so many chips and scratches on them that they looked as if they had been attacked with a chisel.

Jim led me right through the kitchen to the family room which was not much different, except that the furniture changed from a tired white table to a tired brown couch and armchair.

"No television?" I said.

"In the closet."

"That's where you watch it?"

"I take it out."

"For Christmas eve or Oscar night?"

Jim smiled.

"When the Red Sox are playing, although the reception is never that good."

"At last something in common with the other boys."

"I like baseball," he said, "it's slow and deliberate. There's a stillness to it that brings time to a stop . . . and stops you from thinking."

"Whew," I said, "you're beginning to sound a lot like Beany."

Jim shook his head, as if he was trying to shake off a cobweb.

"Are you a baseball fan?" he asked.

"Not really."

"Sports?"

"I like hiking."

"So do I."

The strangest thing for me as I looked around was that I didn't see one photograph. No picture of his mother, his first pet or the old neighborhood, nothing at all from the past, nothing that might personalize the room. All that hung on the wall, at least downstairs, were two prints of some winter ice skating scenes that were obviously put up long ago by a prior resident.

I looked up at Jim as he appeared to stare off into space. Although the house appeared to be sparsely furnished, it felt crowded with memories that had nothing to do with any of the prior occupants.

"You weren't kidding," I said, "about the house. Now that you own it, are you planning to put your considerable talents to use?"

Jim shrugged.

"Not right now," he said. "Right now I'm planning to go upstairs to straighten out the mess in my bedroom."

"Have some high expectations about tonight, do you?"

"As long as you don't," Jim said. "You're the first woman who's ever been here."

"I'm honored and you're the first man . . . or woman . . . that I've been alone with in quite some time."

"How about Beany?"

"Only at the restaurant."

"I don't know if I can handle the pressure," Jim said, sounding half serious.

"I expect it's like riding a bicycle," I said with a smile.

I felt as if we were a couple of servants of God getting ready to renounce our vows.

"Where's Beany's desk?" I asked.

"Upstairs," Jim said, backing up the stairs, "just give me a moment."

"Let me help."

"No, I'm way too embarrassed. Why don't you just sit in that old armchair and read your letter. It's the only comfortable seat in the house."

So I sat down and while I sank deep into the cushions, the springs poking me from behind, I marveled at some of the obvious parallels. Jim's workshop was clearly more his home than this house, much the way my kitchen was for me. Neither one of us appeared very concerned about comfort, which suggested that we both lived more in our minds than our bodies. From the books scattered about, mostly history, it was evident that Jim was a reader like me, and considering what brought us both to this spot at this moment, it would suggest that our biological urges were second-class citizens.

"Are you all right?" he called out from upstairs.

"You mean have I run away?"

"Yes."

"No, I'm still here."

"I won't be too long."

"Take your time, I like order and cleanliness."

"I've noticed."

My mother used to say that messiness was a failure of will and a sign of disaffection.

"Excuse the noise," Jim said, his footsteps echoing through the entire house.

I leaned back on the chair until I found a fairly comfortable position and opened Beany's next letter. It was dated November 11, 1988 and addressed to Evan. Beany was now 66 years old and it was hard for me to believe that he was still having these one-way conversations. Can you still believe in the possibility of love at that age, reborn or renew, after studiously avoiding it for so long? I had my doubts, since I felt as if Jim might be my last chance, and I was barely past 30. At Beany's age, it must have been like looking through the wrong end of the binoculars, everything appearing so much smaller and distant than it once did.

For a moment, I wished that I was back at the restaurant with a bottle of wine and with no need to communicate with anyone other than myself. I knew Jim would gladly take me home if I asked him; perhaps he'd even be a bit relieved, but I've always been one to finish what I start, so I cleared my mind and turned to Beany's letter.

Dear Evan,

Congratulations on Bush. Your Presidential candidates seem to be on a roll these days, although if you ask me the Republican Party could have done better. He's wishy-washy at best and has no charisma, not like President Reagan. I doubt he will make it to a second term, although I am not sure who is out there from the Democratic Party capable of challenging him. Perhaps some dark horse will emerge to surprise everyone like Cuomo or Biden, or perhaps another unknown governor like Jimmy Carter. Now that was a man who deserved a second chance.

I've not been well as of late, nothing serious, just a chronic prostate problem that I've been assured is normal for a man in his mid-60s. I am up so often at night trudging to the bathroom that I don't even bother to open my eyes anymore. I know that the wine and my new affinity for spicy food is not helping, but I have denied myself enough of life's pleasures (as I suspect you have as well), and both are definitely worth the discomfort. I hope you are not suffering the same, although I bet if they did a study they would find it to be a common side effect of years of abstinence. After all, it has to go somewhere, so why not to enlarging the prostate.

I am soon to publish a new book that will undoubtedly be the one they refer to in my obituary. I can see it now: Professor Roger J. Beanstock, a confirmed bachelor teaching at a female college, which probably says more than anyone would need to know about me, was the author of the definitive collection of Romantic Poets of the 19th Century, aptly named "The Immortal Ones." A minor poet on his own, having published two slim volumes of depressing poetry entitled "When the Soft Voices Die" and "Looks that Oppress," Professor Beanstock will best be remembered for his efforts, exemplified in this collection, to bring poetry to the masses. As he stated in the book's introduction, "Anyone who has ever loved, suffered or thought needs and seeks poetry." That should cover everyone, I think, even chemists. I don't see a best seller in my future, but I am hoping it might find its way into the textbook catalogues so that I can earn enough in royalties for a modest vacation once every other year. Not bad for five years of research and writing? Such are the expectations of an English professor, this English professor anyway, which are certainly much lower than they have ever been.

I saw your recent article in Organic Chemistry Today – no, I am not a regular subscriber – and judging from the number of patents you have accumulated and the co-authorship with a scientist from Merck working on drugs to combat plaque, and not the kind that inhabits our teeth, I suspect that you are profiting handsomely from your research on lipids. Bravo, as I remember wealth was another one of your goals, although I am curious how you could find any time to spend it, and what you could possibly be interested in spending it on, other than more test tubes and chemical apparatus. One of these day, perhaps you will accept how your own personal chemistry works and write back to me.

I could not believe that Evan hadn't responded once in all the years or that Beany persisted, even if it was every 10 years or so. Obviously Evan was stubborn and insistent on sticking to his youthful decision or just one of the world's biggest cowards. If it wasn't for his obituary, I would have bet that he married a woman, like so many others back then did, genuflecting to society's norms, and had a family. But he didn't, according to his obituary, so why not drop Beany a short note, if only to tell him that he was content with the life he'd chosen so stop writing? Could he have been that fearful for his reputation? Certainly it didn't matter by 1988. Perhaps it was just a case of letting sleeping dogs lie . . . or perhaps he liked it that way . . . a sort of slow, lifelong, literary courtship.

It hardly seems fair that the homosexual community, challenged as it has been over the years by all the different gatekeepers of society, is now tested by AIDS, which has turned love, albeit its physical manifestations, into a struggle between life and death. I imagine that this is back page news in Nebraska, buried behind the exploits of yet another top-ten football team, but here it hits hard. In the past year, I have watched a history professor waste away, the husband of an administrator who apparently had a secret life like so many used to years ago and a painter of some note. It is an ugly illness that takes people slowly, but with great flair and drama. It is almost a justification for cheating death by taking leave on your own accord.

But if Beany didn't have AIDS or some other terminal illness, what made him choose to go when he did, I wondered. There weren't too many letters left and I hoped that the answer would be in one of them.

I guess we have found our reward for our abstinence, a lifetime of love exchanged for a few extra years of placid existence. Do you still stand by your decision, I wonder? Of course, I have no way of knowing, since your silence can mean almost anything. In any event, perhaps you should consider abandoning your lipids after all these years and focusing instead on the HIV virus. Wouldn't it be ironic if you found the cure that could once again set the gay community free?

I will close with a poem that was written by someone who is HIV positive, which is not quite AIDS yet, although it appears inevitable since it seems all the men of science can do at this point is delay its arrival. He is a tradesman with no formal education beyond secondary school, and I came across it in the local underground paper. He has done quite an admirable job and if I ever decide to put together a collection entitled "The Mortal Poets," I will certainly include it.

Time is never constant
Night is much slower than the day
Perhaps because it moves so cautiously in the dark
A rainy day never measures up to a clear one
Nor will anticipation to memory
It will stand still when you want it to fly
And fly when age tries to slow it down
It's a friend and an enemy
A lover and a parent
It's immune to flattery and anxiety
It never feels abandoned
Needs no friends
Never regrets the news
And will set you free
Without intimacy

And without notice
Time is never constant
Almost invisible
But never out of mind.

Regards,
Roger

Why did Beany do it, I kept asking myself? Why did he keep writing? Did he really hope for a thaw? Evan had clearly sold his soul to his lab. All I could think of was another short story Beany once told me about. It was by a Southern writer I had heard of but never read, Flannery O'Connor. It involved a family on a vacation trip, a husband and wife, two children, and a battle axe of an old grandmother, who couldn't stop complaining and criticizing, and apparently was like that as long as anyone could remember. They take a wrong turn and wind up on a deserted country road where they are taken prisoner by an escaped convict with a gun. It's clear he wants the car and intends to kill them all, and in the last few moments the grandmother grows quiet and understanding and helps each member of the family meet their end, as she is the last to go. She exits quietly with dignity and self-respect.

"What a terrible story," I remember saying.

"You have to look past the plot to the characters and the theme."

The point, according to Beany, was that the grandmother could have been a good woman, and would have been a good woman, if only she had lived her whole life at the point of a gun.

"That's what some people need," Beany said.

Perhaps that was Beany's secret, he needed the heartache and emptiness Evan provided to be the kind of professor, poet, and scholar he wanted to be.

"So what did Professor Beanstock have to say tonight?" Jim said, walking down the stairs. He had changed from his jeans and brown corduroy shirt into shorts and a T-shirt. His legs were lean and the muscles well-defined. I could feel my Kinsey meter definitely pulling to the left.

"Just looking at you in that outfit makes me shiver."

"It's all mind over temperature."

"I have this sudden urge to start making soup."

"The cupboard's pretty bare, empty actually."

We both looked toward the kitchen.

"I don't think the stove's been used in years for anything but boiling water."

The thought of a classic stove like that abandoned and ignored sent a shiver down my spine.

"The bedroom is warmer," Jim said.

"That's your pick-up line?" I said.

"It's the truth . . . besides, I'm out of practice."

I stood up and walked toward the stairs.

"What was in the letter?" he asked.

"The usual stuff."

"What's the usual stuff?"

"The world according to Beany."

I had given Jim more than enough information about Beany and me at this point and I didn't feel like giving out much more, at least not until he started reciprocating. Not surprisingly, he was sensitive enough to let it go.

"Is the bed also 100 years old?" I said, as we climbed the stairs slowly like an old married couple.

"That was the only thing I had to buy."

"So it doesn't creak?"

"I don't know. I've never actually put it to the test."

While I was comfortable about spending the night, I still wasn't sure what that meant. It could mean our faces flush and our hearts racing with physical intimacy, both of us are out of shape and out of practice, the way it might be scripted if we were making a movie, or it could mean our faces flush and our hearts racing with a different kind of intimacy, a motionless intimacy, where what's being stroked and stimulated by words and revelations are feelings and memories. A lot of truth can be let out in a bed in the stillness of the late night. It's a perfect place for trust and solemn sympathy, side by side, eyes on the ceiling watching shadow after shadow, our sensibilities held steady by the nearness, warmth and support of someone other than ourselves and the rationalization we've come to depend on. Of course, it could be some combination of the two.

The bedroom was sparse as well, the furniture consisting of one relatively new regulation queen size bed, albeit with a old quilt, which he probably got from his mother, a worn out old chest, another descendant no doubt of the house's original settlers, one of Jim's handmade rockers, a small end table, and a pole lamp.

All the clutter was squeezed into the corner, including some dirty clothes and a pile of trade magazines. Instead of a closet, there was an old armoire, tilting slightly, as if one leg was about to give out, overburdened as it were by its own thoughts and memories.

"How's the Colrain library?" I asked, looking over at the pile of library books on the end table.

"There's not much there. I use the Northampton library."

I looked at the titles - more history, a book on Winston Churchill and FDR, and a biography of John Adams.

"Not a big fiction reader," I said.

"I like biographies. I figure that if you can't live your own life, you might as well live someone else's."

I stared back at Jim in response to that one, although he didn't look up from the books.

"I don't think you've had enough soup yet tonight."

He looked up with a half-smile.

"Enough to get up the nerve to ask you over."

I knew that wasn't easy and I also knew that it had nothing to do with Jim being shy.

I sat down on the bed and surveyed the room . . . still no photographs, nothing on the small end table, like a photo of his mother or a favorite pet, nothing that would give anything away.

"Don't own any cameras I take it?"

"No."

"You have a moral issue with photography?"

Jim shrugged.

"Like those tribes in Africa who think that every photograph steals a piece of their soul?"

"I don't believe in the soul," he said, turning his eyes away from mine and staring out the window.

"I have to believe that there's more to life than what we can see and feel."

"I hope you're right," Jim said, tossing me a flannel shirt and pointing me in the direction of the bathroom.

"Where's Beany's desk?" I asked.

"It's in the room you'll pass it on the way to the bathroom."

It was the only thing in the room, sitting in the center like a museum piece on display. It was a big desk, the kind that would make anyone who sits down behind it feel important and productive, like some successful chief executive. It had a solid mahogany floating top that extended beyond the base. There were hand-carved columns on the front and sides and deep drawers in back with hand-carved ribbon and flower pulls. I imagined Beany sitting behind it, a bottle of wine towering over the scattered books and paper as he worked on his next book or poem. I imagined it sitting in the living room by the fireplace. I wished that I had been inside Beany's house to see it in its natural habitat.

I really didn't believe Jim's remark about not believing in the spirit and the soul, which I thought about while I washed up and brushed my teeth with my finger. At least, I didn't believe that he completely believed it. That's a place a lot of people go to hide when bad things happen. It's a place of denial, but it's not necessarily your true place. How can anyone not believe that there's more to life than just their mass? Even an agnostic or an atheist can't deny that there are forces that can't be seen, like energy and anti-matter, whatever that is. Life is like the horizon, it's just the limit of our sight. It's that space beyond it, that unseen place that I want my soup to reach.

"You have a soul," I said, coming back into the bedroom, "everyone does and it's not like Tinkerbell, you don't need to believe to keep it alive. It's a force, an energy that can never die. That's why your own body may seem foreign to you sometimes."

"It's my mind and heart that seems foreign to me," Jim said, "not my body."

"For me, it's my body."

"Well, it doesn't look foreign to me," Jim said. "And it certainly looks better in that shirt than I do."

"Having decided to fall off the wagon, you don't want to waste any time."

"Do you?"

I didn't, which was a relief, since I wasn't sure that the hormones were still all there.

"No, but I think we need to talk some more first . . . to see where this leads." I said. "I'm not finished with your soul yet."

"It'll still be there afterward? Besides, I'm not used to talking this much at night . . . at all really."

He pulled back the quilt and we both climbed into bed.

"Seriously," I asked, "how long have you felt this way?"

"About talking at night or how I look in that shirt?"

"You know what I mean, about your soul."

Jim rolled onto his side so we were face to face.

"Maybe I was being a bit too dramatic," he said. "Maybe what I really mean is that I'm not a big fan of organized religion."

"I wouldn't disagree with you on that."

"I don't believe there's a purpose to everything that happens. Some things are just bad luck . . . the wrong time and the wrong place . . . and some things are just our fault."

OK, I thought to myself, he made a terrible mistake - like everyone else at one time or another -and hasn't been able to forgive himself.

"That's what free will is all about," I said. "But that doesn't negate some greater purpose to life."

"Is this the way foreplay is these days?" Jim said and I laughed.

"It's a part of it," I said, "at least for the mature woman."

"Isn't that what we've been doing for the past month?"

With that I shut up, moved closer and let Jim put his arm around me. I listened to his breathing. You can tell a lot about your own state of mind by listening to your own breath. His sounded labored and anything but relaxed, like he was having a change of heart. My breathing was much easier, unconscious, not the least bit apprehensive. Perhaps because for me the hard part was over, if we fell asleep like this I'd be content.

I stared up, but there was nothing to see. Not a single shadow crossed the ceiling, because not a single car was on the road at this hour in Colrain.

"What are you thinking?" Jim asked.

"I'm enjoying the stillness I feel in your arms," I said. "What about you?"

Jim took a deep breath and drew me closer. What had been absent was now present – the beat of his heart.

"What am I waiting for?" he said. "I've thought a lot about this."

"We can just lie here," I said, thinking about all the things we'd both lived through that we didn't know. It felt as if some empty and lonely spaces were slowly filling in.

"I once read that every moment is really two moments."

"In what way?" I asked.

"A moment of time and a moment of space."

"I suspect the trick is trying to be in both moments at the same time."

With that Jim lifted his head and kissed me and I didn't try to push or pull him back into the moment. I left it up to him and to whatever our bodies believed.

The sex was good. How could it not be after such a long drought, although I had too many things on my mind to really let go, and I suspect Jim did as well, so it wasn't all that it could be. Then again, what ever is? What was particularly nice for me was lying afterward in his arms, the silence comforting and sleepy, that kind of silence that comes from fullness, and I drifted off to sleep without a single thought about all the things that had kept me up over the past year.

"The difficult realities and self-delusions," Beany used to call them, "that hold us back."

I wanted Jim to fall asleep first and waited for his breathing to slow down and grow shallow, but it didn't. It remained deep and thoughtful until I finally fell asleep.

Jim was down in the kitchen when I woke up and the smell of strong coffee filled the house.

"So how was it?" he said, when I walked down wearing his flannel shirt.

"The sex or the sleep?"

"The sleep, I'm afraid to ask about the other."

"It was the best night's rest I've had in a long time."

Jim smiled.

"And the sex was the best I've had in a long time," I added.

"That's very diplomatic."

I didn't return the question. It's not something a woman normally asks, perhaps because we don't look at it as a competitive sport. In any event, I knew I was better at putting my partners to sleep than making the earth move and I was content with that.

"How did you sleep?" I asked.

"I'm not a good sleeper. I haven't been for a long time."

"A long time being the last 4 or 5 years?"

Jim didn't respond.

"Do you want to talk about it?"

"I'd need a couple of gallons of soup for that."

"Well, I'm the person who can make it for you."

"It'll have to wait because I've got a bunch of deliveries to make and I've got to drop you off at Northampton on the way."

Jim put a cup of coffee down in front of me.

"Sorry, but I don't have anything around to eat for breakfast. I usually grab something on the road."

"Don't worry about it," I said. "I own a restaurant in case you've forgotten so I never go hungry for long."

Jim kissed me lightly on the lips when he dropped me off.

"See you on Thursday," I said, when he didn't say anything about coming down to Northampton any sooner. Without a car there was not much I could do.

"Sure," Jim said, like a man who was beginning to feel guilty, which put me in a bad mood for the rest of the morning, at least until I started thinking about what kind of special soup I could make for next Thursday.

CHAPTER TWENTY-FOUR

The next day I got a lot more attention than my soup board. Captain Dale was in early, before we even opened, to pick up some soup to take with him to his monthly meeting with the other police departments in the county.

"You look great Tess," he said with a big smile.

He didn't say another word, but the way he looked at me, like a beaming father whose daughter had just successfully completed the triple axel, made it clear that he knew.

"Thank you," I said, "but I'm a little tired."

He just gave me a wink and a thumbs-up.

"What did you tell him?" I asked Georgina after he left.

"Nothing."

"Don't give me that, what did you say?"

"Not much," Georgina said with a grin of her own, "just that the curse has been broken."

"Very nice, I really appreciate it."

Georgina chuckled.

"Seriously, why should everyone know my business?"

"First," Georgina said, as she walked around straightening out the chairs, "you don't think everyone already knows."

"About last night?"

"About Jim taking over Beany's Thursday night table," she said. "Joe saw it, Lisa knows. It's a small town. The winter's long. Everyone needs something to talk about."

"I don't want to be that something."

"Then don't run the most popular soup kitchen in town."

Lisa Montero was in the moment we opened for business and she didn't even order any soup.

"Did I tell you I had a feeling about you two?" she said and I nodded. "So how was it? Is he as good as he looks?"

"I don't kiss and tell," I said.

Lisa looked at Georgina and Georgina looked back, like they shared a secret that they weren't thinking about letting me in on.

"Now that you popped your cherry," she said, "I'd play the field a bit to see what's out there."

"I appreciate the advice."

"I've got a lot of names in here," she said, holding up her black book. "Not that you need my help with that soup of yours."

"You'll be the first I call," I said, "when I'm ready to look."

Lisa looked at Georgina and then back at me.

"Just be careful," Lisa said, backing out toward the door. She was already a little late for opening up her shop.

"Why?"

"Because you're like a child sometimes and I don't want you to get hurt again and decide to close Circa and move to New York City, because I'm addicted to the soup . . . we all are."

With that Lisa left before I could say another word.

"What is she worried about?" I asked Georgina.

"She's been asking around about him."

"Jesus," I said, "despite what you and Lisa might think I'm not a child. I can take care of myself."

Georgina turned around and refolded one of the napkins. Then she moved over to some of the other tables and squared up the chairs.

"OK," I said, "what did she find out?"

"That's that point," Georgina said spinning quickly around and knocking the napkins to the floor. "She found out nothing. She couldn't even find where he came from."

"Maine."

"Or why he moved here . . . by himself."

"And I should be careful over what – the fact that Lisa is a lousy detective?"

"Don't you think it's a little odd?" Georgina said, picking up the napkin. "He's a mystery man. Lisa said that type usually has something to hide."

"And what type is that?"

"Dark, quiet . . . sad eyes."

"Did Lisa say that?"

Georgina nodded.

"Tell her I'll wear a helmet next time he's here," I said, walking into the kitchen.

Apparently Orit was the only one who didn't know, probably because the library was not on Tom, Lisa or Joe's route. She found out quick enough when she came in to pick up some soup for dinner and Georgina whispered it into her ear. She nodded like she half-expected it to happen.

"I know Mr. Chapman," she told me. "He's a regular at the library, history book buff, very polite, always returns his books on time."

"Does he strike you as odd?" I asked for Georgina's benefit.

Orit looked surprised by the question and rubbed her ear before answering.

"Not odd, I wouldn't say that . . . he's serious and quiet, but people are like that in libraries as a rule, maybe not kids, but adults. I'd say he's a little sad, but that's not so unusual, I wouldn't call that odd. Why do you ask?"

"No reason."

"I think he may be hiding something," Georgina said.

"Like what?" Orit asked.

"How come a good looking guy like that is still alone?" she said. "He could be hiding something."

"Oh, that's nonsense," Orit said. "There is any number of good reasons why people need time alone."

She picked up her soup and nodded.

"Besides," she added, before turning to leave, "who isn't hiding something or other? It's one of the lessons of life that I've learned over the years . . . you can find it in all kinds of books . . . wisdom is knowing when to keep things to yourself."

Of course, the parade of well wishers didn't stop.

Joe came in at closing to pick up Georgina and repeated his offer to come running if I needed him. I wouldn't have been surprised if he handed me a whistle.

"I appreciate that Joe," I said, "but I don't think I'm going to need any protection."

"You never know. You probably ought to get a car so you're not stuck up there, you know if something gets out of hand."

"You can call me anytime," Georgina interrupted in case Joe was planning to use the opportunity to make a sale.

"Thank you, but don't hold your breath."

"I was never her type," I heard Joe say to Georgina on their way out, "too much to say I guess and too lively."

Georgina laughed and held tight onto Joe's arm as they left the restaurant.

Even Matt called me later that evening to check on the computers, but he quickly turned the conversation to Jim.

"I bumped into Georgina," he told me. "Did you tell him?"

"Yes, I did. I'm not going to start off with a big secret."

Of course, as soon as I said that I realized that Jim was still holding on to his secret and no relationship could go forward as long as he did.

We talked some more about what would happen, now that my resolve had been broken, the first time I met a woman I couldn't resist. Matt still didn't believe in bi-sexuality and was certain that I was gay trying to masquerade as straight.

"Even if you're right," I said, "don't you think I can resist temptation out of a sense of loyalty and love? Husbands and wives do that all the time?"

I heard Matt chuckle on the other end of the phone.

"And look how much success they have," he said. "What's the divorce rate now 50%? Besides, at our age we're all helpless to the sensation."

I disagreed and begged off the phone so I could think some more about the special soup I wanted to make for next Thursday. I actually didn't decide until the day before, but I ultimately went with a soup I had never made before that I'd found about three months earlier when I was in the library researching Southeast Asian soups.

I was looking into Laos, where soup is served with every proper meal, when I came across a small book published by the British Ambassador to Laos in the early 70s, which contained the recipes of Chaleunsilp Phia Sing, the royal chef to King Sisavang Vong, the last crowned monarch of Laos. According to Mr. Davidson, Sing was a Southeast Asian Leonardo Da Vinci - a physician, architect, choreographer, sculptor, painter and poet, in addition to serving as the royal chef.

When Sing was born in the 1890s, his country was still misty, mountainous and tropical, with teak forests, fruit trees, brilliant flowers, bamboo, wild orchids, monks in saffron robes and houses on stilts. When he died in 1968, American troops were about to begin dumping herbicides on Laos' borders to destroy the vegetation and improve the visibility for military operations.

There were 115 recipes in the book, 20 of them for soups, which says something about the spirituality of the Laotian culture, because soup is the most spiritual of foods as far as I'm concerned. It takes a diverse group of ingredients, breaks them all down and mixes them all together so that they are basically unrecognizable, visible only in taste and concept.

Many of the ingredients in the book were exotic for American tastes including banana leaves, water buffalo, ant eggs, birds, water snails, green algae, sting ray and jelly mushrooms, and some of his soups contained bold combinations of ingredients such as fish cooked in pork broth, chicken with dried squid, and cabbage and eggs.

Recipe number 69, always an auspicious number, was called Keng Jeeg Kai, which meant Shredded Chicken Soup. It called for chicken, although I could never duplicate the fresh, free-roaming chicken that would have been available to Sing, not the way preservatives, hormones and pesticides find their way into the feed we throw at our chickens these days, even the ones we sell as organically grown. It had to simmer for about 30 minutes before being skinned, removed from the bone and shredded. It also called for scallions, fresh sprigs of cilantro, salt, onions, shallots, peeled and cut into lengthwise pieces, garlic and fish sauce.

Sing noted that this soup would clear the head and warm the heart whatever the weather or the mood. Cooking, Sing told Mr. Davidson, whether for the Royal Family or your own family is Het Bun Dai Bun, which means "whoever does good, the beautiful or the right, will receive the same gift in return." So I decided that Keng Jeeg Kai would be my good, beautiful, and right gift for my customers and for Jim, selfishly hoping for something in return – Jim's secret.

I added a 17th century English soup that I had made before, which I discovered in one of Samuel Pepy's diaries. Pepy kept his diary in shorthand over a 10-year period from the restoration of King Charles II in 1660 to the death of his wife Elizabeth at age 29 in 1669. His Pea Soup recipe called for green peas, of course, leeks, bacon, parsley, chervil, butter, spinach, sorrel, lettuce, cabbage, celery, mint, mace (which is the outer covering of the nutmeg), and cloves.

"Ladle the soup over a piece of toast," he wrote, "and you will have a meal strong enough to vent those vile tumors that build up in the mind."

Finally, I wanted a heavier, meatier soup, something to strengthen resolve and temper sadness, even if it meant beef, and I settled on a recipe I got from a friend's German grandmother called Föhn Beef Noodle Soup. The Föhn is a warm wind that sometimes appears on the southern side of the Alps distorting the view and making the mountains that are hundreds of miles away seem much closer. It's a soup that can bring the most distant angst, another German word, well within reach, and it's only when it's within reach that we can do anything to dissipate it.

Jim arrived right on time and I prepared a sampler of the three special soups for Georgina to bring out, which I'd never done before. I don't do samplers. My customers can read the ingredients and my own notes as to what beneficial effects each soup is supposed to have and then it's up to them to make a choice, knowing how they are feeling when they come in.

"A three-pronged attack," Georgina said, "on his heart, mind and spirit?"

I nodded.

"He doesn't stand a chance."

Georgina had been increasingly critical of Jim during the past week when he didn't call or come for a visit.

"If you sleep with a guy and it takes," she said, "then he'll be all over you for at least the first month or two."

"In college maybe," I said, "when you're all living the same lives and experiencing the same things . . . wait until you each start carrying around a lot of different emotional baggage."

"Maybe what you really need to add to his soup," Georgina said, "is some sodium pentothal."

Of course, that was what I was trying to do - use nature's ingredients as a kind of truth serum.

"Is he trying all three," I asked Georgina during one of her trips back to the kitchen, "or is he eating one at a time?"

One at a time was the sign of a disciplined, well-ordered mind, a stable down-to-earth personality, not prone to spontaneous outbursts, or the need for constant stimulation.

"One at a time."

"Good," I said and Georgina gave me her fish eye.

"I don't think he's wild about the pea soup though. He's been taking his sweet time with that one."

Not a good sign, I thought.

"Tell him to finish it."

Georgina laughed. "What am I, his mother?"

"Don't take it away the bowl until it's empty."

"Yes mother."

"I'm serious."

"Do the peas help you forget or help you remember?" Georgina said a bit facetiously.

"They help you let go, so you can release whatever it is that's blocking you from moving ahead."

"Apparently he's not ready to let it go."

That was clear.

It was almost 11 by the time the restaurant emptied out and I could send Georgina home. Jim was sipping some coffee, but he still looked like he was about to fall asleep.

"Busy day?" I asked, sitting down with my glass of red wine.

"I had a delivery in Boston. I used to like going to Boston when I was young. Now I hate it, too many cars and too easy to get lost."

"I think you're still young."

"Younger."

"I heard you didn't like the pea soup."

"I'm not a big fan of the pea . . . but I ate it."

"I wasn't coming out unless you did. Peas are good for venting."

"That can be taken a number of ways," Jim said with a laugh.

"You know the way I mean."

"Are you trying to drug me with your soup?"

"I'm trying to drug everyone."

We sat quietly a while, sipping our coffee and wine. I wondered what Jim was thinking or whether he was thinking at all. The men I've known over the years, particularly Nick and Jake, had this ability to wipe their minds clean sometimes and stare off into the distance, as if they were one for a few moments with the vast vacuum of outer space. I've never been able to zone out like that, not with someone beside me, at least not without the help of grass or alcohol. Not even soup these days can completely silence this inner monologue I have that's always waiting around for a quiet moment to be heard, which is why I suppose I like to keep busy.

My thoughts as I sipped my wine, watching Jim stare out the window, was whether this was how my new and perhaps last shot at romance was going to end - with a bowl of unappreciated pea soup and an unrevealed secret.

"Do you want to come back tonight?" Jim asked.

It was a question I'd thought about a lot during the week.

"I don't mind a Thursday night friend," I said, "but I'm not sure I want a Thursday night lover. I'd be cheating myself . . . and you. It's like driving around with a nail in your tire. Sooner or later it's going to go flat."

"Am I the nail?"

I shrugged.

"It sounds like something Beany would have said," Jim said. "It was all or nothing for him too . . . right, nothing in the end because he couldn't have what's his name?"

"Evan. His decision was more complicated than that. Evan moved across the country and the world was very different back then. It wasn't a very friendly place."

Jim nodded.

"I understand," he said, "I just need time. I've got to do this slowly. I don't know any other way . . . it's the way I've always done things."

"I can see that."

"By the way I eat?"

"Among other things," I said, "but I'm not in a hurry. If we're going to have a relationship, more than just a regularly scheduled appointment, which don't get me wrong I liked, the windows need to be opened wide and the secrets aired out. I can wait until you're ready and maybe you won't ever be ready. I can understand that too. I just don't want to get too deep into this and find out it's never going to happen."

Jim nodded and stood up to leave.

"Wait," I said, going back into the kitchen and bringing out a container of pea soup to take home with him. "Give it another chance, it may help."

"You mean hold my nose and force it down like medicine?"

"If that's what it takes."

"I'll try," Jim said with a little smile.

Even his little smiles brightened his eyes.

He left with a light kiss on the lips and I sat back down to finish my wine, disappointed and a little depressed at the thought that Jim might never be ready. I wished that I had Beany around to talk to. He always had these pithy things to say when I was feeling down or confused. I suppose because he had said them often enough to himself. I particularly liked the one he borrowed from Peanuts.

"I'm a big believer in the Charles Schulz philosophy of life," Beany once told me. "I only dread one day at a time."

Once when I gave him a dozen excuses why whatever it was I wanted to do with my life made sense, throwing up one rationalization after another hoping that one would stick, he waved his hand and said he didn't need to hear any more, this time quoting a Yiddish saying he liked: "If you don't want to do something, one excuse is as good as another."

CHAPTER TWENTY-FIVE

If I didn't have Beany at least I had his next letter, which I pulled out after Jim left, although I wasn't happy to see that the supply was dwindling. This letter was dated December 31, 1990. New Year's Eve and presidential elections seemed to be Beany's most sentimental moments, at least when it came to Evan.

Dear Evan,

No Presidential election to write about, but I thought I'd write anyway, because as I sit here waiting for the clock to strike twelve, having declined the half-dozen faculty parties I am always invited to - years ago in an effort to set me up with some unattached female scholar and now out of pity - I cannot help but reflect on some of the amazing events that 1990 brought. Nelson Mandela walking free is perhaps the most remarkable of all. In my most idealistic moment, I think of it as heralding a new age of tolerance that will extend from race and religion to all the other myriad differences that define the human race, differences that should unite instead of divide us. Germany reuniting into a single country again was equally significant and unexpected considering the length of the Cold War. If East and West can find each other after all these years, perhaps there is still hope for us.

Margaret Thatcher, as you undoubtedly know, resigned. I'm sure she was one of your favorites, although I must confess I liked her as well, notwithstanding her frumpiness and dowdiness. I liked her plain and direct talk and I liked the fact that she was a woman. Who knows, one day perhaps we may have a gay man or woman leading this nation. A world governed by such people would surely be a more peaceful place, or at least one more focused on inflicting pleasure as opposed to pain. Certainly, it would be a better-dressed world. Of course, there is Martina Navratilova, who won her 9th Wimbledon at the advanced age of 33. Why anyone thinks that's old is beyond me. I suppose it does confirm that as long as we are still breathing, there is hope for us.

Instead of trying to come up with resolutions, I have been thinking about what three characteristics of my personality have most defined my life. For example, with respect to you I would have to say your love of science is first, followed by your desire for success. The third would be your fear of the unpredictable and unexpected, which is probably not all that uncommon among scientists. I'm not all that different with respect to the first two. I substitute love of literature for science and worship success and accomplishment as well, although with a literary measure, not a monetary one. The third, however, is very different. You cannot love literature without embracing the unpredictable and unexpected. For me, the third would have to be my desire to remain invisible in my day to day life, not my professional one, even though that means foregoing much of what literature supposedly teaches as the reason for living. Fear is not the motivation here as much as loyalty and stubbornness.

Beany certainly kept his anguish to himself during our Thursday night sessions. Of course, I knew he was lonely and introspective, poet or not. Who wouldn't be living alone at his age? He drank like that for a reason and when he came to the restaurant he needed soup as badly as a parched man needs water. Still, I thought his angst was more existential and philosophical, the product of immersing himself into the suffering of hundreds of other writers, not in significant part to one unrequited love.

The question I asked myself was whether Beany would have made the same choice if he had to do it all over again in today's Northampton, where one's sexual persuasion is no more defining or limiting than one's height and weight. What bothered me was the thought that Beany might have made the same decision anyway. He may have put invisibility as one of his top three personality characteristics, trying to make it sound like a choice, but I think it was a basic part of his genetic make-up. Beany was one of those people born to live life from a distance, to pick up the bodies after the battle was over and study what's been written about other people's love affairs. Evan moving across the country just made it that much easier.

I felt differently. I liked being in the heart of things, if only to dole out my soup. I wanted to keep things simple if I could, but I was beginning to realize that didn't necessarily mean separate and apart. I couldn't live at a distance, not forever, and I didn't have to if I could decide on one person and stick with him . . . or her. Despite what Matt believed, I believe that I could resist those other attractive complications the same way I do salty foods and sweets. I was built like Beany with respect to denial, but the denial of others, not necessarily myself. Beany, on the other hand, was skilled at both.

I have also been thinking about this fall's senior seminar on poetry. We finished with two poems on the theme of a "wasted life." The first was "Lying in a Hammock at William Duffy's Farm in Pine Island, Minnesota" by James Wright. I suppose the title gives some of it away.

Over my head, I see the bronze butterfly,
Asleep on the black trunk,

Blowing like a leaf in green shadow.
Down the ravine behind the empty house,
The cowbells follow one another
Into the distance of the afternoon.
To my right,
In a field of sunlight between two pines,
The droppings of last year's horses
Blazing up into golden stones.
I lean back, as the evening darkens and comes on.
A chicken hawk floats over, looking for home.
I have wasted my life.

The last line, particularly the suddenness of it, has kept many a student . . . and professor . . . up late at night. Is he feeling guilty for not working harder? After all, Americans live and die for their jobs. Certainly, you and I are good examples. Or is he saying that he has worked too hard and lying there on the hammock watching the things he hasn't noticed before suddenly makes him realize just how much time he has wasted?

The other poem that my class, and now perhaps you, had to wrestle with is by Robert Bly, a well-known poet, who happened to be James Wright's friend and neighbor. It is entitled "Watering the Horse."

How strange to think of giving up all ambition!
Suddenly I see with such clear eyes
The white flake of snow
That has just fallen in the horse's mane!

Is Bly suggesting that we give up all ambition? That's the first question I ask the class to get the discussion started. You and I know full well how we would have responded to that suggestion as young men. Would we respond the same way now if we had it to do all over again? Yet when he decides to do so, he suddenly sees with clear eyes, suggesting perhaps by way of hyperbole that we all need to live in more than one dimension. Or is he really telling us that it's not so bad to reach old age, provided we can let go of our ambitions?

Did Beany select these poems because they suggested - better a life than a career or a career within a life, as opposed to a life within a career. Was this, I wondered, the beginning of regret, a first step down the road to suicide?

Well, my dear boy, we enter the last decade before the new millennium pretty much where we were during the prior four. The world is changing and, of course, we need not and will not change with it. At our age, we can remain old-fashioned and out of step and no one will notice or care. However, I do remain hopeful that before we reach the new millennium, I will at last hear from you, perhaps even see you, and that we can resume a friendship that I have never relinquished.

I leave you with a short poem from Lao Tsu: "If nothing is done, then all will be well."

Don't believe it, he didn't.
With kindest regards,
Roger

I wondered if Beany's letters to Evan would have been much different if he had been writing to God instead. Did Evan really have to exist? He could have been an imaginary friend and accomplished the same purpose. If Beany really wanted to be invisible, what did the reasons or excuses matter. Of course, we don't always know what we really want until we get what we think we did . . . and then it's often too late.

CHAPTER TWENTY-SIX

I did get a note from Jim in the mail early the next week.

"Had the pea soup, got it down and didn't gag. Although it didn't help, I did sleep through the night for the second time in a long time. You were the first."

So it did help, I thought. But when he didn't show up the next Thursday, I wondered if he wasn't developing a resistance to my soup like an over-prescribed antibiotic. He did call and speak to Georgina, because I was too busy in the kitchen to come to the telephone.

"He said he was having trouble with his truck," she said.

I nodded.

"But I don't believe him," she added.

"Why is that?"

"Because it sounded rehearsed."

"How does one single sentence about a truck breaking down sound rehearsed?"

"When it comes out in one breath."

"So tell me, Dear Abby, what do you think the real reason is? He's going out with Lisa on the side or has he had enough soup?"

"He's falling for you and getting cold feet. Guys like that hate commitment."

"All he's committing to is soup on Thursday nights."

"Yeah, right, and sleeping with the cook is your standard tip. It's not easy for a confirmed bachelor."

"Beany was a confirmed bachelor," I said. "You can't be a confirmed bachelor at 30."

"What's the right age?"

"45," I said, picking the first number that popped into my head.

Georgina laughed.

"Maybe his secrets are getting the best of him," she said.

I nodded, that I could agree with.

"You mark my words," she said, "if he doesn't show up next week, it's because he's decided to go back into his shell. I'm sure he can find an occasional tumble in any one of the bars up there in the mountains. There's not much else for them to do at night unless they have a satellite dish."

"And if he shows up next Thursday?"

"You can reel him in, hook, line, and sinker."

"And tell me again just how much experience you've had with men?" I asked.

"Counting all my mother's husbands?"

We both laughed.

Georgina stayed around to help me clean up, probably because she felt badly about leaving me alone.

"What do you think his big secret is?" she asked.

"I have no idea."

"Maybe he had a sex change operation," Georgina said with a big grin, "and his real name is Jaime."

I suppose that would be perfect for me, I thought.

"I've seen the equipment . . . it's original issue."

We both laughed.

"Something to do with his mother or father, that's my guess," I said. "She died young and Jim doesn't speak to his father anymore."

"I doubt that's it," Georgina said. "Everyone has parent problems, they're a dime a dozen. I think it's an old girlfriend. It's always another woman."

"Experience talking again?"

"Do I get to count how many times I've been dumped? I can beat your three by a mile."

"Two weeks doesn't count as a meaningful relationship."

"What if she dumped him and he did something awful to her," Georgina said, "like throwing lye in her face."

"You've been reading too many romance magazines."

"What if she dumped him for his best friend?"

"I don't see Jim as the vengeful type."

"What if it was an accident and he was high on drugs? What if he was in jail?"

"Rehabilitated, it wouldn't bother me."

"Wouldn't it depend on what he was in for?"

"If it was something really bad, he'd still be there."

I tried to think of something Jim could have done that would make a difference, but I couldn't, which was a sure sign that my Kinsey meter had moved decidedly off center.

Beany's letter that Thursday was relatively short and was dated February 2, 1994, Groundhog Day. Apparently, he didn't write Evan when Bill Clinton won the Presidency or if he did, he didn't include it in my inheritance. He clearly culled out the letters he wanted me to read, still the professor trying to control the direction of his class even from the great beyond. It was written to someone whose name I didn't recognize, but it wasn't hard to figure out that he was an attorney.

Dear Harold,

Thank you for taking the time to consult with me on Monday with respect to my estate. I am now 72 and while I still enjoy my corporeal existence, especially when it comes to food and drink, and have no immediate plans to depart, I do recognize that at my age the train might leave the station at any moment. As I have no relatives, at least none close enough to require a Christmas card I do need to decide on what to do with my house, which has grown remarkably in value over the years, its furnishings, which have kept pace, and my meager, yet respectable savings.

I have thought about some of the charities that you mentioned, but my contribution would be a drop in the proverbial bucket. I have thought about endowing a chair at the college, but the professors around here do too much sitting as it is. I even thought about a scholarship, but have decided to leave that up to the government and the Financial Aid Department. Instead, what I would like you to do is endow a Smith College poetry contest entitled the Poetry of Loss. Submissions will require a collection of 20 or more poems all dealing with the theme of loss with a monetary prize and a private printing of the winning collection. Oh yes, the contestants must all be over 50. I will leave the details up to the contest judges, who should be from the college. I will give it some more thought, but I think the judges should be the Chairpersons of the Science, English and Physical Education Departments; the mind, the heart, and the body, an apt combination of the mental, emotional, and physical that ought to make for some passionate debate and interesting decisions.

As for my remains, cremate them and scatter them off Race Point in Provincetown. I've always enjoyed my visits there. I will leave it up to you to find someone the estate can pay to take care of that.

Let me know when the documents are ready for execution.

Respectfully,

Roger Beanstock

I didn't know that Beany was a fan of Provincetown, but it didn't surprise me. He could be invisible there, a spectator, a reader of sorts, studying everyone else's life, exactly the way he liked it.

I sat there drinking my wine for quite a while wondering why Beany included this letter in my packet, perhaps to confirm that he approached death the same way he did life, dispassionately and decisively. I would have just given the money, not surprisingly, to the nearest soup kitchen. Feeding the hungry could be my legacy, although the more I thought about it the more I realized that Beany had the same idea, except he wanted to feed the hungry mind instead of the body. Limiting it to aspiring poets over 50 was a nice touch.

In the end, I think the real reason Beany included this letter was to show me just how lonely the road he had chosen was, particularly as he approached the end and had to strain to find a way to dispose of his assets, as well as his remains.

The letter made me think of this one Thursday night. It was early spring and the world was filled with buds and mud. I had made three pleasant spring soups, Cauliflower and Spinach with Tarragon, Golden Beet and Pea with Fennel and Asparagus with Turnip Greens and Red Potatoes, relatively airy soups that can help rekindle love and life.

Beany was a little sad to say goodbye to the winter soups, which were his favorite, not surprisingly since they were hearty soups made to strengthen resolve and fortitude in the dark and sometimes lonely winter months; although little did I know that he'd never have another one of my winter soups again. Maybe he had a sense of that. Beany used to say that the big decisions in his life simmered for a long time, like my soup, except in his subconscious instead of on the stove, and popped out fully formed when they were ready.

Anyway, this was the first really warm night of the spring, long in coming, since the nights usually remained cool and crisp for quite some time in this part of Massachusetts. Beany was overdressed in his long wool coat and hat, so he started off hot and a bit irascible. The soup and wine dulled the edge a bit.

"How's my young protégé this evening," he said, when I came out with my empty glass, which Beany promptly filled. After I started refusing to accept payment for the soup, he insisted on supplying my wine for the evening, so he always brought along two bottles. Sharing one would not have been enough for him.

"The same as I was last Thursday evening."

"Now some people would say that's good, the ones who worship consistency and routine . . . like me. But I think you're different."

"No, I'm not," I said, and I really believed it at the time. Why else was I considering a life of abstinence and working seven days a week making soup? It was a life of routines, which would also explain why I needed my Thursday nights with Beany.

"Have you ever noticed how different your voice sounds when you hear it recorded?" he said.

"I can barely recognize myself," I said, "I always sound so squeaky."

"That's my point," he said, "it is the same thing with personalities. The hardest thing for anyone to see is their own true self. I've got a much better vantage point out here and I say without the slightest hesitation or doubt that you're not afraid of surprises. Indeed, I'd go so far as to say that you like the unexpected. Sure, you need some routine and consistency in life like everyone else, but you don't crave it the way I do. That's how you were able to jump so easily from Nick to Jake to Jolene, and from Plattsburgh to San Francisco to Northampton. You can handle the everyday accidents and changes in this mundane world. Perhaps with a little help from your soups. I never had that in me. Soup or no soup, I can't bear uncertainty."

"That's a crock," I said. "Isn't that what you teach your students, how to handle life unexpected through books and poetry?"

"The authors do that, I don't. I study and I write. I'm all about myself and my solitude. Teaching is a necessary evil. I do it to make a living and I do it in a place and on a subject well removed from real life. It's not like I'm teaching elementary school. You're very different than I am; you won't get very far down my road without drowning in regrets."

"You're in a good mood tonight," I said.

"A mood for truth; the spring brings it up like skunk grass."

"Wouldn't crocuses be a better analogy?"

"Simile, more fragrant perhaps, but not better, the truth is rarely very flowery. More often it is a weed."

"Well, I think you are wrong about me. I think I will make a great old maid."

"Oh, I'm sure you could play the part well; you're intelligent, not quick to anger, a good traveler, a real journeyman – journeywoman of sorts, not the type to wallow in self-pity, or let great ambitions depress you, and certainly not the type to carry your emotions out in front of you all the time like a burning candle."

"It's the soup."

"It's more than the soup. It's your make-up, it's who you are. You might play a great old maid, but you will never be a happy or contented one . . . not like me."

"And you're content?"

Beany lifted his glass.

"With the soup, yes, but the wine is a little too oaky for my taste."

"Seriously."

"Seriously," Beany said with a smile.

Now Beany often tried to gently dissuade me from following in his footsteps, but he had never been this direct or adamant, and I suspected that he might have started his drinking that evening a little earlier than usual.

"So should I flip a coin," I said, "heads heterosexual, tails homosexual, or should I just stick with both? I could take turns. It'll be like spending my life stuck in a revolving door."

"Pick one, stick with it."

"Easier said than done."

"Who promised you easy?" Beany said.

"A bit didactic tonight for the Socratic professor, don't you think?"

"Sometimes near the end of the semester you have to give out an answer or two."

"If I can't discover it for myself, I haven't learned it."

Beany sighed, which he didn't often do, finished his glass of wine, which was half full, and refilled it along with mine.

"Are you all right?" I asked.

"Forget what I said. You will do what you want. That much we have in common."

Suddenly, I saw something in his eyes, a fresh sadness, something new and raw.

"Did something happen today?" I asked.

"I am sure that something did somewhere in the world, but except for a few parking tickets and a late paper or two, I'm not sure much happened at Smith."

Beany's pupils grew smaller as he tried a smile, which lingered on his face long after the effort, like something left etched in the sand. Beany suddenly looked very tired.

"Some more soup?" I asked.

He shook his head no. Sometimes it's like refusing an aspirin when you have a headache, you're not quite ready to give up on the pain and prefer to let it run its course. I didn't push it and we polished off the second bottle of wine in silence with Beany staring out the window, while I stared at him wondering about the anxiety that must take hold of someone his age – and in his circumstance – from time to time, because of what can be lost so suddenly and the dreams that still remain out of reach. Of course, I thought that dream was his place in the world of poetry among the immortal ones.

CHAPTER TWENTY-SEVEN

I think I agreed with Georgina that what Jim did that next Thursday would either make or break our relationship, and I was honestly uncertain whether he would decide to come or not, especially since I didn't hear from him at all during the week, either on the telephone or by mail, and he clearly knew where to find me.

"The betting line is 3 to 2 against you," Georgina said during the height of the dinner hour, while she was waiting for me to fill up some bowls with soup.

"Who's making the book Lisa or Joe?"

"Neither, I am, and the only one betting he'll show is Joe. He says no guy can pass up free soup and sex."

"What makes him think the soup is free?" I said.

Georgina made a face.

"It's still early."

"But it's getting late fast," she said, picking up two bowls of soup and heading back into the dining room.

The next time there was a lull she came back into the kitchen to chase me away from the window.

"Which soup did you make for him?"

"What makes you think I made anything special for him?"

"You did for Beany."

"That was different," I said.

"No it's not," Georgina said, "you specialize in soup for lost souls . . . Jim's just replaced Beany's, except he's a friend with privileges."

"You are so . . . so . . . ."

"So what?"

"So young."

"So which soup is for him?" Georgina said.

"The Tuscan Bean."

A basic soup for a basic decision - fresh beans, firm to the eye and tender in the mouth, onions, carrots, garlic, olive oil and fresh sage – a dense, earthy soup to help loosen that seemingly irresistible hold that the past sometimes has on us. Some cooks will add elbow macaroni or diced potatoes, but I don't. I'm a purist with Tuscan Bean and when I'm having difficulty shaking something from my mind it's one of my first choices.

"It gives me gas," Georgina said.

"To good benefit," I said and we both laughed.

"If he doesn't show up tonight," she said, "I'm not letting him back in here again."

"I think there are a few tables in there that need more bread," I said, placing some extra focaccia on her tray.

"It's almost ten," Georgina said the next time she came back into the kitchen.

There were only a few tables still occupied.

"He's not the kind of guy who's a slave to a schedule. He doesn't even wear a wristwatch."

"We're talking about a date here, not a job interview."

"And he has a ways to drive."

She walked over to the door and peered into the dining room. Somehow I knew Jim was coming, call it soup intuition.

"You know," Georgina said, "I think you'd do well if you got an espresso machine."

"I don't want to encourage coffee."

"I know, I know, too much caffeine can dilute the benefits of the soup."

"We're plenty busy as it is," I said. "And besides, the town has plenty of coffee shops."

"Starbucks is the only one that stays open late."

"I don't want to become a hangout for the college crowd pulling all-nighters."

Georgina looked at her watch and then stared through the kitchen door window.

"He'll be here," I said.

I remember my mother once telling me that if you say something forcefully and out loud it's more likely to come true – the opposite of wishing on a star. I'm sure she told me that to make sure I didn't keep anything from her, but I was a little girl and that irrational belief has sort of stuck with me.

"How many tables are left?" I asked.

"Two," she said, her face pressed against the window. "Wait, someone's coming in."

I busied myself checking out the list of ingredients I needed for tomorrow.

"It's him," Georgina said, grabbing some focaccia and a big bowl and handing it to me to fill with Tuscan Bean. She also poured me a glass of wine from the bottle I had opened earlier in the evening.

"You want me to stick around and help clean up."

"Tomorrow is fine," I said. "You can leave as soon as those two tables do."

"But I want all the details."

Jim had two bowls of soup by the time Georgina left and I finished up in the kitchen. I took off my apron and joined him, wine in hand.

"I wasn't sure you'd come," I said.

"I wasn't either for a while, but not because I didn't want to."

"I understand."

"Because I did and do, I just didn't know if I could live up to your conditions."

"Telling me the truth?"

Jim nodded and looked down at the soup.

"Truth serum?" he asked.

"Tuscan Bean . . . helps let go of the past. Of course, it takes some willingness and effort on your part."

"I'm here."

"You most certainly are and I'm ready whenever you are."

Jim ate the soup slowly.

"This is incredible," he said, "whether it works or not."

I just sat quietly watching him eat.

"What's that herb?"

"Sage."

"You can almost feel it."

"It's been used over the years for everything from snakebites to menstrual cramps."

"Well, I've got neither."

"As well as depression."

Jim nodded thoughtfully, while he continued to eat the soup

"Would you come back to my place?" he said.

I must have looked a bit confused, because he didn't wait for me to respond but explained that it would be easier for him there than here.

"This place is all about you," he said. "I love being here and I don't want to bring those feelings into Circa."

I didn't have to think about it for more than a few seconds.

"I'll get my bag," I said, "it's in the kitchen."

"You always come prepared?"

"Like a girl scout, and I'll put together a bag with some ingredients to make a soup."

"In case we get hungry?"

"I can make a soup while you talk. I'll be a better listener if I'm cooking and eating it will make it easier for both of us . . . however things turn out."

"What kind of soup?"

"Something simple that doesn't require pureeing, because I assume you don't have a mixer or a blender."

"No."

"How about a Vegetarian Jambalaya, onions, celery, green pepper, mushrooms, tomatoes, long grain rice, garlic, olive oil, parsley, paprika, cayenne pepper and chili powder."

"You have that all in the back?"

"It's on tomorrow's menu," I said. "It's easy to make and it tastes great."

"And?"

"It's a good soup if you're feeling indecisive and need a little push . . . or a big push."

"How come I'm not surprised," Jim said with a smile.

I went in back and filled a grocery bag with what I needed. I also grabbed a loaf of Semolina. It was a day old, but that didn't matter when it came to Jambalaya.

Jim kept the conversation light on the ride up talking about some of the new furniture orders he was working on. He was doing a whole reading room for a bed and breakfast that involved a couple of big oak rockers, a desk and four walls filled with bookcases. He was also doing another dining room table that would seat 20 and not the expandable kind. With inlays, he said, which would present a big challenge since he'd be working with some rare woods he'd never worked with before. It would be the most expensive piece he'd ever made.

"I wish I were as good with people as wood," he said.

"If you can do one thing well, you can do everything well," I said.

"Beany?"

"My grandmother used to tell me that all the time."

"I suppose the opposite would be true as well," Jim said. "If you let one thing stop you, then everything will."

"Not everything works in reverse," I said. "It's not the way I would look at it."

"Because you tend to look at the positive, while I look at the negative."

"I don't believe that."

"It's true," Jim said his shoulders slumped forward over the wheel.

"Two people who like what they do as much as we do, already have more in common than most of the couples I've met."

"I don't think the problem is you and me together," Jim said, as we pulled into his driveway.

"So what do you think the problem is?"

"It's not you. I don't care who you're attracted to, as long as it includes me."

"And you already know that it does," I said quietly. "I don't usually sleep with my customers, no matter how much they like the soup."

Jim smiled, one of his genuine smiles that did reach his eyes.

"I know," he said, "I heard all about your automotive sweetheart."

"It's nice to know Lisa is such a good gossip."

"Every small town needs someone to spread the news."

Jim turned off the engine and we sat there a moment overcome by the sudden silence, which in a place like Colrain can take your breath away, like a gust of frigid wind.

"I'm the problem," Jim said.

"Nothing you did or didn't do is going to change how I feel," I said.

"I know that, which is why I'm the problem. I don't know if I could live through it again."

"Bad things happen to everyone. You have to be able to leave the wreckage on the side of the road and move on."

"That's my point," Jim said, and I didn't like the sound of that at all. They sounded like the words of someone who at one time had seriously considered doing what it took Beany 60 years to accomplish.

I followed Jim into the house.

"You turned the heat up," I said, "so my coming back wasn't all that much of a surprise."

"A boy scout is always prepared," he said with a smile.

"I'm going to run upstairs to change into something comfortable then I'm coming down to start the soup."

"You need a big pot?"

"Oops," I said, "I forgot about that. What have you got?"

"There's an old one in the barn. I'll be right back."

I hoped Jim didn't have his hopes up, because I wasn't changing into some flimsy negligee. I brought my favorite flannel pajamas, the ones with feet, despite the fact that they hid all my curves and made me look more like a little boy or maybe because of it. Jim might as well see me at my worst, especially if I was about to see him at his.

When I got down to the kitchen, Jim was scrubbing at a big pot that had to be fifty years old.

"How do I look?" I asked, opening my arms so he could get a full view of the flowers on the pajamas that covered me from head to toe.

"Like a farm girl in a meadow."

"Perfect."

"Is this pot OK?"

"It's better than OK, but stop scrubbing it," I said rushing over to take it from his hands. "It's just like the old cast iron pot my grandmother had."

I examined the inside for cracks. There were none.

"You can't buy these, except at a flea market. They're great for soups. They cook evenly and consistently, and they hold onto the heat."

"Don't they stick?"

"Are you kidding, not if they're seasoned; cast iron is naturally non-stick. All I need is a little olive oil to re-season it. It gets absorbed right in."

"I don't have any olive oil."

"I brought some."

Jim sat down at the kitchen table to get out of my way.

I loved the way the pot felt in my hand and I loved its age. I could read its history in the dings and scratches, and almost smell traces of the old soups it once held. It seemed very appropriate to this old kitchen with its faded and cracked linoleum floor and single overhead light fixture.

"Can I help?" Jim asked.

"Just step out of the way. This is my workshop and using the tools without training can be dangerous . . . to the soup."

Jim smiled and leaned back on his chair. I noticed a second chair, its equal in terms of age and abuse, now sitting on the other side of the table. The last time I was here there was only one.

"Can I at least help chop?" Jim asked.

"No, when I make a soup, at least at home, I have to do everything. This way I can block out any other distractions. It's part of the healing process. Just sit there and keep me company."

The truth is that I needed to keep focused on preparing the soup to keep my balance since I had no idea what to expect from Jim. Before I started I took out a bottle of wine, opened it with the corkscrew I brought in case Jim didn't have one, and found a clean mug to use as a wine glass.

"Would you like any?" I asked in case his refusal to drink was only limited to outside the home.

Jim shook his head no and I set about curing the pot with olive oil. While I waited for the oil to heat up, I chopped the onions and celery, and sliced the garlic as thin as I could with the one dull kitchen knife I found in the utensil drawer. I then emptied out the olive oil and wiped the residue into the pot with a paper towel. Once that was done I tossed in the butter, which melted quickly, and began sautéing the onions and garlic. Nothing turns a chilly, bare room into a home quicker than the smells of onions and garlic.

"I don't remember anymore how to cook for two," I said, "so you're going to have enough soup for the entire week."

"Good, I'm tired of the supermarket's roast chicken."

I started chopping the green peppers and tomatoes, and measuring out the rice. I liked having all my ingredients ready and waiting.

"I brought my own vegetable stock," I said, bringing out a container of broth that I had grabbed from the freezer. It was still not completely defrosted.

"Frozen? That doesn't sound like you."

"I make it fresh in big batches on Mondays and then freeze it. If I had to make the broth from scratch every day I'd have to move into the restaurant."

Jim smiled. He had a nice, easy smile when he let it go, when he wasn't fully conscious of what was hiding behind it.

"You know," I said, "you're the one who's supposed to be doing the talking tonight, not me."

The smile disappeared and Jim took a deep breath.

"You sure you don't want a sip of wine to get you started?"

Jim shook his head slowly from side to side

"So tell me why," I said to get things started, "you once thought about following in Beany's footsteps . . . and I don't just mean by living alone."

Jim cleared his throat, stood up and walked over to the window. He pushed aside the curtain, which looked like it had once been much thicker and a brighter color, perhaps yellow, but had grown thin and transparent with age, and bleached a dull white by years of sunlight. It was dark outside with no moon and not a single star, the kind of night that can make a person living alone feel trapped, like they've been taken captive by something they can't even see. Jim pressed his ear against the window, as if he were trying to hear something or someone in some kind of ghostly proximity on the other side.

I put in the vegetable stock to thaw and turned down the flame. I half expected Jim to just blurt it out like - "I once killed a man" - but I knew it wasn't going to be that quick or easy. He needed to find a way to get at the disappointment and anger. Of course, it never stopped squeezing his heart, but it had been hiding for so long behind his detachment and vagueness that it had to be hard to reach. The things we carry around silently within us may not always have our undivided attention, but they always have a voice and they can't ever be trusted. They become more possessive and defiant over time unless you do something. Dislodging them is a slow, difficult process, but that's the nature of most important things in life from preparing soup to building a meaningful relationship.

"I always thought I would live my whole life in Maine," Jim finally said, turning from the window, "not near my old man, but somewhere along the coast. I never liked flat sandy beaches as much as rocky ones. There's something about lying down to catch the sun on one of those giant rocks that the ocean has worn smooth and tossed up against the shore like a pebble, the pulse of the sea beating in your ears, the smells from distant shores in the air that makes you so aware that you're alive . . . and how little you really know."

"Were you this existential back then?" I asked.

"I could never put into words what I felt back then, maybe because I never thought much about it. I've had a lot of quiet time over the last five years to make up for it. Of course, now I do nothing else but read and think . . . except when I'm working in the shop."

"Which is why I'm in the kitchen seven days a week," I said. "Too much uninterrupted thinking turns everything silent and still."

Jim nodded.

"Sometimes I think so much my head hurts."

"Sometimes all that thinking makes you feel lonelier," I said, "even when you're around other people."

"Not just sometimes," Jim said.

I stopped my preparations and looked over at Jim hoping to catch his eye, but he just continued to stare out the window behind a dark, distant gaze.

"All the more reason," I said, "that lovers need to be completely honest. I never want you . . . or any partner . . . to feel lonely around me."

"I don't, I never have, that's just the thing, I don't know why . . . not from that very first night at Circa when you came out of the kitchen. It's what makes it seem OK. Maybe it was the soup . . . or just the way you looked at me . . . like you saw something no one else did, like it was meant to be."

I nodded, too choked up to speak.

"Which is the reason I decided to choose life."

"Life?"

It scared me a bit to hear Jim talk in terms of life like that, as if it were some loose thread you could cut away with a snip of the scissors or some meaningless possession you could discard like a week-old newspaper.

"I don't like the sound of that," I added.

Jim cleared his throat.

"I didn't mean it the way it sounded," he said. "I mean life as in being out there again with someone else; love would probably have been a better word. I've decided in favor of love, as opposed to against it."

Jim looked down at his hands as if to make sure.

"You were talking about the Maine coast," I said to bring Jim back to where he left off.

He nodded and tried to smile. It wasn't one of his easy ones.

"Do you know that Maine is the country's biggest exporter of blueberries and tooth picks?"

"Essential for pancake houses everywhere."

"Most of the nation thinks we must all be strange to want to live in a place with such long, severe winters, but I think that's one of the reasons we do. I love to see my breath in the mornings and hear the sound of the ice cracking in the pine trees at night. It makes the other seasons that much sweeter."

"The way suffering and pain helps us appreciate pleasure."

"I suppose," Jim said, turning to look at me, "but the winter has its own pleasure, its own beauty and it's anything but still. There are birds that actually fly south to winter in Maine. I loved the challenge of living in the Maine winter. It's like nothing else can ever destroy you after that."

Jim took a breath and looked up again at the empty sky out the window. I don't know what he was trying to see, since everything was black and hidden away by a low layer of dark, invisible clouds. Maybe he just needed the blank background to help bring his past into better focus.

I turned back to the soup and immediately realized that I had been a bit too generous with the spices. I never use measurements when it comes to seasoning, relying instead on my intuition, which had been too distracted by Jim's words to pay close attention. I stirred the soup vigorously to hide the evidence and decided to simmer it longer than usual to reduce its potency. Heat and time will do that to just about anything, as well as anyone.

Jim walked away from the window and sat back down on the chair.

"I always liked to build things with my hands. I built my own tree house when I was 10 without any help from my father, who said it was a useless project. I had to scavenge for wood and nails and my mother helped with the roof by finding some old shingles. It was right before she got sick. I lived out there for about week after she died."

"That must have been hard on you."

Jim nodded, his mouth closed so tight it looked like a long scar.

"Particularly on someone with a father like that," I said.

"I couldn't wait to get out of there and away from him," Jim said. "I didn't know where I was going after high school, but it was away. I thought about the military, but I didn't want to trade one tyrant for another. I had been yelled at and ordered around enough for one life."

"Where did you go?"

"I moved a couple of mountains away with a buddy of mine to this small town and took a job in a lumber yard cutting 2 by 4s and stacking plywood. I was happy to be on my own."

"Did something happen at the lumberyard?"

"Like what?"

"Someone's always cutting off an arm in the movies."

"No, about the worst thing I can remember happening was getting sawdust in my eye. I hated wearing those safety goggles. I was a kid, so what did I know."

"Are you going to make me guess?" I asked.

The infinite patience I had for myself while making soup wasn't transferring as easily to Jim.

"I'm sorry," I said, before Jim could respond. "Take your time. I'm just a little anxious."

Jim wiped his palms on his pants. His cheeks were flushed and I could see this small vein on his temple beating along with his heart.

"No, you're right," he said, rocking forward on the chair and then falling back against it. He stared at his hands, turning them over and over as if they held the key. I remembered reading once how people can sometimes feel a memory as much as they can visualize it. Why shouldn't touch be as strong as smell or sight when it comes to bringing back the past?

"I was once married," Jim said without looking up, the numbness of her absence in his hands, and I swallowed hard as I turned to stir the soup.

It wasn't hard to figure out what was coming.

"It seems so long ago and so far away, although it wasn't . . . and isn't."

Jim looked up. His eyes were as dark and heavy as the low, black clouds outside.

"How did you meet?"

"I met Maggie about a year after high school," Jim said, squeezing his hands into fists and then opening them slowly. "I called her Magpie. She was from Orono, a small town on the other side of the mountain. I knew the town, because I made some lumber deliveries there and did a little carpentry work on my own time for a guy who was opening up a coffee shop, you know, framing walls and building shelves."

It's strange, I thought, the way small details like that become such an important part of a memory, almost as if they're necessary to protect someone – the listener or the speaker - from too sudden an exposure, a sort of safeguard against the danger of sudden, intimate recall.

"I went to the movies with my old high school buddy, Steve Mills. We were talking about moving together down to Kennebunkport. His cousin knew a general contractor down there who was looking for a couple of young guys willing to work cheap. Steve wanted to be an electrician. I wanted to be a carpenter."

Jim closed his eyes, as if he needed some stillness to catch his breath. I tried not to make a sound, although every breath I took seemed to echo around the kitchen.

"Maggie was with a friend who Steve knew and we wound up at a bar afterward drinking beers."

Jim smiled, not at me, because his eyes were still closed, but at the picture I imagined he was seeing of the four of them sitting in a booth in the dim light, a bowl of pretzels and a pitcher of beer on the table, their words floating to the ceiling, hardly noticeable as the static electricity crackled each time their eyes met or their feet lightly brushed against each other under the table.

"Maggie had just graduated high school, although she looked all of about 16. She had this great laugh that seemed to come from someplace deep inside her, that made her eyes water and her long, curly red hair shake."

Jim stopped for a moment like there was something important he was trying to remember.

"She could hardly sit still most of the time, like she was always about ready to jump up and do something, and when she talked her hands danced in the air. She kept touching me on the forearm when she wanted to make a point."

Jim looked up at me.

"It was the weirdest thing - all I wanted that first night was her approval. I searched for it every time she looked into my eyes and I knew it as soon as I saw it . . . it was almost like looking at tomorrow. I hadn't had that feeling since before my mother died. I certainly never got it from my father."

"That's really beautiful," I said. "It's as good a definition of love as I've ever heard."

"I see tomorrow when I look at you as well," he said, which went down better than any soup I've ever made. It wasn't a line, Jim wasn't just saying that. I could feel that. Besides, I really did believe in the truth of what he was saying, because there are many souls in each life that we can love and who can love us. Each love has its own logic and momentum, and whether I admitted it or not some of what Beany had talked about did sink in. The heart has a limitless capacity, if only you don't bar the door and board up the windows.

"Maggie wasn't all that pretty."

"People are beautiful because we love them. We don't love them because they're beautiful."

Jim nodded.

I had to resist my natural inclination to reach out and touch Jim's forearm, because I didn't want to intrude on his memory of Maggie doing that.

"She was short and a bit wide around the hips and she always complained that her features were too close together," Jim said with a real smile this time. "She said she had a crayon face . . . like a child might draw, but she didn't. There were so many cute things about her, like the way she used to crinkle her nose when she wasn't sure about something and blush bright red when she was surprised. And when she smiled, her whole face smiled, even her eyebrows. People liked to be with her. I think it was because she was so comfortable in her own skin. You know what I mean?"

I nodded. I've always envied people like that. They always know what to say and they always seem so content with themselves.

"You could see it in her eyes . . . she was never the least bit self-conscious. Aside from my mother, I had never met a girl so easy to talk to."

Jim looked up at me and smiled.

"Don't say it," I said.

"But you are easy to talk to."

"You're more mature now. It gets easier as you get older, especially after I dope you up with my soup."

"Well, I'm going to need some soon," he said. "How is it coming?"

"Slowly, like you. You can't rush soup."

Jim walked over to the pot and lifted the plate I was using as a lid.

"It smells great."

"If I could figure out how to turn that into an air freshener, I'd make a fortune."

Jim rested his hand on my back for a moment and then walked over to the window again.

"What a dark night," he said, pulling the curtain to one side. "I hate it when there are no stars."

Jim stared outside for a while as if he were waiting for the energy to leave the moment again and return to the past.

"You know what first love is like," he said.

"What about all your girlfriends in high school?" I asked. "I'm sure there were plenty of those."

"We hung out in packs, broke off in pairs from time to time, but nothing lasted very long or seemed all that meaningful. Besides, my father kept me pretty busy with chores."

Jim took a deep breath, held it in for a moment and then let it out slowly.

"We went out the next night and the night after that, and Steve wound up moving to Kennebunkport without me."

I added the mushrooms and rice, which were the last ingredients to go in, while Jim went on to describe their courtship. They were one of those combinations that clicked from the start, like leeks and potatoes, and mushrooms and barley. The ones that take longer, like peas and ham, and Jim and I, are more an acquired taste. They're less predictable, but no less rewarding in the end.

"We got married about six months later," Jim said. "We were really young and poor, but there was nothing to stop us. I was living alone and Maggie had been planning to move in with one of her girlfriends. She couldn't wait to get started with real life, as she put it. Besides, we were in love."

"Which is all that matters," I said.

"People don't wait to get on with their lives in Maine, not like they do around here, so we moved to this small house in Machias, which is on the coast near the Canadian border. It was the cutest little place with one bedroom and a kitchen that you could barely turn around in, but the rent was cheap, in part because I agreed to fix it up. I was doing general carpentry full time by then, working for a couple of builders and Magpie took a job at the town elementary school as a teacher's assistant.

"After a couple of weeks, I felt as if I knew every one of the kids in her class. She couldn't stop talking about them. From that moment on she knew exactly what she wanted to do and she started taking courses at the community college to get a teaching degree. Maggie loved little children and little dogs, anything she could wrap her arms around."

"Did you guys get a dog?"

"We got a mutt from the shelter, part terrier and part beagle. He was Maggie's dog really, she took care of him. She called him Fortune, short for fortunate, because she said we were fortunate to find him."

"What happened to Fortune?"

"He ran away . . . sort of."

Jim's eyes glazed over and he looked toward the window.

"I didn't feel the same way . . . about kids, maybe because I was an only child. Maggie came from a big family, but it didn't matter much to me either way. I'd have gone along with whatever she wanted. I just wasn't sure what kind of father I'd be, since I didn't have much of an example growing up."

"I think you'd be a great father," I said, in part to hear myself speak, as well as to drown out my own heart, which was beating in my ears.

"I think I'd be all right now, but that was back then when I was younger . . . and stupider. Anyway, Maggie was a planner and she had everything planned out, even the date when she wanted to get pregnant. She was going to get her teaching degree first and get a job. It was going to be the summer after her first year of teaching. This way she could work another half a year and take a maternity leave."

CHAPTER TWENTY-EIGHT

I looked at Jim hunched over the table staring down at his hands and refilled my cup with wine.

"Are you a planner?" Jim asked looking up.

"Only when it comes to soup and the restaurant."

"I'm like that too when I'm building something. You have to know what you need and how you're going to get from point A to point B. I'm terrible when it comes to everything else. I never know what I'm going to eat until five minutes before I eat it."

"Well, you do now."

"It smells really good. I can't believe that I'm hungry again."

"About another half hour, take a deep breathe though it'll be good for you."

So Jim walked over to the stove and did, smiling weakly as he returned to his seat.

"We can go into the living room if you want while it simmers," I said. "I can just come back once in a while to stir it."

"I'm OK here. I like watching you cook."

So I stirred the soup and added some dill to look busy.

"We were doing pretty well for a couple of kids. I was always busy and they really liked Maggie at school. The principal said he'd hire her as a teacher as soon as she graduated, but then the plan got a bit derailed."

"What happened?"

Jim's eyes, damp and dim, disappeared almost as if he had turned them around so they were looking in instead of out. He said something, but I couldn't make it out, not with the plate rattling on top of the pot as the soup simmered.

"What did you just say?"

"Maggie got pregnant," Jim said, louder this time.

"Thank God," I said, without thinking. "I was afraid it was cancer."

"What made you think that?"

"Because I know this isn't going to have a happy ending."

Jim bit down on his lower lip while nodding slowly.

"It was one of those Saturday nights, when we had a little too much to drink and Maggie thought it was safe. You know, right before her period or right after, I don't really remember which."

"Neither is completely safe."

"We learned that soon enough. You'd think they'd teach a few useful things like that in high school."

Jim didn't say another word for the next few minutes, spending most of that time gazing down at his hands.

"Did she get an abortion?" I finally asked to bring him back to the present.

When Jim looked up his face was red, as if he had just come in from the cold or he was the one actually drinking a whole bottle of wine.

"No, Maggie would never do anything like that. She was quiet for about a day or two, before she came up with her new plan. She would continue working and taking classes while she was pregnant and after she had the baby, she'd take a part-time job in a daycare center. Babies can go anywhere, she said, and at night I could watch the baby while she went to school. After she got her degree and started teaching, we'd be able to afford full-time daycare and teaching hours were so good that it would be easy."

Jim sighed and hesitated.

"That must have seemed a little scary," I said catching his eye.

"It was, I mean we were doing OK between the two of us, but I was all of 23."

I turned around to look at the soup. I can always tell when it's ready by the color. You can do that with a lot of foods. When I cook spaghetti I never have to time it or taste it; al dente has a look about it that I can readily see, although it's hard to describe. Since I could see that the soup was just about ready, I turned the burner down as low as possible.

Jim stood up and walked back over to the window.

"It was a starless night, just like tonight. Nothing moved. The sun had set early and it was as if all at once everything went dark. There's no twilight during the winter in Maine. Even the ocean was still, too still, eerily still. I like it better when the wind blows and the waves are crashing against the rocks. I bet there's a storm coming, I said to Maggie."

Jim looked around the room for a moment, as if he had lost something.

"It was Maggie's 21st birthday - legal drinking age - and I insisted we go out for a drink. It really didn't mean that much, since she'd been drinking with me at the local bars since we got there. Pretty much every bartender knew us and no one cared. Who's going to tell a married woman she's too young to drink?

"She wasn't drinking much, because of the baby. She was about 4 and 1/2 months pregnant and just beginning to show. I think she had one glass of wine, maybe two. She had read somewhere that wine was safer for the fetus. I was strictly drinking beer back then. I must have put in about 10 days straight on this house some Boston Brahmin was building as a weekend retreat."

Jim turned from the window and caught me staring at him.

"Do you really want to hear this?"

"I do," I said. "It's as important for you to say it as it is for me to hear it. When's the last time you talked about any of this with anyone?"

"This will be both the first time . . . and hopefully the last time."

Jim walked back to the chair and sat down. His breathing slowed and he sat there a few moments lost in thought.

"We were at Hunter's Bar, which was about four miles up Storm Mountain Road. It was Maggie's favorite, because dogs were allowed so we got to bring Fortune with us. It was about 10 o'clock, early for a Friday night; usually we'd hang out until after midnight. A lot of people we knew were there, some guys from work, a couple of Maggie's friends from school, and she was having a great time showing off her belly and her birthday present."

"What was it?"

"Did you see that little box in the bedroom?"

"No."

Jim ran upstairs. When he came back he was holding a beautiful mahogany jewelry box about the size of his hand with an inlay on top in the shape of a heart.

"I made it for her out of the scrap wood from the job I was on. I worked on it in the basement after she went to bed. Maggie was an early sleeper."

Jim handed it to me to look at. It was beautiful - an early indication of what his hands would be capable of doing in the future. Their initials were carved on the bottom and there was a gouge on one side that I didn't want to think about.

"It's a work of art," I said. "What was it for?"

"A ruby necklace someday, I told her. Maggie loved rubies because of the ruby slippers in *The Wizard of Oz*."

"She must have loved it."

Jim nodded.

"It's the only thing I have left."

"No photographs?"

He shook his head and swallowed hard.

"I destroyed them all one night when I got really drunk."

I gave Jim back the box and he put it down on the table. He didn't take his eyes off it as he continued talking.

"I was tired and all I wanted to do was go home, turn on the TV and fall asleep on the couch. Fortune was barking at something outside, which got the other dogs barking."

Jim sighed and touched the box.

"Maggie really didn't want to go, I could tell, but she would never say so. That's the way she was, she always wanted to do what everyone else wanted to do. Making you happy made her happy."

Jim looked up.

"I wasn't too tired to drive and I wasn't drunk. I'd driven like that a hundred times before and a lot worse." Jim looked up at me as if to make sure I was following. "If we had stayed one minute longer . . . even if I had gone to the bathroom . . . it would have all turned out differently. Why should a few seconds make such a difference? How can everything turn on a single instant?"

Jim looked down at his hands again. I remembered reading once in a psychology text in college that people near death, whether their own or someone else's, often stare at their hands, as a focal point to distract them from the pain. I thought about walking over to Jim and putting my arm around him, but I've never been good at knowing what's best at moments like this.

"It was cold, but it had been cold all day, so the snow hadn't melted and refrozen and the roads were dry. I wasn't driving fast, not any faster than I'd driven down that road a hundred times before."

Jim stared straight ahead, as if he was driving down that mountain again.

"Maybe if the radio wasn't blasting, Maggie had it turned way up, you know how you listened to music at that age. Maybe I would have heard something."

So now he avoids music, I thought, thinking about the silence that filled Jim's car and workshop, along with alcohol.

"What would you have heard?" I asked. "Was it a blow-out? Did you run over something and lose control?"

Jim stood up and walked over to the window. He looked over his shoulder at me. He looked like a little boy afraid of the night. I took one of the bowls, filled it with soup and put it on the table.

"Have a little soup," I said. "Maybe it'll help."

Jim sat down at the table, looked down at the bowl, but made no effort to pick up the spoon.

"Did you ever see a moose up close, Tess?"

"No."

"This bull was at least 6 feet tall and over 1600 pounds, that's what the sheriff told me. It was the biggest moose he'd ever seen. He was standing there right in the middle of the road when we came around the curve . . . as if he was taking in the scenery, except it was black out, but maybe they see well in the dark, I don't know. Maybe he heard the car or saw the reflection of the headlights off the snow and he froze."

Jim stood up and walked back over to the window.

"Moose are oddly built," he said. "They have this large, heavy body suspended on long, spindly legs, so when the bumper hits them they go flying up into the windshield."

He parted the curtains and looked up and out.

"Maggie was killed instantly. She never said a word. She didn't even have time to scream. I think she might have had her eyes closed. She could have been sleeping. I hope so. I hope she didn't see it coming. I did . . . and I walked away with barely a scratch."

I was the one who sat down and ate some soup. Of course, it didn't help, certainly not enough to keep my hand from shaking.

"My hands were bleeding," Jim said, looking down at them, "but the flying glass missed my face . . . because I ducked, I instinctively ducked, and when I reached over to pull Maggie down . . ."

Jim's chest heaved and he gasped for breath.

"She was dead?" I said to finish the thought for him, trying to make it a little easier if I could.

"Her head was gone."

With that Jim rested his head against the window.

I stood up, walked over and held him from the back.

"It wasn't your fault," I whispered. "It happened so quickly. That's the way accidents happen."

"I never got to say goodbye."

I pressed up against him.

"I should have gone with her."

Jim's breathing was erratic, shallow and uneven.

"It was a little girl," he said, so low I could barely hear him.

"How did you find out?"

"I asked . . . I wanted to give her a name. Maggie would have wanted that."

"What did you call her?"

"Maya, after Maggie, I made the coffin myself. They were buried together."

I led Jim back to the table and made him sit down. I pushed the soup in front of him, but he just stared at it. His eyes had lost their color, the blue fading to a flat white. I thought about that Chinese saying Beany once told me that all of life is a dream walking and all of death is a going home, but I couldn't bring myself to disturb Jim's silence.

"Sometimes when I close my eyes," he said, after what seemed like an hour, "I can't see her anymore, no matter how hard I try. I can see her hands fly as she talks, but I can't see her face . . . not clearly enough."

"Then don't try. Some people you see best with your heart."

Jim didn't respond, but he absentmindedly ate a little soup.

The rest of the evening was far less dramatic. Jim explained that he moved to Northampton about three months later. Everyone in town was as kind as they could be, but he just couldn't take the way they looked at him when they thought he wouldn't notice, as if he had a thread loose and was in danger of unraveling. He could feel their eyes sometimes burning his back like the noon, summer sun. He also hated the way conversations suddenly stopped or changed when he came into a room.

"I didn't want to do carpentry any longer. I wanted to build things on my own in Maggie's honor, as a way of reaffirming her life."

"Reincarnations in Wood," I said, "it's a beautiful name."

"Because there's a little bit of the two of them in everything I make."

"And everything you are," I said, placing my hand on top of his, "which maybe one day someone else can add to. There's always room for another ingredient in any good soup."

"You make it sound like a religion sometimes."

"It's as good a basis as any."

Jim tried to smile.

"What about your father?" I asked.

"He came to the funeral. He must have heard about it from someone, because I didn't call him. He came up to me afterward when no one else was around and asked me what I was thinking drinking and driving like that. He looked at me like no matter what anyone else said he knew it had to be my fault."

We both had some more soup and then went to bed, where I held Jim until he fell asleep. After his breathing grew shallow and his eyelids stopped fluttering, I let go and tried to fall asleep, although I kept thinking about Maggie. I wasn't jealous in the least, I was grateful to her for helping make Jim who he is now. I wouldn't have fallen for the Jim that she knew, just like Jim wouldn't have fallen for me the way he once was.

It's a little like making a soup, I thought as I drifted off. You start with a broth, to which you add genes and family history, sprinkle in a variety of experiences and then let it all simmer together. What you wind up with is the person you meet in the moment you meet them, a person who will change as new experiences are added, just the way soup does with every new spice and every additional ingredient. We all are a mix of various ingredients cooked over time in our own pot and the results are always different and always changing.

CHAPTER TWENTY-NINE

Jim seemed noticeably more at ease when he drove me home early the next morning. He held my hand as we walked to his truck and thanked me. I thanked him for opening up to me. He promised to call, but he didn't think he could get down to Northampton until Thursday because of a big order that he had to work on. I think he just wanted to go slow and wanted some time to recuperate, which was all right with me. I liked the fact that we both had separate lives to go along with what might be a new joint one. It felt healthier than any of my other relationships, male or female, which were so all-consuming and demanding that there was barely time to be alone.

Of course, it wasn't until I got home that I realized I had forgotten to read Beany's next letter. So I sat down in the small kitchen in my apartment, which I hardly used since I took most of my meals at Circa, and took it out to read. I knew I was down to a precious few, but I was surprised to see that this letter jumped 10 years into the future. It was dated April 15, 2004, about six months before Beany walked into my restaurant.

My Dear Boy,

I can still call you boy after all these years, because until last weekend you remained fixed that way in my imagination. So am I, by the way, which is why my heart almost stops every time I have the misfortune of passing a mirror. I don't care what you think you look like and I certainly hardly noticed your limp; behind the eyes of this well-respected, spectacled, grey-haired chemist stood my young friend just back from the war.

I was so happy to read that Evan and Beany had finally reconnected that I looked around for someone to tell. I even tried calling Jim, but he didn't answer, and I didn't want to leave a message.

What were the odds that we would both be in Boston on the same day, at the same time, in the same hotel, you attending yet another conference on how lipids can save the world and me a guest lecturer at yet another poetry seminar discussing that great paradox of human nature – why all experiences, even the most painful ones, when translated into art or poetry somehow seem wonderful. To experience those anguished and traumatic feelings through the words of another is to be intensely alive and touched by the mysteries of their life and thus your own, and to be intensely alive is the opposite of being dead, and since we met I feel intensely alive.

I wondered how that sentiment would apply to Jim. His wooden creations were works of art, no different than a poem or a novel, imbued with his experiences, particularly that terrible night of Maggie's birthday. Surely his pain seeps into his work and contributes to their beauty and meaning. The part Beany doesn't mention in his letter, but which is equally important and paradoxical, is why translating one's pain into art is itself a release, more so than talking to any therapist or taking a hundred pills. It's what has kept Jim going to this point and probably what drives me in the kitchen.

To the rest of the world we are two harmless old men, about as interesting as a couple of blades of grass. Fine, let them overlook us, while we enjoy the mystery that comes at the beginning and end of life. Here is what I propose - following up our discussion in the bar – we should meet for two weeks this summer, longer if you can get away, not in Boston, New York, or Los Angeles, but in Provincetown. I will arrange for a lovely little cottage that I have stayed at on the East End, which is filled with wonderful art galleries and restaurants and has a porch overlooking the bay where you can watch the sun rise and set by simply turning your gaze. It will stand your lipids on their head . . . well, perhaps not all of them. For that we will have the miracle of modern pharmaceuticals. The following summer, of course, will require three weeks. You know where that is heading.

How is it that I couldn't detect any trace of this non-academic, guttural happiness in Beany that first fall Thursday he came in to begin our year of soup? Perhaps he was saddened by the fact that the summer was over and their two week idyll already seemed so long ago, or perhaps because Evan insisted that their communications be kept to a minimum during the school year. Those two glorious weeks during the summer would hardly suffice for Beany after all those barren years. Besides, the next summer recess was almost a year away and a year was far stronger and darker at his age.

Now we should not try to make up for lost time, nor cry over spilled milk. (I am not normally such a repository of the world's clichés, but I am eager to get this letter to you, which means there is no time to agonize or be overly-

creative.) The poets tell us instead to make the most of the moments we do have and to live as best we can in the present. I am reminded of a stanza from a poem I have always loved by Emily Bronte entitled "Remembrance:"

But when the days of golden dreams had perished
And even Despair was powerless to destroy,
Then did I learn how existence could be cherished,
Strengthened and fed without the aid of joy.

My classes over the years have always found that poem depressing and that stanza in particular, but I do not. It is a reminder that no matter how much we lose in the living, no matter how happiness is tempered by time, there is much to cherish in the moment, even without that wild exuberance of our youth. So we shall do that and fill those remaining moments that we have with tales from our last 50 years apart, which, contrary to Ms. Bronte's experience, will bring us some measure of joy and laughter.

Let me know what dates work best for you for next summer.

With fondest regards,

Rog

CHAPTER THIRTY

I couldn't wait to show Jim the letter and to read the entire poem, which I found later that morning in the Northampton Library with some help from Orit.

"I know Bronte was one of the professor's favorites," she said.

"Did he come here a lot?"

"Not really, only on those occasions when he wanted to avoid his students. He'd always come by my office to say hello and talk about whatever it was that he was working on, and he was always working on something."

"Were you ever curious about him . . . about how he lived?"

"I knew exactly who Professor Beanstock was," Orit said, very seriously and very quietly.

I thought of asking her about Evan, but she quickly put down the slim volume of Emily Bronte's poetry I was looking for and went back to her office.

It appeared from the preface that she had written "Remembrance" near the end of her life, and that she had died very young. Bronte had apparently lost her true love at a young age, like Jim lost Maggie and, in a way, Beany lost Evan. In one of the middle stanzas, immediately before the one quoted by Beany, she wrote:

No other Sun has lightened up my heaven;
No other Star has ever shone for me;
All my life's bliss from thy dear life was given-
All my life's bliss is in the grave with thee.

Pretty dark and dismissal stuff, as Jim agreed when I read it to him over the telephone, but it was the last two stanzas that I think Beany had in mind for him and me.

Then did I check the tears of useless passion,
Weaned my young soul from yearning after thine;
Sternly denied its burning wish to hasten
Down to the tomb already more than mine!

And even yet, I dare not let it languish,
Dare not indulge in Memory's rapturous pain;

Once drinking deep of that divinest anguish,
How could I seek the empty world again?

Now I'm sure there are many ways to interpret that, but it seemed clear to me that Emily Bronte was telling us that you can't dwell forever on the empty world of pain and memory, and while it's always there and always a part of you, there comes a time to move on. The paradox of the heart is that while sometimes it seems to be made of glass, it isn't, it's unbreakable, and while it sometimes seems completely full, it never is, there is always room for more.

I couldn't tell whether Jim agreed with my interpretation, although I think he did agree with the sentiment. It was time to move on, to look ahead not back and to recognize that you have to live in the moment or not at all. Jim had come to the realization, as had I, that neither one of us was built for one, not entirely, not to be alone in every aspect of life. Beany knew that all along.

Jim called every night that week, always near quitting time, and we talked so long that I sometimes asked Georgina to stay later to help straighten up the kitchen and get things ready for the next day. Jim did most of the talking and I did most of the listening, because that's what he needed after so many years of silence. Besides, I was far better at listening. Georgina said that I did most of my talking with my soup.

"Some people tell you everything," she said, "every thought in their head, like their religion is talk, but not you, you're all about soup."

Then she smiled and said, "well, maybe not ALL anymore."

Jim talked about the orders he was working on and the new ones he was getting, everyday kinds of things that a man might tell his wife when he returned home from work. He had bottled up his thoughts and words for so long that it probably felt good to air them out. When he ran out of everyday conversation and wasn't ready to say goodnight, he'd speak a bit about Maggie and his mother and what it was like growing up without her, and as he did he'd pause sometimes as if some little epiphany had just hit him, as I'm sure it had now that he was bringing these moments out into the light.

Beany once told me that if I thought our pasts were always fixed and unchanging, far from that uncertain edge inhabited by the present and future, I would be sitting in the corner wearing a dunce cap.

"What you see when you look back changes as you get older, along with your feelings and beliefs," he said. "Everything looks different when viewed with old age. It's an entirely new perspective, like looking back from the top of the mountain. You can see a lot more at one time and all the little details that once seemed so troublesome become a lot smaller in the distance."

He used to call it "withering away into the truth," which I think Beany said was a line from a poem by Yeats.

Jim had a lot of memories and thoughts he needed to share and I was happy to listen. I knew when the time was right I would share some of mine as well, including my concern that I would wind up like my mother, because I was unable to sustain a relationship beyond the magic number of 3 years.

Georgina, who could hear bits and pieces of our conversations as she worked around the restaurant, never missed an opportunity to comment on them afterward.

"Are you like his girlfriend or his mother?" she asked one night.

"Some of both, I suppose. Isn't that what all women are in a relationship with a man?"

"I don't know about the guys you've gone out with, but the guys I go out with certainly aren't looking for their mother. At least, I hope not."

"That'll change once they get a little older."

"Well, I hope you're more girlfriend than mother, unless you want to wind up a servant like mine. Any man that I marry is going to know how to cook, clean and do laundry."

"I don't think that will be a problem. Jim has been living on his own now for quite some time."

"And it's a pigsty in there; you said so yourself."

"It's not a pigsty. It's just typically male and messy."

"And watch out that he isn't just dumping all his bad karma on you so he can lighten his load and look around for some younger, happy-go-lucky chick."

"I'll be careful."

Jim came for soup that Wednesday, since he had a big delivery in New Hampshire the next day, and he promised to pick me up Friday night so we could spend the weekend together, which meant that I had the restaurant to myself Thursday night for

Beany's next to last letter. It was another New Year's Eve missive, this time dated December 31, 2004, about three months into our year of soup.

Dearest Evan,
In the deserts of the heart
Let the healing fountain start,
In the prison of his days
Teach the free man how to praise.

It's the last stanza from a long elegy by W. H. Auden written in memory of Yeats. It comes to mind tonight because I've been thinking about the prison of our old age from which we were furloughed for a brief time this past summer, and will be again for a longer period next summer. It is what Robert Frost meant I think when he asked "what to make of this diminished thing," being what's left of our life.

I started the new fall term feeling full of praise, which my students undoubtedly noticed, but it faded as fast as my wrinkled tan. The brilliant colors of fall only served to remind me of the three seasons standing between us and brought a melancholy I hadn't known for quite some time. It was the worst on Thursdays, since I had no classes on Fridays to fill the day and the loneliness always seemed to catch me unaware, the empty space between classes, like the empty space between summers, like the empty space between the stars scaring me almost as much as my own deserted place (don't think me too clever, it's Frost again, which is what comes of having spent the last two weeks before break studying his poetry).

So I went out walking one Thursday night hoping the chill in the air would numb my thoughts and came across a lovely new restaurant devoted to soups. My mother used to call soup the food of the heart, because like all good liquids it could fill even the smallest empty space. She had a poetic soul as well and what's more she was right. I felt much better having supped with soup and, more importantly, I made a new friend, the first in so many years, in the proprietor and chef, a young woman with her own relationship and gender issues. I have returned every Thursday since because it gives me the strength to face up to yet another weekend alone grading papers and counting the days until we next meet (remember we agreed on at least three weeks this time).

Thursday always seems to be the day when I am best acquainted with the night (yes, another Frost), and the time spent with Tess and her soup (and a bottle of wine of course), helps immeasurably. Instead of sitting alone dodging my thoughts, I spend the evening with nothing at all to explain. It is so much easier listening to someone else's thoughts and plans and nodding as if to confirm that some sort of magical wisdom has seeped in along with the age spots and insomnia. What you and I both know is that what is confusing when you are young remains just as confusing when you are old, the only difference now is that it seems so much less important.

Anyway, if youth believes that by virtue of reaching this gray and paunchy state we have become Solomon-like, as well as content, I am willing to accommodate them. Besides, it is a role I enjoy playing, at least for an evening. All I have to do is repeat in one form or another that time is neither wrong nor right, and love and need are one. Had enough Frost? Well, at least it helps me get through the weekend, which used to be a lot easier when you were just a distant memory, instead of a lingering aftertaste, and a much anticipated one as well, but that is the nature of need, whether young or old.

I don't know why it should be a surprise that Beany needed me on those Thursday nights as much as I needed him. I knew he was using my soup to try to fill at least temporarily some of those spaces in his heart, although I thought they were more the short spaces of diminished time and the long spaces of old memories, more than the space between encounters.

I suppose that's why Beany was so insistent that I pick - either male or female - and not let my ambivalence root me to one spot, unable or unwilling to take a chance, as it did with him. The deserted spaces in Beany's heart I now realized were conspicuous by absence, as opposed to presence; they were more than pauses, they were great empty stretches, enormous and accusatory, made more noticeable by the two weeks spent with Evan during the summer of 2004.

At least I now knew that the two weeks in Provincetown were a big success. I felt good about that.

I always thought that a large part of Beany's Thursday night melancholy, which he couldn't completely hide from me, was due to his age and the fact that so many of his contemporaries were gone, which would distract anyone from the moment, as well as his regret for all the years he refused to connect with anyone. Of course, I didn't realize at the time that it was not anyone, but anyone else. He'd connected once with Evan, but without any other relationships Beany didn't have enough memories to fill the spaces of a long life. The summer holiday with Evan must have made that even more poignant. If poetry had taught Beany anything, it was that the richer and more varied his experiences, painful or not, the sweeter his short time with Evan would be, and the easier to accept its limitations. I guess that's the whole point of living, instead of waiting around.

Beany never talked about any of this during our Thursday nights together, possibly because I never gave him too many still moments to jump in, focused as I was on my own ideas and plans, and when I did he preferred to talk about his literary interests. More likely, he probably didn't see much point in it at this diminished stage of his life. He was escaping himself on Thursday nights, and his Fridays without classes, and the soup and conversation worked much better without facing up to what never was and never could be.

Next summer I think we should discuss lightening our academic load a bit, perhaps to one semester a year. Lord knows the English Department could use some fresh blood. We could spend some time in the winter traveling. Italy would be nice. Of course, I know how obsessed you are, did I say obsessed, I meant close, how close you are to that great lipid breakthrough you talked about last summer and I am sure it would be difficult for you to give up even one day of research. After all, humanity should always come first, although I'm sure that your colleagues and graduate candidates could carry on for a bit without you. You cannot help humanity if you completely ignore your own humanity. All I am suggesting is that you think about it. I know that I am.

Always,
Rog

Of course, I knew how this all turned out. I didn't remember the exact date that Evan died, but I did remember that it was sometime in the spring of 2005, so there was no second summer. If Evan was uncomfortable with anyone knowing his sexuality, which would have been hard to change after a lifetime of denial and resignation, then he might not have written Beany back, not often anyway, or encouraged him to call. That might mean Beany didn't find out until sometime later, perhaps when he called to confirm their summer plans or perhaps when picking up some periodical for university educators and scanning for news out of the University of Nebraska.

Beany resented computers, he said, because of the way that they sped up time and fractured space. I wasn't surprised that he preferred the world the way it once was. Who that age wouldn't be nostalgic for their distant youth? Of course, his complaints always seemed more literary than anything else.

"Everything is written these days sitting in front of a screen in a small room with the telephone ringing and music playing," he complained one night. "No one takes the time anymore to sit and watch the world with a pad and pencil. Writing used to be a slow process from brain and heart to hand and paper – like cooking soup – each word carefully measured and never added before its time, because you couldn't just press the delete button and replace it in a nano-second, as if it were never there."

He liked to say that the modern world no longer looked out on the horizon and life was "all about your own space." He had a computer, but he swore that he hardly used it and certainly never for his writing. So I was fairly confident that Beany wasn't e-mailing with Evan, who, as a scientist, probably embraced computers from their infancy, so he wasn't likely to have read about Evan's sudden death in the University of Nebraska online news.

There was that one Thursday night, probably in the late spring, when Beany left early because he had too much to drink. He must have known by then. It was undoubtedly on that night that the seeds of what he would do a few months later were planted in his brain.

Jim disagreed with me on this point, and I suppose he ought to know. He said a thought like that takes a long while to germinate.

"Years," he said, "not months."

It lies there for quite some time unnoticed at first before it becomes a minor irritant like a pebble in your shoe. Jim said the first time he really felt it was after his mother died and then it grew in his subconscious as a way of striking back at his father. Ultimately he decided that his father wouldn't care. Of course, it went into hibernation once Maggie came into his life.

"It never completely disappears," he said, "once it takes root."

Of course, it began to grow again after she died.

"Maybe if I had been Beany's age," Jim said, "it might have turned out differently."

Meaning he wouldn't have been able to resist it as he did by moving away.

Jim suspected that the idea probably popped into Beany's head during the war as he scurried about collecting the bodies of young boys. Afterward, it might have been nourished by some of the poetry Beany studied, as well as Evan leaving for Nebraska and breaking off all communications. Evan's death, he said, after that summer holiday must have finally made the time seem right.

"It's the way the book would have ended," Jim said, "if Beany had been writing it."

"You make suicide sound like a lifestyle choice, like moving in to assisted living."

"I suppose in some ways it is, although that's not what I meant. I meant that he probably couldn't come up with enough reasons not to do it. He didn't have that one big argument that seems to trump most everything else, particularly when you're younger."

"What's that?"

"That there are still so many possibilities ahead."

"There's always a reason, even at Beany's age. Just think about the sunsets that still lie ahead . . . even if it's just one more."

"I'm not disagreeing with you. It's just that Beany probably wasn't thinking that way. He wasn't a linear thinker, as far as I can tell. I don't think time flowed for him in just one direction."

"What makes you say that?"

"One of his poems I found. Have you read any of his stuff?"

"Just his letters."

Jim pulled a folded piece of paper out of his wallet.

"I came across this in his desk. It was stuck in that back drawer. I bet he would have removed it when he emptied the desk but missed it. I meant to show it to you the other day, but we got sort of busy."

We both smiled.

"It has no title," he said, "but it looks like his handwriting."

"It is," I murmured, as I cleared my throat to read it out loud.

Time is never the same
One moment to the next
One thought to another
Or as dreams die
With you and without you
Before, during and after

Nothing is the same
But time most of all

"The thing about suicidal thoughts," Jim said, "is that they have to simmer for a while until they're done."

I hated the soup analogy, which Jim must have seen on my face, because he apologized right away.

"Of course there are instances where a person commits suicide in response to a specific event," Jim said.

"Like the death of a spouse or a long-suffering love."

Jim nodded.

"But for someone like Beany to think along those lines - as a morally justifiable alternative - the idea had to be sitting there for a long time, even if only in his subconscious."

Who was I to argue, since the thought of killing myself had never seriously crossed my mind.

CHAPTER THIRTY-ONE

Jim and I fell into a fast and easy routine. It wasn't just Thursday nights any longer. He'd come by the restaurant a couple of nights a week for soup and conversation. Sometimes I'd go back with him and sometimes he'd spend the night at my place. Sometimes he'd go home by himself, because he had some early deliveries and I had a big market day. Sometimes we just needed some time alone. It's not something you have to ask for at our age, you can just sense when it's time.

We didn't talk much more about Maggie or our pasts, not as much as we talked about us and the present. In some ways, we were already like an old married couple, comfortable in each other's company, not the least bit self-conscious or put off by the silent moments. To both of our amazement, we liked the feeling of being part of something bigger than ourselves again. We had no major secrets left, yet there were still plenty of little things to learn about each other, like the difficulty Jim had falling asleep and my need to constantly keep busy. Little discoveries like that are always helpful in keeping a relationship fresh and alive.

The sex was fine, but I'm not sure it set his heart pounding any more than it did mine. It's not like I stood there in Circa's kitchen with images of Jim in bed glowing before me. I thought more about the two of us talking quietly in bed, listening to the soft notes of tenderness in his voice, or just lying in his arms feeling as if I had found a place I had once thought lost.

Everything about us, including the sex, quickly fell into a routine. I told Jim that was because I spread routines like viruses, which made him laugh.

"I'm just not oversexed," I said, "like all the other girls."

"What other girls?"

Jim said he'd rather be over-souped than oversexed, and I'm sure he really meant it.

"I'm very well endowed," I said, "when it comes to soup hormones."

Jim took me in his arms and kissed me lightly on the lips.

"Besides," he said, "the sex is almost as good as the soup and that's saying a lot."

There was only one Beany letter left at this point and I saved it for a Thursday when Jim was up in Vermont installing cabinets in the home of an expatriate Russian writer. It was, as I already knew from peeking ahead, dated October 4, 2005, the night before his suicide, and it was addressed to me.

My Dear Tess,

You and your soup, but mostly you, have made the last year a triumph for me, which I know you will not believe in light of why I am writing this letter. Knowing you as I do after a year of Thursdays, which is more than a little and less than a lot, I am sure that you read my letters chronologically, over time, which means that you now know more than a little and less than a lot about me. I am sorry that I was not more forthcoming with you, particularly with respect to Evan, but the pleasure for me, beside the good company and good soup, was sharing your life in the twilight of mine. Mine no longer interested me as much, I'm not sure it ever really did, certainly not for a long time, which is what I think I love most about literature. It's always about other people's lives.

I poured myself another glass of wine and looked over at the table where Beany used to sit. I didn't want to rush this last letter. Indeed, I had bought the most expensive bottle of red that I could find at the local liquor store from a vineyard in Napa called Opus One and I had decanted it earlier in the evening to give it time to breathe. I planned to drink it very slowly, every drop of it.

I made Georgina try a little before she left and she made a toast.

"To the learned professor of English, Roger Beanstock, more than just a wordsmith, but a human being as well . . . may he find in heaven what he missed in life."

"How do you know he missed anything?" I said, since I hadn't really talked with her about the details of my conversations with Beany or the contents of his letters.

Georgina rolled her eyes in response.

"OK, I get it." I said. "It was a nice toast."

"This is good," Georgina said, holding her glass up to the light.

"It ought to be at that price."

We stood there side by side staring at Beany's empty chair.

"Do you believe in heaven?" I asked.

"I don't know," she said. "I haven't given it too much thought. I guess I figure it's too far off for an opinion or a plan. My mother says the fact that so many people do has to account for something. I suppose it's as good a proof as any."

"Belief by definition doesn't require proof."

"Do you believe in heaven?" Georgina asked.

"I do," I said without hesitation, "but not the way they preach about it. I believe in the energy of existence . . . and the spirit. Nothing ever disappears completely."

"Whatever that means," Georgina said, gathering up her stuff because she had a hot date with a senior chemistry major, things with Joe having cooled, "although the thought of coming back as mulch doesn't particularly excite me. I hope Beany is enjoying himself wherever or whatever he is, although I'll take my heaven on earth if I have a choice."

"Obsessed with immediate gratification like everyone else?"

"Don't knock it until you've tried it," Georgina said with a smile. With that she drained her glass, kissed me on the cheek and left. I went back to reading.

I cannot resist leaving you with another poem that has become a recent favorite. It's called Funeral Blues by W. H. Auden, who I have always liked and not just because of his sexual orientation.

Stop all the clocks, cut off the telephone
Prevent the dog from barking with a juicy bone
Silence the pianos and with muffled drum
Bring out the coffin, let the mourners come.
Let aeroplanes circle moaning overhead
Scribbling on the sky the message
He is Dead.
Put the crepe bows round the white necks of the public doves
Let the traffic policeman wear black cotton gloves
He was my North, my South, my East and West
My working week and my Sunday rest
My noon, my midnight, my talk, my song;
I thought that love would last forever.
I was wrong.
The stars are not wanted now;
Put out every one
Pack up the moon and dismantle the sun
Pour away the ocean and sweep up the woods;
For nothing now can ever come to any good.

I never told anyone about Evan, so I did not see any point in starting with you. I found out when I called on May 2nd to tell him what I had found for our summer rendezvous in Provincetown – the first three weeks in July. It was a charming little 100-year old cabin overlooking the dunes and the ocean with a fireplace and the largest hydrangea bush I'd ever seen. It was expensive, but what else did I have to do with my money. I had, of course, already made the reservation and paid for the rental, so I assume the house sat empty those three weeks in memory of us. How many 'us' have failed to show over the years? I imagine it must be sad for the house, sort of like being left standing at the altar, if you can anthropomorphize a thing like that.

I had to look that one up. It meant to attribute human characteristics to something inanimate.

It was Wednesday when I called and I wasn't sure at first that I would make it to Thursday. It's not that my everyday life was going to change all that much, but my everyday thoughts would, at least my recent ones. It was as if the universe, my universe, was rapidly shrinking, while at the same time everything else was receding at the speed of light. I looked around, but there was no longer anything beyond the horizon, not anything I could sense or feel. If not for you and that asparagus soup of yours, I don't think I would have waited another minute, let alone another few months.

I thought a lot about it over the last few weeks, hoarding my pills so I'd have more than enough to enjoy with my final bottle of wine, but it's important that you hear what it is I am not saying. I am not saying that this was my response to the moment. It is something I have been thinking about for quite some time, since I started spending those beautiful spring days collecting bouquets of dead faces, flowering boys whose sudden glimpse of the eternity ahead had drained all the color from their lips and cheeks. I started thinking about it more because of the ones who didn't appear so frightened, who looked peaceful and serene, as if they had lain down to take a nap and were relieved to be released at last from the forces that held their feet to the ground. Once a thought like that is hatched, you cannot ever put it back in the egg.

So be sure that this decision is much more than a simple reaction to Evan's death, although that certainly is a part of it. It's also the realization that some of the things I once thought possible were really impossible, and some of the things I once thought impossible had actually been possible all the time.

I have always thought it was possible to live a full, productive life alone, immersed in study and nourished by words, without sustained love and companionship, and that loving one person for a moment, however brief and long ago would be enough. Perhaps that might explain why I was never more than a second-rate poet. I always knew something was missing from my poetry. It wasn't suffering, I had that. It wasn't intelligence or perspiration. It wasn't motivation. It was the ability to touch someone else's heart. You need to be touched more than once to be able to do that. You need to be touched often to know how to touch back.

I always thought it was impossible to forgive yourself, to tell the difference between what was real and what you believed and to escape the constant ache of memory. But time has a way of bringing body and soul together. And certain things you do or don't do make a difference, just as what I do now. You need to be as open-minded in life as in literature.

When you reach that stage of life when your ideas are as confused as your senses, then it's time to move on. The time has come for me to follow my heart at last and since, as Auden put it, I have reached the point at which "nothing can ever come to any good," I have loosened that grip around it and let my heart beat for itself.

Going through old age alone must really suck, I thought to myself, thinking also of my mother and those last few years of her life when I was away in college and she was alone, which must have seemed like another world. It must be particularly hard if you don't have a fortune in memories to spend, like a rich monthly pension.

Of course, I didn't come to this decision without some scholarly research.

What I discovered was very interesting. The Ancient Greeks rejected suicide because it was a release of ourselves – our souls – from the bodies the gods have placed us in as some sort of test or punishment. Aristotle considered it a great wrong against the state.

I had to open another bottle of wine because the Opus One was empty and I needed more. I was out since I no longer kept a supply in the restaurant now that Beany was gone and Jim didn't drink. Fortunately, all I had to do was walk home, which I did and had another full glass before I resumed reading.

Rome, however, was different. Seneca himself committed suicide because he believed that a wise person "lives as long as he ought, not as long as he can." When we lose the things nature meant for us to have and there is nothing good in the moment or the moments to come, when all that you love has disappeared, then, the Stoics believed, it's a reasonable choice to make. Private factors had to be weighed, not just the social ones.

Of course that makes killing yourself, I thought, addressing Beany in my head, much too easy to justify. Who ever gets everything out of life that nature intended? If everyone jumped off a cliff every time it seemed that there was nothing good left to come, there wouldn't be enough of us around to propagate the species. Of course, the certainty of that feeling must be very different in your 80's, than it is in your 30's.

Still, I didn't buy Beany's or Seneca's rationale for a minute. Consciousness itself is enough of a reason to stick around. As long as you can watch a sunset or listen to a bird calling out an early spring morning, why does it matter if it's a life without a long term purpose? Although I'm sure Beany, never much of a naturalist, would respond that's all fine and good so long as consciousness hasn't become too hobbled to appreciate that sunset or too blinded by blame and resolve to see beyond its own skin. But that can change, I'd have said, anything can change, and the thing about change is that it's instantaneous and has a mind of its own. I think I could have held my own here in a discussion with Beany, if only he had given me a chance.

Christianity, of course, found suicide to be contrary to the laws of nature (mandating self-preservation), of reason (harmful to the community), and of God. But if it were contrary to the law of nature, John Donne pointed out, why weren't all acts of self-denial or deprivation similarly unlawful? Clearly there are circumstances where reason would recommend ending one's life early, such as the Jews did at Masada to avoid being tortured and murdered by the victorious Roman army. There is nothing in the Scriptures that clearly condemns suicide. Indeed, Christian doctrine permits other forms of killing, including martyrdom, capital punishment and holy war.

Of course, poets have been leaders in championing this kind of self-determination to put it in democratic terms. I am sure that analogy will send you running to the kitchen for a hefty bowl of one of the soups of the day.

Actually, it sent me back to the wine bottle to pour another glass. I couldn't bear to continue listening to Beany justify killing himself, any more than I could have listened to Jim on that subject, and I was tempted to stop reading and go to bed, convinced that I would never understand or appreciate why he did what he did, but fortunately Beany was ready to move on to another subject, one that was much more interesting to me - love.

I do not want to leave you, Tess, without discussing the counterpoint, because if death is one side of the argument, love is the other. It's a strange, overused word. It's been bandied about in literature and life for so long that its meaning has been totally obscured. If you ask 100 people for their definition of love, I am sure you would get 200 different answers.

There were so many different definitions of love that I've read over the years that I started writing some of them down. I thought you might be interested in a few of my favorites. The one I think you'll like best is that love is the immortal yearning to merge oneself into the totality of things visible and invisible, to extend oneself into the illimitable of space and to prolong oneself into the infinite of time. There's something onomatopoetic about it. It almost sounds like love. It transcends death, which is why I think you will like it. And although you might not admit it, it does make death seem much less significant, and my decision of little cosmic consequence. I like it for a different reason, however, because it doesn't really need another person. Love, by that definition, can be achieved in many ways, it can be found in art and in your self . . . others are not always required.

Beany was right; that was a definition I once would have embraced in the abstract before Jim, before I've started thinking of love more like soup, a mixture of various ingredients to create something that nourishes and calms, something certain, warm and comforting that occupies the absent places the way good soup can warm the empty spaces in your heart.

How about love as that ineffable and inescapable sensation that one is trembling on the brink of something else? Of course, that seems to me more like the symptom than the disease. Then there's love as the mastery of infinitesimal detail, which I remember writing down because it reminded me of how I felt when Evan and I first met. He had this way of pushing his hair out of his eyes and tapping his right foot while he was waiting that made me tremble and eager for time to pass – time together - so I could discover new details about him to admire. And I did for a while, when it seemed as if every little Evan detail was created not to be part of the background, but to need one. If love is in the details, what happens when there are no new details, when time and space makes it impossible to see anything new except with the mind's eye? Can love survive that kind of distance? It certainly doesn't sound like it from that definition.

Is it possible to love someone despaired of heart?

Yes, I said to Beany's letter, thinking of Jim, because the heart heals itself over time, not completely, but enough for it to beat on. You don't have to live in despair, just with it, the same way you might live with hardship and poverty.

I think so. The real issue is whether it is possible for the despaired of heart to love? That's a much harder question. I think the answer may be no, not without forgiveness and not without a little luck. A little luck is important in just about everything, and sometimes all you need is time for that 'little luck' to find you, time I don't have. Age figures significantly in my decision, Tess, I want you to know that.

I do, I said.

I once read that the last trap the ego falls into in its search for absolute truth is sentimentality. The absolute truth is that I could not watch myself descend into sentimentality, any more than I could stare too long at the faces of those dead boys, and with the strength and resolve I got from our year of soup and with reruns on the way, I am even more certain that the time is right.

So my soup, which made Beany easier for him to go on, also made it easier for him to let go. It made some sense in a strange way, if you believe that soup can help you gather the strength to do whatever it is you need to do. Beany never struck me as a very sentimental individual and that thought must have frightened him, although if he had stuck around and let the end of his life descend into a bit of sentimentality, probably inevitable for anyone that age, not just him, I suspect he might have written some of his best poems.

One thing about love is that it seems to provide as good a reason to live as to die . . . in literature as well as in life. It's funny though how these tremendous abstractions, which I once loved to ponder over, have grown so remote and indifferent. They appear to have lost as much interest in me, as I in them.

I never loved abstractions, I thought to myself, not nearly as much as soup. Cooking is a lot simpler than trying to explain the universe.

A mid-list poet once wrote that there exists in love and truth no more solid foundation for happiness than in loneliness and falsehood.

I wondered if that mid-list poet was Beany.

Anyway, thanks for the warm and nourishing send-off.
With love,
Roger

CHAPTER THIRTY-TWO

I told Jim about Beany's last letter, his suicide note, although I didn't show it to him, and he didn't ask to see it. He felt reassured, as was I, that Beany's suicide was not an impulsive, spur-of-the-moment act. On the other hand, he appeared uneasy with the idea that the thought was like a perennial that once planted returns year after year.

"It's different for you," I said. "For Beany it was a philosophical question, like some classic work of art that had to be revisited again and again to explore new shades of meaning. It wasn't the result of a single blow, but a part of his everyday life. It was how he viewed existence . . . his existence. Being a college professor is an odd way to live. You grow older and wiser, but everyone else stays 18, dizzy with pleasure. It will never hold the same fascination for you as it did for Beany."

"Because of you," Jim said, stroking my arm.

"No, because of you," I said, "and who you are. You're a builder and a creator of beauty. Beany was a critic, who took things apart and couldn't always be bothered to put them back together. He was a loner who suffered from his writing and the war, missed too many opportunities, and was never really comfortable with himself. He couldn't freely be who he was at the time when it mattered most, when he was a young man. And despite all that, he still lived to a ripe old age."

"Don't worry," Jim said, "I'm not planning to take any short cuts."

Of course, things happen that we don't plan, they always do.

Georgina was more inquisitive about Beany and his last letter.

"So why did he do it?" she asked the next day, as soon as she walked into the restaurant.

It was hard to distill down to one reason, I told her. There seemed to be a number of reasons, ranging from the philosophical to the practical.

"What was the practical?"

"He was close enough to the end that it didn't really matter. I think his exact words were that there was no good to come anymore."

"That sounds like him. And you consider that practical?"

"For an academic."

"And what was the philosophical reason?" she asked.

"Free will . . . the fact that he could decide when and didn't have to live any longer than he wanted to."

"Those aren't reasons, they're excuses. Only a professor could think like that."

Georgina rubbed her chin and tapped her foot.

"There has to be another reason you're not telling me," she said.

"Like what?"

"If the practical reason relates to the mind and the philosophical one relates to the spirit, then what about the heart? There had to be a romantic reason there somewhere. That's the only pain I could ever imagine being unbearable enough to do something like that."

"Even that's not enough."

"So," Georgina said, while she nodded in agreement, "what was it?"

"There was the end of love as well," I said.

"How did his love end?"

"The same way it began, I suppose, with something bursting inside his chest."

"You make love sound like a heart attack."

I shrugged. It sounded like a definition Beany might have added to his list.

"So instead of being on life support for three months, he was on soup support."

"There's a limit to what soup can do," I said with a little smile.

I moped around for a week or two until Jim threatened to start making his own soup for me right out of a can. He suggested a way for me to snap out of it, much the way he did by focusing on an intricate piece of furniture.

"Create a special soup for Beany," he said, "a one-of-a-kind world premiere and then serve it on a special night for him at the restaurant."

I loved the idea immediately and enlisted Georgina, Orit, Tom, Joe and Lisa to post notices around the campus and town that the following Thursday would be Beany night at Circa when I would be unveiling a new soup created in his honor, which would be free to anyone who brought in a copy of his or her favorite poem.

Georgina said to be prepared for a line around the block, so I decided to offer the soup for take-out only and set about trying to create a fitting new soup; one that would acknowledge the importance of both the preparation, as well as the sharing; a soup that would recognize the role of food in the circle of life; a soup that wouldn't simply disappear down the throat into the stomach, but would linger, its scent a sort of compromise that could both bind up a memory and set it free; a soup that is the opposite of death and despair, that whispers words of peace and puts you at ease, helping you to remember that love and happiness is never about deserving, but all about accepting.

I didn't want it to be a variation on a theme, minestrone with a twist, pea soup with turkey instead of ham, but an entirely new creation. Of course, there isn't much that hasn't been done in the world of soup, considering that there was already such a thing as stone soup, yes, made with stones, but I felt up to the challenge and decided that the only way to do it was to start from scratch.

I tried beginning with the name, which was a mistake, even though a soup's name doesn't need to reflect any of its ingredients. I thought about Beany's Memory Soup and Beany's Pondering Life Soup, but they sounded too pretentious and complicated. Great names like great soups should be simple and easy to remember, so I gave up and decided that its creation should come first.

I kept careful notes as I experimented, since creating a soup is part serendipity and part instinct. I decided that it would need to represent all four basic elements - earth, air, fire, and water, as well as both genders, so I began by consulting an older cookbook I had inherited from my great-grandmother, who, according to my grandmother, could make people laugh or cry with a single spoonful. She supposedly told her that love and forgiveness had to be added to a soup like any other ingredient, which she did with smiles, tears and sighs.

The story in the family was that she was a descendent of one of the witches of Salem, not that I believed in such things, or that I knew her well enough to have an opinion since she died before I turned two. Still, there were notes in the margins about all kinds of herbs, plants and spices, and their effects on people, some of which seemed a bit too magical even for my taste. Much of it, I suppose, was derived from folklore. Although no one could seriously dispute the fact that nature's creations have various remedial properties and psychological effects, wine and tea being two obvious examples.

I didn't get much sleep that weekend and wound up closing the restaurant on Monday, Tuesday, and Wednesday so I could focus on Thursday. Jim called regularly, but kept his distance, as did Georgina who popped in from time to time with something for me to eat. I didn't finish until Wednesday afternoon and needed every second to prepare for Thursday night.

Of course, I wasn't completely happy with the result, what cook or artist ever is, but it was good, clearly a keeper that would evolve over time into something even better. The name came to me Thursday morning – Beany's Secret Soup - with a nod to my grandmother's Soup of Secrets. Aside from the fact that I intended to keep the recipe secret for the time being, I decided it was an appropriate name, because what I was really going for was a soup that in addition to being nourishing and warming could help people find a place to rest their secrets, so they could stand alongside of them for a while, instead of underneath them. Obviously, secrets weighed heavily on Beany's life, as they did on Jim. They do for all of us. Finding a way to share them is the best way, I think, to lighten the load.

The broth is the first and most basic part of any soup, and although I considered something radical like goat's milk or fruit juice, I decided to start with the first of the four basic elements - water. I could thicken and flavor it by using beef, poultry, herbs, spices or vegetables. Beany liked his beef, I know that, but beef is a barrier, it keeps things out and holds them in. It doesn't just hold you it holds you down, making it harder to move on.

Poultry was a possibility. It's lighter and easier to penetrate, but it will still slow you down a bit and dull the senses, which can, of course, be useful at times, although it wasn't the feeling I was going for. So I decided to rely initially on herbs, spices and vegetables to try to create the taste that I wanted, which I couldn't have described, at least not in words. I wanted a combination of flavors, something hard to label and understand, but clear and very likeable - a taste-bud symphony of sorts, sweet and spicy, strong and subtle, sharp, vague, serious, funny, a little bit of everything for a life that was anything but, a taste that would be soothing and releasing, while at the same time energizing, and leave your mouth, as well as your mind and heart, tingling and alive.

I started with dill and fennel, both according to my great-grandmother's book representing the element of fire and according to her margin notes masculine as well. Dill is a short-lived annual herb that's very aromatic with a flavor somewhat similar to caraway. It has to be fresh, since it loses its potency rapidly after drying. In the Middle Ages, it was used to ward off evil and protect against witchcraft.

Fennel is a perennial that is also very aromatic with a taste similar to anise. It was used in the nineteenth century to make absinthe, an alcoholic mixture said to be good for upset stomachs and troubled minds. Fennel is also used in Asia as a breath freshener and to improve the milk supply of breast-feeding mothers, which made me wonder why it was considered a masculine herb in my great-grandmother's soup book.

I thought a while about the next flavor to add and being a big citrus fan I settled on lemongrass, which also represented the third element –Air. It is a perennial herb with a lemony flavor that's used in teas and soups and a favorite in Thai cooking. In addition to being used as a pesticide and in cosmetics, it is said to calm the central nervous system. I found fresh stalks at the Asian grocer, which is essential since when bruised and added whole, the juice sacs will release the most concentrated form of its aromatic oils.

I decided to try a bit of mugwort or St. John's plant, a perennial herb which I rarely used, but which represented the fourth of the basic elements - Earth. Mugwort was popular during the Middle Ages for flavoring beer before they discovered hops. Witches and psychics used it to increase the intensity of dreams, as well as to bring on lucid dreams, which are dream states where the sleeper is aware and able to control her behavior. It was also used to ward off fatigue and stimulate the central nervous system, which made for a nice counterbalance to the lemongrass. Mugwort added a very earthy, moss green color to the broth, which was unusual and which I liked very much. The color added a sort of earthy quietness to the soup that seemed both encouraging and sympathetic.

At this point, it tasted less like a soup than some sort of tea, but it was early in the process and tea and soup are first cousins in my mind. If a good homemade soup is not readily available, then tea is always my next best option. I added thyme next, which my great-grandmother considered feminine in her margin notes. Thyme is a perennial herb that is an important nectar source for honeybees. It has to be added early on to allow time for the oils to be released. It is supposed to guard against respiratory infections, although it has a very long and varied history. The ancient Greeks considered thyme to be a source of courage and the Romans used it to purify their homes. In the Middle Ages, it was used as an aid to sleep and to ward off nightmares, as well as being placed in coffins to assure a smooth passage to the next life.

I won't go into all the ingredients I used for the broth, otherwise it wouldn't be much of a secret recipe, but I did include some lavender also to represent the element of Air. I liked its slightly sweet and floral taste. I used the dried buds, which are rich in its oil. Lavender is considered an anti-inflammatory, which aids in relaxation and sleep. It helps with headaches and during the Middle Ages was used to ward off the plague. Since it does repel fleas and flies, there was probably some truth to that.

I added cloves, for protection and love, and rosemary, a stimulant and a mild analgesic, to improve memory. It is called by some the herb of remembrance and also used to be thrown into coffins to help the dead remember life on their journey to the hereafter. And I couldn't ignore ginger since I like its pungent taste. It is also good for settling nervous stomachs and helps people who have suffered a blow to recover their strength.

I added a number of other spices and oils, and some red wine of course, and in the end the broth was as cloudy as an overcast day, as dark a green as a frog pond in the middle of summer, but with a taste as bright and clear as a sunny afternoon. It was understated, but with obvious foreshadows of some good fortune ahead. It left me feeling serene and fortified, ready to move forward. It released a certain store of energy and confidence and encouraged acceptance, although something was still missing. It needed more body and weight.

In the end I decided it needed some chicken flavor, although not the flesh. Its flavor is always a heart-warming antidote to the past, allowing bad memories to resonate in the air as they rise to the heavens. I put some legs, thighs and breasts in to simmer with their skin on for about two hours before removing them. The fat, which we all need to some degree, particularly when we're upset, gave it what it needed, a little more compassion and substance, and a point of presence.

Now I was ready to add the vegetables. I wanted something simple, because the reasons we hold tight to our secrets and eventually realize we can let them go are often simple, sometimes as simple as a beautiful spring day. So I settled on tomatoes, carrots, potatoes, celery, turnips, leeks, peppers and dried black Russian mushrooms.

About an hour before it was ready to be served, I added some English elderberries, which I stumbled upon in the market and hadn't seen for quite some time. Of course, I saw it as a sign. It is rumored to be a sad plant, because of the role it allegedly played in providing the wood for the Cross upon which Jesus was crucified, which I thought appropriate since every soup like every life has to accept some tears. Elderberry has a strong taste and even a hint of it may be enough to begin to peel away the layers that build up around our central core like those surrounding the core of an onion. Elderberries are good for colds for that very reason,

Georgina and Jim were my guinea pigs Thursday afternoon. Jim smiled as he inhaled the steam and his eyes were moist after he finished.

"Beany would have loved it," he said.

Georgina sighed and finished the bowl without saying a word, which was unusual for her.

"It's delicious," she said afterward, "but I don't think I could eat it very often. It makes me want to cry."

"Because you probably have a secret," I said, "you need to let go of."

"Who doesn't?"

When we opened the line was around the block, composed mostly of students, professors and college employees, and I had just enough to provide everyone with a small container to take home. I didn't know what anyone thought, although I did get a few letters of thanks and a number of requests for more over the next few weeks, but it was too emotional a soup for me to make more than once a year.

CHAPTER THIRTY-THREE

I actually didn't make the soup again for over 3 years when I made it again to celebrate the date Beany came in to start the year of soup, and the fact that Jim and I had broken the 3 year jinx, which he celebrated by making a beautiful, hand-carved table for the waiting area in the restaurant, something he knew I'd wanted for quite some time.

"You're not disappointed that it's not something more personal?" he asked.

"Like a jewelry box?"

He nodded.

"You can't get any more personal with me than with my soup."

It took me a long time to go through all the poems we received in exchange. Of course, there were all kinds, ranging from Chaucer and Milton to Keats and Ogden Nash, too many to go through them all here. There was one though that I framed and hung by the prep table in the kitchen. It was by E. E. Cummings entitled "*Love Is More Thicker Than Forget.*"

love is more thicker than forget
more thinner than recall
more seldom than a wave is wet
more frequent than to fail

it is most mad and moonly
and less it shall unbe
than all the sea which only
is deeper than the sea

love is less always than to win
less never than alive
less bigger than the least begin
less littler than forgive

it is most sane and sunly
and more it cannot die
than all the sky which only
is higher than the sky

I'm sure Beany could find a couple of noteworthy definitions of love in that one, although I'm sure his take would be different than mine. I would say that E. E. Cummings saw love as unexplainable . . . an almost nonsensical force that is as irresistible as gravity. Beany would probably say that Cummings saw love as an idea, everywhere, in everything, that was beyond anyone's ability to understand it or possess it. The difference might explain why our two lives will turn out to be very different in the end.

I close Circa now two days a week – Monday and Tuesday – and for four weeks in the summer and a week over Christmas. Jim and I like to spend some of that time traveling. Jim is always on the lookout for new furniture ideas, and I am always looking for soup inspiration. I have come across a couple of other secret soups, a broken-hearted soup and a forgetful soup, so clearly there are a lot of us out there who appreciate soup's power.

In the end, I gave up trying to understand why Beany did what he did and why he lived the way he lived and just accepted it. That was his choice in light of his time and his circumstances. He had two weeks near the end with Evan which probably did not measure up to his expectations in light of the years and memories he had to measure it against. He had a year of soup, which was like discovering a new poet, and I think he left on a high note.

Whatever happens between Jim and me, I have found a home here and a life's work. We travel from one end of the rainbow to the other and, however we get there, by whatever path, the most important things are to know when to let go and move on, to be in the moment, to feel the tremors of love and to try to enjoy the ride, which I learned not from Beany, but because of him – the mark of a great teacher.

###

Questions for Discussion

*Do you think that Tess' reasons for wanting to remain celibate make sense? What reasons, if any, would motivate you to remain alone like that?

*Why do you think she chose to open a soup restaurant in a town like Northampton? Do you think she'd have been able to keep her vow if not for the professor and Jim?

*Tess talks a lot about the medicinal almost magical quality of soup. Do you believe that food can have that effect on people? Is there anything in the professor's life that had a similar healing quality for him? Is there anything in your life that has a similar power or influence? If so, how did you discover it and what sort of comfort does it provide you with?

*Tess's relationship with Professor Beanstock seems to be a guiding force throughout this story. Why do you think Professor Beanstock chooses to bequeath the letters to Tess? Why do you think he chooses to let her learn about his past via these letters rather than in person during their year of soup? What it is about Professor Beanstock that immediately puts Tess at ease and allows her to open up so readily when she clearly doesn't do this with anyone else?

*What do you think about Professor Beanstock's relationship with Evan and how it evolves over the years? How differently do you think their lives would have evolved if they were young professors today? Why was Professor Beanstock so reluctant to come out even at the end of his life?

*Why do you think Professor Beanstock chooses to take his own life? Is it solely because of Evan or are there other factors involved? He clearly was able to live without Evan as a regular presence in his life for so many years, so why does he make the decision now? Do you think there comes a time when you have lived enough and it's time to go? How do you know when that is? Do you believe in taking your own life when the circumstances warrant, at least as you see them? Is that a personal decision we are each entitled to make?

*Do you think Tess come to terms with her three failed relationships and her bisexuality? What does she learn from these failed relationships and from her relationship with Professor Beanstock that will help her move forward with Jim?

*Will Tess and Jim be able to heal one another and move forward together?

*How do you move forward after something like what happened to Jim? Is it just time or do you need to find someone else to love? Can you really prevent that from happening or is finding another love inevitable at that age?

Sample:

A Family Institution

Ira's expectations are lower than they once were. He is satisfied with the flimsiest of promises - a train that runs on time, faint praise from a superior, or the passing smile of a pretty woman. When the conversation at parties turns to the old college days or early married life, as compared to middle age in suburbia, as it frequently does, he's the first to volunteer that it's better now.

"It's those little certainties in life that really matter," he'd say to the eyebrows raised in response.

Most of them would profess to disagree citing the thrilling discovery of love and the limitless energy of their innocent youth, but not without nodding unconsciously at the same time, as if some deeper, more honest self recognized it was all a delusion. This was the point where Ira would excuse himself to get more wine counting the little certainties in his head as he did so. It was never very difficult. First, there was the warm bed he shared with his wife, Ellen, who was asleep most work nights long before he found the energy to get up from the den couch, turn off the TV and head to bed. She always felt so warm and welcoming when he slid in beside her.

Second, he would add the animated discussions with Jaime and Scott about school, friends, and the latest gadget that they can't live without, conversations that spring to life like the old pop-up books the moment he walks through the door. Then there are the lazy weekend mornings in bed, breakfasts out, shopping expeditions, Saturday night movies followed by Saturday night embraces, holidays, snowstorms warmed by movie rentals and microwave popcorn, swimming in the town pool, and endless nights of cable filled with action adventures and steamy romances for the late nights. Of course Ira would also have to include their growing savings backed by the full faith and credit of the United States government.

He can't recall when it dawned on him that it was a lot easier moving with a force instead of against it or when he learned that thinking too precisely about things just made them difficult to accept. It was probably after they were married and Jaime was born. It was around that time he realized that he couldn't satisfy everyone all of the time, not even himself; you just had to put the past behind you and move forward. It was obviously a sign of maturity.

Ira was always quick to give Ellen much of the credit. Disappointment and failure was as common as a cold to a third-grade teacher, especially when you were dealing with 28 kids from all different kinds of families, many as nutty as his.

"If you don't move quickly past the failures and disappointments," Ellen always says, "you'll just burn out . . . as quickly as a shooting star."

Shooting stars were pretty and dramatic, but a man needs to last longer than that. Lasting itself was a kind of success. Ellen believed that as well. You can't be disappointed, she said, by a life well lived.

Of course it has all been a little disappointing to his mother, Selma, the high priestess of great expectations, who foretold his name in lights. She expected a Nobel Prize or at least a show at the Metropolitan Museum of Art.

"I'd have settled for a doctor or even a lawyer," Selma said when he told her that he intended to make advertising his career, "or a dentist for crying out loud."

Of course, she didn't really consider what he did, creating coupon campaigns, to be advertising. It certainly wasn't the kind of thing, she said, that real advertising men did, like producing commercials and writing jingles. Selma considered coupons to be at the bottom of the advertising food chain. She said he was like one of those guys in the street handing out circulars, except he did it in the newspaper.

"He could've been a genius Murray," she liked to say to the ceiling fan in the kitchen, where the spirit of Ira's father had revolved since his death fifteen years earlier.

She loved to remind him about her great Uncle Johann, who supposedly invented the thumbtack, and her father's second cousin, who wrote a sonata for the left-handed piano player.

Ellen told him to ignore his mother when she got like that. She called it Selma's ancestral refrain.

When his mother really wanted to put on the finishing touch, she'll repeat his name slowly; I . . . RA . . . I . . . RA, turning her head each time from side to side with a little sigh like she was letting out some gas at the same time.

She knew how much he hated his name. It didn't sound intellectual or athletic, and it didn't slide off the tongue like Charles or Andrew. It was the first-person singular I followed by RA, the ancient Egyptian sun god and the symbol for radium. Unfortunately, he didn't have a heavenly body, and he certainly didn't glow.

Ira was in charge of couponing at American Family Care Products and the father of the tip-in coupon, lightly glued to the page of a magazine so that the consumer could simply rip it off. It's far more expensive than the traditional printed-on-a-page coupon - the kind you cut out - but it has a much higher redemption rate. It is especially good for new products. Ira specialized in over-the-counter drugs and his biggest successes to date have come with colds and hemorrhoids.

"My son provides relief from itching at both ends," was the way Selma liked to describe it to her friends.

Ira liked what he did. He liked coupons. They had a single, clear purpose. He liked dealing with things that had expiration dates. You know what to expect and when to expect it. He took great delight in patrolling the refrigerator, tossing out milk, cottage cheese, or anything else on the exact date stamped on the container. Even though Ellen insisted that the stamped date was only the last sale date and that it remained edible for days afterward, he refused to treat them that lightly.

About eight months ago Ira turned forty. He's always been a little chubby, so the few extra pounds he's put on over the last five years weren't really that noticeable. Although his once fiery reddish-brown hair has faded like the den curtains and the top of his head had begun to rise to the surface like a wild mushroom.

His father, of course, his mother often pointed out, had a full head of dark hair until the day he died. Not a hint of grey, although his mother wasn't around to remind him of all his failings. She had died before he even married Selma.

Ira's eyes were still dark and clear, framed by crow's feet like his mother, which she never said a word about. His nose bent slightly to the left, as if it had grown up in the face of a stiff breeze, perhaps because he always sat to the left of his mother at the dinner table. He had a mustache left over from college and a large mouth, the kind that needed something to keep it busy like a pipe or gum. It dominated his whole face like Jimmy Carter, but without the toothy smile.

Ira considered his life safe, secure, certain, and relatively satisfying, as predictable and episodic as a television sitcom.

Unfortunately, it was about to be preempted by, of all things, a tombstone.

It all started on a Monday, always an unwelcome day.

Monday

Ira could barely make his tie in the morning. The knot kept coming out too small, leaving the back way too long, like Jaime always made it for him when she insisted on trying. She had his small hands, which made it difficult, although he knew she'd eventually get it since she had Ellen's concentration and determination. She stared so intently at her fingers when she tried that it seemed as if her eyes were controlling them instead of her brain. He could look right into them unobserved, which made him feel like a Peeping Tom, but he liked what he saw . . . she enjoyed the challenge and was unafraid of failure, another one of Ellen's traits. A good teacher needs that.

It took four tries for him to get the knot right, not a good way to start the week, which meant he had to hurry to catch the train. He grabbed his brief case and rushed into Jamie's room. The floor was strewn with outfits and books. Jaime always looked neat, her face washed, her hair combed, her clothes coordinated just like her mother, but everything else around her was always a mess and she always left a mess when she left a room. He liked to call her Pigpen, after the Peanuts character. He bent down to give her a kiss on her forehead. Her lips were slightly parted and fell naturally into a mysterious little grin. She didn't stir as Ira brushed a strand of hair away from her eyes; she never did. Jamie has always been a good sleeper.

Scott is nine and you could perform open-heart surgery on the floor of his room. He won't go to sleep if there's a piece of paper on the floor or anything out of place. Every drawer is shut tight, not a single sock or shirt sticking out. His comic books are neatly stacked on the bookcase, and the pictures on the dresser all arranged in neat rows.

There was always a little tension in Scott's face while he slept, particularly around the eyes. He was troubled by dreams that forced him to make impossible choices between people he loved, choices that always seemed to make the difference between life and death. Ira knew the feeling. His bad dreams didn't disappear until 5 years after he moved out of his house and away from his mother. They didn't really stop until he married Ellen.

Scott was a light sleeper, probably because he was always afraid of missing something, so he didn't get too close. Ira just blew him a kiss and tiptoed out of the room. Even so, Scott lifted his head slightly and looked up at him with a vague sense of recognition before mumbling something about a falling rock. Fortunately, he turned onto his side away from the door and instantly fell back asleep.

Ira went back to their bedroom to say good-bye to Ellen, who looked pale under the bent spotlight thrown by the 75-watt light bulb in the hall. Sleep always deepened the lines in her forehead, making her look more thoughtful. The static lifted a few strands of hair like little hands calling out in school for attention.

Not even sleep could hide that third-grade teacher cuteness. Those big, cheerful eyes filled with kindness when opened and intensely occupied by whatever or whoever was in front of them. A little circular nose and a wide, comfortable mouth that brought her students a great rush of affection with each smile, just as it did with Ira.

Ellen had the petite body of a model from the waist up, but from the waist down it's been the slow escalation of the Vietnam War. The groves in her thighs have grown more committed and intransigent every year. Sometimes she stared at them in the mirror and wondered out loud whether they were actually turning into Jell-o. Then she slapped them together and laughed because it sounded almost as if they were clapping. Ira has always been jealous of her complete lack of self-consciousness.

He bent down to kiss her good-bye, another one of his rituals, and she reflexively covered her mouth to hide her bad breath. He kissed her forehead instead.

By seven-twenty he had his paper and stood waiting for the seven-twenty-eight train. It was the same time every day, give or take a minute or two, and the platform was crowded as always. Everyone was facing north waiting for that first glimpse of the train as it came around the bend. When it did there would be the usual cacophony of folding newspapers, opening and closing attaché cases, and dropped conversations, as well-dressed feet fluttered like birds to the spots on the platform where they'd be close to the opening doors.

The seven-twenty-eight is one of the new trains with state-of-the-art features like a red emergency stop button instead of a cord. The seats don't flip like the older cars, half face one way and half the other, so you either watch where you're going or watch where you've been. Since most people pick the former, on days when Ira's not fast enough he winds up traveling backwards. He doesn't like watching the past recede quickly like that and it makes him a little nauseous.

Today's ride to Grand Central took the usual forty-two minutes. He read *the New York Times*, skimmed it really, and near the end of the ride turned to the business section to check his American Family's stock. It was the only stock he owned, not counting some mutual funds, the contents of which were a mystery to him, and he was glad to see that it was slowly creeping back up after dropping a month ago because of disappointing earnings.

He noticed that the lottery was up to forty million. Ira never played, but he'd been thinking about starting and fantasized about how his life would change if he won. He'd have more time to spend with Jaime and Scott for one thing. He'd be waiting for them when they got home from school with a warm snack. He could meet Ellen for lunch sometimes. Maybe open a small business near home or do absolutely nothing.

He knew that would make his mother proud.

He wasn't much of a get-rich-quick schemer or dreamer, so he attributed his recent thoughts to the lunacy of turning forty. Decades were like lines in the sand that sometimes you crossed with the promise - or threat - of living the rest of life somehow differently. However, like most promises and threats, it never amounted to much, nothing ever changed.

Ira wondered how he could live the rest of his life somehow differently and all he could come up with was going back to art. He had dreamed about being a cartoonist in high school. It was delusional to think of becoming an artist at his age with household expenses so high and Jaime and Scott not all that many years away from college. He used to work on the sets for the plays in high school and do caricatures for the yearbook. He took some art classes in college, but it was clear that he only had a small talent at best. He was good with landscapes, but terrible with people, just like in real life.

He felt worse the more he thought about it, not because he couldn't come up with another viable idea about something different to do, but because he knew there was no chance he'd try even if he had. Maybe he was just overreacting to the widow Selma, who never hid her disappointment.

"Your father," she told him when she handed him his fortieth birthday gift, a book entitled The Ten Best Ways To Stay Motivated, "may he rest in peace, didn't have your advantages. He grew up without a nickel in his pocket, but by the time he was your age he had his own accounting practice. Now that's motivation."

"He worked day and night," he said.

"So I could stay home with you."

Ira remembered that all too well.

"I hate numbers; I like advertising."

Selma rolled her eyes upward like she expected Murray to smack him on the back of his head on his next pass around the ceiling.

Today, Ira had to begin finalizing the coupon campaign for American Family's newest cold medicine, Sinoral. He had planned hundreds of coupon campaigns, the kind that people rip out of Sunday supplements and had devised some great rebate programs that compelled people to soak labels off jars and cut bar codes from almost indestructible containers. Selling over-the-counter drugs in America was very competitive and coupons were a major weapon in every company's arsenal. The distribution of manufacturer's cents-off coupons exceeded one hundred billion dollars last year. A successful coupon campaign had about a two-percent rate of return. Ira has had a half dozen as high as four percent.

For some reason Selma always found that funny.

She wasn't impressed that the first coupon promotion was in 1880 by C.W. Post of Battle Creek. He gave out one-cent coupons to encourage people to try Grape-Nuts. She didn't care that the Nielsen people, the same ones who monitored television ratings, accumulated and published annual figures on coupon redemption. Most of all she didn't care that the last industry-wide innovation, the tip-in coupon, was Ira's creation.

"Try creating something the world can't live without, "she once said, "like the thumbtack."

Ira was at lunch in the cafeteria with Tom and some of the other guys from marketing. They were talking football but Ira wasn't paying much attention in part because he was a one-sport fan. If it wasn't baseball, he wasn't interested. He was wondering instead about what they'd be having for dinner and whether his favorite show on TV tonight would be a rerun. If it was, he might take Scott to buy that skateboard he wanted. Selma would flip out when she heard, because she thought that they were far too dangerous. She wouldn't let Ira have a bicycle when he was growing up, because she was sure that he'd kill himself. Ellen called it the only child syndrome.

He did listen when the conversation switched to Tom's new secretary.

"They defy gravity."

"It's like they're staring up at me."

"I swear that her nipples stood up and saluted the other day when I walked by."

Heads turned in the cafeteria wondering what was so uproariously funny.

As they were just finishing lunch, the super was letting the police into his grandmother's apartment. His aunt had been calling for over two hours. They found her on the floor in the bathroom still in her nightgown. By the time Ira got back to the office, the police had notified his aunt and the required calls were being made.

Ira was in the middle of proofing the final Sinoral coupon design. There are lots of cardinal rules for coupons. Keep them dollar-bill size since odd shapes create problems for consumers and retailers. Make them simple and clear. Don't use the coupon itself to advertise, but show a picture of the product on the coupon. The face value must be in large type in the top corners. The expiration date must be clearly visible and allow for adequate time, since a short expiration angers consumers and they'll simply rip off the date. Retailers don't care because a manufacturer will accept a coupon until the end of time.

Ira was running through his checklist when he got the call. An acid heart attack, quick and to the point. The funeral was the next morning. His mother didn't believe in wasting time.

"Have Tom finish the Sinoral layout," he told his secretary. "And don't forget to tell Paul what happened. I'll be back the day after tomorrow."

He couldn't focus on his book on the way home or even think about the coupon layouts he'd brought home with him. He kept thinking about Grandma Sadie. They lived with her until he was five. His father was just getting established and money was tight. He remembered warm milk at night that knocked him out like a sucker punch and bedtime stories about what happened to little boys who wandered away at the grocery store or didn't do as they were told.

She was an old woman as long as he could remember with a proud posture and regal, gray hair. She buried her parents and two brothers in Russia and her husband, Ira's grandfather, at a very early age. Although she had a tough exterior, she was the kindest person he knew, not manipulative, not judgmental, and easily pleased, at least by him. She was the opposite of his mother who must have inherited her demanding gene from some pagan ancestor.

Grandma Sadie had three children. His mother was the youngest. She had Sadie's deep-set eyes, overhung by thick eyebrows as sharp as a rocky ledge, so like Ira's that it was almost frightening. Obviously not the personality marker one might think.

His Aunt Sarah was the oldest. Ira has always been very close to her. She spent a lot of time at his house while he was growing up, telling Selma to "leave the poor boy alone already." His late Uncle Max, the middle one, lived in the Midwest and looked nothing like his grandmother. He had a small mouth and always wore a salesman's smile. Max had two girls that he hardly knew who grew up in Sheboygan, Wisconsin.

Ira was always his grandmother's favorite. He always thought it was because he lived closer, but the events that were about to unfold proved to him that there was more to it than that.

Ellen and the kids were upset, of course, but they had a very different relationship with his grandmother. She used to visit three or four times a week when he was growing up in the city, but she didn't travel to the suburbs very often. When she did, the kids didn't sit still, or if they did it was in front of the television. They didn't have time to listen to her stories.

Ira had this peculiar funny feeling in his mouth that night, a kind of tingling in his gums, as if they were tired of holding on to his teeth, as if they were about to let go, so he kept pushing in on his teeth, as if to prevent them from popping out.

"What's wrong with your mouth?" Ellen asked him as he climbed into bed.

He ran his tongue along his gums.

"I don't know. They just feel funny."

"Well pushing in on them isn't going to help. Call the dentist."

"Tonight?"

"No, tomorrow after the funeral."

Ira nodded but he wasn't going to call. He'd let it pass and it would go away, funny feelings like that – stress-related probably – generally did. Besides, the Sinoral campaign was going to keep him busy and he couldn’t afford to take off any time for the dentist, certainly not for the next two weeks.

That night Ira dreamt that he was in the dentist's chair.

"So you've finally found your teeth," the dentist said, except it wasn’t his dentist it was his late Uncle Max.

"What does that mean?"

"People become aware of their teeth when they reach middle age."

Ira pushed in on his teeth and he could feel them move.

"Unfortunately," Max said, "once they do that feeling never goes away.

Tuesday

His teeth still felt strange in the morning. He had braces when he was ten to straighten out an overbite that was "barely noticeable" according to the orthodontist, because his mother couldn't live with the imperfection. Now it felt as if they were getting even by pushing back out where nature intended them to be.

They left early and had to wait in the car for the funeral home to open. Ira hated being late, which is probably what comes from living life according to a train schedule and growing up with a mother who considered "Thou Shalt Be On Time" to be the eleventh commandment.

A directory out front listed the recently departed like the menu in a drive-in restaurant. Sadie was on top. His mother wouldn't have had it any other way. Her casket was already at the front of the chapel, sealed tight, his aunt having already made the necessary identification. The room itself was meant to suggest a living room with red drapes on the walls and maroon carpet on the floor. But the line of folding chairs and the heavy chandelier made if feel more like a cheap hotel ballroom.

The service started promptly at nine. There were very few old faces, since Sadie had outlived most of her friends. A rabbi no one knew recited some well-turned phrases, but Ira didn't listen. Instead, he heard her insisting that he eat more in that soft yet unyielding voice of hers. He also smelled the onions, butter, and chicken that attached to all her housedresses like lint.

There should be a *Reader's Digest* in there, he thought, opened to "Personal Glimpses."

The rabbi recited the names of the mourners, which he received moments before from Selma, and called him Ida. He said nothing about the pogroms in Russia, the murder of her two brothers by the White Army, the arranged marriage to her second cousin, Ira's grandfather, his early death, or her refusal to eat anything until everyone else had seconds. Of course, there was not a word about her bedtime stories.

Ira's mother sat with her military posture, eyes straight ahead, wearing that hard, enduring look he first noticed as a child. He used to think it was anger and determination; now he saw it more as disbelief and disappointment. Aunt Sarah, on the other hand, looked around and smiled at him. At least until the coffin creaked and everyone jumped, even the Rabbi. Ira half-hoped that the lid would make a loud pop like a newly opened vacuum-sealed jar, and Sadie would sit up to say it was all a big mistake.

The Rabbi went back to his sermon and Ira thought back to that winter when he turned eight and forced his grandmother to sleep with him whenever she came for a visit. It was because of the light fixture in his room, the Methuselah of all light fixtures, with three naked bulbs for eyes and a nose and a decorative braided line below that looked like an angry little mouth. Perhaps it was originally designed to hold candles in one of those dark torture chambers in the castles of matinee movies and was murderously angry because some fool had electrified it.

Sometimes at night he swore he could hear it thinking.

Most nights he slept under the covers barely able to breathe, but when Grandma Sadie was over, he felt safe pressed up against her. She was big and warm and impervious to fear. No evil spirit could penetrate that force field of chicken and mothballs. Her slow, heavy breathing completely drowned out the whispers from above.

"Don't baby him," Selma would say.

"It's just for a few minutes until he falls asleep."

It was never just for a few minutes.

It got so bad that Ira was afraid to go into his room even in daylight. The problem disappeared once his grandmother convinced his father, over his mother's objection, to change the fixture. He never figured out how she knew, because he never said a word to anyone.

The rabbi finished the sermon by talking about Sadie's living memory. He went on and on about how she wasn't really dead, but alive in each of them, seeing the world through the eyes of her children and experiencing the joy of life through her grandchildren.

Seeing the world through the eyes of Selma was not a very comforting thought.

His mother insisted that Ira ride with her and Aunt Sarah in the limousine, which came, Selma pointed out, "as part of the package."

"It'll be strange without her," Sarah said as they pulled away from the curb.

Selma barely nodded. She just stared straight ahead her mouth snapped shut like her purse and her chin out, as if her jaw had been wired shut.

"She's always been there," Sarah said to Ira. "And I've never been far away."

In fact, Sarah lived with her mother until about 20 years ago, when she finally moved out to a similar apartment two blocks away.

"I spoke to her two or three times a day."

Ira tried touching Aunt Sarah lightly on the arm, the way he'd seen Ellen do a thousand times, but it turned out more like a pat. He didn't know what else to do or say so he stared out the window.

"It's unhealthy to call that often," Selma said.

Sarah sighed.

Ira thought about how death polarizes things. Clear becomes ambiguous and uncertain turns into inevitable. Far away seems so close and near much further away. It's life through both ends of the binoculars. Fortunately, this state of confusion and doubt doesn't last very long.

He was second now, he realized, in the natural order of things, right behind his mother. Instead of depressing him, it made him wonder why he bothered spending two and one half hours every day on a train to nowhere. It couldn't go anywhere because the tracks ended at Grand Central Station. Why spend every waking hour making money for nameless, faceless shareholders?

"It's good to have family at times like this."

Sarah took Ira's hand and held it in her lap. All three of them stared at his hand.

"I liked that coupon for the rash cream. What was the name again?"

"Dermacure."

"That's the one. I liked the funny face. Did you draw it?"

"No."

"Like someone tortured by an itch."

"Exactly."

Ira looked over at his mother who was staring out the window now. She looked smaller when she wasn't speaking.

Wouldn't everyone be surprised if he quit and enrolled in art school.

He closed his eyes and took back his hand. He knew better than to make a decision at a time like this, when death has stirred up all the sediment. He wondered what Ellen, Jaime, and Scott were talking about in the car behind. He hoped it wasn't about death. Of course, Ellen didn't believe in avoiding awkward subjects.

"She had a hard life," Sarah said.

"Who doesn't?" Selma said turning her head away from the window.

"Not like hers."

"It's not a contest. You don't measure life by who you bury and how young."

"Or how sorry you feel about yourself," Sarah said.

They rode the rest of the way in silence.

At the graveside, Sarah and his mother stood apart, arms intertwined like promenading partners at a square dance. Aunt Sarah couldn't remain angry for very long, nor would Selma have let her. The two of them stood there whispering one-syllable words that Ira couldn't quite make out, shaking their heads, and occasionally looking in his direction.

Of course, looking back now, he wondered how he could have missed all the signs over the years. Quiet conversations that stopped the moment he entered the room, eyes scrutinizing him behind his back, hands always fixing his collar, brushing down his hair, and picking lint off his sweater, as though looking for that loose thread that might unravel everything.

The wind was cold and Ira huddled with Ellen and the kids. He could smell Ellen's hair. It had a sandy, ocean smell. The same way it smelled when they first met.

The rabbi droned on and on in a language that no one understood, but which sounded familiar. All eyes were on the frozen hole in the ground.

"From dust to dust, we commend her to your care . . ."

The cemetery also reminded him of the beach. Maybe it was the absence of a skyline or the sea of stones under a gray, rolling horizon. Maybe it was the missing noises of commerce and daily life.

". . . to everlasting happiness and repose . . ."

The cold amplified the breathing of the mourners, almost like the sound of the surf through a seashell.

". . .to eternal fulfillment and reward . . ."

His mother moved perilously close to the edge of the grave, the dirt lapping up against her feet like the tide. She was like that, often standing right in your face during a conversation. No one said a word, but everyone thought the worst. What if she fell in? Of course things like that only happened in the movies.

It was overcast and the gray clouds were scalloped like brain matter. They rumbled softly, as if from a distant storm, or perhaps the reflected sound of some truck from a highway in the distance.

". . .and let us say AMEN."

"Amen," everyone said in unison.

The rabbi closed the book, picked up some dirt, and recited a prayer. Three large men leaning on shovels tried to appear solemn, but only succeeded in looking cold and impatient. They shifted their weight back and forth from foot to foot and kicked at their shovels as if to keep them in line.

There must be a dozen other souls waiting to take up residence today on Paradise Lane and Restful Way.

The rabbi dropped his handful of dirt on the coffin and disappeared. Selma was next. She took a fistful and practically threw it at the coffin. It sounded like the crack of a bat against the ball.

Aunt Sarah went next, followed by Ellen, and then the kids. Everyone took a turn throwing dirt on the coffin before returning to the cars.

Ira waited until the end. The gravediggers coiled their hands around their shovels and cleared their throats, but he ignored them. His handful of dirt barely landed on the coffin before they started shoveling. Furiously, almost frantically, as if too much longer and she might climb back out of the grave.

Their dirt hit the coffin like a gunshot at first until the layers reduced the sound to a dull thud. He wanted to wait until she was completely buried, like a spring bulb and backed up past her stone, which was blank on one side and engraved on the other for his grandfather, Issac Portnoy. He died over forty years earlier and gave Ira the "I" for his name.

There were about fifty graves in this small, walled-in area dedicated to members of the Mozur Lodge. Mozur was a small town in Russia that emptied out after the revolution. There didn't appear to be many vacancies.

He drifted farther back until he stood on a patch of grass that must have been meant for Aunt Sarah. His mother waved him to the car, but he pretended not to see her. She raised her arms higher, but he looked away. Perhaps it was bad luck to stand on an empty grave. His mother knew every superstition and honored them all. He moved over to the next grave and looked down at the stone.

"Eva Portnoy, beloved daughter of Issac and Sadie, born December 12, 1918-died December 12, 1968."

His first thought was that the poor woman died on her fiftieth birthday. The he read the stone again. Something was very odd, but he couldn't put his finger on it. He couldn't focus at first. Perhaps it was the gust of frigid air or the sounds of the gravediggers as they filled the hole where she'd spent the rest of eternity. Out of the corner of his eye, he saw Selma whispering to Scott, who started running toward him.

It seemed as if he were in a movie with the camera retreating so that Scott never seemed to get any closer.

He looked down again at Eva's stone and another gust of wind blew some fine particles of dirt into his eyes. It came right off his grandmother's grave, as if she didn't want him to look again, but it was too late, he'd already figured it out.

How could Eva have been his aunt? Sarah was the oldest, born in 1916. Max, dead ten years, was born four years later. His mother was the last, born in 1923. If Eva came between Aunt Sarah and Max, Ira realized, which meant that he was twenty when she died, how is it that he never heard her name? How is it that no one casually mentioned her during those long Sunday afternoons around the kitchen table when Sarah and his mother tried to describe what it was like growing up in the Bronx? How is that possible that she wasn't in a single photograph?

Scott tugged on his jacket.

"Come on Dad it's getting cold. Grandma wants to go. We're blocking cars. Dad?"

He looked down at Scott. He loved the color of his hair, a shade of brown somewhere between sand and earth. Could he hide him? Erase him from human memory?

He gave him a hug and Scott looked up with tears in his eyes.

"I'm cold," he said.

"Let's go."

Ira put his arm around his shoulder and walked him to the car. He didn't look back once.

Everyone returned to his mother's house, which was filled with fruit baskets, jars of nuts, boxes of cookies, and platters of cold cuts. There was a big bouquet of flowers from his office.

"You're supposed to send food to the house and flowers to the funeral home," Selma said when she read the card.

"They're nice flowers," he said.

"Inappropriate," Selma said turning and walking to the door to greet some recent arrivals.

People sat around eating and discussing Florida vacation spots, inexpensive restaurants, World War II battles, and a host of other subjects, like they were trying out for *Jeopardy*. There was almost a party atmosphere.

His mother played the hostess better than the grieving daughter.

"What's the point," she said. "It won't change anything."

The present always came first for her, followed by the future. The past was a distant third.

He sat quietly in the corner of the living room briefly conversing with the mourners as they left the kitchen plates piled high with roast beef and potato salad. It was the perfect spot - not enough room for anyone to sit comfortably beside him and no lengthy conversations possible with so much food close at hand.

"Sorry about your grandmother."

"Thank you."

"We should all make it to eighty-two."

Ira nodded. That was the most popular line.

Then they raised their plates in benediction and promised to find him later.

He wasn't being sociable, but he's never been good at parties. He's uncomfortable with small talk. He has to think about it too much. He never knows how to fill the silences, whether it's a time of celebration, illness, or death. He can handle the nodding and looking interested part well enough, smiling or frowning depending on what's appropriate, but he normally relies on Ellen to carry the conversation forward. She was, however, busy helping in the kitchen.

That's what attracted him to Ellen the very first time they met. He didn't have to think about what to say next. It was as if she were writing the dialogue and all he had to do was read it, like it was hanging up there in a comic strip balloon. Every response felt spontaneous and sounded right. For a lot of people, that's as good a reason as any to fall in love.

Ira was never sure what Ellen saw in him that day at the coffee shop, but he bet it was the home in the suburbs and the two kids. A life without surprises, although she said it was the look in his eyes, like a little kid hoping that the present was for him.

Ira was startled by Aunt Sarah, who squeezed in beside him.

"You're not eating."

"I had something before."

It was a lie, but safer than saying he wasn't hungry. You didn't skip meals in his family, because it could only be an early sign of illness.

"There's cake."

"Maybe later."

Selma insisted that Sarah was very beautiful when she was young, although it's hard to tell from the few black-and-white pictures that remain and impossible to imagine from the way she looked now. Her eyes, which still looked kindly as they fell on him, carried two big bags around with them these days like they were homeless, and they didn't open that wide anymore, swollen as they were by two cataract operations. Sometimes they filled with tears in the normal course of a conversation, as if they had worries and troubles of their own. Her good-natured mouth has also begun to sag as well. Her entire face seemed to be losing its shape, the years erasing the child-like symmetry that had once defined her features. Selma said it was because she retained too much water.

"She turned down a lot of perfectly good marriage proposals," Selma said, "because she waited too long for Mr. Perfect."

Still, Aunt Sarah didn't complain, didn't criticize, and always kept busy. She worked up until a few years ago in the administrative offices of the garment workers union and the day after retiring she joined the senior citizen's center. Unlike his mother, who filled her days thinking about all the things that could go wrong, Sarah attended Broadway shows, traveled to Atlantic City, and did arts and crafts. Ira's house was full of her clay bowls and potholders.

"She was a good mother and grandmother," Sarah said brushing the hair from the front of Ira's face.

"The best," he said.

"Everyone liked her."

Effortlessly, he thought, just like Ellen.

"Did I ever tell you about this Italian woman who worked with her in the garment center?" Sarah said.

"About a thousand times."

"Sadie helped her find a place to live and she named her first daughter after her. Can you imagine, somewhere in the city there's an Italian girl named Sadie."

They both smiled and stared straight ahead at Selma, who moved constantly, keeping to the edge of everyone's conversation like a moth circling the light.

"Aunt Sarah."

"Yes darling?"

"Who was Eva?"

Sarah's whole body contracted in an instant, like it was a single muscle. Her breathing stopped and then resumed with a start, like a car thrown too quickly into gear.

"She was your sister," he said. "I saw her headstone at the cemetery."

Aunt Sarah watched Selma work the room, heading slowly in their direction.

"Eva was two years younger than me. Grandma had to put her in an institution."

"How old was she?"

"Eighteen. She stayed there for the rest of her life."

"What was wrong with her?"

"Behavioral problems."

"They don't put people away for life for behavioral problems."

"Things were different back then."

"What institution?"

"What's the difference?"

"I'm curious. I suddenly discover at the age of forty that my mother had a sister who died when I was twenty who I didn't even know existed. Don't you think that's a little strange?"

"The world didn't have to know everybody's business back then, not like today."

"Well, this is today and I'd like to know."

"You know all you need to know," Sarah said.

"You sound like my mother."

Sarah shuddered.

"I'm sorry," Ira said.

"Just don't ask her about Eva."

"Why?"

"Because your mother was the youngest and Max and I were in school. My mother had to work, so Eva wound up taking care of her. She took care of your mother until the day they took her away."

"How old was she?"

"Who?"

"My mother . . . when they took Eva away?"

"Eleven. She never saw her again."

"She didn't visit?"

"No."

"Why not?"

"It was hard for her."

"Did you visit?"

"In the beginning."

"It was hard for you."

"I was much older."

Selma was getting closer.

"What's the name of the institution?"

"Your mother is coming."

"Tell me . . . or I'll ask her."

Aunt Sarah swayed back and forth as if the upper part of her body were balancing on a spring.

"I want to know."

The desperation in his voice must have surprised her. It certainly surprised him. He wouldn't have asked his mother - not yet anyway - and certainly not now . . . maybe never, he'd have discussed it with Ellen first.

Selma stopped about ten feet away and rested her hand on the shoulder of one of her cousins. She said something to him, but looked right at Sarah and Ira.

"The name?"

"Pilgrim State Hospital."

"Where is that?"

"Not now."

"Where?"

"Long Island."

"So what are you two whispering about?" Selma said.

"You," Sarah said.

"What about me?"

"How well you handle these things."

"I've had practice."

"You don't get better with practice at things like this."

"You two were whispering like a couple of criminals planning a robbery. What else have you been talking about?"

"This new course I'm taking at the center," Sarah said.

"What about?"

"Knitting."

"Sweaters?"

"Afghans."

"Sweaters would be more useful," Selma said. She had an opinion about everything.

"I've made enough sweaters to last a lifetime," Sarah said.

"No one ever has enough sweaters."

Sarah didn't argue. She knew better.

"And that's the big conspiracy?"

Sarah nodded.

"I don't believe you for a minute."

Sarah laughed.

"But I don't have time to stand here and find out," his mother said. "Ira, there's so much food in the kitchen, I want you to take some home."

"We don't need anything."

"I've already made up a platter for you. It's in the refrigerator."

"Fine."

"When are you going to learn to make a tie?" Selma said, bending down to straighten the knot. "Go get some dessert in the kitchen. I want to talk to Aunt Sarah."

Ira jumped up.

"And don't forget to tuck the tie into your shirt while you're eating," she said. "The way your father always did. He saved a fortune on dry-cleaning."

Ira ate a big piece of chocolate cake in the kitchen, letting his tie swing dangerously close to the frosting. He was almost elated to learn that his mother's family wasn't perfect and that they weren't an unbroken string of well-adjusted, success stories. There was a big failure carefully hidden away by his mother, lest she become a yardstick to measure his own accomplishments.

They didn't get home until after ten. They were all exhausted. Ellen and the kids went right to bed, but Ira couldn't sleep. He had this urge to do something domestic, so he sat at the kitchen table balancing the checkbook.

He tried not to think about Eva. It was hard enough comparing the amount on each check with the scribble in the checkbook. He also needed to spend a few minutes looking over the budget for the Sinoral campaign. He'd lost a day already and it had to be finalized by Friday. The big question, as always, was how many consecutive Sundays to run it and how far up front in the supplement.

Ellen didn't know about Eva. There hadn't been a quiet moment to tell her since the cemetery. Besides, he wasn't ready to talk. The whole thing still seemed too bizarre and personal. He needed to think about it awhile and work some answers out in his head in terms of what he wanted to do before talking it over with Ellen, especially since he knew what she was likely to say. She'll try to convince him to respect Aunt Sarah's wishes. Every family has a black sheep, she'll say, some skeleton hidden in the closet. What was your grandmother supposed to do, advertise the fact that her daughter had been committed to a mental institution?

Ellen respects the past. She believes in leaving well enough alone. He's always loved that about her. He usually felt the same way, except not tonight, tonight he felt as if Eva needed to be rescued from obscurity. He felt the passion begin to burn and everyone needed a burning passion from time to time. Lord knows, it's been so long since he's had one.

For a long time it used to be his art. In high school, it was the caricatures of the teachers that he drew senior year for the yearbook. In college, it was the sketching courses, fruits, landscapes and nudes. There were some really talented students, both real and representational, and it quickly became clear that he wasn't one of them. He had the technique, but not the vision. He was pretty good with trees and rocks. Once or twice he caught the light just right surprising even himself. His mother has one of those landscapes in her den. He was a passable artist, but not nearly as good as Selma believes. She didn't see all the failures.

"He could've been another Rockwell, drawing pictures instead of coupons," she occasionally told the kitchen fan, when he was near enough to overhear it.

She couldn't possibly understand that a small talent can be a curse, in some ways worse than no talent at all.

Ira finally climbed into bed about three in the morning. He dreamt that he was at some kind of resort that looked more like a college campus. He had to leave, he was late for something, but he couldn't find his way out. He walked in the same direction for hours, however, the campus never ended. He finally stopped to ask someone for help, an attractive girl in her early twenties with long, curly hair and crystal-clear blue eyes, so blue that it was like looking into the reflection of a mountain lake. She had one flaw, a large mouth, which made her smile look a little silly.

"Don't you know where you are?" she said her voice very soft and sweet, almost melodic.

"On vacation? In college?"

He was sure it was one or the other.

"No Ira, you're in a mental institution."

When he looked down he saw that he was in a straight jacket.

"How do you know my name?"

She looked disappointed and kissed him on the forehead.

Then he woke up.

About the Author

A Year of Soup is Howard Reiss' second novel inspired during a dinner at a small restaurant in Northhampton, Mass. when an old professorial looking gentlemen with a bottle of wine in a paper bag sat down at a table in the corner and was immediately joined by the young, female proprietor and chef. Although he couldn't hear their conversation, he tried to imagine it and their stories as well.

Howard Reiss' first novel, *A Family Institution,* published in 2011, was based on a true incident involving the discovery of an aunt he didn't know existed who spent most of her life in Pilgrim State Hospital. The main character's quest for the truth about his family takes him to Pilgrim State where he takes a job in the records department, learns a lot about how the mentally ill and, in particular, his aunt was treated in the 1950s, and in the process turns his life and family upside down. It's a serious subject approached with a strong comic touch and has been a growing favorite of book clubs around the country.

Howard Reiss is a graduate of Dartmouth College and Columbia Law School and the father of two girls. He helped found a soup kitchen in Nyack, New York where he lives and runs, supports book publishers by buying more books than he can possibly find the time to read, and is somewhere north of 50.

Connect with Me Online

Website: http://www.howardreiss.com

Facebook: http://www.facebook.com/HowardReissAuthor

Twitter: @HoRoRe

20887214R00168

Made in the USA
San Bernardino, CA
30 April 2015